No Graves As Yet

By Anne Perry
Published by The Random House Publishing Group

FEATURING WILLIAM MONK

The Face of a Stranger
A Dangerous Mourning
Defend and Betray
A Sudden, Fearful Death
The Sins of the Wolf
Cain His Brother
Weighed in the Balance
The Silent Cry
A Breach of Promise
The Twisted Root
Slaves of Obsession
Funeral in Blue
Death of a Stranger

FEATURING THOMAS AND CHARLOTTE PITT

The Cater Street Hangman
Callander Square
Paragon Walk
Resurrection Row
Bluegate Fields
Rutland Place
Death in the Devil's Acre
Cardington Crescent
Silence in Hanover Close
Bethlehem Road
Highgate Rise
Belgrave Square
Farriers' Lane
The Hyde Park Headsman
Traitors Gate
Pentecost Alley
Ashworth Hall
Brunswick Gardens
Bedford Square
Half Moon Street
The Whitechapel Conspiracy
Southampton Row
Seven Dials

No Graves As Yet

A Novel of World War I

ANNE PERRY

BALLANTINE BOOKS • NEW YORK

A Ballantine Book
Published by The Random House Publishing Group

www.ballantinebooks.com

Library of Congress Cataloging-in-Publication Data
Perry, Anne.
No graves as yet : a novel of World War I / Anne Perry.— 1st ed.
p. cm.
ISBN 0-345-45652-1 (alk. paper)
1. Great Britain—History—George V, 1910–1936—Fiction. 2. World War, 1914–1918—England—Fiction. I. Title.
PR6066.E693N6 2003
823'.914—dc21
2003052233

Design by Julie Schroeder

Manufactured in the United States of America

First Edition: September 2003

2 4 6 8 10 9 7 5 3 1

Dedicated to
my grandfather,
Captain Joseph Reavley,
who served as chaplain in the trenches
during the Great War

And they that rule in England,
In stately conclave met,
Alas, alas for England
They have no graves as yet.

—G. K. Chesterton

No Graves As Yet

CHAPTER

ONE

It was a golden afternoon in late June, a perfect day for cricket. The sun burned in a cloudless sky, and the breeze was barely sufficient to stir the slender, pale skirts of the women as they stood on the grass at Fenner's Field, parasols in hand. The men, in white flannels, were relaxed and smiling.

St. John's were batting and Gonville and Caius were fielding. The bowler pounded up to the crease and sent the ball down fast, but a bit short and wide. Elwyn Allard leaned forward, and with an elegant cover drive, dispatched the ball to the boundary for four runs.

Joseph Reavley joined in the applause. Elwyn was one of his students, rather more graceful with the bat than with the pen. He had little of the scholastic brilliance of his brother, Sebastian, but he had a manner that was easy to like, and a sense of honor that drove him like a spur.

St. John's still had four more batsmen to play, young men from all over England who had come to Cambridge and, for one reason or another, remained at college through the long summer vacation.

Elwyn hit a modest two. The heat was stirred by a faint breath of wind from across the fenlands with their dykes and marshes, flat under the vast skies stretching eastward to the sea. It was old land, quiet, cut by secret waterways, Saxon churches marking each village. It had been the last stronghold of resistance against the Norman invasion eight and a half centuries ago.

On the field one of the boys just missed a catch. There was a gasp and then a letting out of breath. All this mattered. Such things could win or lose a match, and they would be playing against Oxford again soon. To be beaten would be catastrophic.

Across the town behind them, the clock on the north tower at Trinity struck three, each chime on the large A-flat bell, then followed the instant after on the smaller E-flat. Joseph thought how out of place it seemed, to think of time on an eternal afternoon like this. A few feet away, Harry Beecher caught his eye and smiled. Beecher had been a Trinity man in his own years as a student, and it was a long-standing joke that the Trinity clock struck once for itself and once for St. John's.

A cheer went up as the ball hit the stumps and Elwyn was bowled out with a very respectable score of eighty-three. He walked off with a little wave of acknowledgment and was replaced at the crease by Lucian Foubister, who was a little too bony, but Joseph knew his awkwardness was deceiving. He was more tenacious than many gave him credit for, and he had flashes of extraordinary grace.

Play resumed with the sharp crack of a strike and the momentary cheers under the burning blue of the sky.

Aidan Thyer, master of St. John's, stood motionless a few yards from Joseph, his hair flaxen in the sun, his thoughts apparently far away. His wife Connie, standing next to him, glanced across and gave a little shrug. Her dress was white broderie anglaise, falling loosely in a flare below the hip, and the fashionable slender skirt reached to the ground. She looked as elegant and feminine as a spray of daisies, even though it was the hottest summer in England for years.

At the far end of the pitch Foubister struck an awkward shot, elbows in all the wrong places, and sent the ball right to the boundary. There was a shout of approval, and everyone clapped.

Joseph was aware of a movement somewhere behind him and half turned, expecting a grounds official, perhaps to say it was time for lemonade and cucumber sandwiches. But it was his own brother, Matthew, who was walking toward him, his shoulders tight, no grace in his movement. He was wearing a light gray city suit, as if he had newly arrived from London.

Joseph started across the green, anxiety rising quickly. Why was his brother here in Cambridge, interrupting a match on a Sunday afternoon?

"Matthew! What is it?" he said as he reached him.

Matthew stopped. His face was so pale it seemed almost bloodless. He was twenty-eight, seven years the younger, broader-shouldered, and fair where Joseph was dark. He was steadying himself with difficulty, and he gulped before he found his voice. "It's . . ." He cleared his throat. There was a kind of desperation in his eyes. "It's Mother and Father," he said hoarsely. "There's been an accident."

Joseph refused to grasp what he had said. "An accident?"

Matthew nodded, struggling to govern his ragged breathing. "In the car. They are both . . . dead."

For a moment the words had no meaning for Joseph. Instantly his father's face came to his mind, lean and gentle, blue eyes steady. It was impossible that he could be dead.

"The car went off the road," Matthew was saying. "Just before the Hauxton Mill Bridge." His voice sounded strange and far away.

Behind Joseph they were still playing cricket. He heard the sound of the ball and another burst of applause.

"Joseph . . ." Matthew's hand was on his arm, the grip tight.

Joseph nodded and tried to speak, but his throat was dry.

"I'm sorry," Matthew said quietly. "I wish I hadn't had to tell you like this. I . . ."

"It's all right, Matthew. I'm . . ." He changed his mind, still trying to grasp the reality. "The Hauxton Road? Where were they going?"

Matthew's fingers tightened on his arm. They began to walk slowly, close together, over the sun-baked grass. There was a curious dizziness in the heat. The sweat trickled down Joseph's skin, and inside he was cold.

Matthew stopped again.

"Father telephoned me late yesterday evening," he replied huskily, as if the words were almost unbearable for him. "He said someone had given him a document outlining a conspiracy so hideous it would change the world we know—that it would ruin England and everything we stand for. Forever." He sounded defiant now, the muscles of his neck and jaw clenched as if he barely had mastery of himself.

Joseph's mind whirled. What should he do? The words hardly made sense. John Reavley had been a member of Parliament until 1912, two years ago. He had resigned for reasons he had not discussed, but he had never lost his interest in political affairs, nor his care for honesty in government. Perhaps he had simply been ready to spend more time reading, indulging his love of philosophy, poking around in antique and secondhand shops looking for a bargain. More often he was just talking with people, listening to stories, swapping eccentric jokes, and adding to his collection of limericks.

"A conspiracy to ruin England and everything we stand for?" Joseph repeated incredulously.

"No," Matthew corrected him with precision. "A conspiracy that *would* ruin it. That was not the main purpose, simply a side effect."

"What conspiracy? By whom?" Joseph demanded.

Matthew's skin was so white it was almost gray. "I don't know. He was bringing it to me . . . today."

Joseph started to ask why, and then stopped. The answer was the one thing that made sense. Suddenly at least two facts cohered. John Reavley had wanted Joseph to study medicine, and when his firstborn son had left it for the church, he had then wanted Matthew to become a doctor. But Matthew had read modern history and languages here at Cambridge, and then he joined the Secret Intelligence Service. If there was such a plot, John would understandably have notified his younger son. Not his elder.

Joseph swallowed, the air catching in his throat. "I see."

Matthew's grip eased on him slightly. He had known the news longer and had more time to grasp its truth. He was searching Joseph's face with anxiety, evidently trying to formulate something to say to help him through the pain.

Joseph made an immense effort. "I see," he repeated. "We must go to them. Where . . . are they?"

"At the police station in Great Shelford," Matthew answered. He made a slight movement with his head. "I've got my car."

"Does Judith know?"

Matthew's face tightened. "Yes. They didn't know where to find you or me, so they called her."

That was reasonable—obvious, really. Judith was their younger sister, still living at home. Hannah, between Joseph and Matthew, was married to a naval officer and lived in Portsmouth. It would be the house in Selborne St. Giles that the police would have called. He thought how Judith would be feeling, alone except for the servants, knowing neither her father nor mother would come home again, not tonight, not any night.

His thoughts were interrupted by someone at his elbow. He had not even heard footsteps on the grass. He half turned and saw Harry Beecher standing beside him, his wry, sensitive face puzzled.

"Is everything . . . ?" he began. Then, seeing Joseph's eyes, he stopped. "Can I help?" he said simply.

Joseph shook his head a little. "No . . . no, there isn't anything." He made an effort to pull his thoughts together. "My parents have had an accident." He took a deep breath. "They've been killed." How odd and flat the words sounded. They still carried no reality with them.

Beecher was appalled. "Oh, God! I'm so sorry!"

"Please—" Joseph started.

"Of course," Beecher interrupted. "I'll tell people. Just go." He touched Joseph lightly on the arm. "Let me know if I can do anything."

"Yes, of course. Thank you." Joseph shook his head and started to walk away as Matthew acknowledged Beecher, then turned to cross the wide expanse of grass. Joseph followed him without looking back at the players in their white flannels, bright in the sunlight. They had been the only reality a few moments ago; now there seemed an unbridgeable space between them.

Outside the cricket ground Matthew's Sunbeam Talbot was parked in Gonville Place. In one fluid motion Joseph climbed over the side and into the passenger seat. The car was facing north, as if Matthew had been to St. John's first and then come all the way through town to the cricket ground looking for Joseph. Now he turned southwest again, back along Gonville Place and finally onto the Trumpington Road.

There was nothing to say now; each was cocooned in his own pain, waiting for the moment when they would have to face the physical proof of death. The familiar winding road with its harvest fields shining gold in the heat, the hedgerows, and the motionless trees were like things painted on the other side of a wall that encased the mind. Joseph was aware of them only as a bright blur.

Matthew drove as if it demanded his entire concentration, clutching the steering wheel with hands he had to loosen deliberately now and then.

South of the village they turned left through St. Giles, skirted the side of the hill over the railway bridge into Great Shelford, and pulled up outside the police station. A somber sergeant met them, his face tired, his body hunched, as if he had had to steel himself for the task.

"Oi'm terrible sorry, sir." He looked from one to the other of them, biting his lower lip. "Wouldn't ask it if Oi din't 'ave to."

"I know," Joseph said quickly. He did not want a conversation. Now that they were here, he needed to proceed as quickly as possible, while his self-control lasted.

Matthew made a small gesture forward, and the sergeant turned and led the way the short distance through the streets to the hospital mortuary. It was all very formal, a routine the sergeant must have been through scores of times: sudden death, shocked families moving as if in a dream, murmuring polite words, hardly aware of what they were saying, trying to understand what had happened and at the same time deny it.

They stepped out of the sunlight into the sudden darkness of the building. Joseph went ahead. The windows were open to try to keep the air cool and the closeness less oppressive. The corridors were narrow, echoing, and they smelled of stone and carbolic.

The sergeant opened the door to a side room and ushered Joseph and Matthew in. There were two bodies laid out on trolleys, covered decently in white sheets.

Joseph felt his heart lurch. In a moment it would be real, irreversible, a part of his own life ended. He clung to the second of disbelief, the last, precious instant of *now,* before it all changed.

The sergeant was looking at him, then at Matthew, waiting for them to be ready.

Matthew nodded.

The sergeant pulled back the sheet from the face. It was John Reavley. The familiar aquiline nose looked bigger because his cheeks were sunken, and there was a hollowness about his eyes. The skin on his forehead was broken, but someone had cleaned away the blood. His main injuries must be to his chest—probably from the steering wheel. Joseph blocked out the thought, refusing to picture it in his mind. He wanted to remember his father's face as it was, looking as if he were no more than asleep after an exhausting day. He might still waken and smile.

"Thank you," he said aloud, surprised how steady he sounded.

The sergeant murmured something, but Joseph did not listen. Matthew answered. They went to the other body, and the sergeant lifted the sheet, but only partially, keeping it over one side, his own face crumpled with pity. It was Alys Reavley, her right cheek and brow perfect, skin very pale, but blemishless, eyebrows delicately winged. The other side was concealed.

Joseph heard Matthew draw in his breath sharply, and the room seemed to swing and slide off to one side, as if he were drunk. He grasped Matthew and felt Matthew's hand tighten hard on his wrist.

The sergeant covered Alys Reavley's face again, started to say something, then changed his mind.

Joseph and Matthew stumbled outside and along the corridor to a small, private room. A woman in a starched uniform brought them cups of tea. It was too strong and too sweet for Joseph, and at first he thought he would gag. Then, after a moment, the heat felt good, and he drank some more.

"Oi'm awful sorry," the sergeant said again. "If it's any comfort, it must've been very quick." He looked wretched, his eyes hollow and pink-rimmed. Watching him, Joseph, in spite of himself, started to recall his days as a parish priest, before Eleanor died, when he had had to tell families of tragedy, and try to give them whatever comfort he could, struggling to express a faith that could meet the reality. Everybody was always very polite, strangers trying to reach each other across an abyss of pain.

"What happened?" he said aloud.

"We don't know yet, sir," the sergeant answered. He had said what his name was, but Joseph had forgotten. "The car came off the road just afore the Hauxton Mill Bridge," he went on. "Seems it was going quite fast—"

"That's a straight stretch!" Matthew cut across him.

"Yes, Oi know, sir," the sergeant agreed. "From the marks on the road, it looks as if it happened all of a sudden, like a tire blowing out. Can be hard to keep a hold when that happens. It could even've bin both tires on the one side, if there were something on the road as caused it." He chewed his lip dubiously. "That could take you right off, no matter how good a driver you were."

"Is the car still there?" Matthew asked.

"No, sir." He shook his head. "We're bringing it in. You can see it if you want, o' course, but if you'd rather not . . ."

"What about my father's belongings?" Matthew said abruptly. "His case, whatever was in his pockets?"

Joseph glared at him in surprise. It was a distasteful request, as if possessions could matter now. Then he remembered the document Matthew had mentioned. He looked at the sergeant.

"Yes, sir, o' course," the sergeant agreed. "You can see them now, if you really want, before we . . . clean them." That was almost a question. He was trying to save them hurt and he did not know how to do it without seeming intrusive.

"There's a paper," Matthew explained. "It's important."

"Oh! Yes, sir." The sergeant's face was bleak. "In that case, if you'll come with me?" He glanced at Joseph.

Joseph nodded and followed them out of the room and along the hot, silent corridor, their footsteps self-consciously loud. He wanted to see what this damnable document could possibly be. His first vague thoughts were that it might have something to do with the recent mutiny of British army officers in the Curragh. There was always trouble in Ireland, but this looked uglier than usual—in fact, various politicians had warned it could lead to the worst crisis in over two hundred years. Joseph knew most of the facts, as the newspapers reported them, but at the moment his thoughts were too chaotic to make sense of anything.

The sergeant led them to another small room, where he unlocked one of the several cupboards and pulled out a drawer. He carefully extracted a battered leather attaché case with the initials J.R.R. stamped just below the lock, and then a woman's smart, dark brown leather handbag heavily smeared with blood. No one had yet attempted to clean it.

Joseph felt sick. It did not matter now, but he knew the blood was his mother's. She was dead and beyond pain, but it mattered to him. He was a minister of the Church; he should know to value the spirit above the body. The flesh was temporary, only a tabernacle for the soul, and yet it was absurdly precious. It was powerful, fragile, and intensely real. It was always an inextricable part of someone you loved.

Matthew was opening the attaché case and looking through the papers inside, his fingers moving delicately. There was something to do with insurance, a couple of letters, a bank statement.

Matthew frowned and tipped the case upside down. Another paper slithered out, but it was only a receipt for a pair of shoes—12/6d. He ran his hands down inside the main compartment, then the side pockets, but there was nothing more. He looked across at Joseph and, with fingers trembling, put down the case and reached for the handbag. He was very careful not to touch the blood. At first he just looked inside, as if a paper would be easy to see. Then when he found nothing, he began carefully moving around the contents.

Joseph could see two handkerchiefs, a comb . . . He thought of his mother's soft hair with its gentle, natural curl, and the way it lay on her neck when she had it coiled up. He had to close his eyes to prevent the tears, and there was an ache in his throat so fierce he could not swallow.

When he mastered himself and looked down at the handbag again, Matthew was staring at it in confusion.

"Perhaps it was in his pocket?" Joseph suggested, his voice hoarse, jolting the silence.

Matthew looked across at him, then turned to the sergeant.

The sergeant hesitated.

Joseph looked around. It was bare except for the cupboards, more a storeroom than an office. A simple window faced a delivery yard, and then rooftops beyond.

Reluctantly the sergeant opened another drawer and took out a pile of clothes resting on an oilskin sheet. They were drenched with blood, dark and already stiffening. He did his best to conceal it, handing Matthew only the man's jacket.

His face blanched even whiter, Matthew took it and, with fingers clumsy now, searched through one pocket after another. He found a handkerchief, a penknife, two pipe cleaners, an odd button, and some loose change. There was no paper at all. He looked up at Joseph, a frown between his brows.

"Maybe it's in the car?" Joseph suggested.

"It must be." Matthew stood still for a moment. As if he had spoken it, Joseph knew what he was thinking: Regrettably, he would have to examine the rest of the clothes—just in case. He was startled by how fiercely he did not want to intrude into the intimate, the familiar smell. Death was not real yet, the pain of it only just beginning, but he knew its path; it was like the loss of Eleanor all over again. But they must look. Otherwise they would have to come back and do it later if the document was not in the car.

But of course it was in the car. It had to be. In the glove compartment, or one of the pockets at the side. But how odd not to have put it in the briefcase along with the other papers. Isn't that what anyone would do, automatically?

The sergeant was waiting. He too did not want to inflict that distress.

Matthew blinked several times. "May we have the others, please?" he requested.

The clothes were inspected, as both brothers tried to distance their minds from what their hands were doing. There were no papers except for one small receipt in their father's trouser pocket, soaked with blood and illegible, but there was no way in which it could be called a document. It was barely two or three inches square.

They folded the clothes again and set them in a pile on top of the oilskin. It was an awkward moment. Joseph did not know what to do with them. The sight and touch of the garments knotted up his stomach with grief. He wished he had never had to see them at all. He certainly did not want to keep these clothes. Neither did he want to pass them over to strangers as if they did not matter.

"May we take them?" he asked haltingly.

Matthew jerked his hand up. Then the surprise died out of his face as if he understood.

"Yes, sir, o' course," the sergeant replied. "I'll just wrap 'em up for you."

"If we could see the car, please?" Matthew asked.

But it was still on the way back from Hauxton, and they had to wait another half hour. Two more cups of tea later they were taken to the garage where the familiar yellow Lanchester sat gashed and crumpled. The whole of the engine was twisted sideways and half jammed into the front of the passenger area. All four tires were ripped. No human being could have remained alive inside it.

Matthew stood still, struggling to keep his balance.

Joseph reached out to him, glad to break the physical aloneness.

Matthew righted himself and walked over toward the far side of the car, where the driver's door was hanging open. He took his jacket off and rolled up the sleeves of his shirt.

Joseph went to the windowless frame of the passenger door, keeping his eyes averted from the blood on the seat, and banged the glove compartment to make it open.

There was nothing inside except a small tin of barley sugar and an extra pair of driving gloves. He looked across and saw Matthew's face, wide-eyed and confused. There was no document in the side pocket. Joseph held the road atlas and riffled the pages, but nothing fell out.

They searched the rest of the car as well as they could, forcing themselves to ignore the blood, the torn leather, the twisted metal, and the shards of glass, but there was no document of any sort. Joseph stepped back at last, elbows and shoulders bruised where he had caught himself on the jutting pieces of what had been seats and the misshapen frames of the doors. He had skinned his knuckles and broken a fingernail trying to pry up a piece of metal.

He looked across at Matthew. "There's nothing here," he said.

"No . . ." Matthew frowned. His right sleeve was torn and his face dirty and smeared with blood.

A few years earlier Joseph might have asked his sibling if he was certain of his facts, but Matthew was beyond such brotherly condescension now. The seven years between them were closing fast.

"Where else could it be?" he said instead.

Matthew hesitated, breathing in and out slowly. "I don't know," he admitted. He looked beaten, his eyes hollow and his face shadowed with fatigue from battling the inner shock and grief, trying to keep it from overwhelming him. Perhaps this document was something to cling to, something over which he could have some control.

Joseph understood how it mattered to him. John Reavley had wanted one of his sons to enter the medical profession. He had believed passionately that it was the noblest of callings. Joseph had started medical studies to please his father, and then found himself drowned by his inability to affect all but the smallest part of the suffering he witnessed. He knew his limitations, and he saw what he thought was his strength and his true vocation. He answered the call of the Church, using his gift for languages to study the original Greek and Hebrew of the scriptures. Souls needed healing as well as bodies. John Reavley was content with that, and deferred his dream to his second son.

But Matthew had refused outright and turned his imagination, his intellect, and his eye for detail toward the Secret Intelligence Service. John Reavley had been bitterly disappointed. He despised espionage and all its works, and equally those who occupied themselves with it. That he had called Matthew in his professional capacity to help him with a document he had found was a far more powerful testimony of his judgment of it than anyone else would understand.

It would have been a chance for Matthew to give his father a gift from his chosen calling, and it had slipped away forever. That was part of the pain etched in his face.

Joseph lowered his eyes. Perhaps understanding was intrusive at this raw moment.

"Have you any idea what it is?" he asked, investing his voice with urgency, as if it could matter.

"He said it was a conspiracy," Matthew replied, straightening his back to stand upright. He moved away from the door, coming around the back of the car to where Joseph was, keeping his voice very low. "And that it was the most dishonorable betrayal he had ever seen."

"Betrayal of whom?"

"I don't know. He said it was all in the paper."

"Had he told anyone else?"

"No. He didn't dare. He had no idea who was involved, but it went as high as the royal family." Matthew looked surprised as he said it, as if hearing the words aloud startled him with their enormity. He stared at Joseph, searching for a response, an answer.

Joseph waited a moment too long.

"You don't believe it!" Matthew's voice was hoarse; he himself sounded unsure if it was an accusation or not. Looking at his brother's eyes, Joseph could see that Matthew's own certainty was wavering.

Joseph wanted to save something out of the confusion. "Did he say he was bringing the document or that he would merely tell you about it? Could he have left it at home? In the safe, perhaps?"

"I would have to see it," Matthew argued, rolling his shirtsleeves down and fastening the cuffs again.

"To do what?" Joseph pursued. "Wouldn't it be better for him to tell you what it was—and he was perfectly capable of memorizing it for you—and then decide what to do, but keep it in the meantime?"

It was a sensible suggestion. Matthew's body eased, the stiffness draining out of it. "I suppose so. We'd better go home anyway. We ought to be with Judith. She's alone. I don't even know if she's told Hannah. Someone will have to send her a telegram. She'll come, of course. And we'll need to know her train, to meet it."

"Yes, of course," Joseph conceded. "There'll be a lot of preparations." He did not want to think of them now; they were intimate, final things, an acknowledgment that death was real and that the past could never be brought back. It was the locking of a door.

They drove back from Great Shelford through the quiet lanes. The village of Selborne St. Giles looked just the same as it always had in the soft gold of the evening. They passed the stone mill, its walls flush with the river. The pond was flat as a polished sheet, reflecting the soft enamel blue of the sky. There was an arch of honeysuckle over the lych-gate to the churchyard, and the clock on the tower read just after half past six. In less than two hours they would hold Evensong.

There were half a dozen people in the main street, although the shops were long closed. They passed the doctor with his pony and trap, going at a brisk pace. He waved cheerfully. He could not have heard the news yet.

Joseph stiffened a little. That was one of the tasks that lay ahead, telling people. He was too late to wave back. The doctor would think him rude.

Matthew swung the car left, along the side road to the house. The drive gates were closed, and Joseph got out to open them, then close them again as Matthew pulled up to the front door. Someone had already drawn the curtains downstairs—probably Mrs. Appleton, the housekeeper. Judith would not have thought of it.

Matthew climbed out of the car just as Joseph reached him, and the front door opened. Judith stood on the step. She was fair-skinned like Matthew, but her hair fell in heavy waves and was a warmer brown. She was tall for a woman, and even though he was her brother, Joseph could see that she had a uniquely fierce and vulnerable kind of beauty. The strength inside her had yet to be refined, but it was there in her bones and her level, gray-blue eyes.

Now she was bleached of all color and her eyelids were puffy. She blinked several times to hold back the tears. She looked at Matthew and tried to smile, then took the few steps across the porch onto the gravel to Joseph, and he held her motionless for a moment, then felt her body shake as she let the sobs wrench through her.

He did not try to stop her or find any comforting words. There was no reason that made any sense, and no answer to the pain. He tightened his arms around her, clinging as much to her as she was to him. She was nothing like Alys, not really, yet the softness of her hair, the way it curled, slightly choked the tears in his throat.

Matthew went in ahead of them. His footsteps faded along the wooden floor of the hall, and then they heard his voice murmuring something and Mrs. Appleton replying.

Judith sniffed hard and pulled back a little. She felt in Joseph's pocket for his handkerchief. She took it out and blew her nose, then wiped her eyes, screwing up the linen and clenching it in her hand. She turned away and went inside also, talking to him without looking back.

"I don't know what to do with myself. Isn't it stupid?" She gulped. "I keep walking around from room to room, and going out again, then coming back—as if that would make it any different! I suppose we'll have to tell people?"

Joseph went up the steps behind her.

"I sent Hannah a telegram, but that's all," she went on. "I don't even remember what I said." Inside she swiveled around to face him, ignoring Henry, the cream-haired retriever who came out of the sitting room at the sound of Joseph's voice. "How do you tell people something like this? I can't believe it's real!"

"Not yet," he agreed, bending to touch the dog as it pushed against his hand. He stood in the familiar hallway with its oak staircase curving upward, the light from the landing window catching the watercolors on the wall. "It'll come. Tomorrow morning it will begin." He could remember with sickening clarity the first time he had woken up after Eleanor's death. There was an instant when everything was as it had always been, the whole year of their marriage. Then the truth had washed over him like ice, and something inside him had never been warm again.

There was a fleeting pity in Judith's face, and he knew she was remembering also. He made an effort to force it away. She was twenty-three, almost an afterthought in the family. He should be protecting her, not thinking of himself.

"Don't worry about telling people," he said gently. "I'll do that." He knew how hard it was, almost like making the death itself happen over again each time. "There'll be other things to do. Just ordinary housekeeping, for a start. Practical things."

"Oh, yes." She jerked her attention into focus. "Mrs. Appleton will deal with the cooking and the laundry, but I'll tell Lettie to make up Hannah's room. She'll be here tomorrow. And I suppose there's food to order. I've never done that! Mother always did."

Judith was quite unlike either her mother or Hannah, both of whom loved their kitchens and the smells of cooking, clean linen, beeswax polish, lemon soap. For them, to run a house was an art. To Judith it was a distraction from the real business of living, although to be honest, she was not yet certain for herself what that would prove to be. But Joseph knew it was not domesticity. To their mother's exasperation, she had turned down at least two perfectly good offers of marriage.

But this was not the time for such thoughts.

"Ask Mrs. Appleton," Joseph told her. He steadied his voice with an effort. "We'll have to go through the diaries and cancel any appointments."

"Mother was going to judge the flower show," she said, smiling and biting her lip, tears flooding her eyes. "They'll have to find somebody else. I can't do it, even if they were to ask me."

"And bills," he added. "I'll see the bank, and the solicitor."

She stood stiffly in the middle of the floor, her shoulders rigid. She was wearing a pale blouse and a soft green narrow skirt. She had not yet thought to put on black. "I suppose somebody'll have to sort . . . clothes and things. I—" She gulped. "I haven't been into the bedroom yet. I can't!"

He shook his head. "Too soon. It doesn't matter, for ages."

She relaxed a fraction, as if she had been afraid he was going to force her. "Tea?"

"Yes, please." He was surprised how thirsty he was. His mouth was dry.

Matthew was in the kitchen with Mrs. Appleton, a square, mild-faced woman with a stubborn jaw. Now she was standing at the table with her back to the stove on which a kettle was beginning to whistle. She wore her usual plain blue dress, and her cotton apron was screwed up at the right-hand corner as if she had unthinkingly used it to wipe the tears from her eyes. She sniffed fiercely as she looked first at Judith and then at Joseph, for once not bothering to tell the dog not to come in. She drew in her breath to say something, then decided she could not trust herself to keep her composure. Clearing her throat loudly, she turned to Matthew.

"Oi'll do that, Mr. Matthew. You'll only scald yourself. You weren't never use to man nor beast in the kitchen. Do nothing but take my jam tarts, as if there was no one else in the house to eat 'em. Here!" She snatched the kettle from him and with considerable clattering and banging made the tea.

Lettie, the general housemaid, came in silently, her face pale and tearstained. Judith asked her to make up Hannah's room, and she departed to obey, glad to have something to do.

Reginald, the only indoor manservant, appeared and asked Joseph if they would want wine for dinner and if he should lay out black clothes for him and Matthew.

Joseph declined the wine but accepted the offer to lay out the mourning clothes, and Reginald left. Mrs. Appleton's husband, Albert, was outside working off his grief alone, digging in his beloved garden.

In the kitchen they sat around the scrubbed table in silence, sipping the hot tea, each sunk in thought. The room was as familiar as life itself. All four children had been born in this house, learned to walk and talk here, left through the front gate to go to school. Matthew and Joseph had driven from here to go to university, Hannah to go to her wedding in the village church. Joseph could remember the endless fittings of her dress in the spare bedroom, she standing as still as she could while Alys went around her with pins in her hands and in her mouth, a tuck here, a lift there, determined the gown should be perfect. And it had been.

Now Alys would never be back. Joseph could remember her perfume, always lily-of-the-valley. The bedroom would still smell of it.

Hannah would be devastated. She was so close to her mother, so like her in a score of ways, she would feel robbed of the model for her life. There would be nobody to share with her the small successes and failures in the home, the children's growth, the new things learned. No one else would reassure her anxieties, teach her the simple remedies for a fever or sore throat, or show the easy way to mend, to adapt, to make do. It was a companionship that was gone forever.

For Judith it would be different, an open wound of things not done, not said, and now unable ever to be put right.

Matthew set his cup down and looked across the table at Joseph.

"I think we should go and sort some of the papers and bills." He stood up, scraping his chair on the floor.

Judith seemed not to notice the tremor in his voice or the fact that he was trying to exclude her.

Joseph knew what he meant: It was time to look for the document. If it existed, then it should be here in the house, although why John would have set out to show it to Matthew and then not taken it with him was hard to understand.

"Yes, of course," Joseph agreed, rising as well. They had better give Judith something to do. She had no need to know anything about this yet, and perhaps not at all. He turned to her. "Would you go through the household accounts with Mrs. Appleton and see if there is anything that needs doing? Perhaps some orders should be canceled, or at least reduced. And there may be invitations to be declined."

She nodded, not trusting herself to speak.

"You'll be staying?" Mrs. Appleton said with another sniff. "What'll you be wanting for dinner, Mr. Joseph?"

"Nothing special," he answered. "Whatever you have."

"Oi've got cold salmon and summer pudding," she said a little truculently, as if she were defending Alys's choice. If it was good enough for the master and mistress, it was certainly good enough for the young master, whatever had happened in the world. "And there's some good Ely cheese," she added.

"That would be excellent, thank you." He then followed Matthew, who was already at the door.

They went along the passage and across the hall to John Reavley's study, overlooking the garden. The sun was still well above the horizon and bathing the tops of the orchard trees in gold. The leaves shimmered in the rising wind, and a swirl of starlings rose into the sky, black against the amber and flame, turning in wide spiral arms against the sunset.

Joseph looked around the familiar room, almost like an earlier pattern of his own in Cambridge. There was a simple oak desk, shelves of books covering most of two walls. The books dated back to John's university days. Some were in German. Many were leather-bound, a few well-thumbed cloth or even paper. There was a recently acquired folio of drawings on the table by the window.

A Bonnington seascape hung over the fireplace, its color neither blue nor green, but a luminous gray that holds both at its heart. Looking at it, one could draw a cleaner breath and almost feel the sting of the salt in the wind. John Reavley had loved everything in this room. Each object marked some happiness or beauty he had known, but the Bonnington was special.

Joseph turned away from it. "I'll start over here," he said, taking the first book off the shelf nearest the window.

Matthew began with the desk.

They searched for half an hour before dinner, and all evening afterward. Judith went to bed, and midnight found the two brothers still sifting through papers, looking in books a second or third time, even moving furniture. Finally they admitted defeat and forced themselves into the master bedroom to look with stiff fingers through drawers of clothes, in shelves where toiletries and personal jewelry were kept, in pockets of the clothes hanging in wardrobes. There was no document.

At half past one, head throbbing, eyes stinging as if hot and gritty, Joseph came to the end of places to investigate. He straightened up, moving his shoulders carefully to ease the ache. "It's not here," he said wearily.

Matthew did not answer for several moments. He kept his eyes on the drawer he had been going through for the third time. "Father was very clear," he repeated stubbornly. "He said the effect of it, the daring, was so vast it was beyond most men's imagination. And terrible." He looked up at last, his eyes red-rimmed, angry, as if Joseph were attacking his judgment. "He couldn't trust anyone else because of who was involved."

Joseph's imagination was too tired and too full of pain to be inventive, even to save Matthew's feelings. "Then where is it?" he demanded. "Would he trust it to the bank? Or the solicitor?"

Denial was in Matthew's face, but he clung to the possibility for a few seconds, because he could think of nothing else.

"We'll have to speak to them tomorrow anyway." Joseph sat down on the chair by the desk. Matthew was sitting beside the drawers on the carpet.

"He wouldn't give it to Pettigrew." Matthew pushed his hair back off his forehead. "They're just family solicitors—wills and property."

"Then quite a safe place to hide something valuable and dangerous," Joseph reasoned.

Matthew glared at him. "Are you trying to defend Father? Prove that he wasn't imagining it out of something that was really perfectly harmless?"

Joseph was stung by the accusation. It was exactly what he was doing—defending, denying—and he was confused and dizzy with loss. "Do I need to?" he demanded.

"Stop being so damn reasonable!" Matthew's voice cracked, the emotion raw. "Of course you need to! It wasn't in the car! It isn't in the house." He jerked his hand sharply toward the door and the landing beyond. "Doesn't it sound wild enough to you, unlikely enough? A piece of paper that proves a conspiracy to ruin all we love and believe in—and that goes right up to the royal family—but when we look for it, it vanishes into the air!"

Joseph said nothing. The tag end of an idea pulled at his mind, but he was too exhausted to grasp it.

"What is it?" Matthew said roughly. "What are you thinking?"

"Could it be obvious?" Joseph frowned. "I mean, something we are seeing but not recognizing?"

Matthew looked round the room. "Like what? For God's sake, Joe! A conspiracy of this magnitude! The document is not going to be hung up on the wall along with the pictures!" He put the papers in the drawer, climbed to his feet, and carried it back to the desk. He replaced it in its slots and pushed it closed. "And before you bother, I've taken the backs off all the drawers and looked."

"Well, there are two possibilities." Joseph was driven to the last conclusion. "Either there is such a document or there isn't."

"You have a genius for the obvious!" Matthew said bitterly. "I had worked that out for myself."

"And you concluded that there is? On what basis?"

"No!" Matthew snapped. "I just spent the evening ransacking the house because I have nothing better to do!"

"You *don't* have anything better to do," Joseph answered him. "We had to go through the papers anyway to find what needs attending to." He gestured toward the separated pile. "And the sooner we do it, the less bloody awful it is. We can think of a conspiracy while we look, which is easier than thinking that we are performing a sort of last rite for both our parents."

"All right!" Matthew cut in. "I'm sorry." Again he pushed the thick fair hair off his face. "But honestly, he sounded so certain of it! His voice was charged with emotion, not a bit dry and humorous as it usually is." His mouth pulled a little crooked, and when he spoke again his voice cracked. "I know what it must have cost him to call me on something like that. He hated all the secret services. He wouldn't have said anything if he hadn't been certain."

"Then he put it somewhere we haven't thought of yet," Joseph concluded. He stood up also. "Go to bed now. It's nearly two, and there's a lot we have to do later."

"There was a telegram from Hannah. She's coming on the two-fifteen. Will you go and meet her?" Matthew was rubbing his forehead sore. "She's going to find this pretty hard."

"Yes, I know. I'll meet her. Albert will drive me. Can I take your car?"

"Of course." Matthew shook his head. "I wonder why he didn't drive Father yesterday."

"Or why Mother went," Joseph added. "It's all odd. I'll ask Albert on the way to the station."

The next day was filled with small, unhappy duties. The formal arrangements had to be made for the funeral. Joseph went to see Hallam Kerr, the vicar, and sat in the tidy, rather stiff vicarage parlor watching him trying to think of something to say that would be of spiritual comfort and finding nothing. Instead they spoke of the practicalities: the day, the hour, who should say what, the hymns. It was a timeless ritual that had been conducted in the old church for every death in the village. The very familiarity of it was comfortable, a reassurance that even if one individual journey was ended, life itself was the same and always would be. There was a kind of certainty in it that gave its own peace.

Just before lunch Mr. Pettigrew came from the solicitors' office, small and pale and very neat. He offered his condolences and assured them that everything legal was in order—and that he had been given no papers to keep recently. In fact, not anything this year. A couple of bonds in August of 1913 were the last things. He did not yet mention the will, but they knew it would have to be dealt with in time.

The bank manager, the doctor, and other neighbors called in or left flowers and cards. Nobody knew what to say, but it was done in kindness. Judith offered them tea, and sometimes it was accepted and awkward conversations followed.

In the early afternoon Albert Appleton drove Joseph to the railway station at Cambridge to meet Hannah's train from London. Joseph sat beside him in the front of Matthew's Sunbeam Talbot as they followed the lanes between the late wild roses and the ripening fields of corn already dappled here and there with the scarlet of poppies.

Albert kept his eyes studiously on the road. He looked tired, his skin papery under its dark sunburn, and he had missed a little gray stubble on his cheek when he had shaved this morning. He was not a man to give words to grief, but he had come to St. Giles at eighteen and served John Reavley all his adult life. For him this was the ending of an age.

"Do you know why Father drove himself yesterday?" Joseph asked as they passed into the shade under an avenue of elms.

"No, Mr. Joseph," Albert replied. It would be a long time before he called Joseph "Mr. Reavley," if he ever did. "Except there's a branch on the old plum tree in the orchard hanging low, an' tossled in the grass. He wanted me to see if Oi could save it. Oi propped it up, but that don't always work. Get a bit o' wind an' it goes anyway, but it tears it off rough. Leaves a gash in the trunk, an' kill the whole thing. Get a bit parky an' the frost'll have it anyway."

"I see. Can you save it?"

"Best to take it off."

"Do you know why Mother went with him?"

"Jus' liked to go with him, mebbe." He stared fixedly ahead.

Joseph did not speak again until they reached the station. Albert had always been someone with whom it was possible to sit in amicable silence, ever since Joseph had been a boy nursing his dreams in the garden or the orchard.

Albert parked the car outside the station and Joseph went in and onto the platform to wait. There were half a dozen other people there, but he studiously avoided meeting anyone's eye in case he encountered someone he knew. The last thing he wanted was conversation.

The train was on time, belching steam and grinding to a halt at the platform. The doors clanged open. People shouted greetings and fumbled with baggage. He saw Hannah almost immediately. The few other women were in bright summer colors or delicate pastels. Hannah was in a slim traveling suit of unrelieved black. The tapered hem at her ankles was smudged with dust, and her neat hat was decorated with black feathers. Her face was pale, and with her wide brown eyes and soft features she looked so like Alys that for a moment Joseph felt his emotions lurch out of control and grief engulf him unbearably. He stood motionless as people pushed past him, unable to think or even focus his vision.

Then she was in front of him, portmanteau clutched in her hand and tears spilling down her cheeks. She dropped the bag on the platform and waited for him.

He put his arms around her and held her as close to him as he could. He felt her shivering. He had already tried to work out what to say to her, but now it all slipped away, sounding hollow and predictable. He was a minister, the one of all of them who was supposed to have the faith that answered death and overcame the hollow pain that consumed everything from the inside. But he knew what bereavement was, sharply and recently, and no words had touched more than the surface for him.

Please God, he must find something to say to Hannah! What use was he if, of all people, he could not?

He let go of her at last and picked up her bag, carrying it out to where Albert was waiting with the car.

She stopped, staring at the unfamiliar vehicle, as if she had expected the yellow Lanchester. Then, with a gasp that caught in her throat, she realized why it was not there.

Joseph took her by the elbow and helped her into the backseat, straightening the slender black skirt around her ankles before closing the door and going around to the other side to get in next to her.

Albert got back in and started the engine.

Hannah said nothing. It was up to Joseph to speak before the silence became too difficult. He had already decided not to mention the document. It was an unneeded concern for her.

"Judith will be glad to see you," he started.

She looked at him with slight surprise, and he knew immediately that her thoughts had been inward, absorbed in her own loss. As if she read his perception, she smiled slightly, an admission of guilt.

He put out his hand, palm upward, and she slid hers across and gripped his fingers. For several minutes she was silent, blinking back the tears.

"If you can see sense in it," she said at last, "please don't tell me now. I don't think I could bear it. I don't want to know a God who could do this. Above all I don't want to be told I should love Him. I don't!"

Several answers rose to his lips, all of them rational and scriptural, and none of them answering her need.

"It's all right to hurt," he said instead. "I don't think God expects any of us to take it calmly."

"Yes, He does!" She choked on the words. " 'Thy will be done'!" She shook her head fiercely. "Well, I can't say that. It's stupid and senseless and horrible. There's nothing good in it." She was fighting to make anger conquer the fearful, consuming grief. "Was anyone else killed?" she demanded. "The other car? There must have been another car. Father wouldn't simply have driven off the road, whatever anyone says."

"Nobody else was hurt, and there's no evidence of another car."

"What do you mean, evidence?" she said furiously, the color flooding her face. "Don't be so pedantic! So obscenely reasonable! If nobody saw it, there wouldn't be!"

He did not argue. She needed to rage at someone, and he let her go on until they were through the gates and had drawn up at the front door. She took several long, shuddering breaths, then blew her nose and said she was ready to go inside. She seemed on the edge of saying something more, something gentler, looking steadily at him through brimming eyes. Then she changed her mind and stepped out of the door as Albert held it for her and gave her his hand to steady her.

They ate supper quietly together. Now and again one of them spoke of small, practical things that had to be done, but nobody cared about them. Grief was like a fifth entity in the room, dominating the rest.

Afterward Joseph went to his father's study again and made certain that all the letters had been written to friends to inform them of John and Alys's death and tell them the time of the funeral. He noticed that Matthew had written the one letter he had considered most important, to Shanley Corcoran, his father's closest friend. They had been at university together—Gonville and Caius. Corcoran would be one of the hardest to greet at the church because his pain would be so deep and the memories were so long, woven into so many of the best days right from the beginning.

And yet there were ways in which the sharing would also help. Perhaps afterward they would be able to talk about John in particular. It would keep some part of him alive. Corcoran would never become bored with it or let the memory sink into some pleasant region of the past where the sharpness did not matter anymore.

About half past nine the village constable came by. He was a young man of about Matthew's age, but he looked tired and harassed.

"Oi'm sorry," he said, shaking his head and pursing his lips. "We'll all miss 'em terrible. I never knew better people."

"Thank you," Joseph said sincerely. It was good to hear, even though it twisted the pain. To have said nothing would be like denying they mattered.

"Sunday was a bad day all round," the constable went on, standing uncomfortably in the hall. "Did you hear what happened in Sarajevo?"

"No, what?" Joseph did not care in the slightest, but he did not wish to be rude.

"Some madman shot the archduke of Austria—and the duchess, too." The constable shook his head. "Both dead! Don't suppose you've had time to look at the papers."

"No." Joseph was only half aware of what he was saying. He had not given the newspapers a thought. The rest of the world had seemed removed, not part of their lives. "I'm sorry."

The constable shrugged. "Long way from here, sir. Probably won't mean nothin' for us."

"No. Thank you for coming, Barker."

The constable's eyes flickered down. "I'm real sorry, Mr. Reavley. It won't be the same without 'em."

"Thank you."

CHAPTER

TWO

The funeral of John and Alys Reavley was held on the morning of July 2, in the village church at Selborne St. Giles. It was another hot, still day, and the perfume of the honeysuckle over the lych-gate hung heavy in the air, making one drowsy even before noon. The yew trees in the graveyard looked dusty in the heat.

The cortege came in slowly, two coffins borne by young men from the village. Most of them had been to school with either Joseph or Matthew, at least for the first few years of their lives, played football with them or spent hours on the edge of the river fishing or generally dreaming away the summers. Now they shuffled one foot in front of the other, careful to look straight ahead and balance the weight without stumbling. The tilted stones of the path had been worn uneven by a thousand years of worshipers, mourners, and celebrants from Saxon times to the present day and the modern world of Victoria's grandson, George V.

Joseph walked behind them, Hannah on his arm, barely keeping her composure. She had purchased a new black dress in Cambridge, and a black straw hat with a veil. She kept her chin high, but Joseph had a strong feeling that her eyes were almost closed and she was clinging to him to guide her. She had hated the days of waiting. Every room she went into reminded her of her loss. The kitchen was worst. It was full of memories: cloths Alys had stitched, plates with the wildflowers painted on them that she had loved, the flat basket she used to collect the dried heads from the roses, the corn dolly she had bought at the Madingley fair. The smell of food brought back memories of crumpets and lardy cakes, and hot, savory onion clangers with suet crust.

Alys had liked to buy the blue-veined Double Cottenham cheese and butter by the yard, instead of the modern weights. It was the smallest things that hurt Hannah the most, perhaps because they caught her unaware: Lettie arranging flowers in the wrong jug (one Alys would never have chosen); Horatio the cat sitting in the scullery, where Alys would not have permitted him; the fish delivery boy being cheeky and answering back where he would not have dared to before. All of these were the first marks of irrevocable change.

Matthew walked with Judith a few steps behind, both of them stiff and staring straight ahead. Judith, too, had a veiled hat and a new black dress with sleeves right down to the backs of her hands, and a skirt so slender it obliged her to walk daintily. She did not like it, but it was actually dramatically becoming to her.

Inside the church the air was cooler, musty with the smell of old books and stone and the heavy scent of flowers. Joseph noticed them immediately with a gulp of surprise. The women of the village must have stripped their gardens of every white bloom: roses, phlox, old-fashioned pinks, and bowers of daisies of every size, single and double. They were like a pale foam breaking over the ancient carved woodwork toward the altar, gleaming where the sunlight came in through the stained-glass windows. He knew they were for Alys. She had been all the village wanted her to be: modest, loyal, quick to smile, able to keep a secret, proud of her home and pleased to care for it. She was willing to exchange recipes with Mrs. Worth, garden cuttings with Tucky Spence even though she never stopped talking, patient with Miss Anthony's endless stories about her niece in South Africa.

John had been more difficult for them to understand: a man of intellect who had studied deeply and often traveled abroad. But when he was here his pleasures had been simple enough: his family and his garden, old artifacts, watercolor pictures from the last century that he enjoyed cleaning and reframing. He had delighted in a bargain and searched through antique and curio shops, happy to listen to tales of quaint, ordinary people, and always ready to hear or pass on a joke—the longer and shaggier, the more he relished it.

Joseph's recollections continued as the service began, and he stared at all the long, familiar faces, sad and confused now in their hasty black. He found his throat too tight to sing the hymns.

Then it was time for him to speak, just briefly, as representative of the family. He did not wish to preach; it was not the time. Let someone else do that—Hallam Kerr, if he had a mind to. Joseph was here as a son to remember his parents. This was not about praise, but about love.

It was not easy to keep his voice from breaking, his thoughts in order, and his words clear and simple. But this, after all, was his skill. He knew bereavement intimately, and he had explored it over and over in his mind until it had no more black corners for him.

"We are met together in the heart of the village, perhaps the soul of it, to say goodbye for the moment to two of our number who were your friends, our parents—I speak for myself, and for my brother, Matthew, and my sisters, Hannah and Judith."

He hesitated, struggling to maintain his composure. There was no movement or rustle of whispering among the upturned faces staring at him.

"You all knew them. You met in the street day by day, at the post office, at the shops, over the garden wall. And most of all you met here. They were good people, and we are hurt and diminished by their going."

He stopped for a moment, then began again. "We shall miss my mother's patience, her spirit of hope that was never just easy words, never denial of evil or suffering, but the quiet faith that they could be overcome, and the trust that the future would be bright. We must not fail her by forgetting what she taught us. We should be grateful for every life that has given us happiness, and gratitude is the treasuring of the gift, the nourishing of it, the use, and then to pass it on bright and whole to others."

He saw a movement, a nodding, a hundred familiar faces turned toward him, somber and bruised with the suddenness of grief, each one hurt by its own private memory.

"My father was different," he continued. "His mind was brilliant, but his heart was simple. He knew how to listen to others without leaping to conclusions. He could tell a longer, funnier, more rambling joke than anyone else I know, and they were never grubby or unkind. For him, unkindness was the great sin. You could be brave and honest, obedient and devout, but if you could not be kind, then you had failed."

He found himself smiling as he spoke, even though his voice was so thick with tears it was hard to make his words clear. "He did not care for organized religion. I have known him to fall asleep in church and wake up applauding because he thought for an instant that he was in a theater. He could not bear intolerance, and he thought those who confessed religious faith could be among the worst at this. But he would have defended St. Paul with his own life for his words on love: 'Though I speak with the tongues of men and of angels, and have not charity, I am nothing.'

"He was not perfect, but he was kind. He was gentle with others' weaknesses. I would gladly labor all my life that you would be able to say the same of me when I, too, come to say goodbye—for the time being."

He was shaking with relief as he returned to his seat beside Hannah and felt her hand close over his. But he knew that under her veil she was weeping and would not look at him.

Hallam Kerr took the pulpit, his words sonorous and sure but curiously lacking in conviction, as if he, too, had been swept out of his depth. He continued the service in the familiar way, the words and music woven like a bright thread through the history of life in the village. It was as certain and as rich as the passing seasons, barely changing from year to year down the centuries.

Afterward Joseph again chose the part that was in a way the most harrowing, standing by the church door and shaking hands with people as they fumbled for words, trying to express their grief and support, and few of them knowing how to. In some way the service had not been enough; something was still unsaid. There was a hunger, a need unmet, and Joseph was aware of it as a hollowness within himself. Now, when he needed it most, his words had lost their consuming power. The last shred of certainty in himself melted in his grasp.

Judith and Hannah stood together, still in the shadow of the arched doorway. Matthew had not yet come out. Joseph moved into the sun to speak to Shanley Corcoran, who waited a few yards away. He was not a tall man, and yet the power of his character, the vitality within him, commanded a respect so that no one crowded to him, although most did not even know who he was, let alone the brilliance of his achievements, nor would they have understood had they been told. The word *scientist* would have had to suffice.

He came forward to Joseph now, holding out both his hands, his face crumpled in grief.

"Joseph," he said simply.

Joseph found the warmth of touch and the emotion it evoked almost unbearable. The familiarity of such a close friend was overwhelming. He was unable to speak.

It was Orla Corcoran who rescued him. She was a beautiful woman with a dark, exotic face, and her black silk dress with its elegant waist, flowing jacket to below the hip, and slender skirt beneath was the perfect complement to her delicate bones.

"Joseph knows our grief, my dear," she said, laying her gloved hand on her husband's arm. "We should not struggle to say that for which there can be no words. The village is waiting. This is their turn, and the sooner this duty is accomplished, the sooner the family can go back home and be alone." She looked at Joseph. "Perhaps in a few days we may call and visit with you for a little longer?"

"Of course," Joseph answered impulsively. "Please do. I shall not go back to Cambridge until the end of the week at least. I don't know about Matthew—we haven't discussed it. We just wanted to get today over."

"Naturally," Corcoran agreed, letting go of Joseph's hand at last. "And Hannah will go back to Portsmouth, no doubt." There was a pucker of anxiety between his brows. "I assume Archie is at sea, or he would be here now?"

Joseph nodded. "Yes. But they may grant him compassionate leave when he is next in port." There was nothing he could do for Hannah. She must now face the ordeal of helping her children recover from the pain of their grandparents' death. It was the first big loss in their lives, and they would need her. She had already been away for the larger part of a week.

"Of course, if it's possible," Corcoran acquiesced, still looking at Joseph with the slight frown, his eyes troubled.

"Why should it not be possible?" Joseph said a trifle sharply. "For heaven's sake, his wife has just lost both her parents!"

"I know, I know," Corcoran said gently. "But Archie is a serving officer. I dare say you have been too busy with your own grief to read much of the world news, and that is perfectly natural. However, this assassination in Sarajevo is very ugly."

"Yes," Joseph agreed uncomprehendingly. "They were shot, weren't they?" Did it really matter now? Why was Corcoran even thinking about it—today, of all days? "I'm sorry, but . . ."

Corcoran looked a little stooped. It was so slight as to be indefinable, but the shadow in him was more than grief; there was something yet to come that he feared.

"It wasn't a single lunatic with a gun," he said gravely. "It's far deeper than that."

"Is it?" Joseph said without belief or comprehension.

"There were several assassins," Corcoran said gravely. "The first did nothing. The second threw a bomb, but the chauffeur saw it coming and managed to speed up and around it." His lips tightened. "The man who threw the bomb took some sort of poison, then jumped into the river, but he was pulled out and lived. The bomb exploded and injured several people. They were taken to hospital." His voice was very low, as if he did not want the rest of the people standing in the graveyard to hear, even though it must be public knowledge. Perhaps they had not grasped the meaning of it.

"The archduke continued with his day's agenda," he went on, ignoring Orla's frown. "He spoke to people in the town hall, and later he decided to go and visit the injured, but his chauffeur took a wrong turn and came face-to-face with the final assassin, who leaped on the running board of the car and shot the archduke in the neck and the duchess in the stomach. Both died within minutes."

"I'm sorry." Joseph winced. He could picture it, but the moment he did, their faces changed to those of John and Alys, and the death of two Austrian aristocrats a thousand miles away melted into unimportance.

Corcoran's hand gripped his arm again, and the strength of him seemed to surge through it. "It was chaotically done, but it comes from a groundswell of feeling, Joseph. It could lead to an Austro-Serbian war," he said quietly. "And then Germany might become involved. The kaiser reasserted his alliance with Austria-Hungary yesterday."

It rose to Joseph's lips to argue that it was too unlikely to consider, but he saw in Corcoran's eyes how intensely he meant it. "Really?" he said with puzzlement. "Surely it will just be a matter of punishment, reparation, or something? It is an internal matter for the Austro-Hungarian Empire, isn't it?"

Corcoran nodded, withdrawing his hand. "Perhaps. If there is any sanity in the world, it will."

"Of course it will!" Orla said firmly. "It will be miserable for the Serbs, poor creatures, but it doesn't concern us. Don't alarm Joseph with such thoughts, Shanley." She smiled as she said it. "We have enough grief of our own without borrowing other people's."

He was prevented from replying to her by the arrival of Gerald and Mary Allard, close friends of the family whom Joseph had known for many years. Elwyn was their younger son, but their elder, Sebastian, was a pupil of Joseph's, a young man of remarkable gifts. He seemed to master not only the grammar and the vocabulary of foreign languages but the music of them, the subtlety of meaning and the flavor of the cultures that had given them birth.

It was Joseph who had seen the promise in him and encouraged him to seek a place at Cambridge to study ancient languages, not only biblical but the great classics of culture as well. Sebastian had grasped his opportunity. He worked with zeal and remarkable self-discipline for so young a man, and had become one of the brightest of the students, taking first-class honors. Now he was doing postgraduate studies before moving on to a career as a scholar and philosopher, perhaps even a poet.

Mary caught Joseph's eye and smiled at him, her face full of pity.

Gerald came forward. He was a pleasant, ordinary-seeming man, fair-haired, good-looking in a benign, undistinguished way. Brief introductions were made to the Corcorans, who then excused themselves.

"So sorry," Gerald murmured, shaking his head. "So sorry."

"Thank you." Joseph wished there were something sensible to say, and longed to escape.

"Elwyn is here, of course." She indicated very slightly over her shoulder to where Elwyn Allard was talking to Pettigrew, the lawyer, and trying to escape to join his contemporaries. "And unfortunately Sebastian had to be in London," Mary went on. "A prior commitment he could not break." She was thin, with fierce, striking features, dark hair, and a fine olive complexion. "But I am sure you know how deeply he feels."

Gerald cleared his throat as if to say something—from the shadow in his eyes, possibly a disagreement—but he changed his mind.

Joseph thanked them again and excused himself to speak to someone else.

It seemed to stretch interminably—the kindness, the grief, the awkwardness—but eventually the ordeal was over. He saw Mrs. Appleton, somber and pale-faced, as she said goodbye to the vicar and started back to the house. Everything was already prepared to receive their closest friends. There would be nothing for the staff to do but take the muslin cloths off the food already laid out on the tables. Lettie and Reginald had been given time off also, but they would both be back to help with the clearing away.

The house was a mere six hundred yards from the church, and people straggled slowly under the lych-gate and along the road through the village in the quiet sunlight, turning right toward the Reavley home. They all knew each other and were intimately concerned in each other's lives. They had walked to christenings, weddings, and funerals along these quiet roads; they had quarreled and befriended one another, laughed together, gossiped and interfered for better or worse.

Now they grieved, and few needed to find words for it.

Joseph and Hannah welcomed them at the front door. Matthew and

Judith had already gone inside, she to the drawing room, he presumably to fetch the wine and pour it.

The last person was ushered in, and Joseph turned to follow. He was crossing the hall when Matthew came out of John's study ahead of him, his face puckered with concern.

"Joseph, have you been in here this morning?"

"The study? No. Why? Have you lost something?"

"No. I haven't been in since last night, until just now."

Had his brother looked any less concerned, Joseph would have been impatient with him, but there was an anxiety in Matthew's face that held his attention. "If you haven't lost anything, what's the matter?" he asked.

"I was the last one out of the house this morning," Matthew replied, keeping his voice very low so that it would not carry to anyone in the dining room. "After Mrs. Appleton, and she didn't come back—she was at the funeral all the time."

"Of course she was!"

"Someone's been in here," Matthew answered quietly, but with no hesitation or lift of question in his voice. "I know exactly where I left everything. It's the papers. They're all on the square, and I left some of them poking out a fraction, to mark my place."

"Horatio?" Joseph said, thinking of the cat.

"Door was closed," Matthew answered.

"Mrs. Appleton must have . . . ," Joseph began, then, seeing the gravity in Matthew's eyes, he stopped. "What are you saying?"

"Someone was in here while we were all at the funeral," Matthew replied. "No one would have noticed Henry barking, and he was shut in the garden room. I can't see anything gone . . . and don't tell me it was a sneak thief. I locked up myself, and I didn't miss the back door. And a thief wouldn't go through Father's papers; he'd take the silver and the ornaments that are easy to move. The silver-rimmed crystal bud vase is still on the mantelpiece, and the snuffboxes are on the table, not to mention the Bonnington, which is quite small enough to be carried."

Joseph's mind raced, wild ideas falling over each other, but before he could put words to any of them, Hannah came out of the dining room. She looked from one to the other of them. "What's wrong?" she said quickly.

"Matthew's mislaid something, that's all," Joseph replied. "I'll see if I can help him find it. I'll be in in a moment."

"Does it matter now?" There was an edge to her voice, close to breaking. "For heaven's sake, come and speak to people! They're expecting you! You can't leave me there alone! It's horrible!"

"I'd be happier to look first," Matthew answered her before Joseph found the words. His face was miserable and stubborn. "Have you been upstairs since you came home?"

She was incredulous, her eyes wide. "No, of course I haven't! We have half the village in the house as our guests, or haven't you noticed?"

Matthew glanced at Joseph, then back at Hannah. "It matters," he said quietly. "I'm sorry. I'll be down in a minute. Joe?"

Matthew took a deep breath and walked to the foot of the stairs.

Joseph followed after him, leaving Hannah standing in the hall, fuming. When he reached the landing, Matthew was in the doorway to their parents' bedroom, staring around as if to memorize every article there, every line and shadow, the bright bars of light through the window across the floorboards and the carpet. It was so achingly familiar, exactly as it had been as long as he could remember: the dark oak tallboy with his father's brushes and the leather box Alys had given him for cuff links and collar studs; her dressing table, with the oval mirror on a stand that needed a little piece of paper wedged to keep it at the right angle; the cut-glass trays and bowls for hairpins, powder, combs; the wardrobe with the round hatbox on top.

He had stood here to tell his mother that he was going to leave medicine because he could not bear the helplessness he felt in the face of pain he could do nothing to ease. Joseph knew how disappointed his father would be. John had wanted it so fiercely. He had never explained why. He would say very little, but he would not understand, and his silence would hurt more than any accusation or demand for explanations.

And Joseph had come here later to tell Alys that he was going to marry Eleanor. That had been a winter day, rain spattering the window. She had been putting up her hair after changing for dinner. She had always had beautiful hair.

He forced his mind to the present.

"Is there anything gone?" he said aloud.

"I don't think so." Matthew did not move to go in yet. "But there might be, because it's different somehow."

"Are you certain?" It was a stupid question, because he knew Matthew was not certain. He simply wanted to deny the reality settling more and more firmly in his mind with each second. "I don't see anything," he added.

"Wait a minute." Matthew put up his hand as if to stop Joseph from passing him, although Joseph had not moved. "There is something . . . I just can't put my finger on it. It's . . . tidy. It doesn't look as if someone just left it."

"Mrs. Appleton?" Joseph queried.

"No. She won't come in here yet. It still feels like an intrusion, as if she were doing it behind Mother's back."

"Judith? Or Hannah?"

"No." He sounded quite certain. "Hannah might look, but she wouldn't touch anything, not yet. And Judith won't come in here at all. At least . . . I'll ask, but I don't think so." He drew in a deep breath. "It's the pillows. That's not how Mother had them, and no one here would rearrange them that way."

"Isn't that how most people have them?" Joseph looked over at the big bed with its handmade coverlet and the matching pillow shams just touching. It all looked completely ordinary, like anyone's room. Then a tiny memory prickled as he deliberately brought back the image of telling his mother that Eleanor was expecting their first child. She had been so happy. He pictured her face, and the bed behind her, with the pillows at an angle, one overlapping the other. It looked comfortable, casual, not formal like this.

"Someone has been in here," he agreed, his heart beating so hard he felt out of breath. "They must have searched the house while we were all at the funeral." His pulse was knocking in his ears. "For the document—just as we did?"

"Yes," Matthew replied. "Which means it's real. Father was right—he really did have something." His voice was bright and hard, shaking a little, as if he were expecting to be contradicted. "And they didn't get it from him."

Joseph swallowed, aware of all the multitude of meaning that lay beyond that statement. "They still didn't, because it wasn't here. We searched everywhere. So where is it?"

"I don't know!" Matthew looked oddly blank. Now his mind was racing past his words. "I don't know what he did with it, but they don't have it, or they wouldn't be still searching."

"Who are *they*?" Joseph demanded.

Matthew looked back at him, puzzled, still charged with emotion. "I have no idea. I've told you everything he said to me."

The sound of voices drifted up the stairs. Somewhere toward the kitchen a door closed with a bang. He and Matthew should be down with the guests as well. It was unfair to leave Judith and Hannah to do all the receiving, the thanking, the accepting of condolences. He half turned.

"Joe!"

He looked back. Matthew was staring at him, his eyes dark and fixed, his face gaunt in spite of the high cheekbones so like his own.

"It isn't only what happened to it and what it's about," he said quietly, as if he was concerned someone in the hall below could overhear them. "It's whom it implicates. Where did Father get it? Obviously whoever they are, they know he had it, or they wouldn't have been here searching." He let the words hang between them, his white-knuckled hand on the door frame.

The thought came to Joseph only slowly. It was too vast and too ugly to recognize at once. Then when he knew it, it could not be denied. His mouth was dry. "Was it an accident?"

Matthew did not move; he scarcely seemed to be breathing.

"I don't know. If the document was all he said it was, and whoever he took it from knew he was coming to me with it, then probably not."

There was a footstep at the bottom of the stairs.

Joseph swiveled around. Hannah was standing with her hand on the newel, her face white, struggling to keep her composure. "What's the matter?" she said abruptly. "People are beginning to ask where you are! You've got to talk to them, you can't just run away. We all feel like—"

"We're not," Joseph cut across her, beginning to come down the stairs. There was no point in frightening her with the truth, certainly not now. "Matthew lost something, but he's remembered where he put it."

"You must speak to people," she said as he reached her. "They'll expect us all to. You don't live here anymore, but they were Mother's neighbors, and they loved her."

He slipped his arm lightly around her shoulder. "Yes, of course they did. I know that."

She smiled, but there was still anger and frustration in her face, and too much pain to be held within. Today she had stepped into her mother's shoes, and she hated everything that it meant.

Joseph did not see Matthew alone again until just before dinner. Joseph took Henry into the garden, in the waning light, watching it fade and deepen to gold on the tops of the trees. He stared upward at the massed starlings that swirled like dry leaves, high and wide across the luminous sky, so many dark flecks, storm-tossed on an unseen wind.

He did not hear Matthew come silently over the grass behind him, and was startled when the dog turned, tail wagging.

"I'm going to take Hannah to the station tomorrow morning," Matthew said. "She'll catch the ten-fifteen. That'll get her to Portsmouth comfortably before teatime. There's a good connection."

"I suppose I should get back to Cambridge," Joseph responded. "There's nothing else to do here. Pettigrew will call us if he needs anything. Judith's going to stay on in the house. I expect she told you. Anyway, Mrs. Appleton's got to have someone to look after." He said the last part wryly. He was concerned for Judith, as John and Alys had been. She showed no inclination to settle to anything, and seemed to be largely wasting her time. Now that her parents were no longer here, circumstances would force her to address her own future, but it was too early now to say so to her.

"How long can she run the house on the finances there are before the will is probated?" Matthew asked, pushing his hands into his pockets and following Joseph's gaze across the fields to the copse outlined against the sky.

They were both avoiding saying what they really thought. How would she deal with the hurt? Whom would she rebel against now that Alys was not here? Who would see that she did not let her wild side run out of control until she hurt herself irretrievably? How well did they know each other, to begin the love, the patience, the guiding that suddenly was their responsibility?

It was too soon, all much too soon. None of them was ready for it yet.

"From what Pettigrew said, about a year," Joseph replied. "More, if necessary. But she needs to do something other than spend time with her friends and drive around the countryside in that car of hers. I don't know if Father had any idea where she goes, or how fast!"

"Of course he knew!" Matthew retorted. "Actually, he was rather proud of her skill . . . and the fact that she is a better mechanic than Albert. I'll wager she'll use some of her inheritance to buy a new car," he added with a shrug. "Faster and smarter than the Model T. Just as long as she doesn't go for a racer!"

Joseph held out his hand. "What will you bet on it?"

"Nothing I can't afford to lose!" Matthew responded drily. "I don't suppose we can stop her?"

"How?" Joseph asked. "She's twenty-three. She'll do what she wants."

"She always did what she wanted," Matthew retorted. "Just as long as she understands the realities! The financial ones, I mean." It was not what he meant, and both of them knew it. It was about far more than money. She needed purpose, something to manage grief.

Joseph raised his eyebrows. "Is that a backward way of saying it is my responsibility to tell her that?" Of course it was his. He was the eldest, the one to take their father's place, quite apart from the fact that he lived in Cambridge, only three or four miles away, and Matthew was in London. He resented it because he was unprepared. There was a well of anger inside him he dared not even touch, a hurt that frightened him.

Matthew was grinning at him. "That's right!" he agreed. Then his smile faded and the darkness in him came through. "But there's something we have to do before you go. We should have done it before."

Joseph knew what he was going to say the instant before he did.

"The accident." Matthew used the word loosely. Half of his face was like bronze in the dying light, the other too shadowed to see. "I don't know if we can tell anything now, but we need to try. There's been no rain since it happened. Actually, it's the best summer I can remember."

"Me too." Joseph looked away. "Wimbledon finals were today. No interruptions for weather. Norman Brookes and Anthony Wilding." He could think of nothing that mattered less, but it was easy to say, a skittering away from pain.

"Shearing telephoned me," Matthew answered. "He said Brookes won, and Dorothea Chambers won the women's."

"Thought she would. Who's Shearing?" He was trying to place a family friend, someone calling with apologies for not being here. He ran his hand gently over the dog's head.

"Calder Shearing," Matthew replied. "My boss at Intelligence. Just condolences, and of course he needs to know when I'll be back."

Joseph looked at him again. "And when will you?"

Matthew's eyes were steady. "Tomorrow, after we've been to the Hauxton Road. We can't stay here indefinitely. We all have to go on, and the longer we leave it, the harder it will be."

The thought of such violence being deliberate was horrible. He could not bear to imagine someone planning and carrying out the murder of his parents. Yet the alternative was that John Reavley's sharp and logical mind had slipped out of his control and sent him running from a threat that was not real, dreaming up horrors. That was worse. Joseph refused to believe it.

"And if it wasn't an accident?" Why was it so difficult to say that?

Matthew stared at the last light as the sun kindled fire in the clouds on the horizon, vermilion and amber, tree shadows elongated across the fields. The smell of the twilight wind was heavy with hay, dry earth, and the sweetness of mown grass. It was almost harvest time. There were a handful of scarlet poppies like a graze of blood through the darkening gold. The hawthorn petals were all blown from the hedgerows, and in a few months there would be berries.

"I don't know," Matthew answered. "That's the thing! There's nobody to take it to, because we have no idea whom to trust. Father didn't trust the police with this, or he wouldn't have been bringing it to London. But I still have to look at it. Don't you?"

Joseph thought for a moment. "Yes," he admitted. "Yes. I have to know."

The following afternoon, July 3, Matthew and Joseph stopped by the police station at Great Shelford again and asked if they could be shown on the map exactly where the accident had occurred. Reluctantly the sergeant told them.

"You don't want to go looking at that," he said sadly. "Course you want to understand, but there ain't nothing to see. Weren't no one else there, no brangle, no buck-fisted young feller drunk too much an' going faster than he ought. Let it go, sir, that's moi advoice."

"Thank you," Matthew replied with a forced smile. "Just like to see it. There, you said?" He put his finger on the map.

"That's right, sir. Going south."

"Had accidents there before?"

"Not as Oi know of, sir." The sergeant frowned. "Can't say what happened. But then sometimes that's just how it is. Them Lanchesters is good cars. Get up quite a bit of speed with them. Fifty miles an hour, Oi shouldn't wonder. A sudden puncture could send you off the road. Would do anyone."

"Thank you," Joseph said briskly. He wanted to end this and face looking at the scene. Get it over with. He dreaded it. Whatever they found, his mind would create a picture of what had happened there. The reality of it was the same, regardless of the cause. He turned away and walked out of the police station into the humid air. Clouds were massing in the west, and there were tiny flies settling on his skin, black pinpricks—thunder flies.

He walked to the car and climbed in, waiting for Matthew to follow.

They drove west through Little Shelford and Hauxton and on toward the London road, then turned north to the mill bridge. It was only a matter of three or four miles altogether. Matthew held his foot on the accelerator, trying to race the storm. He did not bother to explain; Joseph understood.

It was only a matter of minutes before they were over the bridge. Matthew was obliged to brake with more force than he had intended in order not to overshoot the place on the map. He pulled in to the side of the road, sending a spray of gravel up from the tires.

"Sorry," he said absently. "We'd better hurry. It's going to rain any minute." He swung out and left Joseph to go after him.

It was only twenty yards, and he could see already the long gouge out of the grass where the car had plowed off the paved road, over the verge and the wide margin, crushing the wild foxgloves and the broom plants. It had torn up a sapling as well and scattered a few stones before crashing into a clump of birch trees, scarring the trunks and tearing off a hanging branch, which lay a few yards further on, its leaves beginning to wither.

Matthew stood beside the broom bushes, staring.

Joseph caught up with him and stopped. Suddenly he felt foolish and more vulnerable with every moment. The police sergeant was right. They should not have come here. It would have been far better to leave it in the imagination. Now he could never forget it.

There was a low rumble of thunder around the western horizon, like the warning growl of some great beast beyond the trees and the breathless fields.

"We can't learn anything from it," Joseph said aloud. "The car came off the road. We won't ever know why."

Matthew ignored him, still staring at the broken wake of the crash.

Joseph followed his gaze. At least death must have been quick, almost instantaneous, a moment of terror as they realized they were out of control, a sense of insane, destructive speed, and then perhaps the sound of tearing metal and pain—then nothing. All gone in seconds, less time than it took to imagine it.

Matthew turned and walked back to the road, beside the churned-up wake, careful to avoid stepping on it—not that there was anything more than broken plants. The ground was too dry for wheel tracks.

Joseph was on the edge of repeating that there was nothing to see when he realized that Matthew had stopped and was staring at the ground. "What is it?" he said sharply. "What have you found?"

"The car was weaving," Matthew answered. "Look there!" He pointed to the edge of the road ten yards further on, where there was another clump of foxgloves mown down. "That's where it came off the road first," he said. "He tried to get it back on again, but he couldn't. A puncture wouldn't do that, not that way. I've had one—I know."

"It was more than one," Joseph reminded him. "All the tires were ripped."

"Then there was something on the road that caused it," Matthew said with conviction. "The possibility of getting four spontaneous punctures at the same moment isn't even worth considering." He started to run until he was level with the first broken foxgloves, then he slowed and began to search the ground.

Joseph followed after him, looking from right to left and back again, and then beyond. It was he who first saw the tiny scratches on the tarmacadam surface. He glanced sideways and saw another less than a foot away, and then another beyond that.

"Matthew!"

"Yes, I see them." Matthew reached the line and bent to his knees. Once he had found them, it was easy to trace the marks right across the road, each less than the width of a car tire from the next. They were only slight scars, except in two places about axle-width apart, where they were deeper, actual gouges in the surface. In the heat of this summer, day after day of sun, the tar would have been softer than usual, more easily marked. In winter there might have been nothing.

"What were they?" Joseph asked, racking his mind for what could have torn tires on a moving car and left this track behind, yet not be here now, nor have been found embedded in the tires themselves. Except, of course, no one had been looking for such things.

Matthew stood up, his face white. "It can't be nails," he said. "How could you put nails on a road to stay point upward and catch only the car you wanted, and not leave them in the tires for police to find if they looked?"

"Wait for them," Joseph answered, his heart knocking in his chest so violently his body shook. A cold, hurting rage engulfed him that anyone could cold-bloodedly place such a weapon across the road, then crouch out of sight, waiting for a car with people in it, and watch it crash. He could hardly breathe as he imagined them walking over to the wreck, ignoring the broken and bleeding bodies, perhaps still alive, and searching for a document. And when they did not find it, they left, simply went away, carefully taking with them whatever had caused the wreck.

He hated them. For a moment the heat of it poured over his skin in sweat. Then he found himself shivering uncontrollably, even though the air was hot and still, damp on the skin. More thunder flies settled on his face and hands.

Matthew had gone back to the side of the road, but opposite from the place where the car had swerved off. On this side there was a deeper ditch, thick with primrose leaves. There was a thin, straight line where they were torn, as if something sharp had ripped through them right from the tarmacadam edge all the way across to the ditch and beyond.

Dizzily, his vision blurred except for a crystal clarity at the center. Through it Joseph saw a birch sapling next to the hedge. A frayed end of rope hung from the trunk, biting into the bark about a foot from the ground. He could imagine the force that had caused that. He could see it—the yellow Lanchester with John Reavley at the wheel and Alys beside him, possibly at something like fifty miles an hour, striking it . . . striking what?

He turned to Matthew, willing him to deny it, wipe away what he imagined.

"Caltrops," Matthew said softly, shaking his head as if he could rid himself of the idea.

"Caltrops?" Joseph asked, puzzled.

"Twists of iron prong," Matthew replied, hooking his fingers together to demonstrate. "Like the things they put in barbed wire, only bigger. They used them in the Middle Ages to bring down knights on horseback."

Thunder rumbled again, closer to them. The air was almost too clammy to breathe.

"On a rope," Matthew went on. He did not look at Joseph, as if he could not bear to. "They must have waited here until they heard the car coming. Then when they knew it was the Lanchester, they sprinted across the road to the far side, and pulled it tight." He bowed his head for a moment. "Even if Father saw it," he said hoarsely, "there would be no way to avoid it." He hesitated a moment, taking a deep breath. "Then afterward they cut the rope—hacked it, by the look of it—and took the whole thing away with them."

It was all clear. Joseph said nothing. It was hideously real now, no more possibility of doubt. John and Alys Reavley had been murdered—he to silence him and retrieve the document, she because she happened to be with him. It was brutal, monstrous! Pain ran through him like fire inside his head. He could see the terror in his mother's face, his father struggling desperately to control the car and knowing he couldn't, the physical destruction, the helplessness. Had they had time to know it was death and they could do nothing for each other, not even time for a touch, a word?

And he could do nothing. It was over, complete, beyond his reach. There was nothing left but blind, bright red fury. They would find whoever had done this. It was his father, his mother, it had happened to. People who were precious and good had been destroyed, taken from him. Who had done it? What kind of people—and why?

They must find them, stop them. This must never happen again.

He would do what he should. He would be kind, obedient, honorable—but never hurt like this again. He could not endure it.

"Is Judith safe?" he said abruptly. "What if they go back to the house?" The thought of having to tell her the truth was ugly, but how could they avoid it?

"They won't go back." Matthew straightened up unsteadily. "They know it's not there. But where the hell is it? I'm damned if I know!" His voice was breaking, threatening to go out of control. He stared at Joseph, willing him to help, to find an answer where he could not.

Thunder cracked across the sky above them, and the first heavy spots of rain fell, splashing large and warm on them and on the road.

Joseph seized Matthew's arm and they turned and ran to the car, sprinting the last few paces and scrambling in, struggling with the roof as the heavens opened and torrential rain swirled across the fields and hedges, blinding the windscreen and drumming on the metal of the car body. Lightning blazed and vanished.

Matthew started the engine, and it was a relief to hear it roar to life. He put the car into gear and inched out onto the swimming road. Neither of them spoke.

When the cloudburst had passed and they could open the windows, the air was filled with the perfume of fresh rain on parched earth. It was a fragrance like no other, so sharp and clean they could hardly draw enough of it. The sun returned, gleaming on wet roads and dripping hedges, every leaf bright.

"What did Father say, exactly?" Joseph asked when at last he had control of himself enough to speak almost levelly.

"I've gone over and over it so many times I'm not sure anymore," Matthew answered, his eyes ahead on the road. "I thought he said he was bringing it, but now I'm not certain. And since they didn't find it, and they must have looked, and so did we, the only alternative seems to be that he hid it somewhere." He was almost calm, addressing it as though it were an intellectual problem he had to solve, and the passion of the reality had never existed.

"We have to tell Judith," Joseph said, watching his face for his reaction. "Apart from keeping the house locked if she's ever in it alone, she has a right to know. And Hannah . . . but perhaps not yet."

Matthew was silent. There was another flare of lightning far away, and then thunder off in the distance to the south.

Joseph was about to repeat what he had said, but finally Matthew spoke.

"I suppose we must, but let me do it."

Joseph did not argue. If Matthew imagined Judith would allow him to evade any of the issues, then he did not know his sister as well as Joseph did.

When they reached St. Giles it started to rain again. They were both glad to leave the car and use getting soaked as an excuse to avoid immediate conversation. It was emotional enough saying goodbye to Hannah as Albert put her luggage into the Ford. She did not want anyone to go to the station with her.

"I'd rather not!" she said quickly. "If I'm going to burst into tears, at least let me do it here, not on the platform!"

No one argued with her. Perhaps they preferred it this way, too. She hugged each of them, not able to find words, or a steady voice to say anything. Then, holding her head so high she all but tripped on the step—even though it had been there all her life—she followed Albert out to the car. Joseph, Matthew, and Judith stood in the doorway watching her until the car was out of sight. Then Joseph walked over the grass to close the gate.

"I know what you're going to say," Judith retorted defensively when they were sitting in the dining room after dinner, Henry asleep on the floor. It was barely dark outside and clear again, the storm long since passed.

"I don't think you do." Matthew set his coffee cup down and regarded her gravely.

She looked at Joseph. "Shouldn't you be the one doing this?" she challenged, anger hard in her voice and her eyes. "Why aren't you telling me what to do? Haven't you the stomach for it? Or do you know it's a waste of time? You're a priest! It's cowardly not even to try! Father always tried!"

It was an accusation that he was not Father, not wise enough, not patient or persistent enough. He knew it already. It was a deep ache inside him and, as with her, an anger, because no one had equipped him to do this. John Reavley had gone leaving a task half done and no one to replace him, as if he did not care.

"Judith . . . ," Matthew began.

"I know!" She swung round to face him, cutting across his words. "The house is Joseph's, but I can live here as long as he doesn't need it, and he doesn't. We've already discussed that. But I can't go on wasting my time. That's a condition. I've either got to get married or find something useful to do, preferably something that pays me enough to at least feed and clothe myself." Her eyes were red-rimmed, full of tears. "Why haven't you the courage to say that to me? Father would have! And I don't need a gardener, a cook, a manservant, and a housemaid to look after me." She stared at him furiously. "I worked that out for myself." She flicked a glance sideways at Joseph, contempt in it.

Joseph felt the sting, but he had no defense. It was true.

"Actually, I wasn't going to say anything of the sort," Matthew said to her tartly. "Joseph told me you were perfectly aware of the situation. I was going to tell you why Father was coming to see me on the day he was killed, and what we have learned since then. I would rather have protected you from it, but I don't think we can afford to do that, and Joseph thinks you have a right to know anyway."

Apology flashed across her face, then fear. She bit her lip. "Know what?" she said huskily.

Briefly Matthew told her about John Reavley's call on the telephone, admitting that he was uncertain now of the exact words. "And when we were at the funeral, someone searched the house," he finished. "That is why Joseph and I were late into the dining room."

"Well, where is it?" she said, looking at one, then the other, her anger added to by confusion and the beginning of sick, urgent fear.

"We don't know," Matthew answered. "We've looked everywhere we can think of. I even tried the laundry, the gun room, and the apple shed this morning, but we haven't found anything."

"Then who has it?" She turned to Joseph. "It is real, isn't it?"

It was a question he was not prepared to face. It challenged too much of the belief in his father, and he refused to be without that. "Yes, it's real," he said with biting certainty. He saw the doubt in her eyes, her struggle to believe and understand it, far more than he was willing to admit. "We went to the stretch of road where it happened," he said in harsh, measured words, like incisions. "We saw where the car began to swerve, and where it finally plowed over the verge and into the trees. . . ."

Matthew started to speak but stopped, blinking rapidly. He turned away.

Judith stared at Joseph, waiting for him to justify what he was telling her.

"Once we understood what had happened, it was quite clear," Joseph continued. "Someone had used a kind of barb, tied to a rope . . . the end of it was still knotted around a sapling trunk . . . and stretched it across the road deliberately. The marks were there in the tarmacadam."

He saw the incredulity in her face. "But that's murder!" she exclaimed.

"Yes, it is."

She started to shake her head, and he thought for a moment she was not going to get her breath. He put out his hand, and she gripped it so hard it bruised the flesh.

"What are you going to do?" she said. "You are going to do something, aren't you?"

"Of course!" Matthew jerked up his head. "Of course we are. But we don't know where to start yet. We can't find the document, and we don't know what's in it."

"Where did he get it?" she said, trying to steady her voice and sound in control. "Whoever gave it to him would know what it was about."

Matthew gave a gesture of helplessness. "No idea! It could be almost anything: government corruption, a financial scandal, even a royal scandal, for that matter. It might be political or diplomatic. It could be some dishonorable solution to the Irish Question."

"There is no solution to the Irish Question, honorable or not," she replied with an edge of hysteria to her voice. "But Father still kept up with quite a few of his old parliamentary colleagues. Maybe one of them gave it to him?"

Matthew leaned forward a little. "Did he? Do you know anyone he was in touch with recently? He'd only had it a few hours when he called me."

"Are you certain?" Joseph asked. "If you are, then that would mean he got it on the Saturday before he died. But if he thought about it a while before calling you, it could have been Friday, or even Thursday."

"Let's start with Saturday," Matthew directed, looking back to Judith. "Do you know what he did on Saturday? Was he here? Did he go out, or did anyone come to see him?"

"I don't know," she said miserably. "I was in and out myself. I can hardly remember now. Albert was supposed to be doing something in the orchard. The only one who would know would be . . . Mother." She swallowed and took a ragged breath. She was still clinging onto Joseph's hand, her knuckles white with the strength of her grip. "But you can't let it go! You're going to do something? If you aren't, then I will! They can't get away with it!"

"Yes, of course I am," Matthew assured her. "Nobody's going to get away with it! But Father said it was a conspiracy. That means several people are involved, and we have no idea whom."

"But . . . ," she started, then stopped. Her voice dropped very low. "I was going to say it couldn't be anyone we know, but that's not true, is it? The opposite is! It had to have been someone who trusted him, or they wouldn't have given him the document in the first place."

He did not answer.

Her rage and misery exploded. "You are in the Secret Intelligence Service! Isn't this the sort of thing you do? What damn use are you if you can't catch the people who killed our family?" She glared at Joseph. "And if you tell me to forgive them, I swear to God I'll hit you!"

"You won't have to," he promised. "I wouldn't tell you to do something I can't do myself."

She searched his face as if seeing him more clearly than ever before. "I've never heard you say that in the past, no matter how hard it's been." She leaned forward and buried her head in his shoulder. "Joe! What's happening to us? How can this be?"

He put his arms around her. "I don't know," he admitted. "I don't know."

Matthew rubbed his eyes, pushing his hair back savagely. "Of course

I'm going to do something!" he repeated. "That's why he was bringing it to me." There was pride and anger in his voice. His face was pinched with loss of what was irretrievable now. He was still struggling to be reasonable. "If it were something the police could deal with, he'd have taken it to them." He looked at Joseph. "We dare not trust anyone," he warned them both. "Judith, you must make sure the house is locked every night, and anytime you and the servants are all out—just as a precaution. I don't think they'll come back, because they've already looked here, and they know we haven't got it. But if you'd rather go and stay—"

"With a friend? No, I wouldn't!" she said quickly.

"Judith . . ."

"If I change my mind, I'll go to the Mannings'," she snapped. "I'll say I'm lonely. They'll understand. I promise! Just don't push me. I'll do what I want."

"There's a novelty!" Matthew said with a sudden, bleary smile, as if he needed to break the taut thread of tension.

She looked at him sharply, then her face softened and her eyes filled with tears.

"I'll find them," he promised, his voice choking. "Not only because they killed Mother and Father, but to stop them doing whatever it was in the document—if we can."

"I'm glad you said *we*." She answered his smile now. "Tell me what I can do."

"When there is anything, I will," he said. "I promise. But call me if there's anything at all! Or Joseph—just to talk if you want. You must do that!"

"Stop telling me what to do!" But there was relief in her voice. A shred of safety had returned, something familiar, even if it was a restriction to fight against. "But of course I will." She reached out to touch him. "Thank you."

CHAPTER

THREE

Joseph found his first day back at St. John's even more difficult than he had anticipated. The ancient beauty of the buildings, mellow brick with castellated front and stone-trimmed windows, soothed his mind. Its calm was indestructible, its dignity timeless. His rooms closed around him like well-fitting armor. He looked with pleasure at the light reflected unevenly on the old glass of the bookcases, knowing intimately every volume within, the thoughts and dreams of great men down the ages. On the wall between the windows overlooking the quadrangle were paintings of Florence and Verona. He remembered choosing them to keep in his heart those streets worn smooth by the footsteps of his heroes. And of course there was the bust of Dante on the shelf, that genius of poetry, imagination, the art of the story, and above all the understanding of the nature of good and evil.

He had been away for long enough for an amount of work to have collected, and the concentration needed to catch up was also a kind of healing. The languages of the Bible were subtle and different from modern speech. Their very nature necessitated that they refer to everyday things common to all mankind: seed time and harvest, the water of physical and spiritual life. The rhythms had time to repeat themselves and let the meaning sink deep into the mind; the flavor and the music of it removed him from the present, and so from his own reality.

It was friends who brought him the sharp reminder of loss. He saw the sympathy in their eyes, the uncertainty whether to speak of it or not, what to say that was not clumsy. Every student seemed to know at least of the deaths, if not the details.

The master, Aidan Thyer, had been very considerate, asking Joseph if he was sure he was ready to come back so soon. He was valued, of course, and irreplaceable, but nevertheless he must take more time if he needed it.

Joseph answered him that he did not. Everything had been done that was required, and his responsibilities to work were a blessing, not a burden. He thanked him and promised to take his first tutorial the following morning.

It was difficult picking up the threads after an absence of almost two weeks, and it required all his effort of mind to make an acceptable job of it. He was exhausted by the end of the day, and happy after dinner to leave the dining hall, the stained-glass windows scattered with the coats of arms of benefactors dating back to the early 1500s, the magnificent timbered ceiling with its carved hammer beams touched with gold, the oak-paneled walls carved in linen-fold, and above all its chattering, well-meaning people. He longed to escape toward the river.

He started across the narrow arch of the Bridge of Sighs with its stone fretwork like frozen lace, a windowed passageway to the fields beyond. He would walk across the smooth grass of the Backs, stretching all the way from Magdalene Bridge past St. John's, Trinity, Gonville and Caius, Clare, and King's College Chapel toward Queen's and the Mathematical Bridge. Perhaps he would go as far as the millpond beyond, and over the causeway to Lammas Land. It was still warm. The long, slow sunset and twilight would last another hour and a half yet, perhaps more.

He was on the slow rise of the bridge, glancing out through the open lattice at the reflections on the water below, when he heard footsteps behind him. He turned to see a young man in his early twenties. His face was beautiful, strong-boned, clear-eyed, his brown hair bleached gold across the top by the long summer.

"Sebastian!" Joseph said with pleasure.

"Dr. Reavley! I . . ." Sebastian Allard stopped, his fair skin a little flushed with consciousness of his inadequacy to say anything that matched the situation, and perhaps also that he had missed the funeral. "I'm so sorry. I can't tell you how bad I feel."

"You don't have to," Joseph said quickly. "I would far rather talk about something else."

Sebastian hesitated, indecision clear in his half-turned shoulder.

Joseph did not want to press him, yet he felt Sebastian had something to say, and he could not rebuff him. Their families had lived in neighboring villages for years, and it was Joseph who had seen the promise in young Sebastian and encouraged him to pursue it. He had been his mentor for the last year while they had both been at St. John's. It had become one of those friendships that blossomed so naturally he could not believe there was ever a possibility it would not have happened.

"I'm going for a walk along the Backs," Joseph said. "If you want to join me, you are welcome." He smiled and began to turn away, so as not to place an obligation on the younger man, as if it were a request.

There were a few moments of silence, then he heard the footsteps quickly and lightly on the bridge after him, and he and Sebastian emerged into the sunlight, almost side by side. The air was still warm, and the smell of cut grass drifted on the slight breeze. The river was flat calm, barely disturbed by three or four punts along the stretch past St. John's and Trinity. In the nearest one a young man in gray flannel trousers and a white shirt stood leaning on the pole with effortless grace, his back to the sun, casting his features into shadow and making an aureole around his head.

A girl with red hair sat in the back looking up at him and laughing. Her muslin dress looked primrose-colored in the fading glow, but in the daylight it could have been ivory, or even white. Her skin was amber where she had defied convention and allowed the long, hot season to touch her with its fire. She was eating from a basket of cherries and dropping the stones into the water one after another.

The young man waved and called out a greeting.

Joseph waved back, and Sebastian answered as well.

"He's a good fellow," Sebastian said a moment later. "He's at Caius, reading physics. All terribly practical." He sounded as if he were about to say something more, then he pushed his hands into his pockets and walked silently on the grass.

Joseph felt no need for speech. The slight splash of punt poles and the current of the river slurping against their wooden sides, the occasional burst of laughter, were a wordless communication. Even grief could not entirely mar its timeless peace.

"We have to protect this!" Sebastian said suddenly and with fierce emotion. His voice was thick, his shoulders tense as he half turned to stare across the shining water at the buildings beyond. "All of it! The ideas, the beauty, the knowledge . . . the freedom to think." He drew in his breath. "To discover the things of the mind. We are accountable to humanity for what we have. To the future."

Joseph was startled. He had been letting himself sink into a sort of vacancy of thought, where emotion was sufficient to carry him. There was a glory here like the best music, filling everything. Now he was jerked back by Sebastian's words. He deserved a considered answer, and it was apparent from the passion in his face that he needed one.

"You mean Cambridge specifically? What do you think endangers it?" Joseph asked, puzzled by the heat in him. "It's been here for over half a millennium, and it seems to be growing stronger rather than weaker."

Sebastian's eyes were grave. His fair skin had been caught by the sun, and in the burning amber light now he looked almost made of gold. "I don't suppose you've had time to read the news," he answered. "Or the inclination, for that matter." He turned his head away, not wanting to intrude into Joseph's feelings, or else hiding his own.

"Not much," Joseph agreed. "But I know about the assassinations in Sarajevo, and that Vienna is unhappy about it. They want some sort of reparation from the Serbs. I suppose it was to be expected."

"If you occupy somebody else's country, it is to be expected that they won't like it!" Sebastian responded savagely. "All sorts of things come to be *expected*." He repeated the word with sarcastic emphasis. "Strike and counterstrike, revenge for this or that—justice, from the other point of view. Isn't it the responsibility of thinking men to stop the cycle and reach for something better?" He swung his arms wide, gesturing toward the exquisite buildings on the farther bank, their western facades glowing pale in the light, the shadows deepening to the east. "Isn't that what all this is for, to teach us something better than 'you hurt me, so I'll hurt you back'? Aren't we supposed to be leading the way toward a higher morality?"

There could be no argument. It was the aim not only of philosophy, but of Christianity as well, and Sebastian knew Joseph would not deny that.

"Yes," he agreed. He sought the supreme comfort of reason. "But there have always been conquests, injustices, and rebellions—or revolutions, if you prefer. They have never endangered the heart of learning."

Sebastian stopped. A burst of laughter came up from the river where two punts almost collided as young men drinking champagne tried to reach across and touch glasses in a toast. One of the boys nearly overbalanced and was perilously close to falling in. His companion grasped him by the back of his shirt, and all he lost was his straw boater, which floated for a moment or two on the shining surface before someone from the other punt caught it on the end of his pole. He presented it to its owner, who took it, dripping wet, and put it back on his head, to shouts of approval and a loud and hilarious guffaw.

It was so good-natured, a celebration of life, that Joseph found himself smiling. The sun was warm on his face, and the smells of the earth and grass were sweet.

"It's not easy to imagine, is it?" Sebastian replied.

"What?"

"Destruction . . . war," Sebastian answered, looking away from the river and back at Joseph, his eyes dark with the weight of his thoughts.

Joseph hesitated. He had not realized Sebastian was so deeply troubled.

"You don't think so?" Sebastian said. "You're mourning a loss, sir, and I am truly sorry for it. But if we get drawn into a European war, every family in England will be mourning, not just for those we loved, but for the whole way of life we've cherished and nurtured for a thousand years. If we let that happen, we would be the true barbarians! And we would be to blame for more than the Goths or the Vandals who sacked Rome. They didn't know any better. We do!" His voice was savage, almost on the point of tears.

Joseph was frightened by the note of hysteria in him. "There was revolution all over Europe in 1848," he said gently, choosing his words with care and unarguable truth. "It didn't destroy civilization. In fact, it didn't even destroy the despotism it was supposed to." This was reason, calm history of fact. "Everything went back to normal within a year."

"You're not saying that was good?" Sebastian challenged him, his eyes bright, assured at least of that. He knew Joseph far too well to suppose he did.

"No, of course not. I'm saying that the order of things is set in very deep foundations, and it will take far more than the assassination of an archduke and his duchess, brutal as it was, to cause any radical change."

Sebastian bent and picked up a twig and hurled it toward the river, but it was too light and fell short. "Do you think so?"

"Yes," Joseph replied with certainty. Private griefs might shake his personal world, tear out the heart of it, but the beauty and the reason of civilization continued, immeasurably greater than the individual.

Sebastian stared across the river, but unseeingly, his eyes clouded by his vision within. "That's what Morel said, too, and Foubister. They think the world won't ever change, or not more than an inch at a time. There are others, like Elwyn, who think that even if there is war, it will all be quick and noble, a rather more dramatic version of a good Rider Haggard story, or Anthony Hope. You know *The Prisoner of Zenda* and that sort of thing? All high honor and clean death at the point of a sword. Do you know much of the truth about the Boer War, sir? What we really did there?"

"A little," Joseph acknowledged. He knew it had been ruthless, and there was a great deal for Britain to be ashamed of. But perhaps there was for the Boers, too. "That was Africa, though," he said aloud. "And perhaps we've learned from it. Europe would be different. But there's no reason to think there'll be war, unless there's more trouble in Ireland and we let it get completely out of hand."

Sebastian said nothing.

"Sarajevo was the isolated act of a group of assassins," Joseph went on. "Europe is hardly going to go to war over it. It was a crime, not an—"

Sebastian turned to him, his eyes astonishingly clear in the waning light. "Not an act of war?" he interrupted. "Are you sure, sir? I'm not. The kaiser restated his alliance with Austria-Hungary last Sunday, you know."

The twilight breeze rippled faintly across the surface of the river. It was still warm, like a soft touch to the skin.

"And Serbia is on Russia's back doorstep," Sebastian continued. "If Austria demands too much reparation, they could get drawn in. And there's always the old enmity between France and Germany. The men who fought the Franco-Prussian War are still alive, and still bitter." He started to walk again, perhaps to avoid the group of students coming toward them across the grass. It was clear he did not want to be caught up in their conversation and interrupted in his infinitely more serious thoughts.

Joseph kept pace with him, moving into the shadow of the trees, their leaves whispering faintly above them. "There may be an unjust suppression of the Serbs," he said, trying to return to the safety of reason. "And the people in general may be punished for the violent acts of a few, which is wrong—of course it is. But it is not the catastrophe for civilization that you are suggesting." He, too, spread his hands to encompass the fading scene in front of them, with its sudden dashes of silver and blue on the water. "All this is safe." He said it with unquestioning certainty. It was a thousand years of unbroken progress toward even greater humanity. "We shall still be here, learning, exploring, creating our own beauty, adding to the richness of mankind."

Sebastian studied him, his face torn with conflicting rage and pity, almost tenderness. "You believe that, don't you?" he said with incredulity verging on despair. Then he continued to walk again without waiting for the answer. Somehow the movement suggested a kind of dismissal.

"What is it you think will happen?" Joseph asked firmly.

"Darkness," Sebastian answered. "Complacency without the vision to see, or the courage to act. And it takes courage! You have to see beyond the obvious, the comfortable morality everyone else agrees with, and understand that at times, terrible times, the end justifies the means." His voice dropped. "Even when the cost is high. Otherwise they'll lead us blindly down the path to a war like nothing we've ever even imagined before." His words were cutting, and without the slightest hesitation. "It won't be a few cavalry charges here and there, a few brave men killed or injured. It'll be everyone—the ordinary man in the street sucked into endless mind- and body-breaking bombardment by even bigger guns. It'll be hunger and fear and hatred until that's all we know." He squinted a little as the sun blazed level with the treetops to the west and painted fire on the top of the walls of Trinity and Caius. "Think of the towns and villages you know—St. Giles, Haslingfield, Grantchester, all the rest—with black on every window, no marriages, no christenings, only deaths." His voice dropped and was filled with a hurting tenderness. "Think of the countryside, the fields with no men to plant them or to reap. Think of the woods in April with no one to see the blossom. Schoolboys won't dream of this." He gestured toward the rooftops. "Only of carrying guns. Their only ambition will be to kill and to survive."

He turned to face Joseph again, his eyes clear as seawater in the long light. "Isn't it worth any price to save us from that? Isn't it what human beings are here for, to nourish and protect what we've been given, and add to it before we pass it on? Look at it!" he demanded. "Don't you love it almost more than you can bear?"

Joseph did not need to look to know his answer. "Yes, I do," he said with the same depth of absolute knowledge. "It is the ultimate sanity of life. In the end, it is all there is to hold on to."

Sebastian winced, his face looking suddenly bruised and hollow. "I'm sorry," he said in a whisper. He moved his hand as if to touch Joseph's arm, then withdrew. "But this is a universal sanity, isn't it? Bigger than any one of us, a purpose, a healing for mankind?" His voice was urgent, begging for assurance.

"Yes, it is," Joseph agreed gently. He meant it more profoundly than he had imagined he would, but as had happened so many times in their friendship, Sebastian put it in exactly the words that framed his own belief. "And yes, it is the duty of those who have seen it and become part of it to protect it with all our power."

Sebastian smiled very slightly and turned away as they started back again. "But you don't fear war, do you, sir? I mean real, literal war."

"I would fear it horribly if I considered it a real danger," Joseph assured him. "But I don't think it is. We've had many wars before, and we've lost many men. We've faced invasion more than once and beaten it off. It hasn't broken us irreparably; if anything, it's made us stronger."

"Not this time," Sebastian said bitterly. "If it happens, it'll be pure, blind destruction."

Joseph looked sideways at him. He could see in Sebastian's face the love for all that was precious and vulnerable, all that could be broken by the unthinking. There was a pain in him that was naked in this strange, fierce light of dusk, which cast such black shadows.

Time and again they had talked of all manner of things, no boundaries of time or place had held them: the men half human, half divine in the epic legends of Egypt and Babylon; the God of the Old Testament, who was the creator of worlds, yet spoke face-to-face with Moses, as one man talks with another. They had basked in the lean, golden classicism of Greece, the teeming magnificence of Rome, the intricate glories of Byzantium, the sophistication of Persia. All had been the furniture of their dreams. Wherever Joseph had led, Sebastian had followed eagerly, grasping after each new experience with insatiable joy.

The light was almost gone. The color burned only on the horizon, the shadows dense on the Backs. The water was pale and polished like old silver, indigo under the bridges.

"We could disappear into the ruins of time if there's war," Sebastian resumed. "In a thousand years' time, scholars from cultures we haven't even imagined, young and curious, could dig up what's left of us, and from a few shards, scraps of writing, try to work out what we were really like. And get it wrong," he added bitterly.

"English would become a dead language, lost, like Aramaic or Etruscan," Sebastian went on with quiet misery. "No more wit of Oscar Wilde, or grandeur of Shakespeare, no more thunder of Milton, music of Keats, or . . . God knows how many more . . . and worst of all, the future culled. All that this generation might do. We have to prevent that—whatever it costs!"

"It is impossible to care too much," Joseph said gently. "It is all infinitely precious." He must bring back reason, ground this fear in the lasting realities.

"There is nothing you or I can do to affect the quarrels of Austria and Serbia," he went on. "There will always be fighting somewhere, from time to time. And as inventions like telephones and wireless get better, we will know of them sooner. A hundred years ago it would have taken weeks for us to learn about it, if we did at all. And by that time it would all have been over. Now we read about it the day after, so we feel it to be more immediate, but it's only a perception. Hold on to the certainties that endure."

Sebastian looked at him, his back to the last of the light, so Joseph could not make out his expression. His voice was rough-edged. "You don't think this is different? A hundred years ago we were nearly conquered by Napoleon."

Joseph realized he had made a tactical error in choosing a hundred years as an example. "Yes, but we weren't," he said confidently. "No French soldier set foot in England, except as a prisoner."

"As you said, sir, things have changed in a hundred years," Sebastian pointed out. "We have steamships, airplanes, guns that can shoot further and destroy more than ever before. A west wind won't keep the navies of Europe locked in harbor now."

"You're allowing your fears to run away with your reason," Joseph chided him. "We have had far more desperate times, but we have always prevailed. And we have grown stronger since the Napoleonic Wars, not weaker. You must have faith in us . . . and in God."

Sebastian gave a little grunt, ironic and dismissive, as if there were some deeper fear he could not explain, one that Joseph seemed to refuse or to be incapable of understanding. "Why?" he said bitterly. "The Israelites were the chosen people, and where are they now? We study their language as a curiosity. It matters only because it is the language of Christ, whom they denied and crucified. If the Bible didn't speak of Him, we wouldn't care about Hebrew. We can't say that of English. Why should anyone remember it if we were conquered? For Shakespeare? We don't remember the language of Aristotle, Homer, Aeschylus. It's taught in the best schools, to the privileged few, as a relic of a great civilization of the past." His voice choked with sudden, uncontrollable anger and his face was twisted with pain. "I don't want to become a relic! I want people a thousand years from now to speak the same tongue that I do, to love the same beauty, to understand my dreams and how they mattered to me. I want to write something, or even do something, that preserves the soul of who we are."

The last of the light was now only a pale wash low across the horizon. "War changes us, even if we win." He turned away from Joseph, as if to hide a nakedness within. "Too many of us become barbarians of the heart. Have you any idea how many could die? How many of those left would be consumed by hate, all over Europe? Everything that was good in them eaten away by the things they had seen and, worse, the things they had been forced to do?"

"It won't happen!" Joseph responded, and the moment the words were gone from his lips he wondered if they were true. "If you can't have faith in people, the leaders of nations, then have faith that God will not allow the world to plunge into the kind of destruction you are thinking of," he said. "What purpose of His could it serve?"

Sebastian's lip curled in a tiny smile. "I've no idea! I don't know the purposes of God! Do you, sir?" The softness of his voice, and the *sir* on the end, robbed it of offense.

"To save the souls of men," Joseph replied without hesitation.

"And what does that mean?" Sebastian turned back to face him. "Do you suppose He sees it the same way I do?" Again the smile touched his lips, this time self-mocking.

Joseph was obliged to smile in answer, although the sadness jolted him as if the fading of the light were in some terrible way a permanent thing. "Not necessarily," he conceded. "But He is more likely to be right."

Sebastian did not reply, and they walked slowly along the grass as the breeze rose a little. All the punts were gone to their moorings, and the spires of stone in the arched top of the Bridge of Sighs were barely darker than the sky beyond.

* * *

Matthew returned to London, going first to his flat. It was exactly as he had left it, except that the maid had tidied it, but it felt different. It should have had the comfort of home. It was where he had lived for the last five years, ever since he had left university and begun working for the Intelligence Service. It was full of the books, drawings, and paintings he had collected. His favorite painting, hanging over the fire, was of cows in the corner of the field. For him their gentle rumination, calm eyes, and slow generosity seemed the ultimate sanity in the world. On the mantel was a silver vase his mother had given him one Christmas, and a Turkish dagger with a highly ornamental scabbard.

But the flat was oddly empty. He felt as if he were returning not to the present but to the past. When he had last sat in the worn leather armchair or eaten at this table, his family was whole, and he knew of no vanishing document that was at the heart of conspiracy, violence, and secrets that brought death. The world had not been exactly safe, but whatever dangers there were lay in places far distant, and only the periphery of them touched England, or Matthew himself.

He spent a long evening deep in thought. It was the first time he had been alone more than to sleep since he had walked across the grass at Fenner's Field to break the news to Joseph. Questions crowded his mind.

John Reavley had called him on Saturday evening, not here at his flat, but at his office in the Intelligence Services. He had been working late, on the Irish problems, as usual. The Liberal government had been trying to pass a Home Rule bill to give Ireland autonomy since the middle of the previous century, and time after time the Protestants of Ulster had blocked it, refusing absolutely to be forcibly separated from Britain and placed in Catholic Ireland. They believed that both their religious freedom and their economic survival depended upon remaining free from such a forced integration, and ultimately subjection.

Government after government had fallen on the issue, and now Arquill's personal Liberal Party required the support of the Irish Parliamentary Party in order to retain power.

Shearing, Matthew's superior, shared the view of many others that there was a great deal of political maneuvering in London behind the mutiny of British troops stationed in the Curragh. When the men of Ulster, solidly backed by their women, had threatened armed rebellion against the Home Rule bill, the British troops had refused to take up arms against them. General Gough had resigned, with all his officers, whereupon Sir John French, chief of the General Staff in London, had resigned also, immediately followed by Sir John Seely, secretary for war in the Cabinet.

Little wonder Shearing and his men worked late. The situation threatened to become a crisis as grave as any in the last three hundred years.

Matthew had been in his office when the call came from John Reavley telling him of the document and that he was going to drive to London with it the following day, expecting to arrive between half past one and two o'clock. He would bring Alys with him, ostensibly for an afternoon in the city, but in order to make his trip unremarkable.

How had anyone else known that he even had the document, let alone that he was taking it to Matthew, and the time of his journey? If he came by car, the route was obvious. There was only one main road from St. Giles to London.

Matthew cast his mind back to that evening, the offices almost silent, hardly anyone there, just half a dozen men, perhaps a couple of clerks. He remembered standing at his desk with the telephone in his hand, the disbelief at what his father had said. Matthew had repeated what his father had said, to make certain he had heard correctly.

The cold ran through him. Was that it? In the quiet office someone had overheard him? That had been enough. Who? He tried to recall who else had been there, but one late night blended into another. He had heard footsteps, voices deliberately kept low so as not to disturb others. He might not have recognized them then; he certainly could not now.

But he could find out, discreetly. He could at least trace the possibly treasonous behavior among his own colleagues—when even a week ago he would have trusted them all without hesitation.

* * *

When he arrived in the morning everything was familiar: the cramped spaces, the echoing wooden floor, the black telephones, the dust motes in the air, the worn surfaces, and the harsh desk lamps, unnecessary now in the sunlight through the windows. Clerks bustled back and forth, shirtsleeves grimy from endless papers and ink, collars stiff and often a trifle crooked.

They wished him good morning and offered their condolences, shy and awkward and, for all he could see, intensely sincere. He thanked them and went to his own small room, where books were wedged into too small a case and papers were locked in drawers. The inkwell and blotting papers were just as usual, not quite straight on his desk, two pens lying beside them. The blotting paper was clean. He never left anything that might be decipherable.

He fished for his keys to unlock the top drawer. At first it did not slide in easily, but took a moment of fiddling. He bent to look more closely, and that was when he saw the finest of scratches on the metal around the keyhole. It had not been there when he left. So someone had searched here, too.

He sat down, his thoughts racing, clouded and skewed by guilt. There was no doubt left in him that it was his words overheard that had sent the assassin after John and Alys Reavley.

His desk was piled with more and more information on the Curragh Mutiny. It was Thursday, July 9, before Calder Shearing sent for him and Matthew reported to his office a little after four o'clock. Like all rooms in the Intelligence Service, it was sparsely furnished, nothing more than the necessities, and those as cheap as possible, but Shearing had added nothing of his own, no family pictures, no personal books or mementos. His papers and volumes for work were untidily stacked, but he knew the precise place of every one of them.

Shearing was not a tall man, but he had a presence more commanding than mere size. His black hair was receding considerably, but one barely noticed it because his brows were heavy and expressive and his eyes were dark and thick-lashed. His jutting nose was a perfect curve and his mouth sensitive, if unsmiling.

He regarded Matthew, assessing his recovery from bereavement and hence his fitness for duty. His question was only a matter of courtesy.

"How are you, Reavley? All matters taken care of?"

"For the time being, sir," Matthew answered, standing to attention.

"Again, are you all right?" Shearing repeated.

"Yes, sir, thank you."

Shearing looked at him a moment longer, then was apparently satisfied. "Good. Sit down. I expect you have caught up with the news? The king of the Belgians is on a state visit to Switzerland, which might be of significance but is more probably a routine affair. Yesterday the government said it might accept the House of Lords' amendment to the Home Rule bill, excluding Ulster."

Matthew had heard the news, but no details. "Peace in Ireland?" he asked, slightly sarcastically.

Shearing looked up at him, his expression incredulous. "If that's what you think, you'd better take more leave. You're obviously not fit for work!"

"Well, a step in the right direction?" Matthew amended.

Shearing pulled his mouth into a thin line. "God knows! I can't see a partition in Ireland helping anyone. But neither will anything else."

Matthew's mind raced. Was that what the conspiracy document concerned—dividing Ireland into two countries, one independent Catholic, the other Protestant and still part of Britain? Even the suggestion of it had already brought British troops to mutiny, robbed the army of its commander in chief, the Cabinet of its secretary of war, and taken Ulster itself to the brink of armed rebellion and civil war. Was that not the perfect ground in which to sow a plot to lead England to ruin and dishonor?

But it was now July and there had been relative peace for weeks. The House of Lords was on the verge of accepting the exclusion of Ulster from the Home Rule bill, and the Ulstermen would be permitted to remain a part of Britain, a right for which they were apparently prepared not only to die themselves but to take with them all the rest of Ireland, not to mention the British army stationed there.

"Reavley!" Shearing snapped, startling Matthew back to the present. "For God's sake, man, if you need more time, take it! You're no use to me off in a daydream!"

"No, sir," Matthew said tartly, feeling his body stiffen, the blood rush warm in his face. "I was thinking about the Irish situation and what difference it will make whether the government accepts the amendment or not. It's an issue that arouses passion far beyond reason."

Shearing's black eyes widened. "I don't need you to tell me that, Reavley. Every Englishman with even half his wits has known that for the last three hundred years." He was watching Matthew intently, trying to judge if his words could possibly be as empty as they sounded. "Do you know something that I don't?" he asked.

Matthew had kept silent on a few occasions, but he had never lied to Shearing. He believed it would be dangerous conduct. Now, for the first time, he considered being deceptive. He had no idea who was involved in the conspiracy, though certainly at least one person here in his office. But he could not tell Shearing that until he had proof. Perhaps not even then.

Who was Catholic? Who was Anglo-Irish? Who had loyalties or vested interests one way or the other? Rebellion in Ireland would hardly change the world, but perhaps John Reavley had felt it was his world. And England's honor would affect the empire, which would be the world, as far as he was concerned. Perhaps he was not so far wrong. And of course there were tens of thousands of Irish men and women in the United States who still felt passionate loyalty to the land of their heritage. Other Celtic peoples—in Wales, Scotland, and Cornwall—might also sympathize. It could tear Britain apart and spread to other colonies around the world.

"No, sir," he said aloud, judging his words carefully. "But I hear whispers from time to time, and it helps to know the issues and where loyalties lie. I'm always hearing mention of conspiracies. . . ." He watched for any shadow of change in Shearing's eyes.

"To do what?" Shearing's voice was low and very careful.

Matthew was on dangerous ground. How far dared he go? If Shearing was aware of the conspiracy, even sympathetic to it, then one slip would mean that Matthew had betrayed himself. The thought struck him with an ugliness that cut deeper than he had expected. He was uniquely alone.

Joseph would not be able to help him, and he could not trust Shearing or anyone else in SIS.

"To unite Ireland," he answered boldly. That was certainly radical enough. Considering the Curragh circumstances, it would rip Britain apart, and possibly sacrifice both army and government in the process, which would provide an interesting opportunity for all Britain's enemies everywhere else—Europe or Asia or Africa. Perhaps John Reavley was not exaggerating after all. It could be the first domino to topple many, the beginning of the disintegration of the empire, which would unquestionably affect all the world.

"What have you heard?" Shearing demanded. "Precisely."

Better to avoid mentioning his father at all, but he could still be accurate about the details. "Odd words about a conspiracy," he said, trying to pitch his tone to exactly the right mixture of caution and concern. "No details, only that it would have very wide effects all over the world—which might be an exaggeration—and that it would ruin England's honor."

"From whom?"

It was on the tip of his tongue to be honest. If he said it was his own father, that would explain so easily and naturally why he had been unable to pursue it any further. But it would also take it a step too close to the truth if Shearing could not be trusted. He would then wonder what else Matthew knew. Far wiser to keep that back. "Overheard it in a club," he lied. It was the first time he had deliberately misled Shearing, and he found it extraordinarily uncomfortable, not only for the deceit to a man he respected, but also because it was dangerous. Shearing was not someone to treat lightly. He had a powerful, incisive mind, an imagination that leaped from one conclusion to another as fast and as easily as his instinct drove it. He forgot almost nothing and forgave very little.

"Said by whom?" Shearing repeated.

Matthew knew that if he gave an unsatisfactory answer or pled ignorance, Shearing would be certain he was lying. It would be the beginning of distrust. Eventually it would lead to his losing his job. Since he actually was lying, his story would have to be very good indeed. Was he equal to that?

Would he ever know if he had succeeded or failed? The answer came even before the question was finished in his mind. No—he would not. Shearing would betray nothing in his demeanor.

"An army officer, a Major Trenton." Matthew named a man from whom he had actually obtained information some weeks ago and who did occasionally attend the same club.

Shearing was silent for several moments. "Could be anything," he said at last. "There are always Irish conspiracies. It's a society divided by religion. If there is a solution to it, we haven't found it in three hundred years, and God help us, we've never stopped trying. But if there is anything specific at the moment, I think it is more likely to lie in politics than any personal plot. And something personal would not dishonor the nation."

"If not Ireland, then what?" Matthew asked. He could not let go. His father had died, broken and bleeding, trying to prevent the tragedy he foresaw.

Shearing stared back at him. "The shootings in Sarajevo," he replied thoughtfully. "Was this before then, or after? You didn't say."

It was like a shaft of light cutting the darkness. "Before," Matthew said, surprised to find his voice a little husky. Was it conceivable his father had somehow got word of that, too late? He must have been killed himself just as it happened. "But that doesn't affect England!" he said, almost before he had weighed the meaning of it. His throat tightened. "Or is there more . . . something else yet to happen that we don't know of?"

A shadow of dark humor crossed Shearing's face and vanished. "There's always more that we don't know of, Reavley. If you haven't learned that yet, then there isn't much hope for you. The kaiser reasserted his alliance with Austro-Hungary four days ago."

"Yes, I heard." Matthew waited, knowing Shearing would go on.

"What do you know about the All-Highest?" Shearing asked, a faint flicker of light dancing in his eyes.

Matthew was lost for words. "I beg your pardon?"

"The kaiser, Reavley! What do you know about Kaiser Wilhelm II of the German Empire?"

"Is that what he is calling himself?" Matthew asked incredulously, scrambling together his thoughts, stories he could repeat about the kaiser's tantrums, his delusions that first his uncle Edward VII and now his cousin George V were deliberately snubbing him, ridiculing and belittling him. There were a great many it might be unwise to retell.

"He's the king's cousin and the czar's," Matthew began, and instantly saw the impatience in Shearing's face. "He's been writing to the czar for some time, and they have become confidants," he went on more boldly. "But he hated King Edward and was convinced he was plotting against him, that he despised him for some reason, and he has transferred that feeling to the present king. He's a temperamental man, very proud and always looking for slights. And he has a withered arm, which is possibly why he is rather bad on horseback. No balance." He waited for Shearing to respond.

Shearing's mouth flickered, as if he thought of smiling and decided against it. "His relationship with France?" he prompted.

Matthew knew what Shearing was expecting. He had read the reports. "Bad," he replied. "He has always wanted to go to Paris, but the French president has never invited him, and it rankles with him. He's . . ." He stopped again. He had been going to say "surrounded by awkward relationships," but perhaps that was a bit presumptuous. He was uncertain of Shearing's regard for royalty, even foreign. The kaiser was closely related to George V.

"More importantly," Shearing pointed out, "he perceives himself to be surrounded by enemies."

Matthew let the weight of that observation sink into his mind. He saw the reflection of it in Shearing's face. "A conspiracy to start a war, beginning in Serbia?" he asked tentatively.

"God knows," Shearing replied. "There are Serbian nationalists who will do anything for freedom, including assassinate an Austrian archduke—obviously—but there are radical socialists all over Europe as well."

"Against war," Matthew cut in. "At least international war. They are all for class war. Surely that couldn't be . . ." He stopped.

"You overheard the remark, Reavley! Could it or not?" Shearing asked tartly. "What about a pan-European socialist revolution? The whole continent is seething with plots and counterplots—Victor Adler in Vienna, Jean Jaurès in France, Rosa Luxemburg everywhere, and God knows who in

Russia. Austria is spoiling for a fight and only wants the excuse, France is afraid of Germany, and the Kaiser is afraid of everyone. And the czar doesn't know a damn thing about any of it. Take your pick."

Matthew looked at Shearing's dark, enigmatic face, filled with a kind of despairing humor, and realized that he had worked with him for over a year but knew almost nothing about him. He knew his intellect and his skills, but his passions he had not even guessed at. He had no idea where he came from, nothing about his family or his education, his tastes or his dreams. He was an intensely private man, but he guarded his inner self so well no one was aware he was doing it. One thought of him only in connection with his work, as if he walked out of the entrance of the building and ceased to exist.

"Perhaps I had better forget it unless something else develops," Matthew said, aware that he had learned nothing and very possibly made himself look incompetent to Shearing. "It doesn't seem to tie in with anything."

"On the contrary, it ties in with everything," Shearing answered. "The air is full of conspiracies, fortunately most of them have nothing to do with us. But go on listening, and advise me if you hear anything that makes sense."

"Yes, sir."

They discussed other projects for a further twenty minutes, particularly who might replace the minister of war, who had resigned over the mutiny. There were two primary candidates, one in favor of peace, even at a high price, the other more belligerent.

"Details," Shearing said pointedly. "All the details you can, Reavley. Weaknesses. Where is Blunden vulnerable? It's our job to know. You can't protect a man until you know where he can be hurt."

"Yes, sir," Matthew agreed. "I know that."

He left, forgetting the minister of war for a moment and pondering what Shearing had said about conspiracy. It seemed as if he did not believe that John Reavley had found anything that was of concern to England.

Matthew walked the long, quiet corridors back to his own office, nodding to this person, wishing a good evening to that one. He felt extraordinarily alone because he realized suddenly that he was profoundly angry.

Shearing had in effect damned John Reavley's perception of truth. If Shearing was right, then Matthew's father had misinterpreted a piece of paper, and he had died horribly for nothing. Matthew was so fiercely defensive of the suggestion that his father was incompetent that his fists were clenched, and he deliberately had to loosen them in order to open the door of his office.

But John Reavley was dead! And there had been the rope on the tree and marks on the road, scars where a row of caltrops had ripped all four tires and sent the car veering one way and then the other until it crashed into the copse. Where did one buy caltrops in the modern world? Or had they been homemade? It might be simple enough, with strong fence wire, wire cutters, and pliers. Any man could do it with a few hours to spare and a knack with his hands.

Someone had searched the house in St. Giles, and his office.

But he could not prove it. The crushed foxgloves would grow back; the marks would be obliterated by rain and dust and other traffic. The rope end tied to the tree could have been put there for any of a dozen reasons. And no one else could say whether objects in the study or the bedroom had been moved or not. The evidence was in remembered details, a sense of disturbance, minute things not as they should be, marks on a lock that he could have made himself.

They would say that John Reavley was a man out of office and out of touch, who dreamed up conspiracies. Matthew and Joseph were deluded by grief. Surely the violent loss of both parents was enough to cause, and to excuse, disjunction of reason in anyone?

It was all true. And the anger inside him turned to a dull, inward ache of confusion. In his mind's eye so clearly he could see his father's keen face. He was an eminently reasonable man, his mind so quick, so very sane. He was the one who curbed Judith's excesses, who was patient with Hannah's being less fluent at expressing herself, who hid his disappointment that neither of his sons had followed the career he so longed for them to embrace.

He had loved the quaint and eccentric things in life. He was endlessly tolerant of difference—and lost his temper with arrogance, and too often with fools who stifled others with petty authority. The real fools, the simple-minded, he could forgive in an instant.

It hurt almost beyond intolerably to believe that his father had utterly misinterpreted one stupid, minor endeavor that would make not even a mark in history, never mind turn the tide of it to ruin a nation and alter the world!

The irony was that he would not have found it as hard to be wrong as Matthew found it for him. Matthew knew that, and it did not help. He stood in the center of his office and had to fight to stop himself from weeping.

CHAPTER

FOUR

Joseph slipped back into the routine of teaching again and found the old pleasure in knowledge easing a little of the pain inside him. The music of words closed out the past, creating their own immediate world.

He stood in the lecture room and saw the earnest faces in front of him, different in features and coloring, but all touched with the shadows of anxiety. Only Sebastian had voiced his fear concerning the possibility of war in Europe, but Joseph heard the echoes of it in them all. There were reports of a French airship making reconnaissance flights over Germany, speculation as to what reparation Austro-Hungary would demand of Serbia, and even discussion of who might be assassinated next.

Joseph had spoken once or twice on the subject to the other students. He had no knowledge beyond the newspaper reports available to everyone else, but since the dean was on a short sabbatical and therefore unavailable, he felt that he should fill his place with the spiritual resources that would have met just such a need as this. There was nothing better than reason with which to answer fear. There was no cause to believe that there would be a conflict involving England. These young men would not be asked to fight, and perhaps to die.

They listened to him politely, waiting for him to answer their needs for assurance, and he knew from their eyes, the tension still there in their voices, that the old power to comfort was not enough.

On Saturday evening he called by at Harry Beecher's rooms and found his colleague reclining in his armchair and reading the current edition of the *Illustrated London News.* Beecher looked up, laying the paper flat immediately. Joseph could see, even upside down, a picture of a theater stage.

Beecher glanced at it and smiled. "*Eugene Onegin,*" he explained.

Joseph was surprised. "Here?"

"No, St. Petersburg. The world is smaller than you think, isn't it! And *Carmen.*" Beecher indicated the picture at the bottom of the page. "But apparently they've revived Boito's *Mefistofele* at Covent Garden, and they say it's very good. The Russian Ballet has *Daphnis and Chloe* at Drury Lane. Not really my kind of thing."

Joseph smiled. "Nor mine," he agreed. "How about a sandwich or a pie and a glass of cider at the Pickerel?" It was the oldest public house in Cambridge, just a few yards along the street, across the Magdalene Bridge. They could sit outside in the fading light and watch the river, as Samuel Pepys might have done when he was a student here in the seventeenth century, or anyone else over the last six hundred years.

"Good idea," Beecher agreed immediately, rising to his feet. The room was a pleasant clutter of books. Latin was his subject, but his interest lay in the icons of faith. He and Joseph had spent many hours positing theory after theory—serious, passionate, or funny—as to what was the concept of holiness. Where did it move from being an aid to concentration, a reminder of faith, into being the object of reverence itself, imbued with miraculous powers?

Beecher picked up his jacket from the back of the old leather chair and followed Joseph out, closing the door behind them. They went down the steps and across the quad to the massive front gate with its smaller door inset, and then out into St. John's Street, and left to the Magdalene Bridge.

The terrace outside the Pickerel was crowded. As usual, there were punts on the river, drifting along toward the bridge, silhouetted for a moment beneath its arch, then gone as they turned and followed the stream.

Joseph ordered cider and cold game pie for both of them, then carried the provisions to a table and sat down.

Beecher regarded him steadily for a moment or two. "Are you all right, Joseph?" he asked gently. "If you need a little more time, I can take some of your work. Really—"

Joseph smiled. "I'm better working, thank you."

Beecher was still watching him. "But?" he questioned.

"Is it so obvious?"

"To someone who knows you, yes." Beecher took a long draft of his cider, then set the glass down. He did not press for an answer. They had been friends since their own student years here, and spent many holidays walking together in the Lake District or along the ancient Roman wall that stretched across Northumberland and Cumbria from the North Sea to the Atlantic. They had imagined the legionaries of the Caesars who had manned it when it was the outer edge of empire against the barbarian.

They had tramped for miles, and sat in the sun staring over the moors in the light and shadow, eaten crusty bread and cheese, and drunk cheap red wine. And they had talked of everything and nothing, and told endless jokes, and laughed.

Joseph wondered whether to say anything to Beecher about his father's death and the fear of a conspiracy of the magnitude he had suggested, but he and Matthew had agreed not to speak of it, even to their closest friends.

"I was contemplating the ugly situation in Europe," he said aloud, "and wondering what sort of future lies ahead for the men who graduate this year. Darker than for us." He looked at his cider, sparkling a little in the long amber light. "When I graduated, the Boer War was over, and the world had all the excitement of a new century. It looked as if nothing would ever change except for the better—greater wisdom, more liberal laws, travel, new art."

Beecher's slightly crooked face was grave. "There are shifts of power all the time, and socialism is a rising force—I don't think anything can stop it," he said.

"Nor should it. We're moving to a real enlightenment, even votes for women in time."

"I was thinking more of the crisis in the Balkans," Joseph said, taking another bite of his pie and talking with his mouth full. "That's what many of our students are worried about." He said *many,* but he was thinking primarily of Sebastian.

"I can't see any of our students joining the army." Beecher spoke just before swallowing the last mouthful of his pastry. "And no matter how heated it gets between Austria and Serbia, it's a long way from us. It's not our concern unless we want to make it so. Young men always worry before leaving university and stepping out into the world." He smiled broadly. "In spite of the competition, there is safety here, and a multitude of distractions. The college is a hotbed of ideas most of them have never even imagined, and of the first temptations of adulthood—but the only real yardstick is your own ability. You may not get a first, but the only person who can prevent you succeeding is yourself. Outside it's different. It's a colder world. The best of them know that." He finished his cider. "Let them worry, Joseph. It's part of growing up."

Again Joseph thought of Sebastian's tortured face as he had stared with such intensity across the burnished water toward the dark outlines of the college. "It wasn't anxiety for himself. It was for what war in Europe would do to civilization in general."

Beecher's face split into a good-natured grin. "Too much poring over dead languages, Joseph. There's always something ineffably sad about a culture whose people have vanished when an echo of their beauty remains, especially if it is part of the music of our own."

"He was thinking of our language being overtaken and our way of thought lost," Joseph told him.

"He?" Beecher's eyebrows rose. "You have someone particular in mind?"

"Sebastian Allard." Joseph had barely finished speaking when he saw a shadow in Beecher's eyes. The still evening light was unchanged. The sound of laughter from a group of young men drifted on the twilight breeze from the green swath of the Backs, but inexplicably the air seemed colder. "He's more aware than the others," he explained.

"He's got a better intellect," Beecher agreed, but he did not look at Joseph.

"It's more than intellect." Joseph felt the need to defend himself, and perhaps Sebastian. "You can have a brilliant brain without delicacy, fire, vision. . . ." He had used the same word again, but there was no other to describe what he knew in Sebastian. In his translations the young man had caught the music and understood not only what the poets and philosophers of the past had written, but the whole regions of passion and dream that lay beyond it. To teach such a mind as his was the wish of all those who wanted to pass on the beauty they themselves had seen. "You know that!" he said with more force than he had intended.

"We're not in any danger of going the way of Carthage or Etruria." Beecher smiled, but it did not reach his eyes. "There are no barbarians at the gates. If they exist, then they are here among us." He looked at his empty glass but did not bother to catch the barman's eye. "I think we are equal to keeping them at bay, at least most of the time."

Joseph heard a note of pain in his voice and knew that it was real, the tip of something he had not seen before. "Not all the time?" he asked gently.

Then into his mind burst back the crushed foxgloves on the verge of the road, the scars of the caltrops on the tarmacadam, the screaming of metal in his imagination, and the blood. And he understood violence and rage completely, and fear.

"Of course not all of it," Beecher replied, his gaze beyond Joseph's head, unaware of the emotion all but drowning his friend. "They are young minds full of energy and promise, but they are also morally undisciplined now and then. They are on the edge of learning about the world, and about themselves. They have the privilege of education in the best school there is, and of being taught—forgive the immodesty—by some of the best mentors in the English language. They live in one of the most subtle and tolerant cultures in Europe. And they have the intellect and the ambition, the drive and the fire to make something of it. At least most of them have."

He turned to meet Joseph's eyes. "It's our job to civilize them as well, Joseph. Teach them forbearance, compassion, how to accept failure as well as success, not to blame others, nor blame themselves too much, but go on and try again, and pretend it didn't hurt. It will happen many times in life. It's necessary to get used to it and put it in its place. That's hard when you are young. They are very proud, and they haven't much sense of proportion yet."

"But they have courage," Joseph said quickly. "And they care—intensely!"

Beecher looked at his hands on the table. "Of course they do. Good God, if the young don't care, there isn't much hope for the rest of us! But they're still selfish at times. More, I think, than you want to believe."

"I know! But it's innocent," Joseph argued, leaning forward a little. "Their generosity is just as powerful, and their idealism. They are discovering the world and it's desperately precious to them! Right now they are frightened they're going to lose it. What can I tell them?" he pleaded. "How can I make that fear bearable?"

"You can't." Beecher shook his head. "You can't carry the world, and you'd only rip a muscle trying—and still probably drop it. Leave it to Atlas!" He pushed his chair back and stood up. "Do you want another cider?" And without waiting for an answer, he took Joseph's glass as well and walked away.

Joseph sat surrounded by murmuring voices, the clink of glass, and the occasional burst of laughter, and he felt alone. He had never realized before that Beecher did not like Sebastian. It was not only the dismissive words; it was the coldness in his face as he said them. Joseph felt distanced by it, cut off from a warmth he had expected.

He did not stay long after that, but excused himself and walked slowly back through the near darkness to St. John's.

Joseph was tired, but he did not sleep well. He rose a little before six and dressed in old clothes, then went outside and down to the river. It was a breathless morning; even the topmost leaves of the trees were still against the blue of the sky. The clear, pale light was so sharp every blade of grass shone with the dew, and there was no mark at all on the shining surface of the water.

He untied one of the small boats and got into it, unlashed the oars, and rowed out past Trinity and on eastward into the spreading light, feeling the warmth on his back. He threw his weight into it, pulling steadily. The rhythm was soothing, and he picked up speed all the way to the Mathematical Bridge before turning to come back. His mind was empty of every thought but the sheer physical pleasure of the effort.

He was back in his rooms, stripped to the waist and shaving, when there was an urgent, almost hysterical banging on his door. He padded over barefoot and opened it wide.

Elwyn Allard was standing on the threshold, his face contorted, his hair flopped over his brow, his right hand raised in a fist ready to hammer on the closed wood again.

"Elwyn!" Joseph was horrified. "Whatever's happened? Come in." He stepped back to make room for him. "You look terrible. What is it?"

Elwyn's body was shuddering. He gasped for breath and started speaking twice before managing to get the words out coherently.

"Sebastian's been shot! He's dead! I'm sure he's dead. You've got to help!"

It took a moment for Joseph to absorb the meaning of the words.

"Help me!" Elwyn begged. He was leaning on the doorpost, needing it to support himself.

"Of course." Joseph reached for his dressing gown from the back of the door and ignored his slippers. To think of bothering with clothes would have been ridiculous. Elwyn must be wrong. There might be time to salvage something—everything. Sebastian was probably ill, or . . . or what? Elwyn had said he had been shot. People did not shoot each other in Cambridge. Nobody had guns! It was unthinkable.

He ran down the steps behind Elwyn and across the silent courtyard, the dew on the grass nearly dry except where the buildings shadowed it. They went in at another door, and Elwyn started to scramble up the stairs, lurching from side to side. At the top he turned right and at the second door hurled his shoulder at it as if he could not turn the handle, although his hands grasped after it.

Joseph passed him and opened it properly.

The curtains were drawn back and the scene was bathed in the hard, clear light of the early sun. Sebastian sat in his chair, leaning back a little.

The low table beside him was spread with books, not littered but lying carefully piled on top of each other in a neat stack, here and there a slip of paper in to mark a place. One book was open in his lap and his hands, slender and strong, brown from the sun, lay loosely on top of it. His head was fallen back, his face perfectly calm, no fear or pain in it. There were a couple of deep scratches on one of them. His eyes were closed. His fair hair seemed barely disturbed. He could have been asleep but for the scarlet wound on his right temple and the blood splattered on the chair arm and floor beyond from the gaping hole at the other side. Elwyn was right. With an injury like that, Sebastian had to be dead.

Joseph went over to the young man, as if even the futile gesture of help were in some way still necessary. Then he stood still, the cold seeping through his body as he stared in sick dismay at the third person he had cared for shatteringly destroyed within the space of two weeks. It was as if he had awakened from one nightmare only to plunge into another.

He reached down and touched Sebastian's cheek. It was colder than life but not yet chill.

A choked gasp from Elwyn tore Joseph out of his stupor. With an intense effort he submerged his own horror and turned to look at the younger man. He was ashen-skinned, the sweat standing out on his lip and brow, his eyes hollow with shock. His whole body trembled, and his breath came raggedly as he struggled to retain some control.

"There's nothing you can do to help him," Joseph said, surprised at how steady his voice sounded in the silence of the room. There was still no one down in the quad, no feet on the stairs outside. "Go and fetch the porter."

Elwyn stood still. "Who . . . who could have done this?" he said, gulping air. "Who would . . . ?" He stopped, his eyes filling with tears.

"I don't know. But we must find out," Joseph replied. There was no gun in Sebastian's hand, nor did one lie on the floor where it would have slipped from his fingers. "Go and fetch the porter," he repeated. "Don't speak to anyone else." He glanced around the room. His mind was beginning to regain some clarity. The clock on the mantel said three minutes to seven. They were one floor up from the ground. The windows were closed and locked, every pane whole. Nothing was forced or broken, nor had the door any marks on it. Already the hideous knowledge was on the edge of Joseph's mind: This had been done by someone inside the college, someone Sebastian knew, and he must have let the person in.

"Yes," Elwyn said obediently. "Yes . . ." Then he turned on his heel and stumbled out, leaving the door open behind him, and Joseph heard his feet loud and clumsy going down.

Joseph went over and closed the door, then turned and stared at Sebastian. His face was peaceful but very tired, as though he had at last shed some terrible burden and allowed sleep to overtake him. Whoever had stood there with a gun in his hand, Sebastian had not had time to realize what he was going to do, or perhaps to believe that he meant it.

Pain was too crippling for anger yet. His mind could not accept it. Who would do such a thing? And why?

Young men were intense, just at the beginning of life and everything was larger to them, more acute: first real love, the brink of ambition realized, triumph and heartbreak so sharp, the power of dreams incalculable, the soaring mind tasting the joy of flight. Passion of all kinds was coming into its own, but violence was only the occasional fistfight, a brawl when someone had had too much to drink.

This had a darkness to it that was alien to everything Joseph knew and loved of Cambridge, to the whole of life here and all it meant. Like a blow, he remembered what Sebastian had said about the heart being changed by war, the beauty and the light of it being destroyed by those who did not understand. It was as if he had in those brief words written his own epitaph.

The door opened behind him, and he turned to see the porter standing in the entrance, his hair ruffled and his face puckered with alarm. He glanced at Joseph, then stared past him at Sebastian, and the color drained from his skin. A gagging sound issued from his throat.

"Mitchell, will you please lock the room here, then take Mr. Allard"—he nodded to indicate Elwyn, a couple of steps behind him on the landing—"and get him a cup of hot tea with a good stiff drop of brandy. Look after him." He took a shivering breath. "We'll have to call the police, so no one else should go up or down this stair, for the time being. Will you tell the other gentlemen who use this way to remain in their rooms until informed otherwise. Tell them there's been an accident. Do you understand?"

"Yes, Dr. Reavley . . . I . . ." Mitchell was a good man who had served at St. John's for over twenty years and was up to meeting most crises appropriately—from drunken brawls and the odd dislocated or broken bone to the occasional overzealous student stuck up on the roof. But the worst crimes had been the theft of a few pounds and, once, cheating at an examination. This was of a different nature, something intruding from outside his world.

"Thank you," Joseph said, stepping onto the landing himself. He looked beyond Mitchell to Elwyn. "I'll go see the master and do everything else that's necessary. You go with Mitchell, stay with him."

"Yes . . . yes . . ." Elwyn's voice tailed off, and he remained motionless until Mitchell locked the door. Then Joseph took him by the arm gently, forcing him to turn away, guiding him to the stairs and down them a step at a time.

Once outside in the quad, Joseph walked briskly across the path to the next quad, which was smaller and quieter, with one slender tree asymmetrically planted to the left. At the farther side was the wrought-iron gate leading through to the Fellows' Garden. At this hour it would be locked, as usual. The master's lodgings had two doors, one from the Fellows' Garden, one from this quad.

He passed into the shadow where the dew was still wet, and suddenly remembered he was barefoot. His feet were cold. He had not even thought to go back to his own room for slippers. It was too late to matter now.

He knocked on the door and ran his fingers through his hair to push it back off his face, suddenly conscious of how he looked if Connie Thyer should answer, not the master himself.

As it was, he had to knock twice more before he heard footsteps. Then the lock turned, and Aidan Thyer stood blinking at him.

"Good God, Reavley! Do you know what time it is?" he demanded. His long, pale face was still dazed with sleep, and his fair hair flopped forward over his brow. He looked at Joseph's dressing gown and his bare feet, then up again quickly, a flicker of alarm shadowing his eyes. "What is it? What's wrong?"

"Sebastian Allard has been shot dead," Joseph replied. The words somehow gave the nightmare a sickening reality. The very act of sharing it increased the number of those for whom it was true. He saw from Thyer's confusion that he had not grasped that Joseph meant violence of the mind as well as of the hand. Joseph had not used the word *murder,* but it was what he meant. "Elwyn just came and told me," he added. "I need to come in."

"Oh!" Thyer jerked to attention, embarrassed. "Yes, of course. I'm sorry." He pulled the door wide and moved back.

Joseph followed him, relieved to step onto carpet after the cold stone of the pathway. He had not realized it, but he was shivering.

"Come into the study." Thyer led the way.

Joseph closed the front door and followed. He sat down in one of the big chairs while Thyer poured him a stiff brandy from the tantalus on the sideboard and passed it to him, then turned back and poured a second one for himself.

"Tell me what happened," he directed. "Where were they?" He glanced at the mahogany clock on the mantel. It was quarter past seven. "Poor Elwyn must be in a state. What about the others who were there?" He shut his eyes for a second. "For God's sake, how did they manage to shoot anyone?"

Joseph was not sure what he was imagining—target practice, a tragic piece of carelessness?

"In his room," he answered. "He must have got up very early to study. He's . . . he was one of my best students." He tried to steady himself. "He was in his chair, alone, apart from whoever shot him. The windows were closed and locked, and there are no marks of forced entry on the door. It was just one shot, to the side of the head, but the gun is not there."

Thyer's face stiffened and his hands clasped the arm of his chair. He sat a little forward. "What are you saying, Joseph?" Unconsciously he slipped into familiarity.

"That someone else shot him and then left, taking the gun with him,"

Joseph answered. "I can't think of any way to explain it except that." How had he come in the space of two weeks to speak of murder as if he understood it?

Thyer sat without moving for several moments. There was a rustle behind him, and Joseph turned to see Connie standing in the open doorway, her dark hair loose around her shoulders and a pale satin wrap covering her from neck to foot.

Both men rose to their feet.

"What is it?" she said quietly. Her face was full of concern, making her look younger and far more vulnerable than the beautiful, self-assured woman she usually was. It was the first time Joseph had seen her when she was not aware, before anything else, of being the master's wife.

"Dr. Reavley, are you all right?" she asked anxiously. "You don't look well. I'm afraid this has been a terrible time for you." She came into the room, ignoring the fact that she was really not dressed suitably to greet anyone. "If I am intruding, please tell me. But if there is anything I can do to help . . . at all?"

Joseph was conscious of the warmth of her—not just her physical nearness, the slight perfume of her hair and skin and the slither of silk as she moved, but of a softness in her face, an understanding of what it is to be hurt.

"Thank you, Mrs. Thyer," Joseph said with an attempt at a smile that failed. "I am afraid something dreadful has happened. I—"

"There is nothing you can do, my dear," Thyer cut in, leaving Joseph feeling as if he had been clumsy. And yet there was no point in protecting her from it. Within a few hours everyone in St. John's would have to know.

"Nonsense!" she said abruptly. "There are always things to do, even if it is only seeing that the domestic arrangements continue. What is it that has happened?"

Thyer's face tightened. "Sebastian Allard has been killed. Apparently it could not have been an accident." He looked at her apologetically, seeing the color drain from her skin.

Joseph stepped toward her, all but losing his own balance as he put out his hands to steady her, and felt the muscles in her arms lock with surprising strength.

"Thank you, Dr. Reavley," she said very quietly but with almost complete control. "I am quite all right. How very dreadful. Do you know who was responsible?"

Thyer moved toward her as well but stopped short of touching her. "No. That is rather what Joseph expects us to do, I imagine—call the police? Isn't it?"

"It is unavoidable, Master," Joseph answered, dropping his hands to his sides. "And if you will excuse me, I must go and see what I can do to help Elwyn. The dean . . ." He did not finish.

Thyer walked from the room to the hall, where there was a telephone on the small table. He lifted it, and Joseph heard him asking the operator to ring the police station for him.

Connie looked at Joseph, her dark eyes searching his, trying to find some answer to the fear that he could see was already beginning inside her.

"I . . . ," he began, and realized he had no idea how to go on. She was expecting him, as a man professing a faith in God, to explain it to her in some terms that at least made sense to him. Idiotic phrases came into his mind that people had said to him after Eleanor's death—things about God's will being beyond the human mind to grasp, that obedience lay in accepting. They had been meaningless to him then, and were even more so now when the violence was deliberate and personal.

"I don't know," he admitted. He saw the confusion in her face. That was not good enough. "You are right." He forced himself to sound certain. "We need to do the ordinary things to help each other. I appreciate your good sense. The students who are here are going to be distressed. We shall need to keep our heads, for their sake. It will be unpleasant having the police here asking questions, but we must endure it with as much dignity as we can."

Her face ironed out, and she smiled very slightly. "Of course. If such a hideous thing had to happen, I am so glad you were here. You always grasp the core of things. Other people only ever seem to touch the edges."

He was embarrassed. She saw more in him than was there. But if it comforted her, he would not indulge in the honesty of denying it at her expense.

"It is good to have something to do, isn't it?" she said wryly. "How wise you are. It will at least get us through the worst of it with some kind of honor. I had better get dressed. I dare say the police will be here almost immediately. The master will inform the poor young man's family, but I should prepare their accommodation here in college, in case that is what they would like. Fortunately at this time of year there are plenty of rooms." She gave a choking little laugh. "The practical and domestic again. I cannot imagine what to say to a woman whose son has been . . . murdered!"

Joseph thought of Mary Allard and how her grief would consume her. No mother can bear the death of her child, but Mary had loved Sebastian with a fierce, all-enveloping pride. She saw in him everything that fed her ambition and her dreams.

He could understand it so easily. Sebastian had possessed an energy of the spirit that lit not only his own vision, but that of others as well. He had touched their lives, whether they wished it or not. It was impossible to believe that his mind did not exist anymore. How could Mary Allard ever bear it?

"Yes," he said, turning to her with sudden urgency. "You will have to look after them, and not be hurt or dismayed if they are in the kind of pain that unintentionally wounds others carelessly, or even on purpose. Sometimes when we are drowning in our own loss we lash out—anger is momentarily easier to cope with." That was hideously true, and yet he was speaking not from his own passion but in the accustomed platitudes he had used for years. He was ashamed of himself, but he did not know what else to say. If he laid open his own feelings, he would allow her to see the rage and confusion inside him, and he could not afford that. She would be repelled by its savagery—and frightened.

"I know." She smiled with great sweetness. "You don't need to tell me . . . or to worry about them." She spoke as if he had answered her need. "Thank you." He had to escape before he broke the grace of her judgment. "Yes . . . thank you. I must see what else I can do." And he excused himself and left, still barefoot and now feeling ridiculous in the broad daylight. He had given no answers at all, not from faith. He had simply provided the advice of common sense: Deal with what one can. At least do something.

He went under the archway into his own quad. Two students returning from early exercise stared at him in amusement and smothered laughter. Did they imagine he was coming back in his pajamas after an assignation? At another time he would have corrected them and left them in no doubt, but now the words died on his tongue. It was as if there were two realities, side by side, glittering, bright as shattered glass, one in which death was violent and terrible, the smell of blood was in the throat, and images floated before the eyes, even when they were closed—and another reality in which he merely looked absurd, wandering around in his dressing gown.

He did not trust himself to speak to the students in case he screamed the dreadful truth. He could hear his own voice inside his head, wild and soaring out of control.

He ran awkwardly across the last few yards to the door, then up the stairs, tripping and stumbling, until he threw open the door to his own room and slammed it behind him.

He stood still, breathing heavily. He must get control of himself. There were things to do, duties—duty always helped. First, he should finish shaving and get dressed. He must make himself look respectable. He would feel better. And eat something! Except that his stomach was churning and his throat ached so abominably he would not be able to swallow.

He took off his dressing gown. It was a flat, baking summer in Cambridge, and he was cold. He could smell blood and fear, as if he were coated with them.

Very carefully, because his hands were stiff, he ran hot water and washed himself, then stared at his face in the glass. Black eyes looked back at him above high cheekbones, a strong, slightly aquiline nose, and a highly individual mouth. His flesh looked gray, even beneath the dark stubble of his half-shaved beard. There was something waxen about him.

Even shaving slowly and carefully, he still cut himself. He put on a clean shirt, and his fingers could not find the buttons or get them through the holes.

It was all absurd, idiotic! The students had thought he was off on some amorous encounter. Looking like this? He was a man walking through a nightmare. And yet he had been so aware of Connie Thyer . . . the warmth of her, the sweet smell, her closeness. How could he even think of such a thing now?

Because he was blindingly, desperately alone! He would have given anything at all to have had Eleanor here, to take her in his arms and cling to her, have her hold him, take some of this unbearable loss from him.

His parents were dead, crushed and tossed aside, for a document. And now Sebastian, his brain destroyed, blasted into wreckage by a bullet.

Everything was slipping away, all that was good and precious and gave light and meaning. What was there left that he dared love anymore? When would God smash that and take it away?

This was the last time he was ever going to let it happen. There was going to be no more pain like this! He could not open himself up to it.

Habit told him that it was not God's fault. How many times had he explained that to other people who were screaming inside because of something they could not bear?

Yes, it was! He could have done something! If He couldn't manage that, why was He God?

And the ice-cold voice of reason said: *There is no God. You are alone.*

That was the worst truth of all: alone. The word was a kind of death.

He stood still for several minutes, no coherent thoughts in his head. The coldness didn't stay. He was too angry. Someone had killed John and Alys Reavley, and he was helpless to find out who or why.

Memories flooded back of pottering quietly in the garden, John telling long, rambling jokes, the smell of lily-of-the-valley, Hannah brushing Alys's hair, Sunday dinner.

He leaned against the mantel and wept, letting go of the self-control at last and freeing the grief to wash over him and take hold.

By midmorning he was still ashen-faced, but composed. His bedder, the elderly woman who tidied and cared for all the rooms on this stair, had been in, shaking and tearful, but she completed her duty. The police had arrived, led by an Inspector Perth, a man of barely average height with receding hair sprinkled with gray, and crooked teeth, two missing. He spoke quietly, but he moved with unswerving purpose. Although he was gentle with the grieving and severely rattled students, he allowed none of his questions to go unanswered.

As soon as Inspector Perth discovered that the dean was absent in Italy but that Joseph was an ordained minister, he asked him to stay at hand. "Might help," he said with a nod. He did not explain if it was to ensure truthfulness among the students or for the comfort of their distress.

"Seems nobody came nor went during the night," Perth said, looking at Joseph with sharp gray eyes. They were alone in the master's lodge, Mitchell having been sent on some errand. "No break-in. My men've bin all over. Sorry, Reverend, but it looks like your young Mr. Allard—the dead one, that is—must've bin shot by someone inside the college here. Police surgeon might be able to tell us what time, but it doesn't make no difference for who could've bin there. He was up an' dressed an' sitting at his books—"

"I touched his cheek," Joseph interrupted him. "When I went in. It wasn't cold . . . I mean, it was . . . cool." He shuddered inside at the memory. That had been three hours ago. Sebastian would be cold now, the spirit, the dreams, and the hunger that made him unique dissolved into—what? He knew what the answer was supposed to be . . . but he had no inner fire that affirmed it to him.

Perth was nodding, biting his lip. "Sounds right, sir. Looks like he knew whoever did it, from what Oi've bin told. You knew him, Reverend. Was he the sort of young gentleman to let in someone he didn't know, at that time—which looks to've bin about half past five—an' while he was studying?"

"No. He was a very serious student," Joseph replied. "He would resent the intrusion. People don't normally call on anyone before breakfast unless it's an emergency."

"What Oi thought," Perth agreed. "An' we've searched all over the room, an' the gun's not there. We'll be going over the whole college for it, of course. Don't look like he put up any sort of a fight. Took by surprise, by all we can see. Someone he trusted."

Joseph had thought the same thing, but until now he had not put it in those words. It was indescribably ugly.

Perth was staring at him. "Spoken to a few of the young gentlemen, sir. Asked if anyone heard a shot, seeing as there must've bin one. One young gentleman said he heard a bang, but he didn't take notice. Thought it was just something in the street, car mebbe, and he doesn't know what time it was. Went back to sleep again." Perth chewed his lip. "An' no one has any thoughts as to why, least none as how they'll own to. All seem took by surprise. But it's early days. D'you know of anyone who had a brangle with him? Jealous, mebbe? He was a very good-looking young man. Clever, too, by accounts—good scholar, one of the best. First-class honors, they say." His expression was carefully unreadable.

"You don't kill people because they outshine you academically!" Joseph said with too much of an edge to his voice. He was being rude and he could not help it. His hands were shaking and he felt dry-mouthed.

"Don't you?" Perth left it as a question unanswered. He sat on the edge of the porter's desk. "Why do you kill someone, then, Reverend? Young gentlemen like these, with every advantage in the world an' their whole lives to look forward to?" He waved at the chair for Joseph to sit down. "What would make one o' them take a gun an' go into someone's rooms afore six in the morning an' shoot him in the head? Must've bin a powerful reason, sir, something for which there weren't no other answer."

Joseph's legs were weak, and he sank into the chair.

"An' it weren't spur of the moment, like," Perth continued. "Someone got up special, took a gun with 'em, an' there was no quarrel, or Mr. Allard wouldn't've bin sitting back all relaxed, with not a book out of place." He stopped and waited, staring curiously at Joseph.

"I don't know." The full enormity of it was settling on him so heavily he could scarcely fill his lungs with air. His mind flickered over the other students closest to Sebastian. Whom could he have let in at that hour and remained seated talking to him instead of getting up and fairly robustly telling him to come back at a more civilized time? Elwyn, of course. And why had Elwyn gone to see him so early? Joseph had not asked him, but no doubt Perth would.

Nigel Eardslie. He and Sebastian had shared an interest in Greek poetry. Eardslie was the better language scholar, he had the vocabulary, but he had less feeling for the music and the rhythm of it, or for the subtlety of the culture. They collaborated well, and both enjoyed it, often publishing the results in one of the college magazines. If Eardslie had also been up early studying and found a particularly good line or phrase, one that he almost gripped but not quite, he would have disturbed Sebastian, even at that time.

But Joseph would not tell Perth that, at least not yet.

And there were Foubister and Morel, good friends to each other, with whom Sebastian and Peter Rattray often made a four for tennis. Rattray was keen on debate, and he and Sebastian had indulged in many all-night arguments, to the intense pleasure of both of them. Although that did not seem a reason for going to anyone's rooms so early.

Who else was there? At least half a dozen others came to his mind, all of whom were still here in college for one reason or another, but he could not imagine any of them even thinking of violence, let alone acting it out.

Perth was watching him, content to wait, patient as a cat at a mousehole.

"I have no idea," Joseph repeated helplessly, aware that Perth would know he was being evasive. How could any man who was trained in the spiritual care of people, living and working with a group of students, be totally blind to a passion so intense it ended in murder? Such terror or hatred does not spring whole into being in a day. How was it that he had not seen it?

"How long've you bin here, Reverend?" Perth asked.

Joseph felt himself blushing, the heat painful in his face. "A little over a year." He had to have seen it, merely refused to recognize it for what it was. How stupid! How totally useless!

"An' you taught Mr. Sebastian Allard? What about his brother, Mr. Elwyn? Did you teach him, too?"

"For a while, for Latin. He dropped it."

"Why?"

"He found it difficult, and he didn't think it was necessary for his career. He was right."

"So he weren't so clever as his brother?"

"Very few were. Sebastian was remarkably gifted. He would have . . ." The words stuck in his throat. Without any warning, the reality of death engulfed him again. All the golden promise he had seen ahead for Sebastian was gone, as if night had obstructed daylight. It took him a moment to regain control of himself so he could continue speaking. "He had a remarkable career ahead of him," he finished.

"Doing what?" Perth raised his eyebrows.

"Almost anything he wanted."

"Schoolmaster?" Perth frowned. "Preacher?"

"Poet, philosopher. In government if he wanted."

"Government? Learning old languages?" Perth was utterly confused.

"A lot of our greatest leaders have begun with a degree in classics," Joseph explained. "Mr. Gladstone is the most obvious example."

"Well, I never knew that!" Perth clearly found it beyond his comprehension.

"You don't understand," Joseph went on. "At university there are always those who are more brilliant than you are, more spectacularly gifted in a particular area. If you didn't know that when you came, you would certainly learn it very quickly. Every student here has sufficient talent and intellect to succeed, if he works. I know of no one foolish enough to carry anything more than a passing moment of envy for a superior mind." He said it with absolute certainty, and it was only when he looked at Perth's expression that he realized how condescending he sounded, but it was too late to retrieve it.

"So you didn't notice anything at all?" Perth observed. It was impossible to tell if he believed that, or what he thought of a teacher and minister who could be so blind.

Joseph felt like a new student chastised for a stupid mistake. "Nothing I thought could lead to more than a passing stiffness, a distance," he defended himself. "Young men are emotional, highly strung sometimes. Exams . . ." He tailed off, not knowing what else to add. He was trying to explain a culture and a way of life to a man for whom it was totally foreign. The gulf between a Cambridge student and a policeman was unbridgeable.

How could Perth possibly understand the passions and dreams that impelled young men from backgrounds of privilege and in most cases a degree of wealth, men whose academic gifts were great enough to earn them places here? He must come from an ordinary home where learning was a luxury, money never quite enough, necessity a constant companion on the heels of labor.

A cold breath touched him—fear that Perth would inevitably come to wrong conclusions about these young men, misunderstand what they said and did, mistake motives, and blame innocence, simply because it was all alien to him. And the damage would be irretrievable.

And then the moment after, his own arrogance struck him like a blow. He belonged to the same world, he had known all of them for at least a year and seen them almost every day during term time, and he had not had even the faintest idea of hatred slowly building until it exploded in lethal violence.

There must have been signs; he had ignored them, misinterpreted them as harmless, and misread everything they meant. He would like to think it had been charity, but it wasn't. To have been blind to the truth was stupidity at best; at worst it was also moral cowardice. "If I can help you, of course I will," he said much more humbly. "I . . . I am as . . . shocked . . ."

"O' course you are, sir," Perth said with surprising gentleness. "Everybody is. No one expects anything like this to happen. Just tell me if you remember anything or if you see anything now. An' no doubt you'll be doing what you can to help the young gentlemen. Some of 'em look pretty frangled."

"Yes, naturally. Is there . . ."

"Nothing, sir," Perth assured him.

Joseph thanked him and left, going outside into the bright, hard sunlight of the quad. Almost immediately he ran into Lucian Foubister, his face white, his dark hair on end as if he had run his hands through it again and again.

"Dr. Reavley!" he gasped. "They think one of us did it! That can't be true. Someone else must've . . ." He stopped in front of Joseph, blocking his way. He did not know how to ask for help, but his eyes were desperate. He was a northerner from the outskirts of Manchester, accustomed to rows of brick houses back to back with each other, cold water and privies. The

Cambridge world of ancient, intricate beauty, space, and leisure had stunned and changed him forever. He could never truly belong here; neither could he return to what he had been before. Now he looked younger than his twenty-two years, and thinner than Joseph had remembered.

"It appears that it was," Joseph said gently. "We may be able to find some other answer, but no one broke in, and Sebastian was sitting quite calmly in his chair, which suggests he was not afraid of whoever entered his room."

"Then it must have been an accident," Foubister said breathlessly. "And . . . and whoever it was is too scared to own up to it. Can't blame him, really. But he'll say, when he realizes the police are thinking it's murder." He stopped again, his eyes searching Joseph's, begging to be reassured.

It was an answer Joseph longed to believe. Whoever had committed such an act would be devastated. To run away was cowardly, and he would be ashamed, but better that than murder. And it would mean Joseph had not been blind to hatred. There had been none to see.

"I hope that's true," he answered, placing a hand on Foubister's arm. "Wait and see what happens. And don't leap to judgment yet."

Foubister nodded, but he said nothing. Joseph watched as he hurried away to the opposite side. As clearly as if he had been told, Joseph knew he was going straight to see his friend Morel.

Gerald and Mary Allard arrived before noon. They had only to come from Haslingfield, about four miles to the southwest. The first shock of the news must have reached them after breakfast, almost certainly leaving them too stunned to react immediately. There may have been people to tell, perhaps a doctor or a priest, and other members of the family.

Joseph dreaded meeting them. He knew Mary's grief would be wild and savage. She would feel all the pent-up, wounding rage that he did. The comforting words that she had said so sincerely to him at his parents' funeral would mean nothing repeated back to her now, just as they had meant nothing to him at the time.

Because he was afraid of the encounter, he went straightaway, within minutes of their car pulling up at the front gate on St. John's Street. He saw Mitchell taking them solemnly through the first quad and the second toward the master's house. Joseph met them a dozen yards from the front door.

Mary was dressed in black, her skirt stained with dust at the hem, her hat wide, shading her veiled face. Beside her, Gerald looked like a man struggling to stand the morning after a drunken binge. His skin was pasty, his eyes bloodshot. He took a moment or two to recognize Joseph, then lurched toward him, momentarily seeming to forget his wife.

"Reavley! Thank God you're here! What happened? I don't understand—it doesn't make sense! Nobody would . . ." He tailed off helplessly, not knowing what else he meant to say. He wanted help, anyone who would tell him it was not true and release him from a grief he could not bear.

Joseph gripped Gerald's hand and steadied his other arm, taking some of his weight as he staggered. "We don't know what happened," he said firmly. "It seems to have been around half past five this morning, and the best thing I can say at the moment is that it was very quick, a couple of seconds, if that. He didn't suffer."

Mary was in front of him, her black eyes blazing even through her veil. "Is that supposed to comfort me?" she demanded, her voice hoarse. "He's dead! Sebastian's dead!"

Her passion was too fierce for Joseph to touch, and yet he was standing here in the middle of the quad in the July sun trying to find words that would be something more than a statement of his own futility. Where was the fire of his faith when he needed it? Anyone could believe on a calm Sunday in a church pew, when life was whole and safe. Faith is real only when there is nothing else between you and the abyss, an unseen thread strong enough to hold the world.

"I know he's dead, Mary," he answered her. "I can't tell you why or how. I don't know who did it, or whether they meant to or not. We may learn everything except the reason, but it will take time."

"It's the reason I want!" Her voice shook with fury. "Why Sebastian? He was . . . beautiful!"

He knew what she meant, not only his face but the brilliance of his mind, the strength of his dreams. "Yes, he was," he agreed.

"So why has your God let some stupid, worthless . . ." She could not think of a word big enough to carry her hatred. "Destroy him?" she spat. "Tell me why, Reverend Reavley!"

"I don't know. Did you think I would be able to tell you? I'm just as human as you are, just as much in need of learning faith, walking with trust, not—"

"Trust in what?" Her thin, black-gloved hand sliced the air. "A God who takes everything from me and lets evil destroy good?"

"Nothing destroys good," he said, wondering if it was true. "If good were never threatened, and even beaten sometimes, then there would be no good, because it would eventually become no more than wisdom, self-interest. If—"

She turned away from him impatiently, snatching her arm back as if he had been holding her, and stalked over the grass toward Connie Thyer, standing at the doorway of the master's house.

"I'm sorry," Gerald muttered helplessly. "She's taking it . . . I . . . I really . . ."

"It's all right." Joseph stopped his fumbling embarrassment. It was painful to see and he wanted it ended for both their sakes. "I understand. You had better go and be with her. She needs you."

"No, she doesn't," Gerald said with an instant's extraordinary bitterness. Then he caught himself, blushed, and walked away after her.

Joseph started back toward the first quad and was almost there when he saw the second woman, also veiled and in black. She was apparently lost, looking through the arch tentatively. She seemed young, from the grace of her posture, yet there was a dignity and natural assurance to her suggesting that in other circumstances she would have been very much in command of herself.

"May I help you?" Joseph asked, startled to see her. He could not imagine what she could be doing here in St. John's, or why Mitchell had ever let her in.

She came forward with relief. "Thank you. That is very kind of you, Mr. . . . ?"

"Reavley, Joseph Reavley," he introduced himself. "You seem uncertain which way to go. Where is it you wish to be?"

"The master's house," she replied. "I believe his name is Mr. Aidan Thyer. Is that correct?"

"Yes, but I am afraid he is engaged at present, and likely to be for some considerable time. An unexpected event has changed everyone's arrangements." There was no need to tell her of the tragedy. "I shall convey any message to him when he is free, and perhaps you can make an appointment to call at another time?"

She stood even straighter. "I am aware of the events, Mr. Reavley. You are referring to the death this morning of Sebastian Allard. My name is Regina Coopersmith. I was his fiancée."

Joseph stared at her as if she had spoken in an alien language. It was not possible! How could Sebastian, the passionate idealist, the scholar whose mind danced to the music of language, have fallen in love and contracted himself to marriage, yet never even mentioned it?

Joseph looked at Regina Coopersmith, knowing he should be offering her some sympathy, but his mind refused to accept what she had said.

"I'm sorry, Miss Coopersmith," he said awkwardly. "I didn't know." He must add something. This superficially composed young woman had lost the man she loved, and in the most appalling circumstances. "I'm deeply sorry for your bereavement." He knew how it felt to face that gulf of loneliness suddenly, without any warning at all. One day one had everything; the next day it was gone.

"Thank you," she replied with the ghost of a smile.

"May I accompany you to the master's house? It is through there." He gestured behind him. "I expect the porter has your bags?"

"Yes, thank you. That would be most courteous."

Joseph turned and walked with the young woman back into the sunlight and along the path. He glanced sideways at her. Her veil hid only part of her face; her mouth and chin were clearly visible. Her features were strong, but pleasant rather than pretty. She had dignity, resolve, but it was not a face of passion. What had made Sebastian fall in love with her? Could she have been Mary Allard's choice for her son, rather than his own? Perhaps she had money and good connections with county families? She would give Sebastian the security and the background he would need for a career in poetry or philosophy, which might not immediately provide such things itself.

Or perhaps there were whole areas of Sebastian's nature about which Joseph had been entirely ignorant.

The midday sun was hot and sharp, casting the shadows with hard edges, like the cutting realities of knowledge.

CHAPTER

FIVE

In a quiet house on Marchmont Street, a man who liked to be known by those he trusted as "the Peacemaker" stood near the mantel shelf in his upstairs sitting room and stared with unconcealed fury at the rigid figure opposite him.

"You searched his office and found nothing!" he said between his gritted teeth.

"Nothing of any interest to us," the other man replied. He spoke English with complete ease, but without colloquialisms. "They concerned things with which we already know. The document was not there."

"Well, it wasn't in the Reavley house," the Peacemaker said bitterly. "That was searched thoroughly."

"Was it?" the other asked skeptically. "When?"

"During the funeral," the Peacemaker replied, a dangerous temper audible in his voice. He did not like being challenged, particularly by someone considerably his junior in rank. It was only his respect for his cousin that made him tolerate this man to the degree he did. He was, after all, his cousin's ally.

"Well, you have the copy Reavley was carrying," the man pointed out. "I'll follow the son. If he knows where it is, I'll find it."

The Peacemaker stood elegantly, looking as if he were at ease to anyone who glanced only casually. More careful scrutiny would have revealed tension in his body so great the fabric of his jacket was straining across his shoulders and his knuckles were white.

"There is no time," he said in a hard, level voice. "Events will not wait. If you can't see that, you're a fool! We must use it within the next few days, or it will be too late."

"One copy—"

"I have to have both! I can hardly offer him one!"

"I'll get another," the man offered.

The Peacemaker's face was white. "You can't!"

The other man straightened as if to leave immediately. "I'll go back tonight."

"It won't help." The Peacemaker held up his hand. "The kaiser is in a rage. You'll get nothing. You might even lose what we have." It was spoken with the unmistakable tone of a command.

The other man breathed in and out slowly several times, but he did not argue. There was anger in his face, and frustration, but it was not with the man known as the Peacemaker; it was with the circumstances he was forced to accept.

"You dealt with the other matter?" the Peacemaker asked, his voice little more than a whisper. There was pain in his face.

"Yes," the man replied.

"How did he get hold of it, anyway?" the Peacemaker asked, sharp frown lines between his brows.

"He was the one who wrote it," the other man answered.

"Wrote?" The demand was peremptory.

"Such things have to be written by hand," the man explained. "It's the law."

"Damn!" the Peacemaker swore, just one word, but it carried a weight of passion, as if it were torn out of him with physical pain. He bent forward a little, his shoulders high, his muscles tight. "It shouldn't have happened this way! We shouldn't have let it! Reavley was a good man, the sort we need alive!"

"Can't be helped," the other explained with resignation.

"It should have been!" the Peacemaker grated, hard bitterness undisguised. "We've got to do better."

The other man flinched a little. "We'll try."

Late on Saturday afternoon Matthew drove from London back to St. Giles. It had been an unpleasant day, not from any cause that he had expected, such as news from Ireland or the Balkans, but from an increasingly immediate domestic problem. A bomb had been found in a church in the heart of Westminster, with the fuse lit. Apparently it had been the work of a group of women who were agitating in increasingly violent ways to be given the right to vote.

Fortunately no one had been hurt, but the possibility of destruction was deeply disturbing. It had meant Matthew had been drawn from his investigation of Blunden and the political weapons that might have been used against him. Instead he had been busy all day with increasing the security in London itself, and had had to ask Shearing for permission to leave, which would not ordinarily have been the case on a weekend.

His sense of exhilaration as he drove out of the heat and enclosure of the city was like an escape from captivity. He felt almost intoxicated as the Sunbeam Talbot accelerated on the open road.

The weather was fine, another golden evening with great puffball clouds piling up in the east, with the sun blazing on them till they drifted like white galleons in the shimmering air, sails full set to the horizon. Beneath them the fields were already ripe with harvest.

The light deepened across the broader skies of the fenland, almost motionless in the amber of sunset.

Matthew drove into St. Giles, along the main street past the shining millpond, and turned along the road to the house. Mrs. Appleton met him at the front door and her face lit with pleasure.

"Oh, Mr. Matthew, it's good you're here. An' you'll be staying?" She stepped back to allow him in, just as Judith came down the stairs, having heard the crunch of car tires on the gravel.

Judith ran down the last couple of steps, Henry at her heels, his tail aloft. She threw her arms around Matthew, giving him a quick, fierce hug. Then she pulled back and looked at him more carefully.

"Yes, of course I'm staying," he said to Mrs. Appleton over Judith's shoulder. "At least until lunchtime tomorrow."

"Is that all?" Judith demanded. "It's Saturday evening now! Do they expect you to work all the time?"

He did not bother to argue. It was a discussion they had had before, and they were unlikely to agree. Matthew had a passion for his work that Judith would probably never understand. If there was anything that fired her will and her imagination enough to give all of herself to it, then she had not yet discovered what it was.

Matthew acknowledged the dog, then followed her into the familiar sitting room with its comfortable furniture and slightly worn carpet, colors muted by time. As soon as the door was closed, Judith asked him if he had discovered anything.

"No," he said patiently, reclining in the big chair that had been his father's. He was self-conscious about sitting in it. He had always taken it when his father was not there, but now it seemed like a statement of ownership. Yet to have sat somewhere else would have been awkward also, a break with habit that was absurd, another difference from the past that had no purpose.

She watched him, a tiny frown on her face.

"I suppose you are trying?" There was a flash of challenge in her eyes.

"That's part of why I came up this weekend . . . and to see you, of course. Have you heard from Joseph?"

"A couple of letters. Have you?"

"Not since he went back." He looked at her, trying to read her feelings from her expression. She sat a little sideways on the couch, with her feet tucked up, the way Alys had criticized and told her was unladylike. Was she as much in control as she looked, with her hair swept back from her calm brow, her smooth cheeks, and her wide, vulnerable mouth?

Or was the emotion bottled up inside her, too raw to touch, but eating away at her will? She was the one of them who was still living here in the house. How often did she come down the stairs and find herself startled that there was no one to greet her except Mrs. Appleton? Did she hear the silence, the missing voices, the footsteps? Did she imagine the familiar touch, the smell of pipe tobacco, the closed study door to indicate that John must not be interrupted? Did she listen for the sound of Alys singing to herself as she arranged flowers and did the dozens of other small things that showed someone in the house loved it?

He could escape. His life was the same as before, except for the occasional telephone call and the visits home. The difference was all inside. It was knowledge he could set aside when he needed to.

It would be like that for Hannah also, and for Joseph. He was worried about them as well, but differently. Hannah had Archie to comfort her and her children to need her and fill her time.

Joseph was different. Since Eleanor's death something within him had retreated from emotions to hide in reason. Matthew had grown up with Joseph, who was seven years older and always seeming cleverer, wiser, and quicker. He had imagined he would catch up, but now in adulthood he began to think that perhaps Joseph had an intellect of extraordinary power. Understanding for which other people labored came to him with ease. He could climb on wings of thought into regions most people only imagined.

But Joseph also retreated from the realities of certain kinds of pain, and in the last year he had escaped more completely. In fleeting, unguarded moments, Matthew had seen this remoteness in his brother's eyes.

Judith was watching him, waiting for him to continue.

"I've been pretty busy lately," he said finally. "Everyone's preoccupied with Ireland, and of course with the Balkan business."

"Ireland I can understand, but why the Balkans?" She raised her eyebrows. "It hasn't anything to do with us. Serbia is miles away—the other side of Italy, for heaven's sake. It's a pretty revolting thought, but won't the Austrians just go in and take whatever they want in reparation, and punish the people responsible? Isn't that what usually happens with revolutions—either they succeed and overthrow the government, or they get suppressed?

Well, anyone who thinks a couple of Serbian assassins are going to overthrow the Austro-Hungarian Empire has to be crazy." She shifted her feet around the other way and settled further into the cushions.

Henry got up from where he had been lying and rearranged himself closer to her.

"It's not they who would do it," Matthew said quietly.

"Who, then?" She frowned. "I thought it was just a few lunatic young men. Is that not true?"

"It seems as if it was," he agreed. "War is just the last in a chain of events that could happen . . . but almost certainly someone will step in with enough sense to stop it. The bankers, if no one else. War would be far too expensive!"

She looked at him very levelly, her gray-blue eyes unflinching. "So why did you mention it?"

He forced himself to smile. "I wish I hadn't. I just wanted you to know I'm not making excuses. I don't know where to begin. I thought I'd go over and see Robert Isenham tomorrow. I expect he'll be at church—I'll see him afterward."

"Sunday lunch?" she said with surprise. "He won't thank you a lot for that! What do you want to ask him?"

He smiled and shook his head. "Nothing so blunt as that. You wouldn't make a detective, would you!"

Her face tightened a little. "What do you think he knows?"

Matthew became serious again. "Maybe nothing, but if Father confided anything at all, it would probably be to Isenham. He might even have mentioned where he was going or whom he was expecting to see. I don't know where to start, other than going through everyone he knew."

"That could take forever." She sat quite still, her face shadowed in thought. "What do you think it could be, Matthew? I mean . . . what would Father have known about? People who plot great conspiracies don't leave documents lying around for anyone to find by chance."

A chill touched him. For an instant he was not quite sure what it was, but the unpleasantness was certain. Then he saw it in her eyes, a fear she could not put words to.

"I know he didn't find it by accident," he answered her. "Unless it belonged to someone he knew very well . . ."

"Like Robert Isenham." She finished the thought for him. "Be careful!" Now the fear was quite open.

"I will," he promised. "There's nothing suspicious in my going to see him. I would do it anyway, sooner or later. He was one of Father's closest friends, geographically if nothing else. I know they disagreed about many things, but they liked each other underneath it."

"You can like people and still betray them," she said, "if it was for a cause you believed in passionately enough. You have to betray other people rather than betray yourself—if that's what it comes to." Then, seeing the surprise in his face, she added, "You told me that."

"I did? I don't remember."

"Yes, you do. It was last Christmas. I didn't agree with you. We had quite a row. You told me I was naive, and idealists put causes before anything else. You told me I was being a woman, thinking of everything personally rather than in larger terms."

"So you don't agree with me, but you'll quote my own words back at me in an argument?"

She bit her lip. "Actually, I do agree with you. I just wasn't going to say so then. You're cocky enough."

"I'll be careful." He relaxed into a smile and leaned forward to touch her for a moment, and her hand closed tightly around his.

The morning was overcast and heavy with the clinging heat of a storm about to break. Matthew went to church, largely because he wanted to catch up with Isenham as if by chance.

The vicar caught sight of him in the congregation just before he began his sermon. Kerr was not a natural speaker, and the presence of overwhelming emotion in a member of his audience, especially one for whom he felt a responsibility, broke his concentration. He was embarrassed, only too obviously remembering the last time he had seen Matthew, which had been at his parents' funeral. He had been unequal to the task then, and he knew he still was.

Sitting in the fifth row back, Matthew could almost feel the sweat break out on Kerr's body at the thought of facing him after the service and scrambling for something appropriate to say. He smiled to himself and stared back expectantly. The only alternative was to leave, and that would be even worse.

Kerr struggled to the end. The last hymn was sung and the benediction pronounced, and row by row the congregation trooped out into the damp, motionless air.

Matthew went straight to Kerr and shook his hand. "Thank you, Vicar," he said courteously. He could not leave without speaking to him, and he did not want to get waylaid and miss the chance to bump into Isenham. "Just came home to see how Judith is."

"Not at church, I'm afraid," Kerr replied dolefully. "Perhaps you could talk to her. Faith is a great solace at times like these."

It was clumsy. There were no other "times like these." How many people have both their parents murdered in a single, hideous crime? Of course Kerr did not know it was murder. But given Judith's character, the last thing poor Kerr needed was an encounter with her! He would attempt desperately to be kind, to say something that would be of value to her, and she would grow more and more impatient with him, until she let him see how useless he was.

"Yes, of course," Matthew murmured. "I'll convey your good wishes to her. Thank you." As he turned and left, he felt that was exactly what his mother would have said—or Joseph. And they would not have meant it any more than he did.

He caught up with Isenham in the lane just beyond the lych-gate. The man was easily recognizable even from behind. He was of average height, but barrel-chested with close-cropped fair hair graying rapidly, and he walked with a slight swagger.

He heard Matthew coming, even though his footsteps were light on the stony surface. He turned and smiled, holding out his hand. "How are you, Matthew? Bearing up?" It was a question, and also half an instruction. Isenham had served twenty years in the army and seen action in the Boer War. He believed profoundly in the Stoic values. Emotion was fine, even necessary, but it should never be given in to, except in the most private of times and places, and then only briefly.

"Yes, sir." Matthew knew what was expected, and he meant this encounter to earn him Isenham's confidence and to learn from it anything John Reavley might have told him, even in the most indirect way. "The last thing Father would have wanted would be for us to fall apart."

"Quite! Quite!" Isenham agreed firmly. "Fine man, your father. We'll all miss him."

Matthew fell into step beside him, as if he had been going that way, although as soon as they came to the end of the lane he would turn the opposite direction to go home.

"I wish I'd known him better." Matthew meant that with an intensity that showed raw through his voice, more than he wanted. He meant to be in control of this conversation. "I expect you were probably as close as anyone," he continued more briskly. "Funny how differently family see a person . . . until you're adult, anyway."

Isenham nodded. "Yes. Never thought of it, but I suppose you're right. Funny thing, that. Look at one's parents in a different light, I suppose." Unconsciously he increased his pace.

Matthew kept up with him easily, as his legs were longer. "You were probably the last person he really talked with," he went on. "I hadn't seen him the previous weekend, nor had Joseph, and Judith was out so often."

"Yes, I suppose I was." Isenham dug his hands deep into his pockets. "It's been a very bad time. Did you hear about Sebastian Allard? Dreadful business." He hesitated an instant. "Joseph will be very upset about that, too. I daresay the boy wouldn't even have gone up to Cambridge, if it weren't for Joseph's encouragement."

"Sebastian Allard?" Matthew was confused.

Isenham turned to look at him, stopping in the road where it had already changed into the long, tree-lined avenue down toward his own house. "Oh, dear. No one told you." He looked a trifle abashed. "I presume they felt you'd had enough to get over. Sebastian Allard was murdered, in Cambridge. Right in college . . . St. John's. Devilish thing. Yesterday morning. I only heard from Hutchinson. He's known the Allards for years. Dreadfully cut up, of course." He pursed his lips. "Can't expect you to feel the same, naturally. I imagine you've got all the grief you can manage at the moment."

"I'm very sorry," Matthew said quietly. There was no sound here in the shelter of the trees and not a breath in the air. "What an appalling tragedy," he said to fill the silence. "I must call in on Joseph before I go back to London. He'll be very grieved. He's known Sebastian for years." He was aware of the numbing pain Joseph would feel, but now he wanted to ask Isenham about John Reavley. He forced all other thoughts out of his mind and kept pace with him in the shade of the ancient elms that closed out the sky above them.

Again the tiny thunder flies were hovering, irritating the eyes and face. Matthew swatted at them, even though he knew it was useless. If only it would hurry up and rain! He did not mind getting wet, and it would be a good excuse to stay at Isenham's house longer. "Actually, it's been a pretty rotten time altogether," he continued. "I know a good few people are worried about this Balkan business."

Isenham took his hands out of his pockets. "Ah! Now there you have a real cause for anxiety," he said, his broad, windburned face intensely serious. "That's very worrying, you know? Yes, I expect you do know . . . I daresay more than I do, eh?" He searched Matthew's eyes intently.

Matthew was a little taken aback. He had not realized that Isenham knew where he worked. Presumably John had said something? In pride, or confiding a shame? The thought stung with all the old sharpness, multiplied by the fact that now Matthew would never be able to prove to his father the value of his profession, and that it was not devious or grubby, full of betrayals and moral compromise.

"Yes," Matthew acknowledged. "Yes, it's pretty ugly. Austria has demanded reparation, and the kaiser has reasserted Germany's alliance with them. And of course the Russians are bound to be loyal to Serbia."

The first heavy drops of rain spattered on the leaves, and far in the distance thunder rattled like a heavy cart over cobbles, jolting and jarring around the horizon.

"War," Isenham said succinctly. "Drag us all in, damn it! Need to get ready for it. Prepare men and guns."

"Did Father know that, do you think?" Matthew asked.

Isenham pursed his lips before responding. "Not sure, honestly." It was an unfinished remark, as if he had stopped before he said too much.

Matthew waited.

Isenham looked unhappy, but he apparently realized he had to continue. "Seemed a trifle odd lately. Nervous, you know? He . . . er . . ." He shook his head. "The day before he died he expected war." He was puzzled. "Not like him, not at all." He increased his pace, his body stiff, shoulders straight. The rain was beating on the canopy of leaves above them and beginning to come through. "Sorry, Matthew, but there it is. Can't lie about it. Definitely odd."

"In what way?" Matthew asked, the words coming automatically as his mind raced to absorb this new information and at the same time defend himself from what it meant.

He was relieved that the weather made it so easy to stay with Isenham, although at the same time it allowed him no excuse to avoid asking still more searching questions. Thank goodness the house was no more than sixty yards away or they would get very wet indeed. Isenham bent forward and began to run. "Come on!" he shouted. "You'll get soaked, man!"

They reached the gate of his garden and dashed through to open the front door. The path was already swimming in water, and the smell of hot, wet earth filled the air. Plants drooped under the fierceness of the storm as it drummed on the leaves.

As Matthew turned to close the gate behind him, he saw a man walking across the lane, coat collar turned up, dark face shining wet. Then the figure disappeared through the trees.

Matthew found Isenham inside and stood dripping in the hallway, surrounded by oak paneling, hunting prints, and leather straps with horse brasses in dozens of different designs.

"Thank you." Matthew accepted the towel Isenham offered him and dried his hands and his face on it. The rain could not have come at a better time if he had designed it. "I think there were certain groups Father was worried about," he went on, picking up the conversation before their dash to the gate.

Isenham lifted his shoulders in a gesture of denial and took the towel back, dropping it on the floor by the cloakroom door along with his own. "He said something about plots, but frankly, Matthew, it was all a bit . . . fanciful." He evidently had struggled to find a polite word, but the real meaning was plain in his face. He shook his head. "Most of our disasters came from good, old-fashioned British blunders. We don't plot our way into wars. We trip over our own feet and fall into them by accident." He winced, looking apologetic, and rubbed his hand over his wet hair. "Win in the end, on the principle that God looks after fools and drunkards. Presumably he has a soft spot for us as well."

"You don't think he could have found something?"

Isenham's face tightened. "No. He lost the thread a bit, honestly. He rambled on about the mutiny in the Curragh—at least that's what I think he was talking about. Wasn't very clear, you know. Said it would get a lot worse, hinted that it would end in a conflagration that could engulf all England, even Europe." He colored with embarrassment. "Nonsense, you see? War minister resigned and all that, I know, but hardly Europe in flames. Don't suppose anyone across the Channel gives a damn about it one way or the other. Got their own problems. You'd better stay for a bite of lunch," he added, looking at Matthew's sodden shoulders and feet. "I've got a telephone. Call Judith and let her know."

He turned and led the way to the dining room, where his housekeeper had laid out cold meat, pickles, fresh bread and butter, a newly baked pie that had barely cooled, and a jug of thick cream.

"Sufficient for two, I think," he pronounced. He ignored his own wet clothes because he could do nothing about Matthew's. It was part of his code of hospitality that he should sit to dine in dripping trouser legs, because his guest was obliged to do so.

"You don't think the Irish situation could escalate?" Matthew said when they were halfway through the excellent cold lamb and he had taken the edge off his hunger.

"To involve Europe? Not a chance of it. Domestic matter. Always has been." Isenham took another mouthful and swallowed before continuing. "I'm sorry, but poor old John was a bit misled. Ran off with the wrong end of things. It *happens*."

It was the note of pity in his voice that Matthew could not bear. He thought of his father and saw his face as vividly as if he had left the room only minutes before, grave and gentle, his eyes as direct as Judith's. He had a quick temper at times and he suffered fools badly, but he was a man without guile. To hear him spoken of with such condescension hurt fiercely, and Matthew was instantly defensive.

"What do you mean?" he demanded. "*What* happens?" He heard the anger inside himself and knew he had to control it. He was sitting in Isenham's house, eating his food, and more important than that, he needed his help. "What was it he was afraid of?"

"Best leave it," Isenham replied, looking down at his plate and very carefully balancing a piece of pickle on the crust of his bread.

"Are you saying he was deluded?" The instant it was out, he wished he had chosen a word less pejorative. He was betraying his own hurt, as well as leaving himself unguarded. It sabotaged his purpose. He was angry with himself. He had more skill than that!

Isenham raised his eyes, hot and miserable. "No, no, of course not. He was just . . . a little jumpy. I daresay we all are, what with the army mutinying, and then all this violence in the Balkans."

"Father didn't know about the archduke," Matthew pointed out. "He and Mother were killed that day themselves."

"Killed?" Isenham asked.

Matthew amended it instantly. "When the car went off the road."

"Of course. I'm . . . I'm sorrier than I can say. Look, wouldn't you rather—"

"No. I'd like to know what he was worried about. You see, he mentioned it to me, but only briefly." Was that a risk? It was a deliberate one. He watched Isenham's face minutely for even a flicker of the eyes that would give away more than the older man had said, but there was none. Isenham was merely embarrassed.

"I don't know what to tell you. I don't want to let down an old friend. Remember him as he was, Matthew."

"Was it really so bad?" It was barely within Matthew's control not to lash back.

Isenham flushed. "No, of course not! Just . . . just a misinterpretation of facts, I think. A touch overdramatic, out of proportion. After all . . ." He was trying to make it better, and failing. "We've always had wars here or there over the last thousand years or so. It's our national spirit, our destiny, if you like." His voice lifted with his own belief. "We'll survive it. We always do. It'll be nasty for a while, but I daresay it won't last more than a few months."

It was clear to Matthew that Isenham was aware of having revealed his friend's weakness to the man's own son, and when John Reavley was not here to defend himself. "I'm sure in a little while he would have seen that," he added lamely.

Matthew leaned forward, elbows on the table. "What was it he thought?" He felt his heart hammering.

"That's it," Isenham said, shaking his head from side to side. "He wasn't clear. Honestly, Matthew, I don't think he knew! I think . . . I didn't want to say this, but you force me to." He looked resentful, his face red even under his windburn. "I think he got hold of half an idea and imagined the rest. He wouldn't tell me what it was because I don't think he could. But it had something to do with honor . . . and he wanted war. There! I'm sorry. I knew it would hurt you, but you insisted."

It was preposterous. John Reavley would never countenance war, no matter what anyone had done. It was barbaric, revolting! It was utterly unlike anything he believed in and had fought for all his life, against all the decency he had treasured, nurtured, every human faith he had professed! The very reason at the heart of his hatred of the intelligence services was what he saw as their dishonesty, then manipulation of people to serve nationalist ends, and ultimately to make war more likely.

"He wouldn't want war!" Matthew said aloud, his voice shaking. The mere idea tore away all that was certain inside him.

But then, how well had he known his father? How many children knew their fathers as men, as fighters, lovers, friends? Do children ever become old enough to see clearly beyond the tie of love?

"He wouldn't ever want war!" Matthew repeated intensely, fixing Isenham with a glare.

Isenham nodded. "He had half a story and he wasn't making sense of it. He was a good man. Remember that, Matthew, and forget the rest." He took another bite of bread and pickle, then helped himself to more meat, speaking with his mouth full. "This kind of tension makes everyone a bit jumpy. Fear does different things to people. Some run away. Some go forward to meet it before it's there—can't bear the suspense. Seems John was one of those. Seen it out on the hunting field sometimes, more in the army. Takes a strong man to wait."

Matthew felt the accusation of weakness scald with a pain almost physical. John Reavley was not weak! Matthew drew in his breath in a gasp, longing to retort with something that would crush the notion out of existence, but he could not find even an idea, let alone words.

"There are no grand conspiracies, only nasty little plots now and then," Isenham continued, as if unaware of the emotions raging inside Matthew. "He wasn't in government anymore, and I think he missed it. But look around you." He waved his free hand. "What could be going on here?"

The truth sank in on Matthew with a slowly crushing weight: Isenham was probably right, and the harder he struggled against the realization, the tighter it coiled around him.

"You should remember the best in him, Matthew," Isenham said. "That was what he was really like."

Then Isenham deliberately changed the subject, and Matthew allowed the conversation to move to other matters: the weather, people in the village, an upcoming cricket match, the daily minutiae of a safe and gentle life in the peace of a perfect summer.

He walked home again when the rain had stopped. The elms were still dripping, and the road steamed in glittering drifts like silken gauze, too faint to catch, and yet weaving brightness around him. The perfume of the earth was almost overpowering. Wet leaves and flowers shone as the sunlight caught them.

Birdsong was sudden and liquid, a beauty of sound, and then gone again.

As he passed the church he saw a man move very quickly into the shadow of the lych-gate, the thick honeysuckle completely hiding him. When Matthew drew level and looked sideways, he was gone. He was certain from his height and the oddly sloping angle of his shoulders that it was the same man he had seen earlier on his way to Isenham's house. Was he going somewhere and had taken shelter from the rain? Without having any reason he could name, Matthew went under the lych-gate and into the churchyard.

There was no one there. He walked a few paces between the gravestones and looked toward the only place where anyone could be concealed. The man had not gone into the church; the door had been in Matthew's sight all the time.

He walked two or three yards farther on, then to the right, and saw the outline of the man half concealed by the trunks of the yew trees. He was standing motionless. There was nothing ahead of him but the churchyard wall, and he was looking not down, as if at headstones, but out across the empty fields.

Matthew bent his head as if reading the gravestone in front of him. He remained motionless for several moments. The man behind the yew tree did not move, either.

Finally Matthew walked over to his parents' grave. There were fresh flowers. Judith must have put them there. There was no stone yet. It looked very raw, very new. This morning two weeks ago they had still been alive.

The world looked just the same, but it wasn't. Everything was altered, as a golden day when suddenly the clouds mass across the sun. All the outlines are the same, but the colors are different, duller, something of the life gone from them.

The caltrop marks on the road had been real, the rope on the sapling, the shredded tires, the searching of the house, and now this man who seemed to be following him.

Or was this exactly what his father had done, added together little pieces that had no connection with each other, and made of them a whole that reflected no reality? Maybe the marks were not caltrops but something else, put there not at the time of the crash but some other time that day.

Perhaps an agricultural implement of some sort had stopped and left scars from the blades of a harrow?

Had there really been anyone in the house, or was it just things rearranged wrongly in the shock of tragedy, a reversal of habit, along with everything else?

And what was to prove the man behind the yews had anything to do with Matthew? He might not want to be seen for a dozen reasons: something as simple as an illicit Sunday afternoon assignation, or a grave to visit privately, to conceal his emotion. Was this how delusion started? A shock, too much time to think, a need to feel as if you understood, so you find yourself weaving everything together, regardless of wherever it fits?

For a moment he considered speaking to the man, a comment on the rain, perhaps, then decided not to intrude on his contemplation. Instead he straightened up and walked back through the lych-gate and out into the lane without looking toward the yews again.

CHAPTER

SIX

A few miles away in Cambridge the Sunday was also quiet and miserable. Thunder threatened all morning, and by the afternoon it rolled in from the west with heavy rain. Joseph spent most of the day alone. Like everyone else, he went to chapel at eleven, and for an hour he drowned all thought in the glory of the music. He ate luncheon in the dining hall; in spite of its magnificence, it was claustrophobic because of the heat and the oppressive weather outside. With an effort he joined in casual conversation with Harry Beecher regarding the latest finds in Egyptology, about which Beecher was wildly enthusiastic. Afterward he went back to his rooms to read. The *Illustrated London News* lay on the table in his study, and he glanced at the theater and arts sections, avoiding the current events, which were dominated by pictures of the funeral of the great statesman Joseph Chamberlain. He had no desire whatever to look at pictures of mourners, whoever they were.

He considered scriptures, then instead lost himself in the familiar glory of Dante's *Inferno*. Its imagery was so sharp it carried him out of the present, and its wisdom was timeless enough, at least for the moment, to lift him above personal grief and confusion.

It was infinitely just—the punishments for sin were not visited from outside, decided by a higher power, but were the sins themselves, perpetuated eternally, stripped of the masks that had made them seductive once. Those who had given in to the selfish storms of passion, regardless of the cost to others, were now battered and driven by unceasing gales, forced to rise before them without rest. And so it was, down through the successive circles, the sins of indulgence, that injured self, the sins of anger that injured others, to the betrayal and corruption of the mind which damaged all mankind. It made infinite sense.

And yet, Joseph reasoned, beauty was there. Christ still "walked the waters of Styx with unwet feet."

If Inspector Perth was working, Joseph did not see him that day. Nor did he see Aidan Thyer or any of the Allard family.

Matthew called in briefly on his way back to London, simply to say how sorry he was about Sebastian. He was gentle, full of a tacit compassion.

"It's rotten," he said briefly, sitting in Joseph's rooms in the last of the twilight. "I'm very sorry."

Hundreds of words turned in Joseph's mind, but none of them seemed important, and certainly none of them helped. He remained in silence, simply glad that Matthew was there.

However, Monday was entirely different. It was July 13. It seemed that on the previous day the prime minister had spoken at length about the failure of the army's present methods of recruitment—a sharp and unpleasant reminder that if the Balkan situation was not resolved and war erupted, then Britain might be unable to defend itself.

Far more immediate to Joseph was Perth's presence in St. John's. The inspector moved about discreetly, speaking to one person after another. Joseph caught glimpses of him, always just going, leaving behind him a wake of deeply troubled young men.

"I hate it!" Elwyn said as he and Joseph met crossing the quad. Elwyn was flustered, as if he were being harried on all sides, trying to do something for everyone and desperate to be alone and deal with his own grief. He stared after Perth's disappearing figure.

"He seems to think it's one of us!" Elwyn said exasperatedly, the disbelief evident in his voice. "Mother's watching him like a hawk. She thinks he's going to produce an answer any minute. But even if he did, it wouldn't bring Sebastian back." He looked down at the ground. "And that's the only thing that would make her happy."

Joseph could see in his face all that he did not say, and imagined it only too easily: Mary Allard wild with pain, lashing out at everyone without realizing what she was doing to her other son, while Gerald offered ineffectual and comforting remarks that only made her worse—and, finally, Elwyn trying desperately to be whatever they expected of him.

"I know it's wretched," Joseph replied. "Do you feel like leaving college for a while? Take a walk into town? I need new socks. I left some of mine at home."

Elwyn's eyes widened. "Oh, God! I forgot about your parents. I'm so sorry!"

Joseph smiled. "It's all right. *I* forget at times. Do you feel like a walk?"

"Yes, sir. Yes, I do. Actually, I need a couple of books. I'll go to Heffer's. You can try Eaden Lilley's. They're about the best for haberdashery around here."

They walked together back across the quad and out of the main gate into St. John's Street, then right into Sydney Street. It was fine and dry after the rain, and the Monday morning traffic included at least half a dozen motorcars, along with delivery vans, drays, and wagons. Cyclists and pedestrians wove in and out of them at practiced speed. It was quieter than term time because the usual gowned figures of students were absent.

"If they don't find anyone, what will happen?" Elwyn said when they had the chance to speak and be heard.

"I suppose they'll give up," Joseph answered. He looked sideways at his companion, seeing the anxiety in his face. He could imagine Mary Allard's fury. Perhaps that was what Elwyn was thinking of, too, and afraid of. "But they will." The instant the words were out, he knew they were a mistake. He saw the bleak pain in Elwyn. He stopped on the footpath, reaching for Elwyn's arm and swinging him round to a standstill also. "Do you know anything?" he asked abruptly. "Are you afraid to say it, in case it would give somebody a motive for killing Sebastian?"

"No, I don't!" Elwyn retorted, his face flushed, his eyes hot. "Sebastian wasn't anything like as perfect as Mother thinks, but he was basically pretty decent. You know that! Of course he said some stupid things, and he could cut you to bits with his tongue, but so can lots of people. You have to live with that. It's like being good at rowing, or boxing, or anything else. You win sometimes, and sometimes you lose. Even those who didn't like Sebastian didn't hate him!" His emotion was overwhelming. "I wish they . . . I wish they didn't have to do this!"

"So do I," Joseph said sincerely. "Perhaps it will turn out to be more of an accident than deliberate."

Elwyn did not dignify that with an answer. "Do you think there'll be war, sir?" he asked instead, beginning to walk again.

Joseph thought of the prime minister's words in the newspaper. "We have to have an army, whether there's war or not," he reasoned. "And the mutiny in the Curragh has shown a few weaknesses."

"I'll say!" Elwyn pushed his hands into his pockets, his shoulders tense. He was broader, more muscular than Sebastian, but there was an echo of his brother in the fair hair and the warm tones of his skin. "He went to Germany in the spring, you know?" he continued.

Joseph was startled. "Sebastian? No, I didn't know. He never mentioned it."

Elwyn shot a glance at him, pleased to have known first. "He loved it," he said with a little smile. "He meant to go back when he could. He was reading Schiller, when he had time. And Goethe, of course. He said you'd have to be a barbarian not to love the music! The whole of human history has produced only one Beethoven."

"I knew he was afraid, of course," Joseph answered him. "We spoke of it just the other day."

Elwyn's head jerked up, his eyes wide. "You mean worried, not afraid! Sebastian wasn't a coward!"

"I know that," Joseph said quickly and honestly. "I meant that he was afraid for the beauty that would be destroyed, not for himself."

"Oh." Elwyn relaxed again. In that single gesture Joseph could see a wealth of Mary's passion, her pride and brittleness, her identification with her sons, especially the elder. "Yes, of course," Elwyn added. "Sorry."

Joseph smiled at him. "Don't think of it. And don't spend your time trying to imagine who hated Sebastian, or why. Leave it to Inspector Perth. Look after yourself . . . and your mother."

"I am," Elwyn answered him. "All that I can."

"I know."

Elwyn nodded unhappily. "Goodbye, sir." He turned away toward the bookshop and left Joseph to continue on his way to the department store to look for socks.

Once inside, he wandered around the tables and the ceiling-high shelves. He was outside again, with a pair of black socks and a pair of dark gray ones, when he bumped into Edgar Morel.

Morel looked flustered. "Sorry, sir," he apologized, stepping aside. "I . . . I was miles away."

"Everyone's upset," Joseph responded, and was about to move when he realized that Morel was still looking at him.

A young woman passed them. She was wearing a navy and white dress, her hair swept up under a straw hat. She hesitated an instant, smiling at Morel. He colored, seemed about to say something, then averted his eyes. The young woman changed her mind and quickened her step.

"I hope she didn't go on my account," Joseph commented.

"No!" Morel said too vehemently. "She . . . she was really more Sebastian's friend than mine. I expect she just wanted to give her condolences."

Joseph thought that was less than the truth. She had looked at Morel with some urgency.

"Did he know her well?" he asked. She had seemed an attractive girl, perhaps a little under twenty, and she carried herself with grace.

"I don't know," Morel replied, and this time Joseph was certain it was a lie. "Sorry for banging into you, sir," he went on. "Excuse me." And before Joseph could say anything else, Morel moved very quickly to the doorway of Eaden Lilley's and disappeared inside.

Joseph walked on farther into the town, stopping for a while in Petty Cury, leading toward the market. He passed Jas. Smith and Sons and then the Star and Garter, dodged a couple of delivery carts and two dangerously speeding bicycles, and came back by Trinity Street to St. John's.

* * *

Tuesday was much the same, a routine of small chores. He saw Inspector Perth coming and going busily, but he managed to put Sebastian's death out of his mind most of the time, until Nigel Eardslie caught up with him crossing the quad early in the afternoon. It was hot and still again; the windows of all the occupied rooms were wide open, and every now and then the sound of music or laughter drifted out.

"Dr. Reavley!"

Joseph stopped.

Eardslie's square face was puckered with anxiety, hazel eyes fixed on Joseph's. "That policeman's just been talking to me, sir, asking a lot of questions about Allard. I really don't know what to say." He looked awkward.

"If you know something that could have a bearing on his death, then you'll have to tell him the truth," Joseph answered.

"I don't know what the truth is!" Eardslie said desperately. "If it's just a matter of where I was or whether I saw this or that, then of course I can answer. But he wanted to know what Allard was like! And how do I answer that decently?"

"You knew him pretty well," Joseph said. "Tell him about his character, how he worked, who his friends were, his hopes and ambitions."

"He didn't get killed for any of those," Eardslie replied, a slight impatience in his voice. "Do I tell him about his sarcasm as well? The way he could cut you raw with his tongue and make you feel like a complete fool?" His face was tight and unhappy.

Joseph wanted to deny it. This was not the man he had known. But then no student would dare exercise his pride or cruelty on a tutor. A bully chooses the easy targets.

"I could tell him how funny Sebastian was," Eardslie was continuing. "He made me laugh sometimes till I couldn't get my breath and my chest hurt, but it could be at someone else's expense, especially if they'd criticized him lately."

Joseph did not reply.

"Do I tell him that he could forgive wonderfully and that he expected to be forgiven, no matter what he'd done, because he was clever and beautiful?" Eardslie rushed on. "And if you borrowed something without asking, even if you lost it or broke it, he could wave it aside and make you think he didn't care, even if it was something he valued." His mouth pinched a little, and the light faded in his eyes. "But if you questioned his judgment or beat him at one of the things that mattered to him, he could carry a grudge further than anyone else I know. He was generous . . . he'd give you anything. But God, he could be cruel!" He stared at Joseph helplessly. "I can't tell the police that. He's dead."

Joseph felt numb. That was not the Sebastian he knew. Was Eardslie's the voice of envy? Or was he speaking the truth Joseph had refused to see?

"You don't believe me, do you!" Eardslie challenged him. "Perth might, but the others won't. Morel knows Sebastian took his girl, Abigail something, and then dumped her. I think he did it simply because he could. She saw Sebastian and thought of him as this sort of young Apollo and he let her believe it. It flattered him."

"You can't help it if someone falls in love with you," Joseph protested, but he remembered the character attributed to the Greek god, the childishness, the vanity, the petty spite, as well as the beauty.

Eardslie looked at him with barely concealed anger. "You can help what you do about it!" he retorted. "You don't take your friend's girl. Would you?" Then he blushed, looking wretched. "I'm sorry, sir. That was rude." He jerked his chin up. "But Perth keeps asking. We want to be decent to the dead, and we want to be fair. But someone killed him, and they say it had to be one of us. I keep looking at everyone and wondering if it was them.

"I met Rattray along the Backs yesterday evening, and I started remembering quarrels he'd had with Sebastian, and wondering if it could be him. He's got a hell of a temper." He blushed. "Then I remembered a quarrel I'd had, and wondered if he was thinking the same thing of me!" His eyes pleaded for some kind of reassurance. "Everybody's changed! Suddenly I don't feel as if I really know anyone . . . and even worse than that, in a way, I don't think anyone trusts me, either. I know who I am and that I didn't do it, but no one else knows!" He took a deep breath. "The friendships I took for granted aren't there anymore. It's done that already!"

"They *are* still there," Joseph said firmly. "Get a grip on your imagination, Eardslie. Of course everyone is upset over Sebastian's death, and frightened. But in a day or two I expect Perth will have it solved, and you'll all realize that your suspicions were unfounded. One person did something tragic and possibly evil, but the rest of you are just what you were before." His voice sounded flat and unreal. He did not believe what he was saying himself—how could Eardslie? He deserved better than that, but Joseph did not have anything to give that was both comforting and even remotely honest.

"Yes, sir," Eardslie said obediently. "Thank you, sir." And he turned and walked away, disappearing through the arch into the second quad, leaving Joseph alone.

The following morning Joseph was sitting in his study again, having written to Hannah, which he had found difficult. It was simple enough to begin, but as soon as he tried to say something honest, he saw her face in his mind and he saw the loneliness in her, the bewilderment she tried to hide and failed. She was not accustomed to grief. The gentleness she had for others was rooted in the certainties of her own life; first her parents and Joseph, then Matthew and Judith, younger than she and relying on her, wanting to be like her. Later it had been Archie, and then her own children.

She reminded him so much of Alys, not only in her looks but in her gestures, the tone of her voice, sometimes even the words she used, the colors she liked, the way she peeled an apple or marked the page in a book she was reading with a folded spill of paper.

Hannah and Eleanor had liked each other immediately, as if they had been friends who had simply not seen each other for a while. He remembered how much pleasure that had given him.

Hannah had been the first one to come to him after Eleanor's death, and she had missed her the most, even though they had lived miles apart.

He knew they had written every week, long letters full of thoughts and feelings, trivial details of domestic life, more a matter of affection than of news. Writing to Hannah now was difficult, full of ghosts.

He had finished, more or less satisfactorily, and was trying to compose a letter to Judith when there was a discreet tap on the door.

Assuming it was a student, he simply called for whoever it was to come in. However, it was Perth who entered and closed the door behind him.

"Morning, Reverend," he said cheerfully. He still wore the same dark suit, slightly stretched at the knees, and a clean, stiff collar. "Sorry if Oi'm interrupting your letters."

"Good morning, Inspector," Joseph replied, rising to his feet, partly from courtesy, but also because he felt startled and at a disadvantage still sitting. "Do you have some news?" He was not even sure what answer he wanted to hear. There had to be a resolution, but he was not yet ready to accept that anyone he knew could have killed Sebastian, even though his brain understood that it had to be true.

"Not really what you'd call news," Perth replied, shaking his head. "Oi bin talking to your young gentlemen, o' course." He ran his fingers over his thin hair. "Trouble is, if a man says he was in bed at half past foive in the morning, who's to know if he's telling the truth or not? But Oi can't afford to take his word for it, you see? Different for you, 'cos Oi know from Dr. Beecher that you was out rowing on the river."

"Oh?" Joseph was surprised. He did not remember seeing Beecher. He invited Perth to sit down. "I'm sorry, but I don't know how to help. There would be no one around in the corridors or on the stairs at that time."

"Unfortunately for us." Perth sat in the large chair opposite the one Joseph had risen from, and Joseph sank back into his own. "No witnesses at all," Perth said dolefully. "Still, people ain't often obliging enough to commit murder when they know someone else is looking at 'em. Usually we can write off a goodly number because o' their being able to show they was somewhere else." He studied Joseph gravely. "We come at a crime, particularly a murder, from three sorts of angles, Reverend." He held up one finger. "First, who had the opportunity? If somebody weren't there at the time, that cuts them out."

"Naturally," Joseph nodded.

Perth regarded him steadily. "Second," he continued, putting up the next finger, "there's the means, in this case a gun. Who had a gun?"

"I have no idea."

"That's a shame, you see, because no one else has neither, leastways not that they're telling of." Perth still had a pleasant air about him, as if he were a lecturer with a bright student, leading him through the points of a piece of logic. "We know it was a small gun, a revolver of some sort, because of the bullet—which we got, by the way."

Joseph winced at the horrible thought of its passage through Sebastian's torn brain, presumably into the wall of the room. He had not looked. Now he was aware of Perth's eyes watching him, but he could not keep the revulsion from his face, or the slight feeling of sickness from his stomach.

"An' o' course it would be awkward like to be carrying a rifle or a shotgun around with you in a place like this," Perth went on, his voice unemotional. "Nowhere to hide it from being seen, except in a case for a trumpet or something like that. But what would anybody be doing with a trumpet at foive o'clock in the morning?"

"Cricket bat," Joseph said instantly. "If . . ."

Perth's eyes widened. "Very clever, Reverend! Oi never thought o' that, but you're right. A nice early practice out on that lovely grass by the river, or even one o' those cricket fields—Fenner's, or what's the other one, Parker's Piece?"

"Parker's Piece belongs to the town," Joseph pointed out. "The university uses Fenner's. But you can't practice cricket by yourself."

"O' course. Town and gown—separate." Perth nodded, pursing his lips. The difference was a gulf between them, uncrossable, and Joseph had inadvertently just reminded him of it. "But then, you see, our fellow might not have bin sticking to the rules," he said stiffly, his expression tight, defensive. "In fact, he might not even have practiced at all, seeing as he would have had a gun in his case, not a bat." He leaned forward. "But since we're having a lot o' trouble finding this gun, which could be anywhere by now, that means we got just the last thing left on which to catch him, doesn't it? Motive!" He held up his third finger.

Joseph should have realized it from the moment Perth had come in. The inspector knew Joseph would have nothing to give him on means or opportunity. He would hardly be here simply to keep Joseph informed. "I see," he said flatly.

"Oi'm sure as you do, Reverend," Perth agreed, a gleam of satisfaction in his eyes. "Not easy to find that out. Not even counting the fact that no one wants to incriminate 'emselves, they don't want to speak ill o' the dead neither. It ain't decent. People talk the greatest rubbish Oi ever heard about a person just because they're dead. Why do you think that is, Reverend? You must come across a lot of that in your line o' work."

"I don't have an active ministry now," Joseph explained, surprised by the pang of guilt it caused him, like a captain having left his ship in bad weather, and before his crew. That was ridiculous; what he was doing here was just as important a job, and one to which he was far better suited.

"Still ordained, though, aren't you." Perth made it a statement.

"Yes."

"You must be a good judge o' folk, an' Oi dare say as they trust you more'n most, tell you things?"

"Sometimes," Joseph said carefully, aware with a biting hollowness that he had been confided in very little, or he would not be as confused as he was by this eruption of violence. "But a confidence is precisely that, Inspector, and I would not break it. However, I can tell you that I have no idea who killed Sebastian Allard, or why."

Perth nodded slowly. "Oi took that for granted, sir. But you know these young men mebbe better'n anyone else."

"I don't know of any reason!" Joseph protested. "Being a minister means that people tend not to tell you their uglier thoughts!" He realized with dismay how profoundly that was true. How many things had he been blind to? For how long? Years? Had his own pain made him retreat from reality into uselessness? Then, without grasping the fullness of what he said, he spoke with sudden intensity. "But I shall find out! I ought to have known!" He meant it, savagely, with the intensity of a drowning man's need for air. Perth might need to solve Sebastian's murder for his professional reputation, or even to prove that town was as good as gown, but Joseph needed to do it for his belief in reason and the power of men to rise above chaos.

Perth nodded slowly, but his eyes were wide and unblinking. "Very good, Reverend." He drew in his breath as if about to add something more, then just nodded again.

After Perth had gone, Joseph began to appreciate the enormity of what he had promised himself. There was no point in waiting for people to reveal some anger or resentment against Sebastian. They had not done so before; they certainly would not now. He had to go and investigate for himself.

The first person he spoke to was Aidan Thyer. He found him at home finishing a late breakfast. He looked tired and flustered, his fair hair more faded by gray than had been apparent at a glance, his face unrefreshed by sleep. He looked up at Joseph in surprise as the maid showed him into the dining room.

"Good morning, Reavley. Nothing wrong, I hope?"

"Nothing new," Joseph replied a trifle drily.

"Tea?" Thyer offered.

"Thank you." Joseph sat down, not because he particularly wanted tea, but it obliged the master to continue the conversation. "How are Gerald and Mary?"

Thyer's face tightened. "Inconsolable. I suppose it's natural. I can't imagine what it is like to lose a son, let alone in such a way." He took another bite of his toast. "Connie's doing everything she can, but nothing makes the slightest difference."

"I suppose one of the worst things is realizing that someone hated him so much they resorted to murder. I admit, I had no idea there was such a passion in anyone." Joseph poured himself tea from the silver pot and sipped it tentatively. It was very hot; obviously someone had refilled it. "Which shows that I was paying far too little attention."

Thyer looked at him with surprise. "I had no idea, either! For God's sake, do you think that if I had—"

"No! Of course not," Joseph said quickly. "But you might at least have been more aware than I of an undercurrent of emotion, a rivalry, an insult, real or imagined, or some kind of a threat." The truth embarrassed him, and it was hard to admit. "I had my head so buried in their academic work that I paid too little attention to their other thoughts or feelings. Perhaps you didn't?"

"You're an idealist," Thyer agreed, picking up his tea, but the sharp perception in his eyes was not unkind.

"And you can't afford to be," Joseph replied. "Who hated Sebastian?"

"That's blunt!"

"I think it would be better if we knew before Perth did, don't you?"

Thyer put down his cup again and regarded Joseph steadily. "Actually, more people than you would care to think. You were very fond of him, knowing the family, and perhaps he showed you the best of himself for that reason."

Joseph took a long breath. "And who saw the other side?" Unwittingly, Harry Beecher's wry, familiar face came to his mind, sitting on the bench in the Pickerel, watching the boats on the river in the evening light, and the sudden tightness in his voice.

Thyer considered for a moment. "Most people, one way or another. Oh, his work was brilliant, you were right about that, and you perceived it long before anyone else. He had the potential to be excellent one day, possibly one of the great poets of the English language. But he had a long way to go to any kind of emotional maturity." He shrugged. "Not that emotional maturity is any necessity for a poet. One could hardly claim it for Byron or Shelley, to name but two. And I rather think that both of them probably escaped murder more by luck than virtue."

"That is not very specific," Joseph said, wishing he could leave it all to Perth and never know more than simply who had done it, not why. But it was already too late for that.

Thyer sighed. "Well, there's always the question of women, I suppose. Sebastian was good-looking, and he enjoyed exercising his charm and the power it gave him. Perhaps in time he would have learned to govern it, or on the other hand it might have grown worse. It takes a very fine character indeed to have power and refrain from using it. He was a long way from that yet." His face tightened until it was curiously bleak. "And of course there is always the possibility that it was not a woman but a man. It happens, particularly in a place like Cambridge. An older man, a student who is full of vitality and dreams, hunger . . ." He stopped. Further explanation was unnecessary.

Joseph heard a sound in the doorway and swiveled around to see Connie standing behind him, her face grave, a flash of anger in her dark eyes.

"Good morning, Dr. Reavley." She came in and closed the door behind her with a snap. She was wearing a deep lavender morning dress, suitable both for the heat and for the tragedy of her houseguests. The sweeping lines of it, impossibly slender at the knees, became her rich figure, and the color flattered her complexion. Even in these circumstances it was a pleasure to look at her.

"Really, Aidan, if you have to be so candid, you might at least do it with more discretion!" she said sharply, coming further into the room. "What if Mrs. Allard had overheard you? She can't bear to hear anything but praise for him, which I suppose is natural enough in the circumstances. I don't suppose the boy was a saint—few of us are—but that is how she needs to see him at the moment. And apart from unnecessary cruelty to her, I don't want a case of hysteria on my hands." She turned away from her husband, possibly without seeing the shadow in his face, as if he had received a blow he half expected. "Would you like some breakfast, Dr. Reavley?" she invited. "It won't be the least difficulty to have Cook prepare you something."

"No, thank you." Joseph felt discomforted for having wanted Thyer to be candid, and a degree of embarrassment at having witnessed a moment of personal pain. "I am afraid the master's comments were my fault," he said to Connie. "I was asking him because I feel we need to have the truth, if possible before the police uncover every mistake of judgment by a student—or one of us, for that matter." He was talking too much, explaining unnecessarily, but he could not stop.

Connie sat down at the head of the table, managing the restriction of her skirts with extraordinary grace, and Joseph was aware of the faint lily-of-the-valley perfume she wore. He felt a wave of loss for Alys that was momentarily overwhelming.

"I suppose you are right," Connie conceded. "Sometimes fear is worse than the truth. At least the truth will destroy only one person. Or am I creating a fool's paradise?"

A flicker of awareness crossed Thyer's face, and he drew in his breath, then changed his mind and did not speak.

This time Joseph was honest. "Yes . . . I'm sorry, but I think you are," he said to her. "Students have asked me whether they should tell the inspector what they know about Sebastian or be loyal to his memory and conceal it. I told them to tell the truth, and because of it Foubister and Morel, who have been friends ever since they came up, have quarreled so bitterly, both feel betrayed. And we have all learned things about each other we were far happier not knowing."

Still not looking at her husband, she reached across and touched her fingers to Joseph's arm. "It seems ignorance is a luxury we can no longer afford. Sebastian was very charming, and he was certainly gifted, but he had uglier sides as well. I know you would prefer not to have seen them, and your charity does you great credit."

"No, it doesn't," he contradicted her miserably. "It was a matter of self-protection, not generosity of spirit. I rather think cowardice is the correct name for it."

"You are too hard on yourself." She was very gentle. There was a softness in her face he had always liked. Now he thought briefly, and with a respect that surprised him, how fortunate a man Aidan Thyer was.

In the evening, Joseph went as usual to the senior common room for a few moments' quiet companionship and time to relax before dinner. Almost as soon as he entered he saw Harry Beecher sitting in a comfortable chair near the window, nursing a glass of what looked like gin and tonic.

Joseph walked toward him with a sudden lift of pleasure. He had shared many years of friendship with Beecher and never found in him meanness of spirit or that self-absorption that makes people blind to the feelings of others.

"Your usual, sir?" the steward asked, and Joseph accepted, sitting down with a deep sense of ease at the sheer luxurious familiarity of the surroundings, the people he had known and found so congenial over the last, difficult year. They thought largely as he did. They had the same heritage and the same values. Disagreements were minor and on the whole added interest to what might otherwise have become flat. The challenge of ideas was the savor of life. Always to be agreed with must surely become an intolerable loneliness in the end, as if anchored by endless mirrors of the mind, sterile of anything new.

"Looks as if the French president is going to Russia to speak to the czar," Beecher remarked, sipping at his glass.

"About Serbia?" Joseph asked, although it was a rhetorical question.

"What a mess." Beecher shook his head. "Walcott thinks there'll be war." Walcott was a lecturer in modern history they both knew moderately well. "I wish to hell he'd be a bit more discreet about his opinions." A flicker of distaste crossed his face. "Everyone's unsettled enough without that."

Joseph took his glass from the steward and thanked him, then waited until the man was out of earshot. "Yes, I know," he said unhappily. "Several of the students have spoken about it. You can hardly blame them for being anxious."

"Even at the worst, I don't suppose it would involve us." Beecher dismissed the idea, taking another sip of his drink. "But if it did—if, say, we were drawn in to help?" His eyebrows lifted with faint humor. "But I don't know whom. I can't see us being overly concerned with the Austrians or the Serbs. Regardless, we don't conscript to the army. It's all volunteer." He smiled lopsidedly. "I think they are rather badly upset about Sebastian Allard's murder, and that's what they are really worried about." His mouth tightened momentarily. "Unfortunately, from the evidence, the murderer has to have been someone here in college." He looked at Joseph with sudden, intense candor. "I suppose you haven't got any idea, have you? You wouldn't consider it your religious duty to protect them . . . ?"

Joseph was startled. "No, I wouldn't!" The hot anger still welled up inside him at the thought of Sebastian's vitality and dreams obliterated. "I don't know anything." He looked at Beecher earnestly. "But I feel I need to. I've gone over everything I can remember of the last few days I saw Sebastian, but I was away, because of my parents' death, for a good while right before he was killed. I couldn't have seen anything."

"You think it was foreseeable?" There was surprise and curiosity sharp in Beecher's eyes. He ignored his unfinished drink.

"I don't know," Joseph admitted. "It can't have happened without some cause that built up over a while. Unless it was an accident—which would be the best possible answer, of course! But I can't imagine how that could happen, can you?"

"No," Beecher said with quiet regret. The evening light through the long windows picked out the tiny lines around his eyes and mouth. He looked more tired than he was admitting, and perhaps a lot more deeply worried. "No, I'm afraid that's a fool's paradise," Beecher said with quiet regret. "Someone killed him because they meant to." He reached out and picked up his drink again, sipping it and rolling it around his mouth, but it obviously gave him no pleasure. "Certainly his work was falling off over the last few weeks. And to be honest"—he looked up at Joseph apologetically—"I've seen a certain harder edge to it, and a lack of delicacy lately. I thought it might be a rather uncomfortable transition from one style to another, made without his usual grace." That was half a question.

"But?" Joseph prompted. He knew Beecher did not like Sebastian, and he didn't relish what his friend would say.

"But on looking back, it was more than just his work," Beecher said. "His temper was fragile, far more than it used to be. I don't think he was sleeping well, and I know of at least a couple of rather stupid quarrels he got involved in."

"Quarrels about what? With whom?"

Beecher's lips pulled tight in the mockery of a smile. "About war and nationalism, false ideas of honor. And with several people, anyone fool enough to get involved in the subject."

"Why didn't you mention it?" Joseph was startled. He had not seen anything of the sort. Had he been blind? Or had Sebastian hidden it from him deliberately? Why? Kindness, a desire not to concern him? Self-protection, because he wanted to preserve the image of him Joseph had, keep one person seeing only the good? Or had he simply not trusted him, and it was only Joseph's imagination and vanity that they had been friends?

"I assumed that Sebastian confided in you," Beecher said. "I realized only the other day that he hadn't. I'm sorry."

"You didn't say anything at the time," Joseph pointed out. "You noticed something was wrong with him, but you didn't ask if I had seen it also, and if I knew what it was. Perhaps together we could have done something to help."

"I didn't like Sebastian nearly as much as you did," Beecher said slowly. "I saw his charm, but I also saw how he used it. I considered asking you if you knew what was causing him such distress, and I believe it was profound. Actually, I did approach it once, but you didn't take me up. We were interrupted by something, and I didn't go back to it. I didn't want to quarrel with you." He raised his eyes, bright and troubled, and for once the humor in him was totally absent.

Joseph was stunned. He had been expecting pain, but this blow hurt far more than anything he had foreseen. Beecher had tried to protect him because he thought Joseph was not strong enough to accept or deal with the truth. He had thought that he would turn aside from a friend rather than look at it honestly.

How could he? What had Joseph ever said or done that even Beecher believed him not only so blind, but such a moral coward?

Was that why Sebastian had not told him? He had spoken of the fear of war and its destruction of the beauty he loved, but surely that was hardly sufficient to disturb him the way Beecher had implied. And it had obviously started weeks before the assassination in Sarajevo.

Elwyn had turned on him instantly when Joseph had said something about fear, denying hotly that Sebastian was a coward, a charge that had never crossed Joseph's mind. Should it have? Had Sebastian been afraid and felt unable to confide it to Joseph, who was supposed to be his friend? What was friendship worth if one had to wear a mask over the thoughts that really hurt?

Not a great deal. Without honesty, compassion, the will to understand, it was no more than an acquaintanceship, and not even a good one at that.

And Beecher's forbearance was no better. There was pity in it, even kindness, but there was no equality, and certainly no respect.

"I wish I had known," Joseph said bitterly. "Now all we are left with is that somebody hated him so uncontrollably they went to his room early in the morning and shot him in the head. That's a very deep hatred, Harry. Not only did we not see it before, we can't even see it now, and God knows I'm looking!"

The next day, late in the morning, Joseph called on Mary and Gerald Allard, still at the master's house, at least until the funeral, which the police had held up because of the investigation. They had been acquaintances a long time. He could think of nothing to say that would ease their pain, but that did not excuse the need at least to express some care. Apart from that, he must learn anything from them he could that would help him to know Sebastian better.

"Come in," Connie said as soon as the maid took Joseph from the front hall into her quiet sitting room. He saw immediately that none of the Allards was there. The moment could be put off a little longer, and he was ashamed of being so relieved.

"Do sit down, Dr. Reavley." She looked at him with a smile, as if she read his thoughts and sympathized with them.

He accepted. The room was wildly eclectic. Of course it was part of the college and could not be fundamentally altered, but Thyer's taste was conservative, and most of the house was furnished accordingly. However, this room was hers, and a Spanish flamenco dancer whirled in a glare of scarlet in the painting over the mantelpiece. It burst with vitality. It was crudely painted and really rather in bad taste, but the colors were gorgeous. Joseph knew Thyer loathed it. He had given her a modern, expensive impressionist painting that he disliked himself, but he thought it would please her, and at least be fit to hang in the house. She had accepted it graciously and put it in the dining room. Perhaps Joseph was the only one who knew that she did not like it, either.

Now he sat down next to the Moroccan blanket in rich earth tones and made himself comfortable, disregarding a tall brass hookah on the table beside him. Oddly, he found the mood of the room both unique and comfortable.

"How is Mrs. Allard?" he asked.

"Plunging between grief and fury," she answered with wry honesty. "I don't know what to do for her. The master has to continue with his duties to the rest of the college, of course, but I have been doing what little I can to offer some physical care to her, though I confess I feel helpless." She gave him a sudden, candid smile. "I'm so glad you've come! I'm at my wits' end. I never know if what I'm saying is right or wrong."

He felt vaguely conspiratorial; it eased the moment. "Where is she?" he asked.

"In the Fellows' Garden," she replied. "That policeman was questioning her yesterday, and she was berating him for his failure to arrest anyone yet." Her eyes became serious, and the soft lines of her mouth pulled a little tighter with pity. "She said there couldn't be more than one or two people who hated Sebastian." Her voice dropped. "I'm afraid that's not really true. He was not always a comfortable person at all. I look at that poor girl, Miss Coopersmith, and I wonder what she is feeling. I can read nothing in her face, and Mrs. Allard is too consumed in her own loss to spare her anything but the most perfunctory attention."

Joseph was not surprised, but he was sorry.

"Poor Elwyn is doing all he can," Connie went on. "But even he cannot console his mother. Although I think he is a considerable strength to his father. I am afraid Gerald is in a private hell of his own." She did not elaborate, but her eyes met Joseph's with the ghost of a smile.

He understood perfectly, but he was not prepared to let her see that, not yet. He had a wrenching pity for Gerald's weakness, and it forced him to conceal it, even from Connie.

He rose to his feet. "Thank you. You have given me a few moments to collect my thoughts. I think I had better go and speak to Mrs. Allard, even if it doesn't do much good."

She nodded and walked with him through to the passage and the side door into the garden. He thanked her again and went out into the sun and the motionless, perfumed heat, where the flowers blazed in a profusion of reds and purples and billowed across the carefully paved walks between the beds. Flaming nasturtiums spilled out of an old terra-cotta urn left on its side. Spires of blue salvia made a solemn background to a riot of pansies, faces jostling for attention. Delphiniums towered almost to eye level, and ragged pinks cast up a giddy perfume. A butterfly staggered by like a happy drunkard, and the droning of bees was a steady, somnolent music in the background.

Mary Allard was standing in the center looking at the dark burgundy moss roses. She was dressed entirely in black, and Joseph could not help thinking how insufferably hot she must have been. In spite of the sun, she had no parasol, and she was also unveiled. The harsh light exposed the tiny lines in her skin, all dragging tight and downward, betraying the pain eating inside her.

"Mrs. Allard," he said quietly.

From the sudden rigidity of her body under the silk, she had obviously not been aware of his presence. She swiveled around to face him. "Reverend Reavley!" There was a challenge in her bearing and the directness of her eyes.

It was going to be more difficult than he had imagined.

"I came by to see you," he began, knowing he was being trite.

"Do you know anything more about who killed Sebastian?" she demanded. "That policeman is useless!"

Joseph changed his mind. Any attempt at comfort was doomed to failure. Instead he would pursue his own need, which was also hers.

"What does he think?" he asked her.

She was startled, as if she had expected him to argue with her and insist that Perth was doing his best, or at the very least defend him by pointing out how difficult his task was.

"He's going around looking for reasons to hate Sebastian," she answered witheringly. "Envy, that's the only reason. I told him that, but he doesn't listen."

"Academic?" he asked. "Personal? Over anything in particular?"

"Why?" She took half a step toward him. "Do you know something?"

"No, I don't," he said. "But I want very much to find out who killed Sebastian, for a lot of reasons."

"To cover your own failure!" She spat the word. "That's all that's left. We sent him here to learn. That was your idea! We trusted you with him, and you let some creature kill him. I want justice!" Tears filled her eyes, and she turned away from him. "Nothing can bring him back," she said hoarsely. "But I want whoever did it to suffer."

Joseph could not defend himself. She was right; he had failed to protect Sebastian because he had seen only what he wanted to see, not any of the darker envies or hatreds that had to have been there. He had thought he was dealing with reality, a higher, saner view of man. In truth, he had been looking for his own comfort.

It was also pointless to argue about justice or to tell her that it would ease nothing. It was morally wrong, and she would almost certainly never know all the truths of what had happened. It would only add to her anger to tell her that mercy was the better part, just as she herself would need mercy when her own judgment should come. She was not listening. And if he was honest, his own rage at violence and senseless death was so close beneath the surface of his words that he would have been a hypocrite to preach to her. He could not forget how he had felt when he stood on the Hauxton Road and realized what the caltrop marks meant, and pictured it in his mind.

"I want them to suffer, too," he confessed quietly.

She lifted her head and turned slowly back to him, her eyes wide.

"I apologize," she whispered. "I thought you were going to come and preach at me. Gerald tells me I shouldn't feel like that. That it's not really me speaking, and I'll regret saying it later."

"Maybe I will as well." He smiled at her. "But that's how I feel now."

Her face crumpled again. "Why would someone do that to him, Joseph? How can anyone envy so much? Shouldn't we love beauty of the mind and want to help it, protect it? I've asked the master if Sebastian was in line for any prizes or honors that might have excluded someone else, but he says he doesn't know of anything." She drew her black eyebrows together. "Do you . . . do you suppose that it could have been some woman? Someone who was in love with him, obsessed with him, and couldn't accept rejection? Girls can be very hysterical. They can imagine that a man has feelings for them when it is only a passing admiration, no more than good manners, really."

"It could be over a woman—" he began.

"Of course it could!" she interrupted eagerly, seizing on the idea, her face lighting up, the rigid line of her body relaxing a little. He could see in the sun the sheen on the silk of her gown and how it pulled over her thin shoulders. "That's the one thing that makes sense! Raging jealousy because a woman was in love with Sebastian, and someone felt betrayed by her!" She put out her hand tentatively and laid it on his arm. "Thank you, Joseph. You have at least made sense out of the darkness. If you came to comfort me, you have succeeded, and I am grateful to you."

It was not how he had intended to succeed, but he did not know how to withdraw. He remembered the girl in the street outside Eaden Lilley's, and what Eardslie had said about Morel, and wished he did not have to know about it.

He was still searching for an answer when Gerald Allard came from the quad gate of the garden, walking carefully along the center of the path between the tumbles of catmint and pinks. It was a moment before Joseph realized that his considered step was due to the fact that he had already partaken of more refreshment than he could absorb. He looked curiously at Joseph, then at his wife.

Mary's eyes narrowed at the sight of him.

"How are you, my dear?" he inquired solicitously. "Good morning, Reavley. Nice of you to call. However, I think we should speak of other things for a little while. It is—"

"Stop it!" Mary said, her teeth clenched. "I can't think of other things! I don't want to try! Sebastian is dead! Someone killed him! Until we know who it was and the person is arrested and hanged, there are no other things!"

"My dear, you should—" he began.

She whirled around, catching the fine silk of her sleeve on a stem of the moss rose. She stormed off, uncaring that she had torn the fabric, and disappeared through the door to the sitting room of the master's house.

"I'm sorry," Gerald said awkwardly. "I really don't know . . ." He did not finish.

"I met Miss Coopersmith," Joseph said suddenly. "She seems a very pleasant young woman."

"Oh . . . Regina? Yes, most agreeable," Gerald concurred. "Good family, known them for years. Her father's got a big estate a few miles away, in the Madingley direction."

"Sebastian never mentioned her."

Gerald pushed his hands deeper into his pockets. "No, I don't suppose he would. I mean . . ." Again he stopped.

This time Joseph waited.

"Well, two separate lives," Gerald went on uncomfortably. "Home and . . . and here. Man's world, this." His arm swept around in a wide, slightly unsteady circle. "Not the place to discuss women, what?"

"Is Mrs. Allard fond of her?"

Gerald's eyebrows shot up. "No idea! Yes! Well, I suppose so. Yes, must have liked the girl."

"You put that in the past," Joseph pointed out.

"Oh! Well . . . Sebastian's dead now, God help us." He gave a little shrug. "Next Christmas will be unbearable. Always spend it with Mary's sister, you know. Fearful woman. Three sons. All successes one way or another. Proud as Lucifer."

Joseph could think of nothing to say. Gerald would probably wish later that he had never made such a remark. It was better not to acknowledge it now. He made the heat an excuse to leave Gerald wandering aimlessly between the flowers and go back into the house.

He went into the sitting room to thank Connie and take his leave, but when he saw the figure of the woman standing by the mantel, in spite of the fact that she was roughly the same height and build as Connie, he knew instantly that it was someone else. The words died on his lips when he saw the black dress, which was fashionable, with a broad sash at the waist and a sort of double tunic in fine pleats over the long, tapering skirt.

She turned around, and her eyes widened with something like relief. "Reverend Reavley! How agreeable to see you."

"Miss Coopersmith. How are you?" He closed the door behind him. He would like the opportunity to speak to her. She had known a side of Sebastian that he had been totally unaware of.

She gave a little shrug, slightly self-deprecatory. "This is difficult. I don't really know what I am doing here. I hoped I could be of some comfort to Mrs. Allard, but I know I'm not succeeding. Mrs. Thyer is very kind, but what do you do with a fiancée who isn't a widow?" Her strong, rather blunt face was touched with self-mocking humor to hide the humiliation. "I'm an impossibility for a hostess." She gave a little laugh, and he realized how close she was to losing her grip on self-control.

"Had you known Sebastian long?" he asked her. "I have, but only the academic side of his life." It was odd to say that aloud; he had not imagined it to be true, but now it was unquestionable.

"That was the biggest side," she replied. "He cared about it more than anything else, I think. That's why he was so terrified there'd be a war."

"Yes. He spoke to me about it a day or two before he . . . died." He remembered that long, slow walk along the Backs in the sunset as if it had been yesterday. How quickly a moment sinks into the past. He could still see quite clearly the evening light on Sebastian's face, the passion in the young man as he spoke of the destruction of beauty that he feared.

"He traveled widely this summer," she went on, looking at the distance, not at Joseph. "He didn't talk about it very much, but when he did you could feel how strongly he cared. I think you taught him that, Reverend, how to see the loveliness and the value in all kinds of people, how to open his mind and look without judgment. He was so excited by it. He wanted intensely to live more . . ." She hunted for the word, "More abundantly than one can being buried by the confines of nationalism."

As she said it, he remembered Sebastian's comments about the richness and diversity of Europe, but he did not interrupt her.

She went on, controlling her trembling voice with difficulty. "For all his excitement at the different cultures, especially the ancient ones, he was terribly English at heart, you know?" She bit her lip to gain a moment's hesitation, trying to control herself before she went on. "He would have given anything he had to protect the beauty of this country—the quaint and funny things, the tolerance and the eccentricity, the grandeur and the small, secret things one discovers alone. He'd have died to save a heath with skylarks, or a bluebell wood." Her voice was trembling. "A cold lake with reed spears in it, a lonely shore where the light falls on pale sandbars." She gulped. "It's hard to believe they are all still just the same, and he can't see them anymore."

He was too full of emotion himself to speak. His thoughts included his father as well, and all the multitude of things his mother had treasured.

"But lots of people love things, don't they?" She was looking intently at him now. "And there were parts of him I didn't know at all. A terrible anger sometimes, when he thought of what some of our politicians were doing, how they were letting Europe slip into war because they are all so busy protecting their own few square miles of territory. He hated jingoism, really hated it. I've seen him white to the lips, almost so choked with it that he couldn't speak." She took a deep, shuddering breath. "Do you think there will be war, Mr. Reavley? Sebastian wanted peace . . . so much!"

Joseph saw Sebastian's face in the fading light again, as clearly as if he had been in the room with them.

"Yes, I know he did."

"I wonder if he would be surprised to see how much turmoil he's left behind." She gave a tiny laugh, almost like a hiccup. "We are tearing ourselves apart trying to find out who killed him, and you know, I'm not sure if I want to succeed. Is that wicked of me, irresponsible?"

"I don't think we have a choice," he answered. "We are going to be forced to know."

"I'm afraid of that!" She stared at him, searching his face.

"Yes," he agreed. "So am I."

CHAPTER

SEVEN

On the evening of Friday, July 17, Matthew again left London and drove north toward Cambridge. It was a fine evening, with a slight wind piling clouds into bright towers of light high up in a cobalt sky—a perfect time to be on the road, once he had left the confines of the city. Long stretches opened up ahead of him, and he increased speed until the wind tore at his hair and stung his cheeks and in his imagination he thought what it would be like to fly.

He reached Cambridge at about quarter past seven. He came in on the Trumpington Road with the river on his left and Lammas Land beyond, past Fitzwilliam, Peterhouse, Pembroke, Corpus Christi, and up the broad elegance of King's Parade with shops and houses to the right, and intricate wrought iron railings to the left. He passed the ornate spires of the screen that walled off the Front Court of King's College, then the classical perfection of the Senate House, with Great Saint Mary's opposite.

He pulled up at the main gate of St. John's and climbed out of the seat. He walked stiffly to the porter's lodge and was about to tell Mitchell who he was and that he had come to see Joseph, when Mitchell recognized him.

Within a quarter of an hour his car was safely parked and he was sitting in Joseph's rooms. The sun made bright patches on the carpet and picked out the gold lettering on the books in the case. The college cat,

Bertie, sat with his eyes closed in the warmth, and every now and again his tail gave a slight twitch.

Joseph sat in shadow. Even so, Matthew could see the weariness and the pain of uncertainty etched in his face. His eyes looked hollow in spite of his high cheekbones. His cheeks were thin and there were shadows that had nothing to do with the darkness of his hair.

"Do they know who killed Sebastian yet?" Matthew asked.

Joseph shook his head.

"How's Mary Allard? Someone told me she came here."

"She and Gerald are staying at the master's house. The funeral was today. It was ghastly."

"They haven't gone home?"

"They're still hoping the police will find something any day."

Matthew looked at him with concern. He seemed to lack all vitality, as if something inside him were exhausted. "Joe, you look bloody awful!" he said abruptly. "Are you going to be all right?" It was a pointless question, but he had to ask. He had some idea of how fond Joseph had been of Sebastian Allard, and of his acute sense of responsibility, perhaps taken too personally. Was this additional blow too much for him?

Joseph raised his eyes. "Probably." He rubbed his hand over his forehead. "It just takes a day or two. There doesn't seem to be any sense in this. I feel as if everything is slithering out of my grasp."

Matthew leaned forward a little. "Sebastian Allard was extraordinarily gifted, and he could be more charming than anyone else I can think of, but he wasn't perfect. Nobody is entirely good—or bad. Someone killed Sebastian, and it's a tragedy, but it's not inexplicable. There'll be an answer that makes as much sense as most things ever do . . . when we know it."

Joseph straightened up. "I expect so. Do you suppose reason is going to be any comfort?" Then before Matthew could answer he went on. "The Allards brought Regina Coopersmith with them."

Matthew was lost. "Who is Regina Coopersmith?"

"Sebastian's fiancée," Joseph replied.

That explained much, Matthew thought. If Joseph had not known of her, he would feel excluded. How odd that Sebastian should not have told him. Usually when a young man was engaged to marry he told everyone. A young woman invariably did.

"His idea, or his mother's?" Matthew asked bluntly.

"I don't know. I've talked with her a little. I should think it's his mother's. But it's probably irrelevant to his death." He changed the subject. "Are you going home?"

"For a day or two," Matthew replied, feeling a sense of darkness inside him as he recalled the anger he had felt listening to Isenham the previous week. The wound was far from healed. He thought of his father and the interpretation Isenham had had of his actions, and it felt like an abscessed tooth. He could almost ignore it until he accidentally touched it, then it throbbed with all the old pain, exacerbated by a new jolt.

Joseph was waiting for him to go on.

"I went to see Isenham when I was up last weekend," Matthew said finally. And then he recounted his conversation with the former army man.

Joseph listened thoughtfully.

"I talked to him for quite a long time," Matthew concluded, "but all he told me that was specific was that Father wanted war."

"What?" Joseph's voice was angry and incredulous. "That's ridiculous! He was the last man on earth to want war. Isenham must have misheard him. Perhaps he said he thought war was inevitable! The question is, was it Ireland or the Balkans?"

"How would Father know anything about either?" Matthew was playing devil's advocate and hoping Joseph could beat him.

"I don't know," Joseph answered. "But that doesn't mean he didn't. You said he was very specific that he had discovered a document outlining a conspiracy that would be dishonorable and change—"

"I know," Matthew cut across him. "I didn't tell Isenham that, but he said Father had been there, and was . . ." He paused.

"What? Losing control of his imagination?" Joseph demanded.

"More or less, yes. He was kinder about it than that, but it comes to the same thing. I know you're angry, Joe. So was I, and I still am. But what is the truth? No one wants to think someone they love is mistaken, losing their grip. But wanting doesn't alter reality."

"Reality is that he and Mother are dead," Joseph said a little unsteadily. "That their car hit a row of caltrops on the Hauxton Road and crashed, killing them both, and whatever document he had, whatever it said, wasn't with him. Presumably whoever killed him searched the car and the bodies and found it."

Matthew was forced to carry on the logic. "Then why did they search the house for it?"

"We only think they did," Joseph said unhappily, then added, "but if they did, then they must have thought it important enough to take the risk of one of us coming back early and catching them. And don't tell me it was a petty thief. No valuables were taken, though the silver vase, the snuff-boxes, the miniatures were all in plain sight."

"But it could still have been a small scandal rather than a major act of espionage affecting the world."

"It was major enough to murder two people in order to hide it," Joseph said, his jaw tight. "And apart from that, Father didn't exaggerate." He made it a simple statement, no additions, no emphasis.

Images raced through Matthew's mind: his father standing in the garden in old clothes, trousers a trifle baggy, mud-stained at the knees, watching Judith picking blackberries; sitting in his armchair in the winter evening by the fire, a book open on his lap as he read them stories; at the dining room table on a Sunday, leaning a little forward in his chair as he argued reasonably; reciting absurd limericks and smiling, singing the Gilbert and Sullivan patter songs as he drove along the road with the top of the old car down in the wind and the sun.

The pain of loss was sweet for all he had been, and almost too sharp to bear because it no longer existed except in memory. It was a moment before Matthew could control his voice enough to speak. "I'll go and see Shanley Corcoran." He took a deep breath. "He was Father's closest friend. I can at last tell him the truth, or most of it."

Joseph hesitated a moment or two before speaking. "Be careful," was all he said.

* * *

Matthew spent the evening at home in St. Giles, and he telephoned Corcoran to ask if he could call the next day. He received an immediate invitation to dinner, which he accepted unhesitatingly.

He was glad of a lazy morning, and he and Judith dealt with a number of small duties. Then in the hot, still afternoon they took Henry and walked together to the churchyard and on through the lanes, Henry scuffling happily in the deep grasses on either side. The wild rose petals had mostly fallen.

Matthew changed for dinner early and was glad to be able to put the top down on the car and drive the ten or twelve miles to Corcoran's magnificent home. As he passed through Grantchester, a dozen or more youths were still practicing cricket in the lengthening sun, to the cheers and occasional shouts of a handful of watchers. Girls in pinafore dresses dangled hats by their ribbons. Three miles further on, children were sailing wooden boats in the village duck pond. A hurdy-gurdy man cranked out music, and an ice cream seller was packing his barrow to go home, his wares gone, his purse heavy.

Matthew crossed the main road between Cambridge and the west, then a mile and a half further along he swung off just short of Madingley, and in through the gates of Corcoran's house. He had barely stepped out of the car when the butler appeared, solemn-faced and punctilious.

"Good evening, Captain Reavley. How pleasant to see you, sir. We have been expecting you. Have you anything you wish carried, sir?"

"No, thank you." Matthew declined with a smile, reaching into the car to pick up the box of Orla's favorite Turkish delight from the passenger seat. "I'll manage these myself."

"Yes, sir. Then if you leave your keys, I'll see that Parley puts your car away safely. If you'd like to come this way, sir?"

Matthew followed him under the portico and up the shallow steps, through the door and into the wide, stone-flagged hallway, black and white squared like a chessboard. A full suit of medieval armor stood beside the carved newel post at the right-hand side of the mahogany staircase, its helmet catching the sun through the oval window on the landing.

Matthew dropped the car keys onto the tray the butler was holding, then turned as the study door opened and Shanley Corcoran appeared.

A wide smile lit Corcoran's face and he came forward, extending both his hands. "I'm so glad you could come," he said enthusiastically, searching Matthew's face. "How are you? Come in and sit down!" He indicated the study doorway, and without waiting for a reply he led the way in.

The room was typical of the man—exuberant. The books and artifacts were highly individual, and there were also scientific curiosities and exquisite works of art. There was a Russian icon, all gold and umber and black. Above the fireplace hung an Italian old master drawing of a man riding a donkey, probably Jesus entering Jerusalem on Palm Sunday. An astrolabe made of silver, polished bright, stood on the mahogany Pembroke table by the wall, and an illustrated copy of Chaucer on the drum table in the center of the room.

"Sit down, sit down," Corcoran invited, gesturing toward the other chair.

Matthew sank back into it, at ease already in the familiar room with its happy memories. It was quarter past seven, and he knew dinner would be served by eight. There was no time to waste on a preparatory conversation. "Did you hear about the death of Sebastian Allard?" he asked. "His family is devastated. I don't suppose it will begin to heal until they find out what happened. I know how they feel."

Corcoran's face darkened. "I understand your grief." His voice was very gentle. "I miss John. He was one of the kindest, most honest men I knew. I can't begin to imagine how you must feel." A frown of puzzlement creased his brow. "But what more is there to know about his death? No one was responsible. Perhaps it was a slick of oil on the road, or something wrong with the steering of the car? I don't drive, personally. I know nothing about the mechanics." He smiled at the irony of it. "I understand airplanes a little, and submarines a lot, but I imagine there are considerable differences."

Matthew attempted to smile in answer. Being here with Corcoran brought back memories with an intensity he had been unprepared for. The veil between past and present was too thin. "Well, neither airplanes nor submarines are going to crash off the road, if that is what you meant. But I don't believe that was what happened. In fact, I'm sure it wasn't." He saw Corcoran's eyes widen slightly. "Joseph and I went to the place," he explained. "We saw the skid marks exactly where the car veered off. There was no oil." He hesitated, then took the plunge. "Only a line of scratches, as if made by a row of iron caltrops across the tarmacadam."

The silence was so heavy in the room that Matthew could hear the ticking of the long-case clock against the far wall as if it were beside him.

"What are you saying, Matthew?" Corcoran said at last.

Matthew leaned forward a little. "Father was on his way to see me in London. He called me up to arrange it the night before. I've never heard him more serious."

"Oh? About what?" If Corcoran already had any idea, there was no indication of it in his face.

"He said he had discovered a conspiracy that was highly dishonorable and would eventually affect the whole world. He wanted my advice on it."

Corcoran's vivid blue eyes were unblinking. "Your professional advice?" he said cautiously.

"Yes."

"You couldn't have misunderstood?"

"No." Matthew was not going to elaborate and perhaps put words into Corcoran's mouth. Suddenly the conversation was no longer easy, or simply between friends.

"I knew he was concerned about something," Corcoran said, looking at Matthew over the top of his steepled fingers. "But he didn't confide in me. In fact, he was politely evasive, so I didn't pursue it."

"What did he say to you, exactly?" Matthew pressed.

Corcoran blinked. "Very little. Only that he was worried about the pressure in the Balkans—which we all are, but he seemed to think it were more explosive than I did." Corcoran's expression tightened, his lips a thin line. "It seems he was right. The assassination of the archduke is very ugly. They'll demand reparation, and of course Serbia won't pay. The Russians will back the Serbs, and Germany will back Austria. That's inevitable."

"And us?" Matthew asked. "That's still a long way from Britain, and it has nothing to do with our honor."

Corcoran was thoughtful for a moment. The ticking of the clock measured the silence in the room.

"The alliances are a web right across Europe," he said at last. "We know some of them, but perhaps not all. It's fears and promises that could be our undoing."

"Do you think Father could possibly have known about the assassination before it happened?" It was a wild thought, but he was reduced to desperation.

Corcoran lifted his shoulders, but there was no incredulity in his face and no ridicule. "I can't think how!" he answered. "If he had any connections with that part of the world, he didn't mention them to me. He knew France and Germany well, and Belgium, too, I think. He had some relative who married a Belgian, I believe, a cousin he was fond of."

"Yes, Aunt Abigail," Matthew confirmed. "But what has Belgium to do with Serbia?"

"Nothing, so far as I know. But what puzzles me far more is that he should want to involve you professionally." He looked apologetic. "I'm sorry, Matthew, but you know as well as I that he hated all secret services."

"Yes, I know!" Matthew cut in sharply. "He wanted Joseph to go into medicine, and when Joseph didn't, he wanted me to. He never really said why. . . ." He stopped, seeing surprise and a swift tenderness in Corcoran's face.

"He didn't tell you?" Corcoran asked.

Matthew shook his head. It was a place inside him that still hurt too much to explore. He had always believed that one day he would have the chance to show his father the value of what he did. Discreetly, it also saved lives; it saved the peace in which people could go about their ordinary, open business without fear. It was one of those professions that, if practiced with great enough skill, one was unaware of. It was visible only when it failed. But John's death had made that proof impossible, and it was an unresolved pain he had no way to deal with.

"It was a long time ago," Corcoran began thoughtfully. "When your father and I were both young. Perhaps it was even something to do with me, I don't know. It was in our first year at Cambridge—"

"I didn't know you were the same year!" Matthew interrupted.

"I was a year older than he. I was there on my father's money, he was on a scholarship. He started in medicine, you know?" Even without Matthew's amazement, it was obvious in Corcoran's face that he knew Matthew had not known. "I was reading physics. We used to spend hours talking and dreaming about what we could do after we graduated."

Matthew tried to visualize the two young men, minds full of the future, of hopes and ambitions. Had John Reavley been happy with what he had achieved? It hurt like a slow, grinding pain in the pit of the stomach to think that perhaps he had not, that he had died a disappointed man.

"Don't," Corcoran said gently, his eyes searching Matthew's face. "He changed his mind because he wanted to go into politics. He thought he could achieve more there, so he read classics instead. That's where most of our leaders come from, the men who learned the discipline of the mind and the history of thought and civilization in the West." He let out his breath slowly. "But there were times when he regretted it. He found politics a hard and often graceless master to serve. In the end he preferred the individual to the mass, and he thought it would give you greater happiness, and far more security."

"But you went on with physics," Matthew said.

Corcoran gave a downwardly twisted smile, self-mocking but also evasive. "I was ambitious in a different way."

"Father thought we were underhand, essentially betrayers—that the intelligence services deliberately used people and had no loyalties. He had no patience with deviousness. He couldn't be bothered to be indirect, to play to people's vanities or use their weaknesses. I don't think he understood how to. And he thought that was what we do."

"Isn't it?" Corcoran asked with a kind of wry regret.

Matthew sighed and leaned back in his chair again, crossing his legs. "Sometimes. Mostly it's just collecting as much information as possible and fitting it together so we see a picture. I wish I could have shown him that."

"Matthew," Corcoran said earnestly, "if he was coming to you for your professional advice, then whatever he had discovered, he must have believed it was profoundly serious and that only one of the secret services could help."

"But you have no idea what it was? What did he say to you? Anything? Names, places, dates, who would be affected . . . anything at all?" Matthew pleaded. "I don't know where to start, and I don't trust anyone, because he said important people were involved." Even to Corcoran he held back that his father had spoken of the royal family. Given how large Queen Victoria's family had been, the net spread very wide indeed.

Corcoran nodded. "Of course," he agreed. "If he could have trusted the ordinary services, then he would have."

There was a knock on the door, and Orla Corcoran came in. She was dressed in a bluish green gown of silk charmeuse with Venetian lace draped around her shoulders. In the fashion of the moment, the waist was high and soft, and the full drape came almost to the ankle before sweeping back to be caught up behind, revealing only a few inches of the plainer skirt beneath. It was decorated with two crimson roses, one just under the bosom, the other on the skirt. Her dark hair was curled loosely and had only a few streaks of gray at the temples; they made her the more striking.

"Matthew, my dear," she said with a smile. "How good it is to see you." She regarded him more closely. "But you are looking a little tired. Have you been working too hard with all this wretched business in eastern Europe? The Austrians don't seem to manage their affairs very well. I do hope they don't draw us all into their mess."

"I'm in good health, thank you," he said, taking her hand and touching it to his lips. "Unfortunately they haven't given me anything so interesting to do. I fear I may be picking up the domestic duties of others who are sent off to exotic parts."

"Oh, you really don't want to go to Serbia!" she said instantly. "It would take you ages to get there, and then you wouldn't understand a word they said." She turned to Corcoran. "Dinner is about to be served. Do come through, and talk about pleasanter things. Have you been to the theater lately? Last week we saw Lady Randolph Churchill's new play at the Prince of Wales." She led the way across the hall, passing a maid dressed in black with a crisp white lace-edged apron apparently without seeing her. "Very mixed, I thought," she went on. "Lots of drama, but a bit thin on skill here and there."

"You are repeating exactly what the reviewers say, my dear," Corcoran remarked with amusement.

"Then perhaps for once they are right!" she retorted, leading the way into the splendid rose-and-gold dining room.

The long mahogany table was very simple, in the classic style of Adam. The mahogany chairs' high, tapered backs echoed the lines of the windows. The curtains were drawn, hiding the view across the garden and the fields beyond.

They took their seats, and the first course was served. Since it was high summer and in the nature of a family meal rather than a formal one, a cold collation was quite acceptable. The second course was grilled trout and fresh vegetables, with a light German wine, dry and very delicate.

Matthew passed the natural compliments to the cook, but he meant them with great sincerity.

The conversation meandered over a dozen subjects: the latest novels published, accounts of travel in North Africa, more local gossip of Cambridgeshire families, the likelihood of a cold winter after such a glorious summer, anything but Ireland or Europe. Eventually they touched on Turkey, but only as a possible site for the ruins of what was once the great city of Troy.

"Wasn't that where Ivor Chetwin went?" Orla asked, turning to Corcoran.

Corcoran glanced at Matthew, then back to his wife. "I don't know," he answered.

"Oh, for goodness' sake!" she said impatiently, spearing a slice of nectarine with her fork. "Matthew knows perfectly well that John quarreled with Ivor. You don't have to tiptoe around it as if it were a hole he would fall into." She turned to Matthew, the fork still in her hand. "Ivor and your father used to be very good friends, nine or ten years ago. They both knew a man called Galliford, Galliard, something like that. He was doing something serious that he shouldn't, I don't know what. They never tell you." She ate the last of the nectarine quickly. "But Ivor told the authorities about it and the man was arrested."

Corcoran drew in his breath, seemingly to interrupt, then apparently changed his mind. The damage was done.

"John never really forgave him for it," Orla continued. "I don't know why—after all, Galliford, or whatever his name was, was guilty of doing it. That was Ivor's chance to join some branch or other of the secret services, and he took it. After that he and John never really spoke to each other, except to be polite. It was a great shame, because Ivor was a lovely man and they used to enjoy each other's company."

"It wasn't that he caught Gallard," Corcoran said quietly. "It was the way in which he did it that John couldn't forgive. John was a very candid man—almost innocent, you might say. He expected a certain standard of honesty from other people." He glanced at Matthew.

"Father never told me about Ivor Chetwin," Matthew said. "Did he go to Turkey?"

"Of course he did!" Orla responded. "But he came back."

"Do you think Father would have seen him again? Recently? In the last week or so before he died?"

Orla looked surprised.

Corcoran understood immediately. "I don't know," he admitted. "It's possible."

Orla had no such hesitation. "Of course it's possible. I know Ivor is at home because he lives in Haslingfield, and I saw him only a couple of weeks ago. I'm sure if your father visited him, he'd be happy to tell you about it."

Corcoran looked at her, then at Matthew, uncertain.

Matthew could not afford to care about old quarrels. High in his mind was the possibility that Ivor Chetwin could be the man behind the conspiracy John Reavley discovered. It was suddenly very important to know if they had met, but he would have to be extremely careful. Whoever it was did not hesitate to kill. Again he was overwhelmed with anger for his father for having been so naive as to trust someone, to think the best of them when it so agonizingly was not true.

"Matthew . . . ," Corcoran began, his face earnest, the lamplight now accentuating the warmth in his features.

"Yes!" Matthew said instantly. "I shall be extremely careful. Father and I are quite different. I trust no one." He wanted to explain to them what he intended to do. However, he did not know yet, and he needed the freedom to change his mind. But above all, he did not want his father's friend watching over his shoulder to see his weaknesses, or his pain if what he found was sad and vulnerable—and private.

"That's not what I was going to say," Corcoran declared. "Ivor Chetwin was a decent man when I knew him. But I doubt your father would have confided anything in him before telling you. Have you considered that this issue your father was so concerned about may have been a piece of politicking that he felt was dishonorable, rather than anything you or I would consider a conspiracy? He was a little . . . idealistic."

"Conspiracy?" Orla looked from Matthew to her husband and back again.

"Probably nothing." Corcoran smiled very slightly. "I daresay he would have found that out if he had had the chance."

Matthew wanted to argue, but he had no weapons. He could not defend his father; he had nothing but remembered words, which he had repeated so often he was hearing his own voice saying them now. There was nothing tangible except death, the awful absence of those he loved, the jolting surprise of the empty rooms, the telephone call no one would answer from the study.

"Of course," he said, not meaning it, nor looking at Corcoran's face. He was agreeing for Orla's sake, so as not to alarm her. Then he changed the subject. "I wish I didn't have to go back to London so soon. It is so timelessly peaceful here."

"Have a glass of port?" Corcoran offered. "I have some real vintage stuff."

Matthew hesitated.

"Oh, it's excellent!" Corcoran assured him. "No cork in it, no crust or sediment, I promise."

Matthew acceded gracefully.

The butler was sent for and dispatched to fetch one of the best bottles. He returned with it cradled in a napkin.

"Right!" Corcoran said enthusiastically. "I'll open this myself! Make sure it's perfect. Thank you, Truscott."

"Yes, sir." The butler handed it over with resignation.

"Really . . . ," Orla protested, but without any belief she would make a difference. "Sorry," she said ruefully to Matthew. "He's rather proud of this."

Matthew smiled. It was obviously a ritual that mattered to Corcoran, and he was happy to observe as Corcoran led them to the kitchen, heated the tongs in the kitchen stove, then grasped the bottle with them, closing them around its neck. Truscott handed him a goose feather and held out a dish of ice. Corcoran passed the feather through the ice, then carefully around the neck of the port.

"There!" he said triumphantly as the glass cracked in a perfect circle, cutting the corked top off cleanly. "You see?"

"Bravo!" Matthew laughed.

Corcoran was grinning widely, his face alight with triumph. "There you are, Truscott! Now you can decant it and bring it to us in the dining room. Mrs. Corcoran will have a Madeira. Come . . ." And he led the procession back to the rose-and-gold room.

It was late on Sunday afternoon when Matthew drove to Haslingfield. Ivor Chetwin did not live in the magnificent manner of the Corcorans, but his home was still extremely agreeable. It was a Georgian manor a mile outside Haslingfield, and the long drive from the road swept around a gracious curve with a stand of silver birches, their leaves shimmering in the breeze, their white trunks leaning with exaggerated grace away from the prevailing wind.

A parlor maid welcomed Matthew, but Chetwin himself appeared almost immediately, an enthusiastic spaniel puppy at his heels.

"I'd have recognized you," Chetwin said without hesitation, extending his hand to Matthew. His voice, unusually deep, still had the echo of music in it from his native Wales. "You resemble your father about the eyes."

The loyalty hardened even more deeply inside Matthew, memory catching him again.

"Thank you for agreeing to see me at such short notice, sir," he replied. "I'm just up for the weekend. I spend most of my time in London now."

"I'm afraid I only get occasional weekends here myself at the moment," Chetwin agreed. Then, followed by the puppy, he turned and led the way into a casual sitting room that opened onto a paved and graveled garden, largely shaded by overhanging trees. It was full of blossom from bushes and shrubs at the sides, and low-growing silvery-gray-leaved plants in clumps in the paving. The extraordinary thing about it was that every flower was white.

Chetwin noticed Matthew staring.

"My white garden," he explained. "I find it very restful. Sit down. Oh, move the cat." He gestured toward a black cat that had settled itself in the middle of the second chair and looked very disinclined to shift.

Matthew stroked the cat gently and felt rather than heard it begin to purr. He lifted it up, and when he had taken the seat, he put it down again on his lap. It rearranged itself slightly and went back to sleep.

"My father intended to come and see you," he said smoothly as if it were true. "I never had the chance to ask him if he actually did."

He watched Chetwin's face. It was dark-eyed, with a strong, round jaw, black hair graying and receding from a high brow. He could read nothing in it. It was a face that could give away exactly what its owner wished it to. There was nothing naive or easily misled in Ivor Chetwin. He was full of imagination and subtlety. Matthew had been here only a few minutes, yet already he had a sense of Chetwin's inner power.

"I'm sorry he didn't," Chetwin replied, and there was sadness in his voice. If he was acting, he was superb. But then Matthew had known men who betrayed their friends, even their families, and though they profoundly regretted what they saw as the necessity, it had not stopped them.

"He didn't contact you at all?" Matthew pressed. He should not have been disappointed, and yet he was. He had hoped Chetwin would have an idea, a thread, however fine, that would lead somewhere. He realized now it was unreasonable. John Reavley would have come to Matthew first before trusting anyone else, even the far more experienced Chetwin.

"I wish he had." Chetwin's face still showed the same sadness. "I would have called on him, but I doubted he would see me." A new bleakness shadowed his eyes. "That's one of the deepest regrets of death: the things you thought of doing and put off, and then suddenly it's too late."

"Yes, I know," Matthew agreed with more emotion than he had meant to expose. He felt as if he were laying a weapon down with the blade toward himself and the handle to a potential enemy. And yet had he shown less, Chetwin would have sensed it and known he was guarding himself.

"I think of something every day I would like to have said to him. I suppose that's really why I called. You knew him during a time when I was so young I thought of him only as my father, not as a person who led any life beyond St. Giles."

"A natural blindness of youth," Chetwin said. "But most of what you would have heard about your father you would have liked." He smiled, which momentarily softened his face. "He was stubborn at times; he had an intellectual arrogance he was not even aware of. It sprang from an effortless intelligence, and yet he had untiring patience for those he perceived as genuinely limited. He treated the old, the poor, the unlearned with dignity. To him the great sin was unkindness." He seemed to retreat further into memory, revisiting the past before his quarrel with John Reavley had bled the pleasure from it.

Matthew took the risk of probing. "I remember him as being completely without guile. Was that true, or just what I wanted to think?"

Chetwin gave a sharp little laugh. "Oh, that was true! He couldn't tell a lie to save himself, and he wasn't about to change what he was to please anyone, or to deceive them, even to gain his own ends." His face became shadowed again, but his dark eyes were unreadable. "That was his weakness as well as his strength. He was incapable of deviousness, and *that* is a politician's main weapon."

Matthew hesitated, wondering if he should admit to being in the intelligence services, and knowing that Chetwin was also. It might be a shortcut to gaining confidences. It would save time, take him nearer the truth. Or should he guard the little ammunition he had? Where were Chetwin's loyalties? He was easy to like, and the ties of the past were strong. But perhaps that was exactly what had cost John Reavley his life.

"He was very worried about the present situation in the Balkans," Matthew said. "Even though he died the day of the assassination, so he didn't hear of it."

"Yes," Chetwin agreed. "I know he used to have a considerable interest in German affairs and had many German friends. He climbed in the Austrian Tyrol now and then when he was younger. He enjoyed Vienna, its music and its culture, and he read German, of course."

"He discussed it with you?"

"Oh, yes. We had many friends in common in those days." There was sadness in his voice and a gentleness that seemed entirely human and vulnerable. But if he was clever, it would do!

"Did he keep up with them, do you know?" Matthew asked. He was going to trail a faint thread of the truth in front of Chetwin, to see if he picked it up, or if he even noticed.

There was nothing guarded in Chetwin's clever face. "I should imagine so. He was a man who kept his friends." He gave a little grimace. "Except in my case, of course. But that was because he did not approve of my change in career. He felt it was immoral—deceitful, if you like."

Matthew drew in his breath. It was like jumping into melted ice. "The intelligence services . . . yes, I know." He saw Chetwin flinch so minutely it was no more than a shadow. Had he not been looking for it, he might not have recognized it as such. "I think it was because of you that he was so disappointed when I joined them as well," he went on, and this time there was no mistaking the surprise. "You didn't know?" he added.

Chetwin breathed out very slowly. "No . . . I didn't."

Matthew was in the presence of a master at guile, and he knew it. But he could play the game, too. "Yes. He didn't approve of it, of course," he said, smiling ruefully. "But he knew that we have our uses. Sometimes there is no one else to turn to."

This time Chetwin hesitated.

Matthew smiled.

"Then he'd changed," Chetwin said slowly. "He used to think there was always a better way. But I suppose you know that, also?"

"Something like that," Matthew said noncommittally. He struggled for something else to pursue. He could not leave Chetwin, possibly the best source of hidden information about his father, without trying every conceivable avenue. "Actually, I think he had changed," he said suddenly. "Something he said to me not long ago made me think he had begun to appreciate the value of discreet information."

Chetwin's eyebrows rose. "Oh?" He did not conceal the interest in his face.

Matthew hesitated, acutely aware of the potential danger of revealing too much to Chetwin. "Just the value of information," he said finally, leaning back a little in his chair. "I never heard the rest of it. I thought it might matter. Whom would he have taken it to?"

"Information about what?" Chetwin asked.

Matthew was very careful. "I'm not sure. Possibly the situation in Germany." That was probably far enough from the troubles in either Ireland or the Balkans to be safe.

Chetwin thought for a moment or two. "Best to go to the man at the top," he said finally. "If it was important, it would reach Dermot Sandwell eventually."

"Sandwell!" Matthew was surprised. Dermot Sandwell was a highly respected minister in the Foreign Office—an outstanding linguist, well traveled, a classicist and scholar. "Yes, I suppose it would. That is excellent advice. Thank you."

Matthew stayed a little longer. Conversation moved from one thing to another: politics, memories, small gossip about Cambridgeshire. Chetwin had a vivid and individual turn of phrase describing people, and a sharp wit. Matthew could see very clearly why his father had liked him.

Half an hour later he rose to go, still uncertain whether his father had confided anything about the document to Chetwin or not, and if he had, whether doing so had been the catalyst for his death.

Matthew drove back to London that evening in heavy, thundery weather, wishing the storm would break and release the gray, choking air into rain to wash it clear.

Thunder rolled menacingly around the western rim of the clouds at about half past six as he was twenty miles south of Cambridge, gliding between deep hedges in full leaf. Then ten minutes later the lightning forked down to the ground and the rain dashed torrentially, bouncing up again from the smooth black road till he felt as if he were drowning under a waterfall. He slowed up, almost blinded by the downpour.

When it was gone, steam rose from the shimmering surface, a silver haze in the sun, and it all smelled like a Turkish bath.

On Monday morning the newspapers told the public that the king had reviewed 260 ships of the Royal Navy at the Spithead base, and that the naval reserves had been called up on orders from the first lord of the Admiralty, Winston Churchill, and the first sea lord, Prince Louis of Battenberg. There was no word whatever of Austria's ultimatum to Serbia on the reparations demanded for the death of the archduke.

Calder Shearing sat at his desk staring grimly ahead of him into the distance. Matthew stood, not yet given permission to sit.

"Means nothing," Shearing said to Matthew darkly. "I'm told there was a secret meeting in Vienna yesterday. I wouldn't be surprised if they push it to the limit. Austria can't be seen to back down. If they did, then all their territories would think they could assassinate people. That's the damn shame of it." He muttered something else under his breath, and Matthew did not ask him to repeat it. "Sit down!" he said impatiently. "Don't hover like that as if you were about to go. You aren't! We've all these reports to go through." He indicated a pile of papers on his desk.

It was a comfortable room, but there were no family photographs, nothing to indicate where he had been born or grown up. Even its functionality was anonymous, clever rather than personal. The Arabic brass dish and bowl were beautiful but of no meaning. Matthew had asked him about them once. Similarly the watercolor paintings of a storm blowing up over the South Downs, and another of dying winter light over the London Docks, the black spars of a clipper sharp and straight against the sky; neither carried any personal significance.

The conversation moved to Ireland and the situation in the Curragh, which was still a cause of anxiety. It was far from resolved.

Shearing swore softly and imaginatively, more to himself than for Matthew's benefit. "How could we be so bloody stupid as to get ourselves into this mess!" he said, his jaw so tight the muscles stood out in his neck. "The Protestants were never going to let themselves be absorbed by the Catholic south. They were bound to resort to violence, and our men would never have fired on them. Any damn fool knows they'll not shoot their own—and so you've got a mutiny!" His dark face was flushed. "And we can't let mutiny go unpunished, so we've painted ourselves into an impossible corner! How stupid do you have to be not to see that coming? It's like being caught by surprise when it snows in January!"

"I thought the government was consulting the king," Matthew replied.

Shearing looked up at him. "Oh, they are! They have! And what happens if the king sides with the Ulster Loyalists? Has anybody thought of that?"

Matthew clenched inside. He had been too consumed with the murder of his father, and the question of the document and what might be in it, to give deeper thought to such an idea. Now he did, and it was appalling. "He can't! Can he?" he demanded.

The anger in Shearing's face was so sharp its power filled the room. "Yes, he damned well can!" he spat, glaring at Matthew.

"When will they reach a decision?"

"Today . . . tomorrow! God knows. Then we'll see what real trouble is." He saw the question in Matthew's eyes. "Yes, Reavley," he said with level, grating calm. "The assassination in Serbia is bad, but believe me, it would be nothing compared with one at home."

"An assassination!" Matthew exclaimed.

Shearing's eyebrows rose. "Why not?" he challenged. "What's the difference? Serbia is a subject part of the Austro-Hungarian Empire, and some of its citizens think assassination of a royal duke is the way to freedom and independence. Ireland is part of the British Empire. Why shouldn't some of its subjects assume that the assassination of a king might earn them the freedom they want?"

"Protestant Northern Ireland wants to remain part of the British Empire," Matthew replied, keeping his voice level with difficulty. "That's what the term *Loyalist* means! They don't want to be swallowed up in Roman Catholic Ireland!" But even as he was saying it he knew the words were empty.

"Very rational," Shearing said sarcastically. "I'm sure if you say that a little louder all the madmen with glory in their brains will put their guns away and go home again." He pulled a thin sheaf of papers out of the drawer in his desk and held it out. "Go and look at those, see what you make of them."

Matthew took them from him. "Yes, sir." He went back to his own office with his fingers numb, his head singing with ideas.

Matthew attempted to work on the papers all day. They were the usual notes on intelligence information intercepted, reports of the movement of men either known or suspected of Irish independence sympathies. He was still looking for any threat to Blunden and his appointment to the War Ministry, with the obvious effect it would have on further military action in Ireland, the need for which seemed almost certain.

If the position went to Wynyard, with his robust opinions and more volatile judgment, it might not only hasten the violence, but make it worse, possibly even spreading it to England itself.

He found it difficult to keep his mind on the subject. It was too nebulous to grasp, the connections too remote. And one name occurred a number of times: Patrick Hannassey. He had been born in Dublin in 1861, the second son of a physician and Irish patriot. His elder brother had gone into law, and died young in a boating disaster off the County Waterford coast. Patrick also had studied law for a while, and he married and had a daughter. Then tragedy had struck again. His wife had been killed in a pointless exchange of violence between Catholic and Protestant, and Patrick, in his grief, had abandoned the slow-moving workings of the law in favor of the swifter struggle of politics, even of civil war.

It would suit his avowed purpose very well to succeed to the War Minister's post, where he could be taunted, defied, and mocked into action that would seem to justify armed retaliation, and the beginning of open warfare. He preached uprising, but he did it subtly, and he was a hard man to catch: elusive, clever, never overreaching himself with arrogance, never betraying those who trusted him, not looking for personal power and certainly not for money.

A little before six Matthew went back to Shearing's office, knowing he would find him still there.

"Yes?" Shearing looked up. His eyes were red-rimmed, his skin colorless.

"Patrick Hannassey," Matthew replied, placing the papers on the desk in front of him. "I'd like your permission to go after him. He is the most serious threat to Blunden, because frankly he's far cleverer. Blunden doesn't react instinctively, but Hannassay's capable of making him look like a coward, compared with Wynyard."

"Denied," Shearing answered him.

"But he's—" Matthew began.

"I know," Shearing cut him off. "And you're right. But we don't know where he is, and his own men will never betray him. For the time being he's disappeared. Learn what you can about him, but discreetly, if there's time. Go after Michael Neill, his lieutenant—you'll get plenty of cooperation on that."

There was a flatness in his voice that alarmed Matthew, a sense of defeat. "What is it?" he asked edgily.

"The king has backed the Loyalists," Shearing answered, watching Matthew, bleak misery in his eyes. "Go and see if you can find out what Neill is up to, and if there's anyone willing to betray him. Anything that will help."

"Sir . . ."

"What?"

Should he mention John Reavley's document? Was this what it was about, and he had the chance now to make it matter? Perhaps even to save the country from plunging into civil war? But Shearing might be part of it.

"Reavley, if you've got something to say, then say it!" Shearing snapped. "I haven't got time to play nursemaid to your feelings! Get on with it, man!"

What could he say? That his father knew there was a conspiracy?

Shearing drew in his breath sharply, with a little hiss between his teeth, impatient, scratchy.

"Only that I think you're right, sir," Matthew said aloud. "One of my informants believed there was a conspiracy."

"Then why the hell didn't you mention it?" Shearing's eyes were hot and black.

"Because he had no facts," Matthew retorted with equal tartness. "No names, no dates, places, nothing but a belief."

"Based on what?" Shearing glared at him, challenging him for a reply.

"I don't know, sir. He was killed before he could tell me." How hard the words were to say, even in anger.

"Killed?" Shearing said softly. Death of one of his own men, honor indirectly so, always hurt him more than Matthew expected. "How? Are you saying he was murdered for this piece of information?" His fury exploded in a snarl, full of helplessness he could no longer conceal. "What the hell's the matter with you that you didn't tell me? If your parents' deaths have robbed you of this much of your wits, then . . ." He stopped.

In that instant Matthew knew that Shearing understood. Had he gone too far? Had he done precisely what his father had warned him against?

"Was it your father, Reavley?" Shearing asked, regret in his face now, something that might even have been pity.

There was no purpose in lying. Shearing would know, if not now, then later. It would destroy his trust and make Matthew look a fool, and it would gain nothing.

"Yes, sir," he admitted. "But he was killed in a car accident on his way to see me. All I know is that he spoke of a conspiracy that would dishonor England." It was ridiculous—he had trouble keeping his voice steady. "And it went as high as the royal family." That was not all of the truth. He omitted the involvement of the world. That was only his father's opinion, and perhaps he put too much importance on England's place in things. He said nothing of the scars on the road and his certainty that it had been murder.

"I see." In the low, slanting sunlight through the windows the tiny lines in Shearing's skin were etched clearly. His emotion and his weariness were naked, but his thoughts were as hidden as always. "Then you'd better follow it up, find out all you can." His lips tightened. It was impossible to imagine his thoughts. "I presume you will anyway. Do it properly."

"And Neill?" Matthew asked. "Blunden?"

Shearing's eyes were bright, as though with amusement he could not share. "I have other men who can do that, Reavley. You are not indispensable. You will be of more use to me doing one job properly than half doing two."

Matthew did not allow his gratitude to show. Shearing should not think him too much in debt. "Thank you, sir. I'll report when I have something." He turned on his heel before Shearing could add anything, and went out, closing the door behind him. He felt a curious sense of freedom, and of danger.

Matthew began immediately and his first call was exactly as Chetwin had suggested, to Dermot Sandwell. Matthew asked if he might see him as a matter of urgency, to do with the king's announcement today of his support for the Ulster Loyalists. He gave his name and rank, and that he was on assignment to the Secret Intelligence Service. There was no point in hiding it because Sandwell could very easily find out and would be extremely unlikely to receive him at all otherwise.

He had to wait only fifteen minutes before he was taken into first the outer office and then the inner. It was a handsome room overlooking Horseguards' Parade, furnished with an extremely individual and pleasing mixture of classical and Middle Eastern styles. A burr walnut desk was flanked by Queen Anne chairs. Turkish brassware sat on an Italian *petra dura* table. Persian miniatures painted on bone decorated one wall, and above the fireplace was a minor Turner of exquisite beauty, and probably worth as much money as Matthew would earn in a decade.

Sandwell himself was tall and very slight, but there was a wiry grace to him that suggested strength. His hair and skin were fair, and his eyes were a uniquely vivid blue. There was an intensity to his face that would have made him unusual even were the rest of him ordinary. It would have held the attention of anyone who had been in his company for more than a few moments.

He came forward and shook Matthew's hand, his grip firm, then he stepped back.

"What can I do for you, Reavley?" He waved at the chair to indicate Matthew was to sit, then sat back again in his own, his eyes not leaving Matthew's face. He continued to create a life and a tension in the room while remaining perfectly motionless. Matthew noticed that there was a mosaic ashtray on the desk, with at least half a dozen cigarette ends in it.

"As you know, sir, His Majesty has expressed his support for the Ulster Loyalists," he began. "And we are concerned that in doing so he may have placed himself in a certain amount of danger from Nationalists."

"I should think that is beyond doubt," Sandwell agreed, with only the smallest flicker of impatience across his face.

"We have cause, insubstantial but sufficient to concern us, that there may be a plot to assassinate him," Matthew went on.

Sandwell was motionless, but something inside him became even more rigid. "Have you, indeed? I admit that in itself it does not surprise me, but I had no idea they were so . . . daring! Do you know who is behind it?"

"That's what I'm working on," Matthew answered. "There are several possibilities, but the one that seems most likely so far is a man named Patrick Hannassey."

"A Nationalist with a long history of activity," Sandwell agreed. "I've had slight dealings with him myself, but not lately."

"No one has seen him for over two months," Matthew said drily. "Which is one of the facts that concerns us. He has dropped out of sight so completely that none of our contacts knows where he is."

"So what is it you want from me?" Sandwell asked.

"Any information you might have on Hannassey's past contacts," Matthew replied. "Anything about him we might not know—foreign connections, friends, enemies, weaknesses . . ." He had decided not to mention Michael Neill. Never pass on information you do not have to.

Finally Sandwell spoke. His voice was quiet and rough-edged. "Hannassey fought in the Boer War . . . on the Boer side, of course. He was captured by the British and held in a concentration camp for some time. I don't know how long, but several months at least. If you'd seen that . . ." His voice cracked. "War can rob men of their humanity. Men you would have sworn were decent and they were before fear, pain, hunger, and the propaganda of hatred stripped away that decency and left only the animal will to survive."

His blue eyes flashed up and held Matthew's with a storm of feeling that his casual, easy elegance had completely masked. "Civilization is thin, Captain Reavley, desperately thin, a veneer like a single coat of paint, but it is all we have between us and the darkness." His long-fingered, almost delicate hands were clenched, the knuckles pale where the skin stretched. "We must hold on to it at any cost, because if we lose it, we face chaos."

His voice was soft, but it contained a contempt he could not control. "Believe me, Captain Reavley, civilization can all be swept away and we can turn into savages so hideous it is a horror you can never wipe from your soul." Now his voice was little more than a whisper. "You wake up sweating in the night, your skin crawling, but the nightmare is inside you, for the possibility that this is what we are all like . . . underneath the smiling masks."

Matthew could offer no argument. Sandwell was speaking about something of which he had no knowledge. He had heard only fragments of accusation and denial, rumors of ugliness that belonged to another world and other, far different people.

Sandwell smiled, but it was a grimace, an attempt to conceal again a little of the passion he had allowed to show itself too nakedly. "We must grasp civilization, Reavley, pay any price to keep it for ourselves and those who come after us. Guard the gates of sanity so madness does not return. We can do that for each other . . . we must. If we can't, there is nothing else worth doing. You want to find Hannassey, I'll help you. If he assassinates the king, God only knows what hatred will follow! We could even end up with martial law, the persecution of thousands of totally innocent Irish people, simply by association. As it is, it's going to take the effort of every good man in Europe to keep the lid on this Austro-Serbian affair, after the assassination of the archduke. Neither side can afford to back down, and they are both gathering allies everywhere they can: Russia for the Serbs, Germany for the Austrians—naturally."

He reached for a black leather cigarette case and took out a cigarette so automatically he seemed unaware of doing it. He lit it and drew in a deep draft of smoke. "As well as the Irish, you might look toward some of the socialist groups," he continued. "Men like Hannassey take their allies anywhere they find them. Socialist aspiration is far greater than many people think. There's Jaurès, Rosa Luxemburg, Adler, unrest everywhere. I'll give you what help I can—all the information this office has is at your disposal—but time is short . . . desperately so."

"Thank you, sir," Matthew said simply. He was profoundly grateful. Suddenly he was lurching forward with a frightening speed. From being alone he had moved to having one of the most discreetly powerful men in foreign affairs willing to listen to him and to share information. Perhaps the truth was only just beyond sight. In days, a week at most, he would face the truth of his parents' death. John Reavley had been right—there was a conspiracy.

"Thank you, sir," he repeated, rising to his feet. "I appreciate that very much." Small words to convey the excitement and the apprehension inside him.

CHAPTER

EIGHT

On Monday, July 20, Joseph spent the morning in a lively albeit erratic discussion with half a dozen students in which he doubted anyone learned very much.

He found himself enervated by the exchange as he walked back across the quad toward his own room, eager for the peace of familiar books and pictures, and above all the silence. He was fourteen or fifteen years older than most of the young men he had been with, but today it seemed more than a generation. They were frightened, perhaps of the thought of war in Europe, even though it was distant and problematical.

Far more immediate was the continuing police investigation of Sebastian Allard's murder. That could not be escaped. It was omnipresent as Sebastian's grieving mother walked the Fellows' Garden in black, waiting for justice, her rage and misery consuming her. She seemed in a self-chosen isolation from the rest of the world. Inspector Perth continued his interrogations, never telling anyone what he had concluded from their answers. And always was the knowledge that one of these gilded scholars, studying the collected thoughts of the ages, had fired the deliberate shot.

Joseph was almost at the door when he heard the light, rapid footsteps behind him and turned to find Perth a couple of yards away. As always, he wore a suit that fitted without elegance or grace. His hair was combed back straight and his mustache trimmed level. He was carrying a pipe by the bowl, as if he was undecided whether to light it or not.

"Oh! Good. Reverend Reavley . . . glad to catch up wi' you, sir," he said cheerfully. "Are you going inside?"

"Yes. I've just finished a debate with some of my students."

"Oi never thought you gentlemen worked so hard, even in holiday times," Perth observed, following Joseph in through the carved stone doorway and past the oak stairs, almost black with age, the middle of the steps hollowed by centuries of feet.

"Quite a few students choose to remain here and do some extra study," Joseph replied, turning the bend and going on up. "And then there are always the undergraduates pursuing other studies."

"Oh, yes, the undergraduates."

They reached the landing and Joseph opened his own door. "Is there something I can do for you, Inspector?"

Perth smiled appreciatively. "Well, since you ask, sir, there is." He stood expectantly on the step.

Joseph surrendered and invited him inside. "What is it?" he asked.

"Oi think it'd be true to say, sir, that you knew Mr. Allard better than any o' the other gentlemen here?"

"Possibly."

Perth put his hands in his pockets. "You see, Reverend, Oi've bin talking to Miss Coopersmith, Mr. Allard's fiancée, as was, if you see what Oi mean? Nice young lady, very collected, no weeping an' wailing, just a quiet sort o' grief. Can't help admiring it, can you?"

"No," Joseph agreed. "She seems a fine young woman."

"Did you know her before, sir? Seeing as you know the Allard family, and Mr. Sebastian especially. People tell me you were very close, gave him lots of advice in his studies, watched over him, as you might say."

"Academically," Joseph pointed out, acutely aware how true that was. "I knew very little of his personal life. I have a number of students, Inspector. Sebastian Allard was one of the brightest, but he was certainly not the only one. I would be deeply ashamed if I had neglected any of the others because they were less gifted than he. And to answer your question, no, I did not know Miss Coopersmith."

Perth nodded, as if that corroborated something he already knew. He closed the door behind him but remained standing in the middle of the floor, as if the room made him uncomfortable. It was alien territory, with its silence and its books. "But you know Mrs. Allard?" he asked.

"A little. What is it you are looking for, Inspector?"

Perth smiled apologetically. "Oi'll come to the point, sir. Mrs. Allard told me what time Sebastian left home to come back to college on Sunday the twenty-eighth o' June. He'd been up in London on the Saturday, but he came home in the evening." His face became very somber. "That were the day of the assassination in Serbia, although o' course we didn't know that then. An' Mr. Mitchell, the porter at the gate, told me what time he got here."

"The purpose?" Joseph reminded him. Since Perth did not, he felt unable to sit down either.

"Oi'm coming to that," Perth said unhappily. "He told his mother as he'd got to come back for a meeting here . . . an' so he had. Six people as'll confirm that."

"He wasn't killed on the twenty-eighth," Joseph pointed out. "It was several days after that—in fact, a week. I remember because it was after my parents' funeral, and I was back here."

Perth's face registered his surprise and then his sympathy. "Oi'm sorry, sir. A dreadful thing. But my point is, like yourself, Mr. and Mrs. Allard live close by, not more'n ten miles. How long would you say it'd take to drive that far, for a young man with a fast car like his?"

"Half an hour," Joseph replied. "Probably less, depending on the traffic. Why?"

"When he left home he told his parents he was going to see Miss Coopersmith for a couple of hours," Perth replied. "But she says that he stayed barely ten minutes with her. He went, going through your village o' St. Giles, an' on toward Cambridge, about three o'clock." He shook his head. He was still holding the pipe by its bowl. "That means he should've bin here by quarter to four, at the outside. Whereas he didn't actually get here, Mr. Mitchell says, until just after six."

"So he went somewhere else," Joseph reasoned. "He changed his mind, met a friend, or stopped in the town before coming on to college. What does it matter?"

"Just an example, sir," Perth said. "Bin asking around a bit. Seems he did things like that quite regular, couple of hours here, couple there. Oi thought as you might know where he spent that time, an' why he lied to folks about it."

"No, I don't." It was an unpleasant thought that Sebastian had regularly done something he had wanted or needed to hide from his friends. But it was drowned in Joseph's mind by another thought, sharp and clear as a knife in sudden light. If Perth was accurate about the time Sebastian had left his home, and that he had driven south to Cambridge through St. Giles, which was the natural and obvious way, then he would have passed the place on the Hauxton Road where John and Alys Reavley were killed, within a few minutes of it happening.

If it had been just before, then it meant nothing; it was merely a coincidence easily explained by circumstance. But if it had been just after, then what had he seen? And why had he said nothing?

Perth was staring at him, bland, patient, as if he could wait forever. Joseph forced himself to meet his eyes, uncomfortably aware of the intelligence in them; Perth was far more astute than he had appreciated until now. "I'm afraid I have no idea," he said. "If I learn anything I shall tell you. Now if you will excuse me, I have an errand to run before my next tutorial." That was not true, but he needed to be alone. He must sort out the turbulence of thought in his mind.

Perth looked a little surprised, as if the possibility had not occurred to him. "Oh. You sure you have no idea what he was doing? You know students better 'n Oi do, sir. What might it've bin? What do these young men do when they ain't studying an' attending lectures and the loike?" He looked at Joseph innocently.

"Talk," Joseph replied. "Go boating sometimes, or to the pub, the library, walk along the Backs. Some go cycling or practice cricket at the nets. And of course there are papers to write."

"Interesting," Perth said, chewing on his pipe. "None of that seems worth lying about, does it?" He smiled, but it was not friendliness so much as satisfaction. "You have a very innocent view o' young men, Reverend." He took the pipe out again, as if suddenly remembering where he was. "Are those the things you did when you was a student? Maybe divinity students are a great deal more righteous-living than most." If there was sarcasm in his voice, it was well concealed.

Joseph found himself uncomfortable, aware not only that he sounded like a prig, but that perhaps he had been as deliberately blind as that made him sound, and that Perth was not. He could remember his own student days perfectly well, and they were not as idealized as the picture he had just painted. Divinity students, along with medical, were among the heaviest drinkers of all, not to mention other even less salubrious pursuits.

"I started in medicine," he said aloud. "But as I recall, none of us appreciated being obliged to account for our free time."

"Really?" Perth was startled. "A medical student? You? Oi din't know that. So you know some o' the less admirable kinds of youthful carry-ons, then?"

"Of course I do," Joseph said a trifle sharply. "You asked me what I know of Sebastian, not what I might reasonably suppose."

"Oi see what you mean," Perth replied. "Thank you for your help, Reverend." He nodded several times. "Then Oi'll just keep on." He turned and went out of the door, at last pulling out a worn, leather tobacco pouch and filling the pipe as he went down the stairs, slipping a bit on the last and most uneven one.

Joseph left a few moments later and walked briskly across the quad and out of the main gate into St. John's Street. But instead of turning right for the town, he went left for a few yards along Bridge Street, across it, along the main road, and eventually onto Jesus Green, looking over to Midsummer Common.

All the time his mind was struggling with the fact that Sebastian had passed by the place in the Hauxton Road where John and Alys Reavley had been killed. The question that burned in his head was this: Had Sebastian witnessed it and known that it was not an accident, possibly even seen whoever it was emerge from the ditch and go over and search the bodies? If so, then he had known too much for his own safety.

Since he too was in a car, he must have been seen by them, and they had to have realized he knew what had happened. Had they tried to follow him?

No, if they were on foot, their car hidden, then they would be unable to go after him. But with any intelligence at all, a few questions and they could have found who owned the car and where he lived. From there on it would be simple enough to trace him to Cambridge.

Had he been aware of that? Was that why he had been so tense, so full of dark thoughts and fears? Had it not really been anything to do with Austria or the destruction that a war in Europe would bring, but the knowledge that he had seen a murder?

Joseph walked across the grass. The sun was hot on his right cheek. There was no traffic on the Chesterton Road, and only a couple of young men in white trousers and cricket sweaters walking side by side a hundred yards away, probably students from Jesus College. They were involved in heated conversation and oblivious of anyone else.

Why had Sebastian said nothing? Even if he had not known at the time that it was John and Alys Reavley who had been killed, he must have known afterward. What was he afraid of? Even if he had weighed the chance of them tracing his car, since he had not recognized them, what threat was he?

Then the answer came to Joseph, ugly and jagged as broken glass. Perhaps Sebastian had known them.

If they were responsible for his death, then there was only one hideous and inescapable conclusion: it was someone here in college! No one had broken in. Whoever murdered Sebastian was one of those already here, someone they all knew and whose presence was part of daily life.

But why had Sebastian told no one? Was it somebody so close, so unbelievable, that he dared not trust anyone with the truth, not even Joseph, whose parents were the victims?

The sun burned in the silence of the mown turf. The traffic seemed to belong to another world. He walked without sense of movement, as if caught in an eddy of time, separate from everyone else.

Was it fear for himself that had kept Sebastian silent? Or defense of whoever it was? Why would he defend them?

Joseph came to the edge of Jesus Green and crossed the road onto Midsummer Common, walking south into the sun.

But if Sebastian thought it was an accident and he had been the one who had reported it, why hide that fact? If he had simply run away, why? Was he such a coward he would not go to the wreck, at least to see if he could help?

Or had he recognized whoever it was who had laid the caltrops and pulled them away afterward, and kept silent because it was someone he knew? To defend them? Or had they threatened him?

And had they killed him afterward anyway?

Was that why he had not come straight to college that day . . . fear?

But what about all the other occasions Perth spoke of? Joseph felt a strange sense of disloyalty even thinking such things. He had known Sebastian for years, met his straight-eyed, passionate gaze as they spoke of dreams and ideas, beauty of thought, music of rhythm and rhyme, the aspirations of men down the ages from the first stumbling recorded words in history. Surely they had trusted each other better than this? Had they been no more than children playing with concepts of honor, as real children built towers of sand to be crashed away by the first wave of reality?

He had to believe it was more than that. Sebastian had come even earlier than Regina Coopersmith said, and passed along the Hauxton Road before the crash. Or he had gone somewhere else altogether, by another route. Whoever had killed him had done so for a reason that had nothing to do with John and Alys Reavley's deaths. That was the only answer he could bear.

Joseph turned back toward St. Johns, increasing his pace. Enough had been said about Sebastian and the injuries people felt they had suffered at his hands that a closer look at some of them would lead either to proving them trivial or, if followed to the very end, to the reason for his death.

One episode that came to his mind first was the curious exchange with Eardslie when they were standing outside Eaden Lilley's and the young woman who walked with such grace had appeared about to speak to them and then changed her mind. It had been suggested that Sebastian had intentionally taken someone else's girl, simply to show that he could, and then cast her aside. Was that true?

It took Joseph half an hour to find Eardslie, who was sitting on the grass on the Backs, leaning against the trunk of a tree with books spread out around him. He looked up at Joseph in surprise and made as if to stand up.

"Don't," Joseph said quickly, sitting down on the ground opposite him, crossing his legs and making himself comfortable. "I wanted to talk to you. Do you remember the young woman who passed us outside Eaden Lilley's the other day?"

Eardslie drew in his breath to deny it.

"Perhaps I shouldn't make that a question," Joseph amended. "It was quite obvious that you did know her, whether it was well or slightly, and that, seeing me there, she decided not to speak to you."

Eardslie looked uncomfortable. He was a serious young man, the oldest son, of whom his family expected a great deal, and the weight of it frequently lay rather heavily on him. Now in particular he seemed conscious of obligation. "Probably a matter of tact, sir," he suggested.

"No doubt. What would she need to be tactful about?"

Eardslie colored slightly. "Her name is Abigail Trethowan," he said unhappily. "She was more or less engaged to Morel, but she met Sebastian, and sort of . . ." He was at a loss to put into words what he meant.

"Fell in love with Sebastian," Joseph finished for him.

Eardslie nodded.

"And you are suggesting that Sebastian brought that about deliberately?" Joseph asked, raising his eyebrows.

Eardslie's color deepened and he looked down. "It certainly looked that way. And then he dropped her. She was very upset."

"And Morel?"

Eardslie raised his eyes. They were wide, golden-flecked, and burning with anger.

"How would you feel, sir?" he said furiously. "Somebody takes your girl from you, just to show you and everybody else that he can? And then he doesn't even want her, so he just dumps her, as if she were unwanted baggage. You can't take her back or you look a complete fool, and she feels . . . like a . . ." He gave up, unable to find a word savage enough.

Joseph realized how much Eardslie himself had cared for Abigail, possibly more than he was admitting.

"Where does she live?" Joseph asked.

Eardslie's eyes widened. "You're not going to say anything to her!" He was horrified. "She'd be humiliated, sir! You can't!"

"Is she the kind of woman who would conceal the truth of a murder rather than face embarrassment?" Joseph asked.

Eardslie's struggle was clear in his face.

Joseph waited.

"She's at the Fitzwilliam, sir. But please, do you have to?"

Joseph stood up. "Would you rather I ask Perth to do it?"

He found Abigail Trethowan in the Fitzwilliam library. He introduced himself and asked if he might speak to her. With considerable apprehension she accompanied him to a tea shop around the corner, and when he had ordered for both of them, he broached the subject.

"I apologize for speaking of what must be painful, Miss Threthowan, but the subject of Sebastian's death is not going to rest until it is solved."

She was sitting straight-backed in her chair, like a schoolgirl with a ruler at her back. Joseph could remember Alys reminding both Hannah and Judith of the importance of posture and poking a wooden spoon through the spokes of the kitchen chairs to demonstrate, catching them in the middle of the spine. Abigail Trethowan looked just as young, proud, and vulnerable as they had. It would be hard to forgive Sebastian if he had done what Eardslie believed.

"I know," she said quietly, her eyes avoiding his.

How could he ask her without being brutal?

All around them was the clatter of china and the murmur of conversation as ladies took tea and exchanged gossip, in many cases bags and boxes of shopping piled near their feet. No one was vulgar enough to look at Joseph and Abigail openly, but he knew without doubt that they were being examined from head to foot, and speculation was rich and highly inventive.

He smiled at Abigail and saw by the flash of humor in her eyes that she was as aware of it as he.

"I could ask you questions," he said frankly. "But wouldn't it be better if you simply told me?"

The color burned up her cheeks, but she did not look away from him. "I'm ashamed of it," she said in a voice that was little above a whisper. "I'd hoped I wouldn't ever have to think of it again, much less tell anyone."

"I'm sorry, but I'm afraid there is no escape. We owe it to everyone else involved."

Once their tea and scones were served, she began her account. "I met Edgar Morel. I liked him very much, and gradually it turned into love—at least I thought it did. I had never really been in love before, and I didn't know what to expect." She glanced up at him and then down at her hands again. She held them clasped in front of her, strong, well-shaped, and bare of rings. "He asked me to marry him, and I was wondering whether to accept. It seemed a little soon." She drew in her breath. "Then I met Sebastian. He was the most beautiful person I had ever seen." She raised her eyes to meet Joseph's, and they were bright, swimming in tears.

He wanted to help her, but there was nothing he could do except listen. If he did not interrupt, it would be over more quickly.

"He was so clever, so quick to understand everything," she went on, rueful now, obviously curious about the irony of it. "And he was funny. I don't think I've ever laughed so much in my life." She looked at him again. "I never really laughed, not just a little giggle but the sort of aching, uncontrollable laughter my mother would think was totally indecent. And it was such fun! We talked about all sorts of things and it was like being able to fly—in your mind. Do you know what I mean, Mr. Reavley?"

"Yes, certainly I do," he said with a catch in his voice, partly for Sebastian, partly for Eleanor, perhaps most of all for inner loneliness for something he needed and did not have.

She sipped her tea.

He took one of the scones and put butter, jam, and cream on it.

"I was in love with Sebastian," she continued with conviction. "It wouldn't matter what Edgar did. I could never feel like that about him. I couldn't marry him. It would have been an impossible lie. I told him, and he was very upset. It was awful!"

"Yes, I'm sure it was," he agreed. "When you are in love, there is not much that hurts as deeply as rejection."

"I know," she whispered.

He waited.

She sniffed a little and sipped her tea again, then set down the cup. "Sebastian rejected me. He said he liked me very much, but he liked Edgar also, and he couldn't do what amounted morally to stealing his girl." She took a shivery breath. "I never saw him alone after that. I was mortified. For ages I didn't want to see anyone. But I suppose it passes. We all survive."

"No, we don't," he corrected her. "Sebastian is dead."

The blood drained from her face, and she stared at him in horror. "You don't . . . you don't think Edgar . . . Oh, no! No! He was upset, but he would never do that! Besides, it really wasn't Sebastian's fault. He didn't do anything to encourage me!"

"Would that make you feel any better if you were in Edgar's place?" he asked. "It wouldn't comfort me to know somebody had taken the woman I loved, without even having to try."

She closed her eyes, and the tears ran down her cheeks. "No," she said huskily. "No, I think I'd feel worse. I still don't believe Edgar would kill him. He didn't love me that much, not to commit murder for. He's a nice man, really nice, just not . . . not alive as Sebastian was."

"It isn't always the value of what is taken that makes us hate," he pointed out. "Sometimes it's just the fact that we've been robbed. It's pride."

"He wouldn't," she repeated. "If you think he did, then you don't know him."

Perhaps she was right, but he wondered if she was defending him because she carried such a burden of guilt for having hurt him. It would be a way of paying some of that debt.

And yet the Morel he knew would not have killed for such a reason. He could easily see him fighting, perhaps punching Sebastian hard enough to kill him by accident, but not deliberately with a gun. For one thing, the sheer physical release of violence would not be in it. It would leave him still empty, and consumed not only with guilt but with fear also.

"No, I don't think he would, either," he agreed.

"Do you have to tell that policeman?"

"I won't unless something happens to change things," he promised. "Unfortunately there are many other possibilities, and very few of us can prove we didn't. Please have one of these scones. They really are excellent."

She smiled at him, blinking hard, and reached out to accept.

On Tuesday afternoon, Joseph took the train to London and was waiting for Matthew when he came home to his flat.

"What are you doing here?" Matthew demanded, coming into the sitting room and seeing Joseph lounging in his own favorite chair. Matthew was in uniform, and he looked tired and harassed, his fair hair untidy and uncharacteristically in need of cutting, his face pale.

"The doorman let me in," Joseph replied, climbing to his feet to leave the chair free. "Have you eaten?" It was past dinnertime. He had found bread and a little cheese in the kitchen and some Belgian pâté, and opened a bottle of red wine. "Can I get you something?"

"Like what?" Matthew said a little sarcastically, but easing himself into the chair and relaxing slowly.

"Bread and pâté?" Joseph replied. "I finished the cheese. Wine or tea?"

"Wine, if you haven't finished that, too! Why have you come? Not for dinner!"

Joseph ignored him until he had cut three slices of the bread and brought it along with butter, pâté, and the bottle of wine and a glass.

"You didn't answer my question. You look like hell. Has something else happened?"

Joseph heard the edge to his voice. "So do you," he said, sitting in the other chair and crossing his legs. "How are you progressing?"

Matthew smiled, half ruefully, and a little of the weariness ironed out of his face. "I know more. I'm not sure how much of it is relevant. The British and Irish parties met at the Palace and failed to reach any agreement. I suppose no one is surprised. The king supported the Loyalists yesterday, but I expect you know that."

"No, I didn't," Joseph said. "But I meant to do with Father's death and the document."

"I know you did. Let me finish! I've spoken to several people—Shanley Corcoran; Ivor Chetwin, who used to be a friend of Father's; my boss, Shearing; and Dermot Sandwell, from the Foreign Office. Sandwell was actually the most helpful. From everything I can gather, an Irish plot to assassinate the king seems most likely. . . ." He stopped, having seen Joseph's face. "It answers all Father's criteria," he said very quietly. "Think of what British reaction would be."

Joseph closed his eyes for a moment. Views of rage, bloodshed, martial law, and oppression filled his mind, sickening him. He had wanted his father to be right, to be justified rather than foolish, but not at this cost. He looked up at Matthew, seeing the grayness in him with an overwhelming understanding. "Is there anything we can do?" he asked.

"I don't know. At least Sandwell is aware of it. I imagine he will warn the king."

"Will he? I mean, would he even be able to get access to see him without alarming . . . ?"

"Oh, yes. I think they're distantly related somewhere along the line. From the marriage of one of Victoria's umpteen children. I just don't know if Sandwell can make the king believe it. No one has ever assassinated a British monarch."

"Not assassinated, perhaps," Joseph agreed. "But we've certainly had a good few murdered, deposed, or executed. But the last was bloodless, and a long time ago: 1688, to be precise."

"Rather beyond living memory," Matthew pointed out. "Did you come to ask what I'd found so far?" He took another bite of his bread and pâté.

"I came to tell you that the police have discovered that Sebastian lied about when he left home to go back to college the day Mother and Father were killed. He actually left a couple of hours earlier."

Matthew was puzzled. "I thought he was killed over a week later. What difference does that make?"

Joseph shook his head. "The point is that he lied about it, and why do that unless there was something he wanted to conceal?"

Matthew shrugged. "So he had a secret," he said with his mouth full. "Probably he was seeing a girl his parents wouldn't approve of, or who was involved with someone else, possibly even someone's wife. Sorry, Joe, but he was a remarkably good-looking young man, which he was well aware of, and he wasn't the saint you like to think."

"He wasn't a saint!" Joseph said a trifle abruptly. "But he could behave perfectly decently where women were concerned, even nobly. And he was engaged to marry Regina Coopersmith, so obviously any involvement with someone else would be something he wouldn't want known. But that isn't why I'm telling you about it. What does matter is that to drive from Haslingfield to Cambridge he would pass along the Hauxton Road, going north, and it now seems that it must have been at pretty much the same time as Father and Mother were going south."

Matthew stiffened, his hand with the bread in it halfway to his mouth, his eyes wide. "Are you saying he could have seen the crash? In God's name, why wouldn't he have said so?"

"Because he was afraid," Joseph replied. He felt the tightness knot inside him. "Perhaps he recognized whoever it was, and knew they had seen him."

Matthew's eyes were fixed on Joseph's. "And they killed him because of what he had seen?"

"Isn't it possible?" Joseph asked. "Someone killed him! Of course, he may have passed before the crash and known nothing at all about it."

"But if he did see it, that would explain his death." Matthew ignored his supper and concentrated on the idea, leaning forward in his chair now, his face tense. "Have you come up with any other motive for what seems to be a pretty cold-blooded shooting?"

"Cold-blooded?"

"Do your students usually call on each other at half past five in the morning carrying guns?"

"They don't have guns," Joseph replied.

"Where did it come from?"

"We don't know where it came from or where it went to. No one has ever seen it."

"Except whoever used it," Matthew pointed out. "But I presume no one left the college after Elwyn Allard found the body, so who left before? Don't they have to pass the porter's lodge at the gate?"

"Yes. And no one did."

"So what happened to the gun?"

"We don't know. The police searched everywhere, of course."

Matthew chewed on his lip. "It begins to look as if you've got someone very dangerous indeed in your college, Joe. Be careful. Don't go wandering around asking questions."

"I don't wander around!" Joseph said a little tartly, stung by the implication not only of aimlessness, but of incompetence to look after himself.

Matthew was deliberately patient. "You mean you are going to tell me this about Sebastian and leave it for me to investigate? I'm not in Cambridge, and anyway, I don't know those people."

"No, of course I don't mean that!" Joseph retorted. "I'm just as capable as you are of asking intelligent and discreet questions, and deducing a rational answer without annoying everybody and arousing their suspicions."

"And you're going to do it?" That seemed to be a question.

"Of course I am! As you pointed out, you are not in a position to. And since Perth knows nothing about it, he won't. What else do you suggest?"

"Just be careful," Matthew warned, his voice edgy. "You're just like Father. You go around assuming that everyone else is as open and honest as you are. You think it's highly moral and charitable to think the best of people. So it is. It's also damn stupid!" His face was angry and tender at the same time. Joseph was so like his father. He had the same long, slightly aquiline face, the dark hair, the kind of immensely reasonable innocence that left him totally unprepared for the deviousness and cruelty of life. Matthew had never been able to protect him and probably never would. Joseph would go on being logical and naive. And the most infuriating thing about it was that Matthew would not really have wished his brother to be different, not if he was honest.

"And I can't afford for you to get yourself killed," he went on. "So you'd better just get on with teaching people and leave the questions to the police. If they catch whoever shot Sebastian, we'll have a lead toward who's behind the conspiracy in the document."

"Very comforting," Joseph replied sarcastically. "I'm sure the queen will feel a lot better."

"What has the queen to do with it?"

"Well, it'll be a trifle late to save the king, don't you think?"

Matthew's eyebrows rose. "And you think finding out who shot Sebastian Allard is going to save the king from the Irish?"

"Frankly, I think it's unlikely anything will save him if they are determined to kill him, except a series of mischances and clumsiness, such as nearly saved the archduke of Austria."

"The Irish falling over their own feet?" Matthew said incredulously. "I'm not happy to rely on that! I imagine rather more is expected of the SIS." He looked at Joseph with a mixture of misery and frustration. "But you stay out of it! You aren't equipped to do this sort of thing."

Joseph was stung by the condescension in him, whether it was intentional or not. Sometimes Matthew seemed to regard him as a benign and otherworldly fool. Part of him knew perfectly well that Matthew was aching inside from the loss of his father just as much as he was himself, and would not admit that he was afraid of losing Joseph as well. Perhaps it was something he would never say aloud.

But Joseph's temper would not be allayed by reason. "Don't be so bloody patronizing!" he snapped. "I've seen just as much of the dark side of human nature as you have. I was a parish priest! If you think that just because people go to church that they behave with Christian charity, then you should try it sometime and disabuse yourself. You'll find reality there ugly enough to give you a microcosm of the world. They don't kill each other, not physically anyway, but all the emotions are there. All they lack is the opportunity to get going with it." He drew in his breath. "And while you're at it, Father wasn't as naive as you think. He was a member of Parliament, after all. He didn't get killed because he was a fool. He discovered something vast and—"

"I know!" Matthew cut him off so sharply that Joseph realized that he had hit a nerve; it was precisely what Matthew feared and could not bear. He recognized it because it was within himself as well: the need to deny and at the same time protect. He could see his father's face as vividly as if he had left the room minutes ago.

"I know," Matthew repeated. He looked away. "I just want you to be careful!"

"I will." This time the promise was made sincerely, with gentleness. "I've no particular desire to get shot. Anyway, one of us has got to keep Judith in some kind of check . . . and you aren't going to!"

Matthew grinned suddenly. "Believe me, Joe, neither are you!"

Joseph picked up the wine bottle and for a few moments did not speak. "If Father was bringing the document to you in London, and whoever killed him took it from the car, what were they searching the house for?"

Matthew thought for a while. "If it really is a plot of some sort to kill the king, Irish or otherwise, perhaps there are at least two copies of it," he replied. "They took the one Father was bringing, but they need the other as well. It's far too dangerous to leave it where someone else might find it—especially if they actually put it into effect."

It made perfect sense. At last there was something about it that fell into place. Intellectually it was a comfort, finally something reason could grasp. Emotionally it was a darkening of the shadows and a waking of a more urgent fear.

CHAPTER

NINE

Joseph returned to Cambridge the following morning, the twenty-second of July. The train pulled away from the streets and rooftops of the city and into the open country northward.

He felt an urgency to be back in college again, and to look with fresh and far more perceptive eyes at the people he knew. He was aware that he would see things he would prefer not to: weaknesses that were impinging on his consciousness, Morel's anger and perhaps jealousy because Abigail had been in love with Sebastian. Had he taken his revenge for that, storing it up until it became unbearable? Or was it the insult to Abigail he avenged? Or was it nothing to do with either of them, but one of the other cruelties? Had someone cheated and been caught? Would a man kill to save his career? To be sent down for cheating was certainly the ruin of all future hope in a profession or society.

Matthew's question about the gun came back again. Where had it come from? Perth had said it was a handgun. Joseph did not know a lot about guns; he disliked them. Even in the open countryside where he lived, close to woods and water, he knew of no one who kept handguns.

As soon as he reached the college, he went to his rooms. After he washed and changed, he started to review the situation. It was like taking the concealing bandages off a wound to find where the infection was, the unhealed part, and how deep it went. If he was to tell himself the truth, he knew it was to the bone.

And it was time he addressed the next issue he was aware of. Had someone cribbed from Sebastian or he from them? The suggestion had been that it was Foubister, and he knew why. Foubister came from a working-class family in the suburbs of Manchester. He had studied at Manchester Grammar School, one of the best in the country, and come to Cambridge on scholarship. His parents must have saved every penny simply to afford his necessities such as clothes and fare. The shock of coming from the narrow, back-to-back houses of the northern industrial city, to the broad countryside of Cambridge, the ancient city steeped in learning, the sheer wealth of centuries of endowment, was something he could not hide.

His mind was outstanding, quick, erratic, highly individual, but his cultural background was of poverty not only in material surroundings, but in art, literature, the history of Western thought and ideas. The leisure to create what was beautiful but essentially of no immediate practical use was as alien an idea to everyone he had known before coming here. It strained the imagination that he should have found the same felicitous phrase to translate a passage from the Greek or Hebrew as Sebastian Allard, whose background was so utterly different, nurtured in the classics from the day he started school.

Joseph stood up with a weariness inside and went to look for Foubister. He found him coming down the stairs from his own rooms. They met at the bottom, just inside the wide oak door open onto the quad.

"Morning, sir," Foubister said unhappily. "That wretched policeman doesn't know anything yet, you know?" His face was pale, his eyes defiant, as if he had already read Joseph's intent. "He's ferreting around in everyone's affairs, asking questions about who said what. He's even gone into past exam results, would you believe?"

So Perth was already pursuing the thought of a cheat! Did he understand that such a charge would follow a man all his life? The whisper of it would deny him a career, blackball him from clubs, even ruin him in society. Was that something a man like Perth would grasp?

Someone had killed Sebastian. If it were not for that, then it was something else equally ugly. Perhaps it would be even worse if it were for a trivial reason?

He looked at Foubister's miserable face, the anger in it, the desperation. He had such a burden of trust, hope, and sacrifice on his shoulders. Added to that, even coming here had opened a world to him he would never forget. The family that had nurtured him and loved him so selflessly was already someplace to which he could never fully return. The gulf widened, every day. He had already lost most of his Lancashire accent; only the odd vowel sound appeared now and then. He must have worked terribly hard to achieve that.

As if he had spoken it aloud, Foubister sensed Joseph's thought. "I didn't crib!" he exclaimed, his face white, his eyes hurt and angry.

"It would be very foolish," Joseph replied. "Your style is nothing like his." Then in case it seemed like an insult he added, "You are quite individual. But do you think it is possible someone else has cribbed, and Sebastian knew it?"

"I suppose it is," Foubister admitted reluctantly, shifting from one foot to the other. "But it would be stupid. You'd have known one style from another, the pattern of thinking, the words, the phrases, the kind of ideas. Even if you weren't sure, you'd suspect."

It was true. Joseph knew each voice as uniquely as the brush stroke of an artist or the musical phrase of a composer.

"Yes, of course," he agreed. "I'm just looking for a reason."

"We all are," Foubister said tensely, holding the book in his hand more tightly. "We're all wandering around tearing ourselves to pieces. He doesn't understand!" He jerked his arm backward to indicate Perth, somewhere in the college behind him. "He doesn't really know anything about us! How could he? He's never been in a world like this." He said it without condescension, but with impatience for those who had placed Perth out of his depth, a feeling he himself must taste every day, even if it was lessening, at least on the surface. But surely, deeper into thought, he must have understood that the thread of it ran through everything—class, manner, words chosen, even dreams.

Joseph drew breath to interrupt, then silenced himself. He should listen. Unguarded talk was exactly what he needed to hear—and weigh. He forced himself to relax and lean a little against the doorjamb.

"Someone mentions an argument, and he thinks it's a fight!" Foubister went on, his wide eyes on Joseph's, expecting understanding. "That's what university is all about, exploring ideas! If you don't question it, try to pick it to pieces, you never really know whether you believe it or not."

Joseph nodded.

"We don't argue to prove a point!" Foubister went on, his voice rising in desperation. "We argue to prove that we exist! Differences of opinion don't mean hate, for heaven's sake—exactly the opposite! You can't be bothered to waste time arguing with someone you don't respect. And respect is about the same thing as liking, isn't it?"

"Almost," Joseph agreed, thinking back to his own college days.

They heard a clatter of feet on a stairway above them, and a moment later a student excused himself and ran past, clutching a pile of books. He glanced at Joseph and Foubister. His eyes were wide with question and suspicion. It was clear in his expression that he thought he understood something. He turned away and sprinted across the quad and through the archway.

"You see?" Foubister challenged, fear rising sharply in his voice. "He thinks I cheated and you're calling me out on it!"

"You can't stop people leaping to conclusions. If you deny it, you'll make it worse," Joseph warned. "He'll find out he's wrong."

"Will he? When? What if they never find out who killed Sebastian? They're not doing very well so far!"

"You said people were arguing and Perth didn't understand," Joseph said levelly. "Who was he thinking of in particular?"

"Morel and Rattray," Foubister answered. "And Elwyn and Rattray, because Rattray doesn't think there'll be war, and Elwyn does. Sometimes he sounds as if he almost looks forward to it! All heroic sort of stuff, like the Charge of the Light Brigade, or Kitchener at Khartoum." His voice betrayed not only fear but disgust. "Sebastian thought there would be war, and that it would be catastrophic, which seems to be what Perth thinks.

Got a face like an undertaker! Elwyn is only afraid it'll all be over before he has a chance to do his bit! But it was just argument!"

He stared at Joseph, his eyes begging for agreement. "You don't kill someone because they disagree with you! Might kill myself if nobody did!" A smile flashed across his face and vanished. "That would be a sure sign I was talking such rubbish nobody cared enough about it, or me, to be bothered contradicting. Either that or I was in hell." He stood motionless, his cotton shirt hanging limply on his body. "Imagine it, Dr. Reavley! Total isolation—no other mind there but your own, echoing back to you exactly what you said! Oblivion would be better. Then at least you wouldn't know you were dead!"

Joseph heard the note of hysteria in his voice.

"Foubister," he said gently. "Everyone is frightened. Something terrible has happened, but we have to face it, and we have to learn the truth. It won't go away until we do."

Foubister steadied a little bit.

"But you should have seen some of the things people have come up with!" He shivered in spite of the breathless heat in the sheltered doorway. "Nobody looks at anyone the way they used to. It's a sort of poison. One of us here actually took a gun, walked into Sebastian's room, and for some dreadful reason shot him in the head." He shrugged, and Joseph noticed how much thinner he was than a month ago.

"We have our faults, and I've seen that in the last couple of weeks more than I ever wanted to." Foubister's face was white with misery, and he hunched as if even in this dazzling summer he could be cold. "I look at fellows I've worked with, sat with at the pub all evening, and wondered if any of them could have killed Sebastian."

Joseph did not interrupt him.

"And even worse than that," Foubister went on, speaking more and more rapidly, "people look at me—all sorts of people, even Morel—and I can see the same thoughts in their eyes, and the same embarrassment afterward. What's going to happen when it's over and we know who it was? Will we ever go back to how we were before? I won't forget who thought it could be me! How can I feel the same about them as I used to? And how could they forgive me, because I, too, have wondered . . . about lots of people!"

"It won't be the same," Joseph said frankly. "But it may still be bearable. Friendships change, but that doesn't have to be bad. We all make mistakes. Think how much you would like your own buried and forgotten, and then do the same for others—and for yourself." He was afraid he sounded trite, because he dared not say what was really in his mind: What if they never found who had shot Sebastian? What if the suspicion and the doubt remained here working their erosion forever, dividing, spoiling, tearing apart?

"Do you think so?" Foubister asked earnestly. He shrugged again and pushed his hands into his pockets. "I doubt it. We're all too damned scared to be idealistic."

"Did you like Sebastian?" Joseph said impulsively, just as Foubister turned to walk away.

"I'm not sure," Foubister replied with painful honesty. "I used to be certain I did. I wouldn't even have questioned it. Everyone liked him, or it seemed that way. He was funny and clever, and he could be extraordinarily kind. And once you start liking someone, it becomes a habit. You don't change, even if they do."

"But?" Joseph prompted.

"When you were with him you saw something good," Foubister said ruefully, "and you believed you could do something that mattered, too. But then sometimes he'd just forget you, or go ahead and do something so much better you felt crushed."

Joseph tried to ignore his own feelings. Sebastian had still needed him, but one day when he didn't, would he have treated Joseph with the same offhand arrogance? He would never know. It was all a matter of belief, and he ought to be able to have some control over that.

"Anyone in particular?" he said aloud.

Foubister's eyes widened. "If you mean do I know who killed him, no, I don't. You don't get a gun and shoot someone because they hurt you or make you feel like a fool, not unless you're mad! You might punch him, or—" He bit his lip. "No, you wouldn't even do that, because you'd be showing everyone how much you hurt. You'd just wear a nice smile as long as anyone was looking at you, and wish you could find a place to hide. Depending on who you are, you either look for something spectacular to do yourself, to show you are just as good, or you take hell out of someone else. I don't know, Dr. Reavley, maybe you do kill. I wish I did know, because it would mean at least that I could stop suspecting everyone else."

"I understand," Joseph said gently.

"Yes, I suppose you do. Thank you at least for saying that." Foubister gave a tiny smile, then turned and walked away, shoulders still tight, his body angular, yet moving with a certain grace.

It was unavoidable now. Joseph must go back to the translations that gnawed at the back of his mind, the occasions when Foubister and Sebastian had struck the same brilliant and unexpected phrase. He hated the thought that Foubister had cheated, but it seemed more and more likely. Was it really only other people's whispers that made Foubister so conscious of suspicion and so afraid, or was it guilt?

He might never know, but he was compelled to look. There were papers he could reread, compare, do all he could to satisfy his own mind. He knew Foubister's work, and he knew Sebastian's. If he had any skill at all, any feeling for the cadence of language, he would know if one man was copying another. If not, then he was no more than a mechanic.

He went back inside and climbed slowly back up the stairs, fingers touching the dark oak of the banister. The first floor up was cooler, airy with its higher ceiling and open window.

Inside, his room was newly tidy from the bedder's ministrations. She was a good woman, neat and quick and pleasant.

He pulled out the appropriate papers and turned his attention to Sebastian's. It was a translation from the Greek, lyrical, full of metaphor and imagery. Sebastian had made a beautiful thing of it, keeping the rhythm swift and light, an excellent mixture of words, long and short, complex and simple, all blending into a perfect whole. And there was the one phrase he remembered: "the bent-limbed trees crowding along the mountain ridge, bearing the burden of the sky upon their backs."

He put it down on the desk and searched for Foubister's translation of the same original. It was in the middle of the page: "the hunch-limbed trees, crawling along the mountain's rim, carrying the sky upon their backs."

The Greeks had described them only as misshapen, silhouetted against the sky. The idea of bearing or carrying was not there, nor the suggestion of human intent. They were too alike for coincidence.

Joseph sat still, the cold grief hardening inside him. He could not ask Sebastian how he had allowed his work to be imitated so closely, and surely there was little point in confronting Foubister. He had just sworn that he had never cheated. If Joseph faced him now with this, would he still deny it? Swear it was just chance? Joseph winced at the thought of seeing it. He liked Foubister and could only imagine what grief it would bring his parents if he were sent down in shame.

But if he had killed Sebastian, that was something that could not possibly be overlooked. He realized with surprise that using those words, even to himself, meant that he had considered ignoring the cheating.

What other explanation was there? Where could he look? Who was there to ask?

His thoughts went immediately to Beecher. He could at least depend on him to be both honest and kind. Perhaps he would even honor Joseph's silence if he was asked to.

He caught up with Beecher on his way across the quad toward the dining hall.

Beecher squinted at him. "You look awful," he said with a half smile. "Anticipating something disgusting in the soup?"

Joseph fell into step beside him. "You've been teaching far longer than I have," he began without ceremony. "What explanation might there be for two students coming up with the same highly individual translation of a passage, other than cheating?"

Beecher looked at him with a frown. "Has this something to do with

Sebastian Allard?" he asked as they walked into the shadow of the archway and turned into the dining hall. Bright patterns of colored light danced on the walls from the coats of arms on the windows. There was a buzz of conversation and expectancy.

Beecher sat down at a table apart from the others, nodding to one or two other people, but giving nothing to his glance to suggest he wished their company.

"Possibly a conversation," he said at last, just as a steward appeared at his elbow to offer him soup. "An experience shared that began a train of thought. They might even have read the same source book for something." He declined the soup, picking up bread instead and breaking it apart.

Joseph also declined the soup. He leaned forward a little across the table. "Have you ever had that happen?"

"You mean is it likely? Whom are we talking about?"

Joseph hesitated.

"For heaven's sake!" Beecher said exasperatedly. "I can't give you an opinion if you don't tell me the facts."

Was Joseph willing to put it to the test? Was it even inevitable now? "Sebastian and Foubister," he said miserably.

Beecher chewed his upper lip. "Unlikely, I agree. Except that Sebastian didn't need to cheat, and I can't see Foubister doing it. He's a decent chap, but he's also not a fool. He's been here long enough to know what it would cost if he were caught. And if he did want to cheat, he'd pick someone less idiosyncratic than Sebastian."

"How do I find out?"

"Ask him! I don't know of anything else." Beecher grinned suddenly. "Logic, my dear fellow! That rigid goddess you admire so much."

"Reason," Joseph corrected. "And she's not rigid—she just doesn't bend very easily."

He went back to Foubister, carrying the paper with him.

"That's an excellent line," he said, disliking the duplicity. "What made you think of it? It's quite a long way from the original."

Foubister smiled. "There's a line of trees a good bit like that," he answered. "Over there in the Gog Magog Hills." He gestured roughly to the south. "Several of us went up that way one Sunday and we saw them, outlined against a clear sky, and then a summer storm came up. It was rather dramatic."

"Good use of opportunity," Joseph observed. "Do it when you can, as long as it doesn't destroy the spirit of the author. The way you have it here, I think it adds to it. It was the right feel."

Foubister beamed. It lit up his dark face, making him suddenly charming. "Thank you, sir."

"Who else was there and saw it?"

Foubister thought for a moment. "Crawley, Hopper, and Sebastian, I think."

Joseph found himself smiling back, an easy, genuine feeling full of warmth. "I should have told you earlier," he said. "It's very good."

In the middle of the afternoon Connie sent Joseph a note inviting him to join Mary Allard and herself for a cold lemonade. He recognized it as a plea for help, and steeled himself to respond. He closed his book, walked across the quad, and went in through the Fellows' Garden, where he found Mary Allard alone.

She turned as she heard his footsteps on the path. "Reverend Reavley," she acknowledged him, but there was no welcome in her eyes or her voice.

"Good afternoon, Mrs. Allard," he replied. "I wish I had something helpful to tell you, but I'm afraid I know nothing of comfort."

"There is nothing," she said, her tone very slightly softening the abruptness of the words. "Unless you can stop them saying such things about my son. Can you do that, Reverend? You knew him as I did!"

"I didn't know him as you did," he reminded her. "For example, I did not know that he was engaged to be married. He never mentioned it."

She looked up at him defiantly. "That is a personal matter. It had been arranged for some time, but obviously he would have completed all his studies first. What I meant was that you, of all people, knew his quality!

You know he had a clarity of mind, of heart, that he was honest in a way most people do not even understand." The anger and the hurt burned through her words. "You knew that he was nobler than ordinary men, his dreams were higher and filled with a beauty they will never see." She looked him up and down as if seeing him clearly for the first time and finding it incomprehensible. "Doesn't it hurt you unbearably that they are questioning his very decency now?" Her contempt was raw and absolute.

At that moment Elwyn came out of the sitting room door and walked toward them. Mary Allard did not turn.

"When you love someone, surely you must also find the courage within yourself to see them with honesty, the light and the darkness as well?" Joseph said to her. He saw her anger gathering to explode. "He was good, Mrs. Allard, and he had amazing promise, but he was not perfect. He had much growth of spirit yet to accomplish, and by refusing to see the shadows in him we reinforced them instead of helping him to overcome them. I am guilty as well, and I wish it were not too late to mend it."

Mary's face held no forgiveness. "Reverend Reavley—"

Elwyn took her by the arm, his eyes meeting Joseph's. He knew his mother was wrong, but her weakness was something he did not know how to face, let alone to overcome. His eyes pleaded with Joseph not to be forced to.

"Let go of me, Elwyn!" Mary said sharply, leaning away from him.

"Mother, we can't help what people are saying! Why don't you come inside? It's hot out here, especially in black."

She whirled on him. "Are you suggesting I shouldn't wear black for your brother? Do you imagine a little discomfort matters a jot to me?"

Elwyn looked as if he had been slapped, but also as if he was used to it. He did not let go of her. "I'd like you to come inside where it is cooler."

She snatched her arm away. She was hurting too deeply to be kind, absorbed in her own pain and careless of his.

Joseph was suddenly angry with her. Her grief was unbearable, but it was also selfish. He turned to Elwyn. "Some pain is intolerable," he said gently. "But it is generous of you to be more concerned for your mother than for yourself, and I admire you for it."

Elwyn flushed deeply. "I loved Sebastian," he said huskily. "We weren't much alike—he was cleverer than I'll ever be—but he always made me feel he respected what I could do, sports and painting. I think a lot of people cared for him."

"I know they did," Joseph agreed. "And I know he admired you, but more than that, he loved you also."

Elwyn turned away, embarrassed by his emotion.

Joseph looked steadily at Mary until a deep stain of color worked up her cheeks. With a look of fury at him for having seen her weakness, she went after her younger son and caught up with him as he reached the steps to the garden door.

Joseph followed her inside, but she barely hesitated in the sitting room. Offering the briefest apology to those there, she hurried after Elwyn through the other door into the hall.

Joseph looked at Thyer, Connie, and Harry Beecher standing uncomfortably in the silence. "I can't think of anything helpful to say," Joseph confessed.

Thyer was by himself, nearest the garden doors, Connie and Beecher at the other side of the room, closer to each other, glasses of lemonade in their hands.

"No one can," Connie said. "Please don't blame yourself."

Thyer smiled slightly. "Particularly her husband, poor devil, and he's trying the hardest." There was pity in his face, and a degree of irritation. "Strange how in times of severest grief some people move further from each other, not closer." His eyes flickered toward Connie and then back to Joseph. "I would like to remind her of her husband's loss as well as her own, but Connie says it would only make it worse."

"Everything makes it worse," Connie answered him. "It's Elwyn I'm sorriest for. Mr. Allard is old enough to look after himself."

"No, he isn't." Beecher contradicted her quietly. "No one is ever old enough to hurt alone. A little tenderness would help him face it, and then begin to recover enough to start again with something like normality."

Connie smiled at him, the warmth filling her eyes, her face. "I don't think Mary is going to see that for a long time. It's a pity. In grieving for what she has lost, she risks forfeiting what she still has."

Beecher's face tightened.

Connie saw it, blushed a little, and looked away.

Joseph heard Thyer draw in his breath, and glanced across at him, but his face was expressionless.

Connie plunged into the silence, talking to Joseph. "We'll do what we can, but I don't think we're going to make much difference. I've tried to reassure Elwyn, but I know a word or two from you now and then would matter to him more."

"He's in an impossible situation," Thyer added. "Neither of them seems to give a damn about him."

Connie put her glass down. "Sometimes what people are is so much woven into their nature and their lives that no outside force, however great, can change them. They were like this long before Sebastian was killed."

It was later the same afternoon that Joseph caught up with Edgar Morel walking on the path along the river.

The conversation began badly.

"I suppose you think I killed him over Abigail!" he challenged Joseph as soon as he caught up with him.

Joseph felt pressed to find the truth before it did any more damage. "I hadn't thought it," he replied.

Morel's face was hard and defensive. "Of course if Sebastian was killed, it has to have been because he knew something foul about someone else, doesn't it?" he said bitterly. "It has to be envy of his brilliance, or his charm or some bloody thing! It couldn't be that he was cheating someone, or stealing, or anything so grubby!" The sarcasm was too overwrought to be truly cutting. "He's far too good for that." Unconsciously he was mimicking Mary Allard's voice. "Nothing's ever his fault. To listen to his mother you'd think he'd been martyred in some holy cause and the rest of us were heretics dancing on his grave."

"Try to have patience with her," Joseph urged. "She has no means of coming to terms with her loss."

"No one has," Morel said with sudden fury. "My mother died last year, just about the time Abigail dumped me for Sebastian. I didn't go around saying everybody else was heartless because they didn't care! The world doesn't stop for anyone's death! And it doesn't excuse making yourself a pain in the arse to everybody else!"

"Morel!" Joseph said sharply, putting out his hand to steady him.

Morel misunderstood the gesture and swung his arm back and let fly with a punch. It caught Joseph glancingly on the cheek, but it knocked him off balance, at least as much with surprise as from the weight of it. He staggered backward and just saved himself from falling.

Morel stood aghast.

Joseph straightened up, feeling painfully foolish. He hoped no one else had seen. He did not wish to pursue the matter, but it would be the end of his authority, and of Morel's respect for him, if he simply let it go. Then the answer came to him instinctively. He took a step forward, and to Morel's total stupefaction, he hit the young man back. Not very hard, but sufficiently to make Morel stagger. He was surprised by the skill he showed; a little more weight and he would have knocked him over.

"Don't do that again," he said as levelly as his pounding heart would allow. "And pull yourself together. Somebody shot Sebastian, and we need to keep our heads and find out who it was, not run around like a lot of schoolgirls getting hysterical."

Morel took a shaky breath, rubbing his jaw. "Yes, sir," he said obediently. "Yes, sir!"

Joseph knew he had handled the situation well, but he felt like a long walk and a drink by himself in some quiet pub where he could be surrounded by the warmth of laughter and friendship without having to participate in it. He was exhausted by other people's emotions. He had more than a sufficient burden of his own. It was not yet a month since both his parents had been killed, and the loss was still raw.

Added to that, since Eleanor's death had shattered his emotional world, taking the energy and the drive out of his faith, he had carefully rebuilt a strength out of reason, impersonal order, the sanity of the mind. It had seemed good, proof against the injuries of grief, loneliness, doubts of all kinds. It had cost him a great deal to create it, but the truth of it was a beauty sufficient to sustain him through anything.

Except that it wasn't working. Everything he knew was still there, still true; it just had no soul. Perhaps hope is unreasonable? Trust is not built on facts. Dealing with man, it is wise not to leap where you cannot see. Dealing with God, it is the final step without which the journey has no purpose.

He dismissed the thoughts and returned to the present, more earthbound troubles. He seesawed between fear that his father had been right and the nagging, aching doubt that perhaps John Reavley had been deluded, losing his grip on reality. That thought hurt with an amazing fierceness.

Added to that, his cheek where Morel had hit him was scratched and definitely tender. He did not want to have to explain that to anyone, especially Beecher. Somehow or other the conversation would get around to the subject of Sebastian and end unpleasantly.

So instead of going to the Pickerel, with its familiar tables by the river and people he knew, he went along the Backs in the opposite direction, almost as far as Lammas Land. He found a small pub overlooking the fields and the millpond, and went into the bar. It was paneled with oak worn dark with time, and pewter tankards hung along the rail above the bar itself, gleaming in the sunlight through the open door. The floor was broad, rough beams and not long ago would have had sawdust over them.

It was early; there were only a couple of elderly men sitting in the corner, and a pretty, fair-skinned barmaid with a wealth of wavy hair tied in a careless knot on the back of her head.

She handed a foaming mug to one of the men, who thanked her for it with ease of habit. Then she turned to Joseph.

"Afternoon, sir," she said cheerfully. She had a soft, pleasing voice, but distinctly broadened with a Cambridgeshire accent. "What can Oi get for you?"

"Cider, please," he answered. "Half a pint." He'd begin with a half, and perhaps have another half later. It was a pleasant place, and the sense of solitude was exactly what he wanted.

"Right y'are, sir." She poured it for him, watching the clear, golden liquid till it stopped just short of the top of the glass. "Haven't seen you here before, sir. We do a fair enough meal, if you'd loike a boite? Just plain, but it's there if you fancy it."

He had not thought he was hungry, but suddenly the idea of sitting here gazing at the flat water of the millpond and the sun setting slowly behind the trees was a far better prospect than going back to the dining hall. There he would have to make polite conversation while knowing perfectly well everyone was wondering what on earth he had done to his face, and making guesses. Sometimes tact was so loud it deafened one. "Thank you," he said. "I probably will."

"You'll be from one of the colleges?" she asked conversationally as she handed him a card with a list of the possibilities for supper.

"St. John's," he replied, reading down the menu. "What sort of pickle?"

"Green tomato, sir. It's homemade, an' if Oi say so when maybe Oi shouldn't, it's the best Oi've ever had, an' most folks agree."

"Then that's what I'll have, please."

"Roight, sir. What sort of cheese? We got Ely cheese, or a good local half an' half." She was referring to the half milk cheese, white and hard, half soft, yellow cream cheese. "Or do you like the French?" she added. "We moight have a bit o' Brie."

"Half and half sounds good."

"It is. All fresh. Tucky Nunn brought it in this morning," she agreed. She hesitated, as if to add something but uncertain if she should.

He waited.

"Did you say St. John's, sir?" There was a faint color in her cheeks, and her soft face was suddenly a little tighter.

"Yes."

"Did . . ." She swallowed. "Did you know Sebastian Allard?"

"Yes, quite well." What could she know of him? "You did, too?" he asked.

She nodded, her eyes flooding with tears.

"I think I'll have my meal outside," he said. "Perhaps you'd be kind enough to bring it to me?"

"Yes, sir, course Oi'll do that," and she turned away quickly, hiding her face.

He walked out into the sun again and found a table set for two. Less than five minutes later the barmaid came with a tray and put it down in front of him. The bread was thick-cut with sharp crusts, cracked where they had broken under the knife. The butter was cut in small chunks off the yard, with a bright sprig of parsley on it, the cheese rich and fresh. The pickle was not one he had seen before, but the pieces were large and the juice of it a dark, ripe color.

"Thank you," he said, taking a moment to appreciate it before he looked up and met her eyes. She was still troubled, hesitant.

"Have they—do they know what happened yet?" she asked.

"No." He gestured to the other chair. "I'm sure the men inside will manage without you for a few minutes. Sit and talk to me. I liked Sebastian very much, but I think I may not have known him as well as I imagined. Did he come along here often?"

She lowered her eyes for a moment before looking up at him with startling candor. "Yes, this summer." She did not add that it was to see her; it was unnecessary. It needed no explaining, for any young man might well have. He wondered with a coldness that still hurt, in spite of his growing acceptance of the facts, if Sebastian had used her completely selfishly, without her having any idea of his engagement to Regina Coopersmith. But surely this charming barmaid could never have imagined she could marry Sebastian Allard. Or could she? Was it possible she had no real idea of the world he came from?

"I am Joseph Reavley," he introduced himself. "I lecture at St. John's in biblical languages."

She smiled shyly. "Oi thought that was who you must be. Sebastian talked about you a lot. He said you made the people o' the past and their ideas and dreams into a whole life that really happened, not like just a lot of words on paper. He said you made it matter. You joined up the past and the present so we're all one, and that makes the future more important, too." She blushed a little self-consciously, aware of using someone else's words, although she obviously understood and believed them herself. "He told me you showed him how beauty lasts, real beauty, the sort of thing that's inside you." She took a ragged breath, controlling herself with difficulty. "And it really matters what you leave behind. He said as it's your thanks to the past, your love of the present, and your gift to the future."

He was surprised, and far more pleased than he wanted to be, because it awoke all the old emotions of friendship, the trust and the hope in Sebastian's integrity that he feared now was slipping out of his hands.

"My name's Flora Whickham," she went on, suddenly aware of not having introduced herself.

"How do you do, Miss Whickham," he replied graciously.

Her face became somber as she returned to the subject. "Do you think it was summink to do with the war?" she asked.

He was mystified. "War?"

"He was terribly scared there was going to be a war in Europe," she explained. "He said everyone was on the edge of it. O' course they still are, only it's worse now since those people were shot in Serbia. But Sebastian said as it would come anyway. The Russians and the Germans want it, and so do the French. Oi hear people in there"—she moved her head slightly to indicate the bar inside—"saying that the bankers and factory owners won't let it happen, there's too much to lose. And they have the power to stop it."

She lowered her eyes, and then looked up at him quickly. "But Sebastian said it would, 'cause it's the nature o' governments, and the army, and they're the ones who have the power. Their heads are stuffed with dreams about glory, and they haven't any idea how it would be for real. He said they were loike a bunch o' blind men tied together, runnin' towards the abyss. He thought millions would die." She searched his face, longing for him to tell her it would not happen.

"No sane person wants war," he said carefully, but with the earnestness that her passion and intelligence deserved. "Not really. A few expeditions here and there, but not out-and-out war. And nobody would kill Sebastian because he didn't, either." He knew as soon as the words were out of his mouth that they were of little use. Why could he not speak to the heart?

"You don't understand," she argued, embarrassed to be contradicting him, and yet her feeling was too strong to be overridden. "He meant to do something about it; he was a pacifist. Oi don't mean he just didn't want to foight—he was going to do something to stop it happening." Her face pinched a little. "Oi know his brother didn't loike that, and his mother would have hated it. She'd think it was cowardice. For her you're loyal and you fight, or you're disloyal, and that means you betray your own people. There's no other way. At least that's what he said."

She looked down at her hands. "But he'd grown away from them. He knew that. His oideas were different, a hundred years after theirs. He wanted Europe to be all one and not ever to foight each other again like the Franco-Prussian War, or all the wars we've had with France."

She raised her eyes and met his with intense seriousness. "That meant more to him than anything else in the world, Mr. Reavley. He knew summink about the Boer War and the way everybody suffered, women and children as well, horrible things. And not only the victims, but what it did to people when they foight like that." Her face was tight and bleak in the soft light. The sun shimmered on the millpond like an old mirror tarnished by the weeds. Dragonflies hovered above it on invisible wings. The evening was so still a dog barking in the distance seemed close enough to touch.

"It changes them inside," she went on, still searching his face to see how much he really understood. "Can you think how you'd feel if it was your brother or husband, someone you loved, who killed people like a butcher—all sorts, women, children, the old, just like your own family?"

Her voice was soft and a little ragged with the pain she could see. "Can you think o' trying to feel like a good person again afterwards? Sitting over the breakfast table talking, just as if it all happened to somebody else and you'd never done all those things? Or telling your children a story, putting flowers in a jug, thinking what to make for dinner, and you were the same person who'd driven a hundred women and children into a concentration camp and let them starve? Sebastian would have done anything at all to stop that happening again—ever. But Oi can't tell that to anybody else. His parents'd hate it; they wouldn't understand at all. They'd see him as a coward." Even saying the word hurt her; it was naked in the soft, sad lines of her face.

"No . . . ," Joseph said slowly, knowing without question that she was right. He could imagine Mary Allard's reaction to such a concept. She would have refused to believe it. No son of hers, especially her beloved Sebastian, could have espoused anything so alien to the kind of patriotism she had believed in all her life, with its devotion to duty, sacrifice, and the innate superiority of her own way of life, her own code of honor. "Did his brother know how he felt?" he added.

She shook her head. "Oi don't think so. He's idealistic, but in a different kind o' way. For him war is all about great battles and glory, that kind of thing. He doesn't think o' being so tired you can't hardly stand up, and hurting all over, and killing other people who are just like you are, and trying to break up their whole life."

"That's not what the Boer War was about," he said quickly. "Is that what Sebastian really believed?"

"More'n anything else in the world," she said simply.

He looked at her calm, tear-filled eyes, her mouth with jaw closed hard to control herself, her lips trembling, and he understood that she had known Sebastian better than he had, and immeasurably better than Mary Allard—or Regina Coopersmith, who probably knew nothing about him at all.

"Thank you for telling me," he said honestly. "Perhaps it does have something to do with that. I really don't know. It seems to make as much sense as anything else."

He stayed in the westering sun and ate his supper, had another glass of cider and a slice of apple pie with thick clotted cream, spoke again with

Flora, remembering happy things. Then in the dusk he walked back along the pale river's edge to St. John's. Perhaps he had discovered where Sebastian went in his unaccounted hours, and it was very easy to understand. He smiled as he thought how simple it was, and that given the same mother, the same imprisoning worship, he would have done so, too.

CHAPTER

TEN

Matthew did not immediately tell Shearing of his intent to continue pursuing Patrick Hannassey as well as Neill. There were too many uncertainties to make a justifiable case for using his time, and he still did not know whom he trusted. If there was a conspiracy to assassinate the king, he could not believe Shearing would be party to it.

And if it was something else—although the more he thought of this, the more did it seem to possess all the qualities of horror and betrayal—then he would be wasting time. He would have to abandon his investigation instantly and change course to pursue whatever new threat loomed. There was no time to waste in explanations.

Special Branch had been set up in the previous century, at the height of the Fenian violence, specifically to deal with Irish problems. Since then it had become involved in every area of threat to the safety or stability of the country—threats of anarchy, treason, or general social upheaval—but the Irish problem remained at the core. Matthew made one or two discreet inquiries among professional friends, and Wednesday lunchtime saw him walking casually across through Hyde Park beside a Lieutenant Winters, who had expressed himself willing to give him all the assistance he could. However, Matthew knew perfectly well that each branch of the intelligence community guarded its information with peculiar jealousy, and it would be easier to pry the teeth out of a crocodile than shake loose any fact they would rather keep to themselves. He cursed the necessity for secrecy that prevented him from telling them the truth. But his father's voice rang in his ears with warning, and he dared not yet ignore it. Once given away, his own secret could never be taken back.

"Hannassey?" Winters said with a grimace. "Remarkably clever man. Sees everything and seems to have a memory like an elephant. What is more important, he can relate one thing to another and deduce a third."

Matthew listened.

"An Irish patriot," Winters went on, staring at the cheerful scene in the park ahead of them. Couples walked arm in arm, the women in high summer fashion, much of it nautical in theme. A hurdy-gurdy man played popular ballads and music hall tunes, smiling as passers-by threw him pennies and threepences. Several children, boys in darker suits, girls in lace-edged pinafores, threw sticks for two little dogs.

"Educated by the Jesuits," Winters continued. "But the interesting thing about him is that to the eye or ear he is not obviously Irish. He has no accent, or at least when he wishes to he can sound like an Englishman. He also speaks fluent German and French, and has traveled very considerably over a great deal of Europe. He is reputed to have good connections with international socialists, although we don't know if he sympathizes with them or merely uses them."

"What about other nationalist groups?" Matthew asked, not sure in which direction he was driving, but thinking primarily of the Serbians because of their recent resort to assassination as a weapon.

"Probably," Winters answered, his cadaverous face furrowed in thought. "Trouble is, he's very difficult to trace because he's so unremarkable to look at. I don't know that he deliberately disguises himself. Nothing so melodramatic as wigs or false mustaches, but a change of clothes, parting the hair on the other side, a different walk, and suddenly you have a different person. No one remembers him or can describe him afterward."

A young man in a Guard's uniform walked past them whistling cheerfully, a smile on his face.

"So he has a sense of proportion, no theatrics," Matthew observed, referring to Hannassey. "Clever."

"He's in it to win," Winters affirmed. "He never loses sight of the main purpose."

"And the main purpose is?"

"Independence for Ireland—first, last, and always. Catholics and Protestants together, willing or not."

"Obsessive?"

Winters thought for a moment. "Not so as to lose balance, no. Why are you asking?"

"I've heard rumors of a plot," Matthew said with studied casualness, adding, "Wondered if Hannassey could be involved."

Winters stiffened slightly. "If it's an Irish plot, you'd better tell me," he said, keeping up his steady, easy pace as they passed an elderly gentleman stopping to light his cigar, cupping his hands around the flame of his match. The breeze was only a whisper, but it was sufficient to blow out the match.

The hurdy-gurdy man changed to a love song, and some of the young people started to sing with him.

"I don't know that it is." Matthew was sorely tempted to tell Winters all he knew. He desperately needed an ally. The loneliness of confusion and responsibility weighed on him almost suffocatingly. "It could be any of several things," he said aloud.

Winters's face was bleak. He was still looking straight ahead and avoiding Matthew's eyes. "How much do you really know what you're talking about, Reavley?"

It was the moment of decision. Matthew took the plunge. "Only that someone uncovered a document outlining a conspiracy that was profoundly serious, and he was killed before he could show it to me," he answered. "The document disappeared. I'm trying to prevent a disaster without knowing what it is. But it seems to me that with the Curragh mutiny, the failure to get any Anglo-Irish agreement, and now the king coming out on the side of the Loyalists, a plot against him fills the outline too well to ignore."

Winters walked in silence for at least fifty yards, which took them around the end of the Serpentine. The sun was hot, baking the ground.

The air was still, carrying the sounds of laughter from the distance, and a thread of music again.

"I don't think so," he said at last. "It wouldn't serve Irish purposes. It's too violent."

"Too violent!" Matthew said in amazement. "Since when has that stopped the Irish Nationalists? Have you forgotten the Phoenix Park murders? Not to mention a score of other acts of terror since! Half the dynamiters in London have been Fenians." He barely refrained from telling Winters he was talking nonsense.

Winters seemed unperturbed. "The Catholic Irish want self-government, independence from Britain," he said patiently, as if it were something he had been obliged to explain too many times, and to men who did not wish to understand. "They want to set up their own nation with its parliament, foreign office, and economy."

"That's impossible without violence. In 1912 over two hundred thousand Ulstermen, and even more women, signed the Solemn League and Covenant to use all means necessary to defeat the present conspiracy to set up a Home Rule parliament in Ireland! If anyone thinks they're going to suppress Ulster without violence, they've never been within a hundred miles of Ireland!"

"Very much my point," Winters said grimly. "To have any hope at all of succeeding, the Irish Nationalists will have to win the cooperation of as many other countries outside Britain as they can. If they assassinate the king, they will be seen as merely criminals and lose all support everywhere—support they know that they need."

They passed an elderly couple walking arm in arm, and nodded politely to them, raising their hats.

"Hannassey is not a fool," Winters continued when they were out of earshot. "If he didn't know that before the assassination in Sarajevo, he certainly knows it now. Europe may not approve of Austria's subjugation of Serbia, and they may get into such a violent and ill-balanced tangle of diplomatic fears and promises that it ends in war. But the one group who will not win will be the Serbian nationalists. That I can promise you. And one thing Hannassey is not is a fool."

Matthew wanted to argue, but even as he drew breath to do so, he realized it was to defend his father rather than because he himself believed it. If Hannassey was as brilliant as Winters said, then he would not choose assassination of the king as a weapon—unless he could be certain it would be attributed to someone else.

"The Irish wouldn't be blamed for it if it appeared to be . . ." He stopped.

Winters raised his eyebrows curiously. "Yes? Whom did you have in mind? Who wouldn't be traced back or betray them, intentionally or not?"

There was no one, and they were both aware of it. It did not really even matter whether the Irish were behind it or not, for they would still be blamed. The whole idea of such a public crime was one they would abhor. They might be even as keen to prevent it as Matthew himself. He was at a dead end.

"I'm sorry," Winters said ruefully. "You're chasing a ghost with this one. Your informant is overzealous." He smiled, perhaps to rob his words of some of their sting. "He's an amateur at this, or he's trying to make himself more important than he is. There are always whispers, bits of paper floating around. The trick is to sort out the real ones. This one's trivial." He gave a bleak little gesture of resignation. "I'm afraid I've got enough real threats to chase. I'd better get back to them. Good day." He increased his pace rapidly, and within a few moments he was lost to sight among the other pedestrians.

Shearing called Matthew into his office the next day, his face grave.

"Sit down," he ordered. He looked tired and impatient, his voice very carefully under control, but the rough edge to it was still audible. "What's this Irish assassination plot you're chasing after?" he demanded. "No, don't bother to answer. If it's not important enough for you to have told me, then you shouldn't be wasting your time on it. Drop it! Do you understand me?"

"I have dropped it," Matthew said tersely. It was the truth, but not all of it. If it was not Irish, then it was something else, and he would continue to investigate the matter.

"Very wise of you," Shearing said. "There are strikes in Russia. Over a hundred and fifty thousand men out in St. Petersburg alone. And apparently on Monday there was another attempt to murder the czarina's mad monk, Rasputin. We haven't got time to chase after private ghosts and goblins." He was still staring at Matthew. "I don't consider you to be a glory seeker, Reavley, but if I find I am mistaken, you'll be out of here so fast your feet will barely touch the ground on your way." There was challenge in his face, and anger. Matthew was overcome for a moment by the chill realization that there was also a shred of fear in it as well, a knowledge that things were out of control.

"The situation in the Balkans is getting worse almost by the day," Shearing went on harshly, glaring at him. "There are rumors that Austria is preparing to invade Serbia. If it does, there is a very real and serious danger that Russia will act to protect Serbia. They are allied in language, culture, and history." His face was tight, and his hands, dark-skinned, immaculate, were clenched on the desk until the knuckles shone white. "If Russia mobilizes, it will be only a matter of days before Germany follows. The kaiser will see himself as ringed by hostile nations, all fully armed, and growing stronger every week. Unbalanced as he is, to a degree he is right. He will face Russia to the east, and inevitably France to the west. Europe will be at war."

"But not us," Matthew said. "We are no threat to anyone, and it's hardly our concern."

"God knows," Shearing replied.

"Isn't that exactly the time the Irish Nationalists would strike?" Matthew could not forget the document and the outrage in his father's voice. He could not let go. "It would be if I were their leader."

"I daresay God knows that, too," Shearing said waspishly. "But you will leave it to the Special Branch. Ireland is their problem. Concentrate on Europe. That is an order, Reavley!" He picked up a small bundle of papers from the top of his desk and held it out. "By the way, C wants you in his office in half an hour." He did not look up as he said it.

Matthew froze. Sir Mansfield Smith-Cumming had been head of the Secret Intelligence Service since 1909. He had begun his career as a sub-lieutenant in the Royal Navy, serving in the East Indies, until he was placed on the inactive list for chronic seasickness. In 1898 he had been recalled and had undertaken many highly successful espionage duties for the Admiralty. Now the agency he led served all branches of the military and the high-level political departments.

"Yes, sir," Matthew said hoarsely, his mind racing. Before Shearing could look up, he turned on his heel and went out into the corridor. He was shaking.

Precisely thirty minutes later Matthew was shown into Smith-Cumming's inner office. Smith-Cumming looked up at him, his face unsmiling.

"Captain Reavley, sir," Matthew said. "You sent for me."

"I did," C agreed.

Matthew waited, his heart pounding, his throat tight. He knew that his entire professional future lay in what he said, or omitted, in this interview.

"Sit down," C ordered. "You are going to remain until you tell me all you know about this conspiracy you are chasing."

Matthew was glad to sit. He pulled the nearest chair around to face C and sank into it.

"Obviously you do not have the documentary proof," C began. "Neither, apparently, does the man who has been shadowing you, and occasionally me."

Matthew sat motionless.

"You did not know that?" C observed.

"I knew someone was following me, sir," Matthew said quickly, swallowing hard. "I did not know anyone had followed you."

C's eyebrows rose, softening a little of the sternness of his face. "Do you know who he is?"

"No, sir." He thought of offering excuses and decided instantly against it.

"He is a German agent named Brandt. Unfortunately we don't know much more about him than that. Where and when did you first hear of this document, and from whom?"

Matthew did not even consider the possibility of lying. "From my father, sir, on the telephone, on the evening of June twenty-seventh."

"Where were you?"

"In my office, sir." He felt his face grow hot as he said it. The crumpled car was sharp in his mind, his father's face, the scream of tires. For a moment he felt sick.

C's face softened. "What did he say to you?"

Matthew kept his voice level with difficulty, but he could not control the hoarseness in it. "That he had found a document in which was outlined a conspiracy that would ruin England's honor forever, and change the world irreparably for the worse."

"Had you heard anything of this before?"

"No, sir."

"Did you find it hard to believe?"

"Yes. Almost impossible." He was ashamed of it, but that was the truth.

"Did you repeat it, to make sure you had understood him?"

"No, sir." Matthew felt the heat burn up his face. "But I did repeat the fact that he was bringing it to me the following day." The admission was damning. The only thing more completely guilty would have been to lie about it now.

C nodded. There was compassion in his eyes. "So whoever overheard you already knew that the document was missing, and that your father had it. That tells us a great deal. What else do you know?"

"My father's car was deliberately ambushed and sent off the road, killing both my parents," Matthew answered. He saw the flash of pity in C's face. He took a deep breath. "When I heard about it from the police, I went to Cambridge to pick up my elder brother, Joseph—"

"He didn't know?" C interrupted. "He was closer, and older than you?"

"Yes, sir. He was at a cricket match. He lost his wife about a year ago. I don't think the police wanted someone from college telling him. The master was at the match as well, and most of his friends."

"I see. So you drove to Cambridge and told him. What then?"

"We identified our parents' bodies, and I searched their effects, and then the wreckage of the car—to find the document. It wasn't there. Then when we got home I searched there also, and asked the bank and our solicitor. When we returned from the funeral, the house had been searched by someone else."

"Unsuccessfully," C added. "They appear to be still looking for it. Presumably a second copy, which would suggest it is some kind of agreement. Your father indicated no names?"

"No, sir."

C stared at him, frowning. For the first time Matthew sensed the depth of his anxiety. "You knew your father, Reavley. What was he interested in? Whom did he know? Where could he have found this document?"

"I've thought about it very hard, sir, and I've spoken to several of his closest friends, and as far as I can tell, they know nothing. When I mentioned plots, they all said Father was naive and out of touch with reality." He was surprised how much that still hurt to say.

C smiled, the amusement reaching all the way to his eyes.

"It seems they did not know your father very well." Then his face hardened. "Resist the temptation to prove that they are wrong, Reavley, whatever it cost you!"

Matthew swallowed. "Yes, sir."

"So you have no idea what this is about?"

"No, sir. I imagined it might be an Irish plot to assassinate the king, but—"

"Yes." C waved his hand briefly, dismissing it. "I know that. Pointless. Hannassey is not a fool. It is European, not Irish. Mr. Brandt is not interested in the independence or otherwise of Ireland, except as it might affect our military abilities. But that is something to consider. If we are involved in civil war in Ireland, our limited resources will be strained to the maximum."

He leaned forward a few inches. "Find it, Reavley. Find out who is behind it. Where did the document come from? For whom was it intended?" He pushed a piece of paper across the top of his desk. "This is a list of German agents in London of whom we know. The first is at the German embassy, the second is a carpet manufacturer, the third is a minor member of the German royal family presently living in London. Be extremely discreet. You should be aware by now that your life depends on it. Confide in no one at all." He met Matthew's eyes in a cold, level gaze. "No one! Not

Shearing, not your brother—no one at all. When you have an answer, bring it to me."

"Yes, sir." Matthew stood up, reached for the paper, read it, and passed it back.

C took it and put it in a drawer. "I'm sorry about your father, Captain Reavley."

"Thank you, sir." Matthew stood to attention for a moment, then turned and left, his mind already racing.

In the upstairs sitting room of the house on Marchmont Street, the Peacemaker stood by the window. He watched as a younger man walked briskly along the pavement, glancing occasionally at the houses to this side. He was reading the numbers. He had been here before, twice to be exact, but on both occasions brought by car, and at night.

The man in the street stopped, glanced up, and satisfied himself that he had found what he was looking for.

The Peacemaker stepped back, just one pace. He did not wish to be seen waiting. He had recognized the man below even before he saw his thick dark hair or the broad brow and wide-set eyes. It was a powerful face, emotional, that of a man who follows his ideals regardless of where they led him . . . over the cliffs of reason and into the abyss, if need be. He knew his easy walk, the mixture of grace and arrogance. He was a northerner, a Yorkshireman, with all the pride and the aggressive stubbornness of the land from which he came.

The doorbell rang, and a moment later it was opened by the butler. There followed a short silence, then footsteps up the stairs—soft, light, those of a man used to climbing the fells and dales—then a tap on the door.

"Come," he answered.

The door opened and Richard Mason came in. He was almost six feet tall, an inch or two less than the Peacemaker, but he was more robust, and his skin had the wind and sunburn of one who travels.

"You sent for me, sir?" he said. His voice was unusual, his diction perfect, as if he had been trained for drama and the love of words. It had a sibilance so slight one was not certain if it was there or not, and one listened to catch it again.

"Yes," the Peacemaker assured him. They both remained standing, as if to be seated was too much a sign of ease for the situation that brought them together. "Events are moving very rapidly."

"I am aware of that," Mason said with only the merest touch of asperity. "Do you have the document?"

"No." That was a tight, hard word carrying a burden of anger in it so great one expected to see his shoulders bend under it. But he remained upright, his face pale. "I've had men searching for it, but we have no idea where it went. It wasn't in the car or on the bodies, and we've tried the house twice."

"Could he have destroyed it?" Mason asked dubiously.

"No." The answer was immediate. "He was"—he gave the merest shrug—"an innocent man in some ways, but he was not a fool. He knew the meaning of the document, and he knew no one would believe him without it. Under his calm manner, he was as stubborn as a mule." His face tightened in the sunlight through the bay windows. "He would never deliberately have defaced it, let alone destroyed it."

Mason stood still, his pulse beating hard. He had some idea of how much was at stake, but the enormities of it stretched into an unimaginable future. The sights of war still haunted his nightmares, but the blood, the pain, and the loss of the past would be no more than a foretaste of what could happen in Europe, and eventually the world. Any risk at all was worth the price in order to prevent that, even this price.

"We can't waste any more time looking," the Peacemaker went on. "Events are overtaking us. I have it from excellent sources that Austria is preparing to invade Serbia. Serbia will resist, we all know that, and then Russia will mobilize. Once Germany enters France it will be over in a matter of days, weeks at the most. Schlieffen has drawn up a plan of absolute exactitude, every move timed to perfection. The German army will be in Paris before the rest of the world has time to react."

"Is there still a chance we will remain out of it?" Mason asked. He was a foreign correspondent. He knew Austria and Germany almost as well as the man who stood opposite him, with his background, his aristocratic connections stretching as high as the junior branches of the royal family on both sides of the North Sea, his brilliance with languages. They shared a rage at the slaughter and destruction of war. The highest goal a man could achieve would be to prevent that from ever happening again, by any means at all.

The Peacemaker chewed his lip, his face strained with tension. "I think so. But there are difficulties. I've got an SIS man breathing down my neck. Reavley's son, actually. He's not important, just a nuisance. I doubt it will be necessary to do anything about him. Don't want to draw attention. Fortunately he's looking in the wrong direction. By the time he realizes it, it won't matter anymore."

"Another copy of the document?" Mason asked. The idea in it was brilliant, more daring than anything he could have imagined. The sheer size of it dazzled him.

When the Peacemaker had first told him of it, it had taken his breath away. They had been walking slowly along the Thames Embankment, the lights dancing on the water, the smell of the incoming tide, the sounds of laughter across the river, the pleasure boats making their slow way upstream toward Kew. He had stood rooted to the spot, lost for words.

Slowly the plan had moved from a dream, lightly touched on, into a wish, and finally a reality. He still felt a little like a man who had created a unicorn in his imagination, only to walk into his garden one day and find one grazing there, milk-white, with cloven hooves and silver horn—a living and breathing animal.

"We haven't found a second copy," the Peacemaker answered grimly. "At least not yet. I've done a certain amount to discredit John Reavley. I wish it hadn't been necessary." He looked sharply at Mason as he saw the alarm in his eyes. "Nothing overt!" he snapped. "We need to give it time for the dust to settle." His mouth pinched unhappily, a shadow in his eyes. "Sometimes the sacrifice is heavy," he said softly. "But if he had understood, I think he would have paid it willingly. He was not an arrogant man, certainly not greedy, and not a fool, but he was simplistic. He believed what he wanted to, and there is no use arguing with a man like that. A pity. We could have used him otherwise."

Mason felt a heaviness settle on him, too, an ache of regret inside him. But he had seen the devastation of war and human cruelty in the Balkans only a year ago, between Turkey and Bulgaria, and the memory of it still soaked his nightmares in horror and he woke trembling and drenched in sweat.

Before that, as a younger man he had gone east and reported the eyewitness accounts of the Japanese sinking of the entire Russian fleet in 1905. Thousands of men were buried in steel coffins under the trackless water, nothing remaining but the stunned loss, the grief of families from half a continent.

Earlier still, on the first foreign assignment of his career, he had watched the farmers on the veldt in Africa, the pitiable dispossessed, wending their slow way across the endless open plains. He had watched the women and children die.

None of it must happen again, Richard Mason vowed to himself. One should not permit such things to happen to other human beings. "A statesman has to think of individuals," he said.

"We have other things to consider," the Peacemaker said. "Without the document war may be inevitable. We must do what we can to make sure that it is quick and clean. There are many possibilities, and I have plans in place, at least on the home front. We can still have tremendous effect."

"I imagine it will be brief," Mason concurred. "Especially if Schlieffen's plan works. But it will be bloody. Thousands will be slaughtered." He used the word bitterly and deliberately.

The Peacemaker's smile was thin. "Then it is even more important that we ensure it is as short as possible. I have been giving it a great deal of thought over the last few days—since the document was taken, in fact." A sudden fury gripped him, clenching his body and draining the blood from his face until his skin was pallid and his eyes glittered. "Damn Reavley!" his voice choked on the name. "Damn him to hell! If he'd just kept out of it, we could have prevented this! Tens of thousands of lives are going to be lost! For what?" He flung his hand out, fingers spread wide enough to have played over an octave with ease. "It didn't have to happen!" He gulped in air and carefully steadied himself, breathing in and out several times until his color returned and his shoulders relaxed.

"I'm sorry, but I can't bear to think of the ruin of a way of life that is the culmination of millennia of civilization—all unnecessary! How many widows will there be? How many orphans? How many mothers waiting for their sons who will never come home from a war they didn't ask for and didn't want?"

"I know," Mason said almost under his breath. "Why do you think I'm doing this? It's like drinking poison, but the only alternative is a slow journey into hell from which we won't come back."

"You're right," the Peacemaker responded, turning toward the light streaming in through the window. "I know! I'm heartsick that we came so close and lost it through an idiotic piece of mischance—a German philosopher with good handwriting and an inquisitive ex-politician who was damned useless at it anyway, and all our plans are jeopardized. But it's too early to despair.

"We must prepare for war, if it comes. And I have several ideas, with the groundwork already laid, just in case. Everything we value depends on our success." He rubbed his hand over his brow. "Goddamn it! The Germans are our natural allies. We come from the same blood, the same language, the same heritage of nature and character!"

He stopped for a moment, regaining his composure. "But perhaps it is no more than a setback. We don't have the document, but neither do they. If they did, Matthew Reavley wouldn't still be looking for it and asking questions." His face hardened again. "We have to see at all costs that he doesn't obtain that document. If it fell into the wrong hands, it would be disastrous!"

"Is Matthew Reavley the only one?" Mason asked.

"Oh, there's another brother, Joseph, but he's completely ineffectual," the Peacemaker replied with a smile. "A scholar, idealist, retreated from life and responsibility. Teaches at Cambridge—biblical languages, of all things! He wouldn't acknowledge the truth if it leaped up and bit him. He's a dreamer. Nothing is going to waken him, because he doesn't want to be disturbed. Reality hurts, Mason, and the Reverend Reavley doesn't like pain. He wants to save the world by preaching a good, carefully thought-out, and well-reasoned sermon to them. He doesn't realize that nobody's listening—not with their hearts or their guts, or willing to pay the price for it. It's up to us."

"Yes," Mason said. "I know that."

"Of course you do." The Peacemaker pushed his hands through his hair. "Go back to your writing. You have a gift. We may need it. Stay with your newspaper. If we can't prevent it and the worst happens, get them to send you everywhere! Every battlefield, every advance or retreat, every town or city that's captured, or where there are negotiations for peace. Become the most brilliant, the most widely read war correspondent in Europe . . . in the world. Do you understand?"

"Oh, yes," Mason said with a soft hiss of breath between his teeth. "Of course I understand."

"Good. Then you'd better go, but keep in touch."

Mason turned and walked slowly to the door and out of it. His footsteps barely sounded on the stairs.

CHAPTER

ELEVEN

In Cambridge, Joseph felt that he was achieving something, but it was all a matter of exclusion. He was no nearer to knowing what had happened, as opposed to what had not. And if Inspector Perth had made progress, he was keeping it to himself. The tension was increasing with every day. Joseph was determined to continue in whatever way he could to discover more about Sebastian and who had had reason to hate or to fear him.

An opportunity came to him when he was discussing a problem of interpretation with Elwyn, who was finding a particular passage of translation difficult.

They had walked from the lecture rooms together, and rather than go inside had chosen to cross the bridge to the Backs. It was a quiet afternoon. As they turned on the gravel path to go toward the shade, bees drifted lazily among the spires of delphiniums and late pinks by the wall of the covered walk. Bertie was rolling on the warm earth in between the snapdragons.

Elwyn was still showing signs of the shock and grief of loss. Joseph knew better than others how one can temporarily forget a cataclysm in one's life, then remember it again with surprise and the renewal of pain. Sometimes one floated in a kind of unreality, as if the disaster were all imagination and in a little while would disappear and life be as it was before.

One was tired without knowing why; concentration slipped from the grasp and slithered away.

It was not surprising that Elwyn was wandering off the point again, unable to keep his mind in control.

"I ought to get back to the master's house," he said anxiously. "Mother may be alone."

"You can't protect her from everything," Joseph told him.

Elwyn's eyes opened abruptly, then his lips tightened and color flooded his face. He looked away. "I've got to. You don't understand how she felt about Sebastian. She'll get over this anger, then she'll be all right. It's just that—" He stopped, staring ahead at the flat, bright water.

Joseph finished the sentence for him. "If she knew who did it, and saw them punished, her anger would be satisfied."

"I suppose so," Elwyn conceded, but there was no conviction in his voice.

Joseph broached the subject he least wanted to. "But perhaps not?"

Elwyn said nothing.

"Why?" Joseph persisted. "Because to do so would force her to see something in Sebastian that she would not wish to?"

The misery in Elwyn's face was unmistakable. "Everyone sees a different side of people. Mother doesn't have any idea what Sebastian was like away from home, or even in it, really."

Joseph felt intrusive, and certain that he, too, wanted to keep his illusions intact, but that was a luxury he could no longer afford. He was being offered a chance to learn, and he dared not turn away from it.

"Did she know about Flora Whickham?" he asked.

Elwyn stiffened, for an instant holding his breath. Then he let it out in a sigh. "He told you?"

"No. I discovered for myself, largely by accident."

Elwyn swung around. "Don't tell Mother! She wouldn't understand. Flora's a nice girl, but she's . . ."

"A barmaid."

Elwyn gave a rueful smile. "Yes, but what I was going to say was that she's a pacifist, I mean a real one, and Mother wouldn't begin to understand that." There was confusion and distaste in his face, and a hurt too tender to probe. He looked away again toward the river, shielding his eyes from Joseph's gaze. "Actually, neither do I. If you love something, belong to it and believe in it, how can you not fight to save it? What kind of a man wouldn't?"

Perhaps he suspected Joseph of that same incomprehensible betrayal. If he did, there would be some truth in it. But then Joseph had read of the Boer War, and his imagination could re-create the unreachable pain, the horror that could not be eased or explained and never, with all the arguments on earth, be justified.

"He was not a coward," Joseph said aloud. "He would fight for what he believed in."

"Probably." There was no certainty in Elwyn's voice or his face.

"Who else knew about Flora?" Joseph asked.

"I don't know."

"Regina Coopersmith?" Joseph asked.

Elwyn froze. "God! I hope not!"

"But you're not certain?"

"No. But I don't really know Regina well. I suppose"—he chewed his lip and looked awkwardly at Joseph—"I don't know women very well. I would feel dreadful, but maybe—" He did not finish.

There were a few moments of silence as they walked side by side over the grass and onto the path under the trees.

"Sebastian had a row with Dr. Beecher," Elwyn went on.

"When?" Joseph felt a sinking inside himself.

"A couple of days before he died."

"Do you know what it was about?"

"No, I don't." He turned to face Joseph. "I thought it was odd, actually, because Dr. Beecher was pretty decent to him."

"Wasn't he to everyone?"

"Of course. I meant more than to the rest of us."

Joseph was puzzled. He remembered Beecher's dislike of Sebastian. "In what way?" he asked. He had meant to be casual, but he heard the harder edge in his voice, and Elwyn must have heard it also.

Elwyn hesitated, uncomfortable. He shuffled his feet on the gravel of the path and sighed. "We all behave badly sometimes—come to a lecture late, turn in sloppy work. You know how it is?"

"I do."

"Well, usually you get disciplined for it—ticked off and made to look an ass in front of the others, or get privileges revoked, or something like that. Well, Dr. Beecher was easier on Sebastian than on most of us. Sebastian sort of took advantage, as if he knew Dr. Beecher wouldn't do anything. He could be an arrogant sod at times. He believed in his own image. . . ." He stopped. Guilt was naked in his face, the stoop of his shoulders, the fidgeting of his right foot as it scuffed the stones. He had said only what was true, but convention decreed that one spoke no ill of the dead. His mother would have seen it as betrayal. "I never thought he liked Sebastian very much," he finished awkwardly.

"But he favored him?" Joseph pressed.

Elwyn stared at the ground. "It makes no sense to me, because it isn't a favor in the long run. You've got to have discipline or you have nothing. And other people get fed up if you keep on getting away with things."

"Did other people notice?" Joseph asked.

"Of course. I think that's what the row was about with Beecher, a day or two before Sebastian's death."

"Why didn't you mention it before?"

Elwyn stared at him. "Because I can't see Dr. Beecher shooting Sebastian for being arrogant and taking advantage of him. Those things are irritating as hell, but you don't kill someone for them!"

"No," Joseph agreed. "Of course you don't." He tried to think of the need to bring Mary Allard toward reality in a way she could manage. He wanted to help, but he could see her fragility, and nothing was going to ease the blow for her if something ugly was exposed in Sebastian. She might even refuse to believe it and blame everyone else for lying. "Try to be patient with your mother," he added. "There is little on earth that hurts more than disillusion."

Elwyn gave a twisted smile. Blinking rapidly to fight his emotion, he nodded and walked away, too close to tears to excuse himself.

Joseph went back to St. John's to look for anyone who could either substantiate or deny what Elwyn had told him. Near the bridge he ran into Rattray.

"Favor him?" Rattray said curiously, looking up from the book he was reading. "I suppose so. Hadn't thought about it much. I got rather used to everyone thinking Sebastian was the next golden poet and all that." The wry, almost challenging look in his eyes very much included Joseph within that group, and Joseph felt the heat burn up his face.

"I was thinking of something a bit more definable than a belief," he said rather tartly.

Rattray sighed. "I suppose he did let Sebastian get away with more than the rest of us," he conceded. "There were times when I thought it was odd."

"Didn't you mind?" Joseph was surprised.

"Of course I minded!" Rattray said hotly. "Once or twice taking advantage of Beecher was clever, and we all thought it would make it easier for the rest of us to skip lectures if we wanted, or turn in stuff late, or whatever. Even came in blotto a couple of times, and poor old Beecher didn't do a damn thing! Then I began to see it was all rather grubby, and in the end stupid as well. I told Sebastian what I thought of it and that I wasn't playing anymore, and he told me to go to hell. Sorry. I'm sure that isn't what you wanted to hear. But your beautiful Sebastian could be a pain in the arse at times."

Joseph said nothing. Actually it was Beecher he was thinking of, and afraid for.

"When he was good, he was marvelous," Rattray said hastily, as if he thought he had gone too far. "Nobody was more fun, a better friend, or honestly a better student. I didn't resent him, if that's what you think. You don't when somebody's really brilliant. You see the good, and you're happy for it—just that it exists. He just changed a bit lately."

"When is lately?"

Rattray thought for a moment. "Two or three months, maybe? And then after the Sunday of the assassination in Sarajevo, he got so wound up I thought he was going to snap. Poor devil, he really thought we were going to war."

"Yes. He talked to me about it."

"Don't you think it's possible, sir?" Rattray looked surprised. "A quick sort of thing, in and out. Settle it?"

"Perhaps," Joseph said uncertainly. Had Sebastian been killed out of some stupid jealousy here, nothing to do with the document or John Reavley's death?

Rattray gave a sudden grin. It lit his rather ordinary face and made it vivid and charming. "We don't owe the Austrians anything, or the Serbs, either. But I wouldn't find a spell in the army so terrible. Could be a wheeze, actually. Spot of adventure before the grind of real life!"

All kinds of warnings came into Joseph's mind, but he realized he actually knew no more than Rattray did. They were both speaking in ignorance, fueled only by other men's experiences.

Before dinner, when he was almost certain to find him alone, Joseph went to Beecher's rooms, bracing himself for a confrontation that could break a friendship he had long valued.

Beecher was surprised to see him, and evidently pleased.

"Come in," he invited him warmly, abandoning his book and welcoming Joseph, offering him the better chair. "Have a drink? I've got some fairly decent sherry."

That was typical of Beecher's understatement. "Fairly decent" actually meant absolutely excellent.

Joseph accepted, embarrassed that he was going to take hospitality in what might prove to be a false understanding.

"I could do with one myself." Beecher went to the sideboard, took the bottle out of the cupboard, and set two elegant engraved crystal glasses on the table. He was fond of glass and collected it now and then, when he found something quaint or very old. "I feel as if I've been dogged by that wretched policeman all week, and God knows the news is bad enough. I can't see any end to this Irish fiasco. Can you?"

"No," Joseph admitted honestly, sitting down. The room had grown familiar over the time he had been here. He knew every book on the shelves and had borrowed many of them. He could have described the view out the window with his eyes closed. He could have named the various members of the family in each of the silver-framed photographs. He knew exactly where the different scenic paintings were drawn, which valley in the Lake District, which castle on the Northumberland coast, which stretch of the South Downs. Each held memories they had shared or recounted at one time or another.

"The police are not getting anywhere, are they?" he said aloud.

"Not so far as I know." Beecher returned with the sherry. "Here's to an end to the investigation, although I'm not sure if we'll like what it uncovers."

"And what might that be?" Joseph asked.

Beecher studied Joseph for some time before replying. "I think we'll discover that somebody had a thoroughly good motive for killing Sebastian Allard, even though they may be hideously sorry now."

Suddenly Joseph was cold, and the aftertaste of the sherry was bitter in his mouth. "What do you think a *good* motive could be?" he asked. "It was in cold blood. Whoever it was took a gun to his room at a quarter after five in the morning." With a jolt of memory so violent it turned his stomach, Joseph recalled exactly the feel of Sebastian's skin, already cool.

Beecher must have been watching him and seen his color bleach. He breathed out slowly. "I'd like to let you go on in your belief that he was as good as you wanted him to be, but he wasn't. He had promise, but he was on the verge of being spoiled. Poor Mary Allard was at least in part responsible."

Now was the moment. "I know," Joseph conceded. "I was responsible as well." He ignored Beecher's look of amusement and compassion. "Elwyn protected him partly for his own sake, partly for his mother's," he went on. "And apparently you let him get away with being rude, late with work, and sometimes sloppy. And yet you didn't like him. Why did you do that?"

Beecher was silent, but the color had paled from his face and his hand holding the sherry glass was trembling very slightly; the golden liquid in it shimmered. He made an effort to control it and lifted it to his lips to take a sip, perhaps to give himself time.

"It was hardly in your interest," Joseph went on. "It was bad for your reputation and your ability to be fair to others and maintain any kind of discipline."

"You favored him yourself!"

"I liked him," Joseph pointed out. "I admit, my judgment was flawed. But you didn't like him. You know the rules as well as I do. Why did you break them for him?"

"I didn't know you had such tenacity," Beecher said drily. "You've changed."

"Rather past time, isn't it?" Joseph said with regret. "But as you said, there is no point in dealing with anything less than the truth."

"No. But I don't propose to discuss it with you. I did not kill Sebastian, and I don't know who did. You'll have to believe that or not, as you wish."

It was not as Joseph wished. He had liked Beecher profoundly almost since they had met. Everything he knew about him, or thought he knew, was decent. Beecher was the ideal professor, learned without being pompous. He taught for the love of his subject, and his students knew it. His pleasures seemed to be mild: old buildings, especially those with quaint or unusual history, and odd dishes from around the world. He had the courage and the curiosity to try anything: mountain climbing, canoeing, potholing, small-boat sailing. Beecher loved old trees, the more individual the better; he had jeopardized his reputation campaigning to save them, to the great annoyance of local authorities. He liked old people and their memories, and odd irrelevant facts. He had spoken of his family now and then. He was particularly fond of certain aunts, all of whom were marvelously eccentric creatures who espoused lost causes with passion and courage, and invariably a sense of humor.

Joseph realized with surprise, and sadness, that Beecher had never spoken of love. He had laughed at himself over one or two youthful fancies, but never anything you could call a commitment, nothing truly of the heart. It was a gaping omission, and the longer Joseph considered it the more it troubled him.

Guardedly he looked at Beecher now, sitting only a few feet away from him, effecting to be relaxed. He was not handsome, but his humor and intelligence made him unusually attractive. He had grace and he dressed with a certain flair. He took care of himself like a man who was not averse to intimate involvement.

And yet he had never spoken of women. If there was no one, why had he not ever mentioned that, perhaps regretted it? The most obvious answer was that had such an attachment existed, it was illicit. If so, he could not afford to tell even his closest friends.

The silence in the room, which would usually have been warm and comfortable, was suddenly distressing. Joseph's thoughts raced in his head. Had Sebastian either stumbled on a secret or gone looking for it and unearthed it deliberately, then used it? It was a thought Joseph would much rather have put away as unworthy, but he could no longer afford to do that.

Whom was it Beecher loved? If he was telling the truth and had not killed Sebastian, nor know who had, then surely the natural person to consider after that would be whoever else was involved in the illicit romance. Or whoever was betrayed by it, if such a person existed.

At last he faced the ultimate ugliness: What if Beecher was lying? What if his illicit lover had been Sebastian himself? The thought was extraordinarily painful, but it fitted all the facts he knew—the undeniable ones, not the dreams or wishes. Perhaps Flora Whickham was merely a friend, a fellow pacifist, and an escape from the inevitable demands of his family?

There were people who could love men and women with equal ease. He had never before considered Sebastian as one such, but then he had not thought deeply about him in that regard at all. It was a private area. Now he was obliged to intrude into it. He would do it as discreetly as possible, and if it led nowhere with regard to Sebastian's death, he would never speak of it. He was accustomed to keeping secrets; it was part of the profession he had chosen.

Beecher was watching him with his characteristic patience until Joseph should be ready to talk again.

Joseph was ashamed of his thoughts. Was this what everyone else was feeling—suspicion, ugly ideas racing through the mind and refusing to be banished?

"Sebastian had a friendship with a local girl, you know?" he said aloud. "A barmaid from the pub along near the millpond."

"Well, that sounds healthy enough!" Then Beecher's face darkened with something very close to anger. "Unless you're suggesting he misused her? Are you?"

"No! No, I really mean a friend!" Joseph corrected him. "It seems they shared political convictions."

"Political convictions!" Beecher was amazed. "I didn't know he had any."

"He was passionately against war." Joseph remembered the emotion shaking Sebastian's voice as he had spoken of the destruction of conflict. "For the ruin it would bring. Not only physically, but culturally, even spiritually. He was prepared to work for peace, not just wish for it."

The contempt in Beecher's face softened. "Then perhaps he was better than I supposed."

Joseph smiled, the old warmth returning. This was the friend he knew. "He saw all the fear and the pain," he said quietly. "The glory of our entire heritage drowned in a sea of violence until we became a lost civilization, and all our wealth of beauty, thought, human wisdom, joy, and experience as buried as Nineveh or Tyre. No more Englishmen, none of our courage or eccentricity, our language or our tolerance left. He loved it intensely. He would have given everything he had to preserve it."

Beecher sighed and leaned backward, gazing up at the ceiling. "Then perhaps he is in some ways fortunate that he won't see the war that's coming," he said softly. "Inspector Perth is sure it will be the worst we've even seen. Worse than the Napoleonic Wars. Make Waterloo look tame."

Joseph was stunned.

Beecher sat up again. "Mind, he's a miserable devil," he said more cheerfully. "A regular Jeremiah. I'll be glad when he finishes his business here and goes to spread alarm and despondency somewhere else. Would you like another glass of sherry? You didn't take much."

"It's enough," Joseph replied. "I can escape reality nicely on one, thank you."

The following day Joseph began his investigation with the worst of all possibilities.

He must begin by learning all he did not already know about Beecher. And surely in this case discretion was the better part of honesty. Candor would ruin Beecher's reputation, and unless it exposed Sebastian's murderer, it was no one else's concern.

The easiest thing to check without speaking to anyone else was with a record of all Beecher's classes, lectures, tutorials, and other engagements for the last six weeks. It was time-consuming but simple enough and easily concealed by finding the same information for everyone and simply extracting that relating to Beecher.

Correlating times and figures was not Joseph's natural talent, but with concentration he compiled a record of where Beecher had been, and with whom, for at least most of the previous month.

He sat back in his chair, ignoring the piles of papers, and considered what it proved and what he should search for next. How did one conduct a secret relationship? Either by meeting alone where no one at all would see you, or where all those who did would be strangers to whom you would mean nothing. Or else by meeting in plain sight, and with a legitimate reason no one would question.

In Cambridge there was no place where everyone would be strangers, nor in the nearby villages. It would be crazy to take such a risk.

Completely uninhabited places were few, and not easily reached. Beecher might bicycle to them, but what about a woman? Unless she was very young and vigorous, she would hardly bicycle far, and a woman who drove a car was very rare. Judith was an exception, not the rule.

That left the last possibility: They met openly, with natural reasons that no one would question. Sebastian knew of their feelings either because he had been more observant than others or because he had accidentally seen something acutely private. Either thought was distasteful.

Surely it would prove to be nonsense, his own overheated imagination. Perhaps Beecher was simply one of those scholarly men who do not form attachments. Such men existed. Joseph's idea that he was not arose simply from his own nature. He failed to imagine living with no desire for intimacy. Possibly Beecher had loved once and could not commit himself again, nor speak of it even to someone like Joseph, who would surely have understood.

And yet even as the thoughts were in his mind, he did not believe them. Beecher was too alive, too physical to have removed himself from any of the richness of passion or experience. They had walked too far, climbed too high, laughed too hard together for him to be mistaken.

Joseph had been hoping to avoid Inspector Perth when he almost bumped into him walking along the path in the middle of the quad, his pipe clenched between his teeth.

He took it out. "Good afternoon, Reverend," he said, this time not standing aside but remaining in front of Joseph, effectively blocking his way.

"Good afternoon, Inspector," Joseph answered, moving a little to the right to go around him.

"Any luck with your questions?" Perth said with what looked like polite interest.

Joseph thought for a moment of denying it, then remembered how frequently he had passed Perth coming or going. He would be lying, but more importantly Perth would know it and then assume he was hiding something—both of which were true. "I keep thinking so, and then realizing it all proves nothing," he answered evasively.

"Oi know exactly what you mean," Perth sympathized, knocking his pipe out on his shoe, examining it to make certain it was empty, then putting it in his pocket. "Oi come up with bits an' pieces, then it slips out o' my hands. But then you know these people, which Oi don't." He smiled pleasantly. "You'd know, fer instance, why Dr. Beecher seems t've made an exception for Mr. Allard, letting him get away with all kinds o' cheek an' lateness an' the loike, where he'd punish someone else." He waited, quite obviously expecting an answer.

Joseph thought quickly. "Can you give me an example?"

Perth replied without hesitation. "Mr. Allard handed in a paper late, an' so did Mr. Morel. He took a mark off Mr. Morel for it, but not off Mr. Allard."

Joseph felt a chill and stared fixedly at Perth, because he was suddenly more afraid of him. He did not want him poking around in Beecher's private affairs. "People can be eccentric in marking sometimes," he said, affecting an ease he was very far from feeling. "I have been guilty of it myself at times. Translation in particular can be a matter of taste as well as exactness."

Perth's eyes widened. "Is that what you think, Reverend?" he said curiously.

Joseph wanted to escape. "It seems probable," he said, moving a little to the right again, intending to go around Perth and continue on his way. He wanted to end this conversation before Perth led him any further into the morass.

Perth smiled as if Joseph had met his prejudices exactly. "Dr. Beecher just loiked Mr. Allard's style, did he? Poor Mr. Morel just ain't in the same class, so when he's late, he's in trouble."

"That would be unfair!" Joseph said hotly. "And it was not what I meant! The difference in mark would have had nothing to do with being late or early."

"Or being cheeky or careless?" Perth persisted. "Discipline's not the same for the clever students from what the way it is for the less clever. You know Mr. Allard's family quite well, don't you?"

It was not himself Joseph was afraid for, it was Beecher, and the thoughts that were darkening in his own mind.

"Yes, I do, and I never allowed him the slightest latitude because of it!" he said with considerable asperity. "This is a place of learning, Inspector, and personal issues have nothing to do with the way a student is taught or the marks given to his work. It is irresponsible and morally repugnant to suggest otherwise. I cannot allow you to say such a thing and be uncorrected. You are slandering a man's reputation, and your office here does not give you immunity to do that!"

Perth did not seem in the least disconcerted. "Oi've just bin going around asking and listening like you have, Reverend," he replied quietly. "And Oi've begun to see that some people thought Dr. Beecher really din't like Mr. Allard very much. But that don't seem to be true, because he bent over backwards to be fair to him, even done him the odd favor. Now why d'yer think that was?"

Joseph had no answer.

"You know these people better'n Oi do, Reverend," Perth went on relentlessly. "Oi'd've thought you'd want the truth o' this, because you can see just how hard everybody's taking it. Suspicion's an evil thing. Turns people against each other, even when there's really no cause for it."

"Of course I do," Joseph responded, then had no idea what to say next.

Perth was smiling. It was amusement and a faint, rather sad compassion. "Hard, ain't it, Reverend?" he said gently. "Discovering that a young man you thought so well of weren't above using a spot o' blackmail now an' then?"

"I don't know anything of the sort!" Joseph protested. It was literally true, but already morally a lie.

"O' course not," Perth agreed. "Because you stopped before you had any proof as you couldn't deny. If you did, then you'd have to face it, and maybe even tell. But you're an interesting man to follow, Reverend, an' not nearly as simple as you'd have me think." He ignored Joseph's expression. "Good thing Dr. Beecher was way along the river when Mr. Allard was killed, or Oi'd have to suspect him, an' of course Oi'd have to find out exactly what it was Mr. Allard knew, although Oi can think of it easy enough. A very handsome woman, Mrs. Thyer, an' mebbe just a little bit lonely, in her own way."

Joseph froze, his heart racing. Beecher and Connie? Could that be true? Images teemed through his mind becoming sharper and sharper—Connie's face, beautiful, warm, vivid.

Perth shook his head. "Don't look at me like that, Reverend. Oi haven't suggested something improper. All men have feelings, an' sometimes we don't want 'em seen by others. Makes us feel kind of . . . naked. Oi wonder what else Mr. Allard's sharp eyes noticed? You wouldn't happen to know, would you?"

"No, I wouldn't!" Joseph snapped, feeling the heat in his face. "And as you say, Dr. Beecher was at least a mile away when Sebastian was shot. I told you that I can't help you, Inspector, and it is the truth. Now would you be good enough to let me pass?"

"Course Oi would, Reverend. You be about your business. But Oi'm telling you, all of you here: You can go round an' round the houses all you like, an' Oi'm still going to find out who did it, whoever he is, no matter what his father paid to have him up here. An' Oi'm going to find out why! Oi may not be able to argue all kinds o' fancy logic like you can, Reverend, but Oi know people, an' Oi know why they do things against the law. An' Oi'll prove it. Law's bigger'n all of us, an' you being a religious man, yer oughta know that!"

Joseph saw Perth's antipathy and understood it. The inspector was out of his depth in surroundings he could never aspire to or be comfortable in. He was being patronized by a number of men considerably younger than he, and they were probably not even aware of what they were doing. The law was both his master and his weapon, perhaps his only one.

"I do know that, Inspector Perth," Joseph said. "And we need you to find the truth. The uncertainty is destroying us."

"Yes," Perth agreed. "It does that to people. But Oi will!" At last he stepped aside, nodding graciously for Joseph to proceed.

Joseph walked on rapidly with the certain knowledge that he had come off second best and that Perth understood him far better than he wished. Once again he had misjudged somebody.

He was invited to dine at the master's lodgings the following day, and accepted because he understood Connie Thyer's desperation to escape the sole responsibility for looking after Gerald and Mary Allard under the weight of their grief. She could hardly offer them anything that could be construed as entertainment, and yet they were her guests. But their unalloyed presence at her table must be almost more than she could bear. Joseph at least was an old family friend, also mourning a close and almost equally recent loss. Also, his religious calling made him extremely suitable. He could hardly refuse.

He arrived a little before eight to find Connie in the drawing room with Mary Allard. As always, Mary was head to toe in black. He thought it was the same dress he had seen her in last time they met, but one black gown looked much like another to him. She certainly appeared even thinner, and there was no doubting the anger in her face. It did not soften in the slightest when she saw Joseph.

"Good evening, Reverend Reavley," she said with polite chill. "I hope you are well?"

"Yes, thank you," he replied. "And you?" It was an absurd exchange. She was obviously suffering intensely. She looked anything but well. One inquired because it was the thing to say.

"I am not sure why you ask," she answered, catching him off guard. "Do I tell you how I feel? Not only has some murderer robbed me of my son, but now vicious tongues are fouling his memory. Or would you feel less guilty if I merely tell you that I am perfectly well, thank you? I have no disease, only wounds!"

Neither of them noticed that Gerald Allard had come into the room, but Joseph heard his swift intake of breath. He waited for Gerald to make some attempt to retrieve his wife's naked rudeness.

The silence prickled as if on the brink of thunder.

Connie looked from one to the other of them.

Gerald cleared his throat.

Mary swung around to him. "You were going to say something?" she accused. "Perhaps to defend your son, since he is lying in his grave and cannot defend himself?"

Gerald flushed a dark red. "I don't think it is fair to accuse Reavley, my dear—" he started.

"Oh, isn't it?" she demanded, her eyes wide. "He is the one who is assisting that dreadful policeman to suggest that Sebastian was blackmailing people, and that is why someone murdered him!" She swiveled back to Joseph, her eyes blazing. "Can you deny it, Reverend?" She loaded the last word with biting sarcasm. "Why? Were you jealous of Sebastian? Afraid he was going to outshine you in your own field? He had more poetry in his soul than you will ever have, and you must realize that. Is that why you are doing this? God! How he'd have despised you for it! He thought you were his friend!"

"Mary!" Gerald said desperately.

She ignored him. "I've listened to him talk about you as if you were flawless!" she said, her voice shaking with contempt, tears glistening in her eyes. "He thought you were wonderful, an unparalleled friend! Poor Sebastian—" She stopped only because her voice was too thick with emotion to continue.

Connie was watching, white-faced, but she did not interrupt.

"Really—" Gerald tried again.

Joseph cut across him. "Sebastian knew I was his friend," he said very clearly. "But I was not as good a friend to him as I would have been had I tried more honestly to see his faults as well as his virtues. I would have served him better had I tried to curb his hubris instead of being blind to it."

"Hubris?" she said icily.

"His pride in his own charm, his feeling of invulnerability," he started to explain.

"I know what the word means, Mr. Reavley!" she snapped. "I was questioning your use of it with reference to my son! I find it intolerable that—"

"You find any criticism of him intolerable." Gerald managed to make himself heard at last. "But somebody killed him!"

"Envy!" she said with absolute conviction. "Some small person who could not endure being eclipsed." She looked at Joseph as she finished.

"Mrs. Allard," Connie said, "we all sympathize with your grief, but that does not excuse you for being both cruel and unjust to another guest in my house, a man who has also lost his closest family almost as recently as you have. I think perhaps in your own loss you had temporarily forgotten that." It was said calmly, even gravely, but it was a bitter rebuke.

Aidan Thyer, who had entered the room during the exchange, looked startled, but he did not intervene, and his expression as he glanced at Connie was unreadable, as if stemming from emotions profound and conflicting. In that instant Joseph wondered if he knew that Beecher was in love with his wife, and if it hurt him or made him fear he could lose what he must surely value intensely. Or did he? What was there, really, behind the habitual courtesy? Joseph glimpsed with pain the possibility of a world of loneliness and pretense.

But the present hauled him back. Mary Allard was furious, but she was too clearly in the wrong to defend herself. She adopted Connie's offer of escape.

"I'm sorry," she said stiffly. "I had forgotten. I daresay your own loss has . . ." She had obviously been going to say something like "cramped your judgment," but realized it made things no better. She left the sentence hanging in the air.

Normally Joseph would have accepted any apology, but not this time. "Made me think more deeply about reality," he finished for her. "And see that no matter how much we love someone or regret lost opportunities to have given them more than we did, lies do not help, even when we would find them more comfortable."

The color drained out of Mary's face, and she looked at him with loathing. Even if she understood anything he said, she was not going to concede it now. "I have no idea what things you may regret," she said coldly. "I do not know you well enough. I have heard no one speak ill of your parents, but if they have, then you should do all within your power to silence them. If you have not loyalty, above all to your own family, then you have nothing! I promise you I will do anything in my power to protect the name and reputation of my dead son from the envy and spite of anyone cowardly enough to attack him in death when they would not have dared to in life."

"There are many loyalties, Mrs. Allard," he answered, his voice grating with the intensity of his feelings: the misery and loneliness of too many losses of his own, the anger at God for hurting him so profoundly and at the dead for leaving him with such a weight to bear, the crush of responsibilities he was not ready for, and above all the fear of disillusion, of the disintegration of the love and beliefs dearest to him. "It is a matter of choosing which to place first. Loving someone does not make them right, and your family is no more important than mine or anyone else's. Your first loyalty ought to be to honor, kindness, and some degree of truth."

The hatred in her face was answer enough without words. She turned to Connie, her skin white, her eyes burning. "I am sure you will understand if I do not choose to remain for dinner. Perhaps you will be good enough to have a tray sent to my room." And with that she swept out through the door in a rustle of black silk taffeta and the faintest perfume of roses.

Connie sighed. "I am sorry, Dr. Reavley. She is finding this investigation very hard indeed. Everyone's nerves are a little raw."

"She idealized him," Gerald said, as much to himself as to anyone else. "It isn't fair. No one could live up to that, nor can the rest of us protect her forever from the truth." He glanced at Joseph, perhaps expecting him to read some apology in it, although Joseph had the feeling he was looking more for acceptance of his own silence. He was sorry for Gerald, a man floundering around in a hopeless task, but he felt far greater pity for Elwyn, trying to defend a brother whose flaws he knew while protecting his mother from truths she could not face and his father from looking impotent and sinking into self-loathing. It was more than anyone should have to do, let alone a young man who was himself bereaved and who should have been supported by his parents, not made to support them in their self-absorbed grief.

He glanced at Connie and saw a reflection of the same pity and anger in her face. But it was Joseph she was looking at, not her husband. Aidan Thyer was averting his gaze, perhaps in order to hide his distaste at Gerald's excuses.

Joseph filled the silence. "Everyone's nerves are a little raw," he agreed. "We suspect each other of things that in our better moments would not even enter our thoughts. Once we know what happened, we will be able to forget them again."

"Do you think so?" Aidan Thyer asked suddenly. "We've pulled off too many masks and seen what is underneath. I don't think we'll forget." He looked momentarily at Connie, then back at Joseph, his pale eyes challenging.

"Perhaps not forget," Joseph amended. "But isn't the art of friendship very much the selecting of what is important and allowing some of the mistakes to drift away until we lose sight of them? We don't forget so much as let the outlines blur, accept that a thing happened, and be sorry. This is how we are today, but it does not have to be tomorrow as well."

"You forgive very easily, Reavley," Thyer said coolly. "I wonder sometimes if you've ever had anything very much to forgive. Or are you too Christian to feel real anger?"

"You mean too anemic to feel anything with real passion," Joseph corrected for him.

Thyer blushed. "I'm sorry. That was irredeemably rude. I do beg your pardon."

"Perhaps I shouldn't weigh things so much before I speak," Joseph said thoughtfully. "It makes me sound pompous, even a little cold. But I am too afraid of what I might say if I don't."

Thyer smiled, an expression of startling warmth.

Connie looked taken by surprise, and she turned away. "Please come in to dinner, Mr. Allard," she invited Gerald, who was moving from one foot to the other and plainly at a total loss. "We will help no one by not eating. We shall need our strength, if only to support each other."

Joseph spent a miserable night, twisting himself round and round in his bed, his thoughts preventing him from sleeping. Small recollections came back to his mind: Connie and Beecher laughing together over some trivial thing, but the sound of it so rich, so full of joy; Connie's face as she had listened to him talking about some esoteric discovery in the Middle East; Beecher's concern when she had a summer cold, his fear that it might be flu or even turn to pneumonia; other, more shadowy incidents that now seemed out of proportion to the casual friendship they claimed.

What had Sebastian known? Had he threatened Beecher openly, or simply allowed fear and guilt to play their part? Was it possible he had been innocent of anything more than a keener observation than others?

But Beecher had been with Connie and Thyer when the Reavleys had been killed—not that Joseph had ever suspected him of that. And Perth said he had been along the Backs when Sebastian was shot, so he could not be guilty.

What about Connie? He could not imagine Connie shooting Sebastian. She was generous, charming, quick to laugh, just as quick to see another's need or loneliness, and to do all she could to answer it. But she was a woman of passion. She might love Beecher profoundly and be trapped by circumstance. If she was discovered in an affair with him and it were made public, he would lose his position, but she would lose everything. A woman divorced for adultery ceased to exist even to her friends, let alone to the rest of society.

Would Sebastian really have done that to her?

The young man Joseph knew would have found it a repulsive thought, cruel, dishonorable, destructive to the soul. But did that man exist outside Joseph's imagination?

He fell asleep not sure of what was certain about anyone, even himself. He woke in the morning with his head pounding, and determined to learn beyond dispute, all the facts that he could. Everything he cared about was slithering out of his grasp; he needed something to hold on to.

It was barely six o'clock, but he would begin immediately. It was an excellent time to walk along the Backs himself and find Carter the boatman, who had apparently spoken with Beecher on the morning of Sebastian's death. He shaved, washed, and dressed in a matter of minutes and set out in the cool clarity of the morning light.

The grass was still drenched with dew, giving it a pearly, almost turquoise sheen, and the motionless trees towered into the air in unbroken silence.

He found Carter down at the mooring, about a mile along the bank.

"Mornin', Dr. Reavley," Carter greeted him cheerfully. "Yer out early, sir."

"Can't sleep," Joseph replied.

"Oi can't these days neither," Carter agreed. "Everybody's frettin'. Newspapers flyin' off the stands. Got to get 'em early to be sure o' one.

Never seen a toime loike it, 'cepting when the old queen were ill." He scratched his head. "Not even then, really."

"It's the best time of the morning," Joseph said, glancing around him at the slow moving river shimmering in the sun.

"It is that," Carter agreed.

"I thought I might see Dr. Beecher along here. He hasn't been this way already, has he?"

"Dr. Beecher? No, sir. Comes occasional loike, but not very often."

"He's a friend of mine."

"Nice gentleman, sir. Friend to a lot o' folk." Carter nodded. "Always got a good word. Talked a bit about them ole riverboats. Interested, 'e is, though between you an' me, Oi think 'e do it only to be agreeable. 'E knows Oi get lonely since moi Bessie died, an' a bit of a chat sets me up for the day."

That was the Beecher that Joseph knew, a man of great kindness, which he always masked as something else so there was never debt.

"You must have been talking together when young Allard was killed," he remarked. How bare that sounded.

"Not that mornin', sir," Carter shook his head. "Oi tole the police gentleman it were, because Oi forgot, but that were the day Oi 'ad the bad puncture. Oi 'ad to fix it, an' it took me an age 'cos it were in two places, an' Oi didn't see it at first. An hour late 'ome, Oi were. O' course Dr. Beecher must've bin 'ere if 'e said so, but Oi didn't see 'im 'cos Oi weren't, if you get me?"

"Yes," Joseph said slowly, his own voice sounding far away, as if it belonged to someone else. "Yes . . . I see. Thank you." And he turned and walked slowly along the grass.

Did he have a moral obligation to tell Perth? He had agreed that the law was above them all, and it was. But he needed to be sure. Right now he was certain of nothing at all.

CHAPTER

TWELVE

On Saturday afternoon Matthew dined with Joseph at the Pickerel, overlooking the river. There were just as many people there as always, sitting around the tables, leaning forward in conversation, but voices were lower than a week earlier, and there was less laughter.

Punts still drifted back and forth on the water, young men balancing in the sterns with long poles clasped, some with grace, others with precarious awkwardness. Girls, wind catching the gossamerlike sleeves of their pale dresses, lay half reclined on the seats. Some wore sweeping hats, or hats decked with flowers to shade their faces; others had parasols of muslin or lace, which dappled the light. One girl, bare-headed, with russet hair, trailed a slender arm into the river, her skin brown from the sun, her fingers shedding bright drops behind her in the golden light.

"One of us ought to go home," Matthew said, reaching his knife into the Belgian pâté and spreading more of it onto his toast. "It ought to be you, and anyway I need to go and see Shanley Corcoran again. With things as they are, he's about the only person I dare trust."

"Are you any further?" Joseph asked, then immediately wished he hadn't. He saw the frustration in Matthew's face and knew the answer.

Matthew ate another mouthful and swallowed the last of his red wine, then poured himself more, before replying.

"Only ideas. Shearing doesn't think it is an Irish plot. He seems to be trying to steer me away from it, although I have to admit his logic is pretty sound." He reached for more butter. "But then of course I don't know beyond any doubt at all that he isn't the one behind it."

"We don't know that about anyone, do we?" Joseph asked.

"Not really," Matthew agreed. "Except Shanley. That's why I need to speak to him. There's . . ." He looked across the river, narrowing his eyes against the brilliance of the lowering sun. "There's a possibility it could be an assassination attempt against the king, although the more I consider it, the less certain I am that anyone would benefit from it. I don't know what I think anymore."

"There *was* a document," Joseph said. "And whatever was in it, it was sufficient for someone to kill Father."

Matthew looked weary. "Perhaps it was evidence of a crime," he said flatly. "Simply a piece of ordinary greed. Maybe we were looking beyond the mark, for something wildly political involving the grand tide of history, and it was only a grubby little bank robbery or fraud."

"Two copies of it?" Joseph said skeptically. Matthew lifted his head, his eyes widening. "It might make sense! Copies for different people? What if it were a stock market scandal or something of that nature! I'm going to see Shanley tomorrow. He'll have connections in the City, and at least he would know where to start. If only Father had said more!" He leaned forward, his food forgotten. "Look, Joe, one of us has got to go and spend a little time with Judith. We've both been neglecting her. Hannah's taken it all very hard, but at least she's got Archie some of the time, and the children. Judith's got nothing, really."

"I know," Joseph agreed quickly, guilt biting deep. He had written to both Judith and Hannah, but since he was only a few miles away, that was not enough.

There was a short burst of laughter from the next table and then a sudden silence. Someone rushed into speech, something completely irrelevant, about a new novel published. No one responded, and he tried again.

"Anything more on Sebastian Allard?" Matthew asked, his face gentle, sensing the slow discovery of ugliness, the falling apart of beliefs that had been held dear for so long.

Joseph hesitated. It would be a relief to share his thoughts, even if as soon as tomorrow he would wish he had not. "Actually . . . yes," he said slowly, looking not at Matthew but beyond him. The light was fading on the river, and the firelike scarlet and yellow poured out across the flat horizon from the trees over by Haslingfield right across to the roofs of Madingley.

"I've discovered Sebastian was capable of blackmail," he said miserably. Even the words hurt. "I think he blackmailed Harry Beecher over his love for the master's wife. For nothing so obvious as money—just for favor, and I think maybe for the taste of power. It would have amused him to exert just a very subtle pressure, but one that Beecher didn't dare resist."

"Are you sure?" Matthew asked, his face puckering with doubt. There was not the denial in his voice Joseph hungered to hear. He had overstated the case deliberately, waiting for Matthew to say it was nonsense. Why didn't he?

"No!" he replied. "No, I'm not sure! But it looks like it. He lied as to where he was. He's engaged to a girl his mother probably picked out for him, but he's got a girlfriend of his own in one of the pubs in Cambridge. . . ." He saw Matthew's look of amusement. "I know you think that's just natural youth," he said angrily. "But Mary Allard won't! And I don't think Regina Coopersmith will, either, if she ever finds out."

"It's a bit shabby," Matthew agreed, the flicker of humor still in his eyes. "A last fling before the doors of propriety close him in forever with Mother's choice. Why hadn't he the guts to say so?"

"I've no idea! I didn't know anything about it! Anyway, he would never have married Flora, for heaven's sake. She's a barmaid. She's also a pacifist."

Matthew's eyebrows shot up. "A pacifist? Or do you mean she agreed with whatever her current admirer happened to say?"

Joseph considered for only a moment. "No, I don't think I do. She seemed to know quite a lot about it."

"For God's sake, Joe!" Matthew sat back with a jerk, sliding the chair legs on the floor. "She doesn't have to be stupid just because she pulls ale for the local lads!"

"Don't be so patronizing!" Joseph snapped back. "I didn't say she was stupid. I said she knew more about pacifism and about Sebastian's views on the subject than to have been merely an agreeable listener. He was drifting away from his roots at a speed that probably frightened him. His mother idolized him. To her he was all she wished her husband could have been—brilliant, beautiful, charming, a dreamer with the passion to achieve his goals."

"Rather a heavy weight to carry—the garment of someone else's dreams," Matthew observed a great deal more gently, and with a note of sadness. "Especially a mother. There'd be no escaping that."

"No," Joseph said thoughtfully. "Except by smashing it, and there would be a strong temptation to do that!" He looked curiously at Matthew to see if he understood. His answer was immediate in the flash of knowledge in Matthew's eyes. "It's not always as simple as we think, is it?" he finished.

"Is that what you believe?" Matthew asked. "Somehow Sebastian was making a bid for freedom, and it went wrong?"

"I really don't know," Joseph admitted, looking away again, across the river. The girl with the bright hair was gone, as was the young man who had balanced with such grace. "But very little I've discovered fits the idea of him I had—which makes me wonder if I was almost as guilty as Mary Allard of building a prison for him to live in."

"Don't be so hard on yourself," Matthew said gently. "He built his own image. It may have been in part an illusion, but he was the chief architect of it. You only helped. And believe me, he was happy to let you. But if he did see what happened on the Hauxton Road, why wouldn't he say something?" His brow furrowed, his eyes shadowed and intense. "Do you think he was mad enough to try blackmail on someone he knew had already killed two people? Was he really such a complete fool?"

Put like that, it sounded not only extreme but dangerous beyond any possible profit. And surely he would have known the people concerned were Joseph's parents—even if not at the time, then later.

"No," he answered, but there was no conviction in his voice. Matthew would never have done such a thing, but he was accustomed to thinking in terms of danger. He was only a few years older than Sebastian, in fact, but in experience it was decades. To Sebastian, death was a concept, not a reality, and he had all the passionate, innocent belief in his own immortality that goes with youth.

Matthew was watching him.

"Be careful, Joe," he warned. "Whatever the reason, someone in college killed him. Don't go poking around in it, please! You aren't equipped!" Anger and frustration flickered in his eyes, and fear. "You're too hurt by it to see straight!"

"I have to try," Joseph said, reasserting reason into its place. It was the one sanity to hold on to. "Suspicion is tearing the college to pieces," he went on. "Everyone is doubting things, friendships are cracking, loyalties are twisted. I need to know for myself. It's my world . . . I have to do something to protect it."

He looked down. "And if Sebastian did see what happened on the Hauxton Road, there may be some way of finding out." He met Matthew's steady blue-gray eyes. "I have to try. Was he saying something to me that last evening on the Backs, and I wasn't listening? The more I think of it, the more I realize he was far more distressed than I understood then. I should have been more sensitive, more available. If I'd known what it was, I might have saved him."

Matthew clasped his hand over Joseph's wrist for a moment, then let go again. "Possibly," he said with doubt. "Or you might have been killed as well. You don't know if it had anything to do with that at all. At least for this weekend, go and see Judith. She's our world, too, and she needs someone, preferably you." It was said gently, but it was a charge, not a suggestion.

Matthew offered to drive him, and no doubt Judith would have brought him back, but Joseph wanted the chance to be alone for the short while it would take him to ride there on his bicycle. He needed time to think before meeting Judith.

He thanked Matthew but declined. He walked briskly back to St. John's to collect a few overnight things such as his razor and clean linen, then took his bicycle and set out.

As soon as he was beyond the town the quiet lanes enclosed him, wrapping him in the shadows of deep hedges, motionless in the twilight. The fields smelled of harvest, that familiar dry sweetness of dust, crushed stalks, and fallen grain. A few starlings were black dots against the blue of the sky, fading gray already to the east. The long light made the shadows of the hay stooks enormous across the stubble.

There was a hurt in the beauty of it, as if something were slipping out of his grip, and nothing he could do would prevent his losing it. Summer always drifted into autumn. It was as it should be. There would be the wild color, the falling of the leaves, the scarlet berries, the smell of turned earth, wood smoke, damp; then winter, stinging cold, freezing the earth, cracking and breaking the clods, ice on the branches like white lace. There would be rain, snow, biting winds, and then spring again, delirious with blossom.

But his own certainties had fallen away. The safety he had built so carefully after Eleanor's death, thinking it the one indestructible thing, the path toward understanding the ways of God, even accepting them, was full of sudden weaknesses. It was a path across the abyss of pain, and it had given way under his weight. He was falling.

And here he was, almost home, where he was supposed to be the kind of strength for Judith that his father would have been. He had not watched closely enough, and John had never spoken of it, never shown him the needs and the words to fill them. He was not ready!

But he was in the main street. The houses were sleepy in the dusk, the windows lit. Here and there a door was open, the air still warm. The sound of voices drifted out. Shummer Munn was pulling weeds in his garden. Grumble Runham was standing on the street corner lighting his clay pipe. He grunted as Joseph passed him, and gave a perfunctory wave.

Joseph slowed. He was almost home. It was too late to find any answers to give Judith, or any wiser, greater strength.

He turned the corner and pedaled the final hundred yards. He arrived as the last light was fading, and put his bicycle away in the garage beside Judith's Model T, finding the space huge and profoundly empty where the Lanchester should have been. He walked around the side and went past the kitchen garden, stopping to pick a handful of sharp, sweet raspberries and eat them, then went in through the back door. Mrs. Appleton was standing over the sink.

"Oh! Mr. Joseph, you give me such a start!" she said abruptly. "Not that Oi i'n't pleased to see you, mind." She squinted at him. "Have you had any supper? Or a glass o' lemonade, mebbe? You look awful hot."

"I cycled over from Cambridge," he explained, smiling at her. The kitchen was familiar, full of comfortable smells.

"Oi'll fetch you some from the pantry." She dried her hands. "Oi dare say as you could eat some scones and butter, too? Oi made 'em today. Oi'll fetch 'em to the sitting room for you. That's where Miss Judith is. She in't expecting you, is she? She din't say nothing to me! But your bed's all made up, loike always."

He already felt the warmth of home settle around him, holding him in a kind of safety. He knew every gleam of the polished wood, just where the dents were, the thin patches worn into carpets by generations of use, the slight dips in the floorboards, which stairs creaked, where the shadows fell at what time of day. He could smell lavender and beeswax polish, flowers, hay on the wind from outside.

Judith was sitting curled up on the couch with her head bent over a book. Her hair was pulled up hastily, a little lopsided. She looked absorbed and unhappy, hunched into herself. She did not hear him come in.

"Good book?" he asked.

"Not bad," she replied, uncurling herself and standing up, letting the book fall closed onto the small table. She looked at him guardedly, keeping her emotions protected. "I like my fairy tales with a little more reality," she added. "This is too sweet to be believable—or I suppose any good, really. Who cares whether the heroine wins if there wasn't any battle?"

"Only herself, I imagine." He looked at her more closely. There were shadows of tiredness around her eyes and very little color in her skin. She was dressed in a pale green skirt, which was flattering because she moved with grace, but very ordinary. Her white cotton blouse was such as most young women choose in country villages: high to the neck, shaped to fit, and with minimum decoration. She was not interested in whether it pleased anyone else or not. He realized with a sense of shock the change in her in a few weeks. The regularity of her features was still there, the gentleness of her mouth, but the vitality that made her beautiful was gone.

"Mrs. Appleton's bringing me some scones and lemonade. Would you like any?" He said it to break the silence; he was thinking how badly he had neglected her.

"No, thanks," she replied. "I've already had some. Did you come home for anything in particular? I suppose they don't know who killed Sebastian Allard yet? I'm sorry about that." She met his eyes, trying to read if he was hurting.

He sat down, deliberately choosing his father's chair. "Not yet. I'm not even sure if they're getting any closer."

She sat down also. "What about Mother and Father?" she asked. "Matthew doesn't tell me anything. Sometimes I think he forgets I even know about it being murder, or about the document. We still get the papers, and the news is awful. Everyone in the village is talking about the possibility of war."

Mrs. Appleton brought in his scones and lemonade, and he thanked her. When she had gone, he looked at Judith again and realized how little he knew her inner strengths and weaknesses. Could she bear the truth that they had no idea who had killed John Reavley, or that his whole judgment of the document could be flawed? He might have died for a simple crime of greed. Could she bear to know that war was a real possibility that nobody could measure? The whole future lay ahead clouded and uncertain—perhaps worse than that, even tragic.

A hard knot of anger clenched inside Joseph against his father. John Reavley should have had more sense than to tell Matthew he had a document that could rock the world, and then to drive unprotected along the road, for someone to kill . . . and not only him, but Alys as well!

"Well, are they right?" Judith demanded, breaking into his thoughts. "Are they right? Is there going to be a war? You can't be so isolated in your ivory tower that you don't know Austria and Serbia are on the brink!"

"I'm not." He said it with the sharpness of his own anger and frustration. "Yes, they are, and I expect Austria will march into Serbia and conquer it again."

"They're talking about Russia getting involved as well if that happens," she persisted.

"It's possible all Europe could be involved," he said, meeting her eyes. "It's not likely, but if it does happen, then we may be drawn in. It's also possible that they will come back from the brink, seeing what it will cost them."

"And if they don't?" She struggled to keep her voice level, but her face was white.

He stood up and walked over to the French windows opening onto the garden.

"Then we'll have to conduct ourselves with honor and do what we've always done—send our armies to the battle," he replied. "I daresay it won't last very long. It's not Africa, where there are vast stretches of open country to hide in."

She must have risen to her feet also, because she spoke from just behind him. "I suppose not." She hesitated a moment. "Joseph, do you think that was what Father knew about? I mean, something to do with the assassination in Sarajevo? Could he have stumbled onto the plan for that?"

Did she want to believe it? It would be far easier than supposing some new danger. It was a moment of judgment. Evasion, or the truth that he did not know? "Perhaps," he agreed, walking out onto the grass. She followed him. The night was balmy and softly scented with the heavy sweetness of pinks and late lilies. "Maybe there was no date on it, and he didn't realize it was planned for that day."

"No, it wasn't," she said grimly. "That doesn't have anything to do with England's honor!" He heard the vibrancy in her voice. She was angry, alive again. "Don't condescend to me, Joseph!" She caught his arm. "I hate it when you do that! Killing an Austrian archduke has got nothing to do with England."

"It was your suggestion," he pointed out, stung by her remark about his condescension, because he knew it was true. Evasion had been a mistake.

"And it was stupid," she went on. "Why can't you tell me I'm stupid honestly? Don't always be so damn polite! I'm not your congregation, and you're not my father! But I suppose you're trying to be, and at least you're somebody I can talk to properly."

"Thank you," he said drily. It was a backhanded compliment he had not deserved, and he was disturbed by how much it mattered to him.

They passed the border and were snared in the warm, sweet perfume. A barn owl swooped low between the trees and disappeared on soundless wings.

"Don't you want to know what the document was?" she asked.

"Of course I do." He said it automatically, and only afterward realized that if it was something their father had misjudged, then perhaps he would rather not.

He stopped at the edge of the lawn and she stood beside him, the moonlight on her face. "Then we ought to be able to find out where he got it, surely," she said. "He can't have had it very long, or he would have taken it to Matthew sooner." Her voice was steady now, some inner resolve asserting itself.

"We've already tried to find out everywhere he went for several days before that," he answered. "He saw the bank manager, Robert Isenham, and old Mr. Frawley, who keeps the curiosity shop up on the Cambridge Road." He looked at her gently. "He and Frawley know each other pretty well. If Father had just discovered anything awful, Frawley would have known there was something wrong."

"Mother went to see Maude Channery the day Father called Matthew," she said seriously.

"Who is Maude Channery?" If he knew, he had forgotten.

"One of Mother's good causes," she answered, struggling for a moment to keep her voice level. "Father couldn't bear her, said she was a fearful old fraud, but he drove Mother there anyway."

"He'd have to, if it was far," he pointed out. "Unless you did—and Mother would never go to visit anyone important in your Model T! Not if the Lanchester was available."

"I could have driven her in the Lanchester," she argued.

"Oh? Since when could you drive that?" he said, surprised. "Or more to the point, since when would Father have let you?"

"Since he couldn't stand Maude Channery," she retorted, a tiny flash of humor in her voice, there and then gone again. "But he didn't. He took Mother. And when they came back he went straight to his study, and Mother and I had supper alone."

He hesitated. The idea was absurd. "Surely you aren't suggesting he got a document of international importance from an old woman who was one of Mother's good causes?"

"I don't know! Can you think of somewhere better to start? You haven't got anything, and neither has Matthew."

"We'll go and see her tomorrow if you like," he offered.

She gave him a wry look, and he knew it was on the tip of her tongue to tell him again not to be so condescending, but instead she simply accepted. She said that they would make it a morning call, before he could change his mind—and she would be ready at ten.

Joseph woke up early. It was a warm, blustery day, the wind full of the fine dust of the first crops being gathered. He walked down to the village and collected the Sunday papers from Cully Teversham at the tobacconists, and exchanged the usual pleasantries—a word about the weather, a spot of local gossip—and left to go home again. He passed a few neighbors on the way, and nodded good morning.

He intended not to open the papers until breakfast, but his curiosity overcame him. The news was worse than he had expected. Serbia had rejected Austrian demands, and diplomatic relations had been broken off. It seemed like the prelude to war. Russia had declared that it would act to protect Serbia's interests. Who would win the Tour de France seemed like an issue from another era already sliding into the past, almost irretrievable even now, and a visit to Maude Channery was the last thing on his mind.

But he had promised Judith, and at least it would make up for some of the time he had been so absorbed with his own emotions that he had forgotten hers.

They set off at ten o'clock, but it took them until after half past to drive as far as Cherry Hinton. After making inquiries at the village shop, they found Fen Cottage on the outskirts, and parked the car just around the corner.

They had knocked twice on the front door before it swung open and they were faced by a short, elderly woman leaning heavily on a walking stick. It was not an elegant cane with a silver tip, but a plain, stout wooden affair, such as a man would use to bear his weight. Her face was set in irritation, and her frizzy white hair was pinned up in a style twenty years out of fashion. Her black skirts brushed the floor and looked as if she had inherited them from someone at least three inches taller.

"If yer lookin' for the Taylors, they moved six months back, an' Oi dunno where to," she said abruptly. "An' if it's anyone else, ask Porky Andrews at the shop. He knows everythin' an'll likely tell you, whether you care or not." She ignored Judith and looked Joseph up and down curiously.

"Mrs. Channery?" he asked. His days as a parish priest came back to his mind with cutting clarity. How often he had called on resentful people who were raw-tongued from pride, guilt, or the need to guard some pain they could neither accommodate nor share. "I'm Joseph Reavley, and this is my sister Judith. I believe you were a great friend of our mother's." He did not make it a question.

"Oh!" She was taken by surprise. The tart remark she had been going to make died on her lips. Something inside her softened. "Yes . . . well . . . well Oi suppose Oi were. Terrible thin'. Oi'm rale sorry. We'll all miss her. Not much point in tellin' you my sympathies. Won't do no good."

"I'd be glad to accept a cup of tea." Joseph was not going to be put off.

"Then you'd better come on in," Mrs. Channery responded. "Oi don't serve on the doorstep." And she turned around and led the way into a remarkably pleasant sitting room, beyond which lay a small, overcrowded garden backing onto the churchyard. He could clearly see a pale carved angel above the hedge, neatly outlined against the dark mass of yew trees.

Mrs. Channery followed his glance. "Humph!" she snorted. "On good days Oi think he's watching over me . . . most times Oi say as he's just snoopin'!" She pointed to the couch and another chair. "If you want tea, Oi et to put the kettle on, so you'd best sit down whoile Oi do. Oi've got biscuits. Oi'm not cuttin' cake at this toime in the mornin'."

Judith swallowed her temper with an effort that was visible, at least to Joseph. "Thank you," she said meekly. "May I help you carry anything?"

"Great heavens, choild!" Mrs. Channery exclaimed. "What d'you think Oi'm bringin'? It's only elevenses."

Anger flushed up Judith's face, but she bit back her response.

Mrs. Channery swiveled on her heel and disappeared into the kitchen.

Judith looked at Joseph. "Mother deserves to be canonized for putting up with her!" she said in a savage whisper.

"I can see why Father loathed her," he agreed. "I wonder why he came."

"With a sword, in case it was necessary, I should think!" Judith retorted. "Or a packet of rat poison!"

Joseph's mind worried at the question. Why had John Reavley come here? Judith could quite easily have driven Alys, and Alys would consider it a useful lesson for her in charitable duty. John tended to avoid unpleasant people, and his tolerance of rudeness was low. He admired his wife's patience, but he had no intention of emulating it.

Mrs. Channery returned, staggering a little under the weight of a large and very well set tea tray. She had kept her word that there was no cake, but there were three different kinds of biscuits, and homemade raisin scones with plenty of butter.

Joseph leaped to his feet to help her, taking the tray before she dropped it, and setting it down on the small table next to a floral jug filled with sweet williams. The ritual of pouring, accepting, passing around the food and making appropriate remarks was all observed to the letter. It was several minutes before Joseph could broach the subject for which they had come. He had given it some thought, but now it seemed foolish. The only thing to be gained by this visit was the time spent with Judith. On the way over they had spoken of odd, unimportant things, but she had seemed to be easier, and once or twice she had actually laughed.

"You have a lovely garden," Joseph remarked.

"It's all over tossled," Mrs. Channery retorted. "Oi can't be frabbed doin' the work, an' I can't be payin' that daft man what does Mrs.

Copthorne's. She pays him twice what he's worth, the more fool her! An' it's still full o' meece! I seen 'em!"

Joseph could sense Judith biting her tongue. "Perhaps that's why I like it," he replied, refusing to be put off.

"Makes yours look good, do it?" Mrs. Channery demanded.

"Yes, it does," he agreed, smiling at her. Out of the corner of his eye he saw Judith's expression of disgust. He noticed an enormous borage plant overtaking its neighbors. "And you have quite a few herbs."

"Gardener, are you?" Mrs. Channery said drily. "Thought you was an airy-fairy sort o' man up at the university."

"One can be both," he pointed out. "My father was, but I expect you know that."

"No idea," she responded. "Scarce saw him. Long enough to be civil, an' then he were off again like Oi'd bit him."

Judith sneezed—at least it sounded something like a sneeze.

"Really?" Joseph said, his attention suddenly held as if in a vise. "He didn't stay with Mother the last time she was here?"

"Din't even stay for tea." She shook her head. Chocolate cake, Oi had. An' Madeira, both. Looked at it loike he hadn't eaten for a week, then went straight out o' the door an' got into that great big yellow car of his. Smelly things, cars," she added. "An' noisy. Dunno why a civilized man can't use an horse an' carriage. Good enough for the queen, God bless her memory." Her lips thinned, and she blinked several times. "Don't get horses goin' mad an' runnin' all off the road into the trees an' killing good folk!"

"Yes, you do!" Judith contradicted her. "Hundreds of horses have taken fright at something and bolted, taking carriages off the road, into trees, hedges, ditches, rivers even. You can't spook a car. It doesn't take fright at thunder, or lightning, or a flapping piece of cloth." She drew in her breath. "And wheels fall off carriages just as often as off cars."

"Thought you'd lost your tongue," Mrs. Channery said with satisfaction. "Found it again, have you? Well, nothin' you say'll get me into one of them machines!"

"Then I shan't try," Judith answered, exactly as if it had been the next thing she had intended. "Do you know where he went?"

"Who? Your father? Do you think Oi asked him, Miss Reavley? That would be very ill-fatched up o' me, now wouldn't it?"

Judith's eyes widened for a moment. "Of course you wouldn't, Mrs. Channery. But he might have said. I imagine it wasn't a secret."

"Then you imagine wrong," Mrs. Channery pronounced with immense pleasure. "It were a secret. Your dear ma asked him, an' he went four wont ways about answerin'. Just said he'd be back for her in an hour . . . an' he weren't! Took him an hour and a half, but she never said a word." She fixed Judith with an accusing eye. "Good woman, your ma was! No one left like her no more."

"I know," Judith said quietly.

Mrs. Channery grunted. "Shouldn't have said that," she apologized. "Not that it ain't true. But it don't do no good cryin'. Not what she'd have wanted. Very sensible woman, she were. Lots o' patience with others what was all but useless, but none for herself. An' she'd have expected you to be like her!"

Judith glared at her, angry not only at what she had said, but that she, of all people, should have known Alys well enough to have understood so much about her.

"You were very fond of her," Joseph observed, to fill the silence more than anything else.

Mrs. Channery's lips trembled for a moment. "O' course Oi were!" she snapped at him. "She knew how to be kind without lookin' down on folks, an' there ain't many what can do that! She never come by without askin' first, an' she ate my cake. Never brought any of her own, like needin' to keep score. But she brought me jam now an' then. Apricot. An' Oi never told her as how the rhubarb jam was horrible. Like so much boiled string, it were. Oi gave it to Diddy Warner, her with the toddy-grass all up in the air like a gummidge. That surprised her. Should have seen the look on her face." She smiled with satisfaction.

"With the hair like a scarecrow?" Judith clarified.

"In't that what I just said?" Mrs. Channery asked.

"I can imagine!" Judith said frankly. "She was the one who gave it to Mother! It was disgusting."

To Joseph's amazement, Mrs. Channery burst into laughter. It was a deep, chesty guffaw of delight, and she laughed so hard he was afraid she was going to choke. The sound was so genuine and so infectious, he found himself joining in, and then after a moment, Judith did also. Suddenly he knew why his mother had bothered with Maude Channery.

They stayed another half hour, and left in surprisingly good spirits.

Walking back to the car, they were serious again.

"He went somewhere," Judith said urgently, catching Joseph's sleeve and forcing him to stop. "How can we find out where? He was different when he returned, and that night he called Matthew. It has to be where he got the document!"

"Perhaps," he agreed, trying to keep his thoughts in check. They started working again. He wanted intensely to believe that there really had been a document of the importance his father had attached to it. And yet if there had been, the implications were enormous, stretching into an uncertain and dangerous future. And where was it now? Had John Reavley managed to put it somewhere safe before he was killed? If so, why had no one found it?

They reached the car.

"What are we going to do?" Judith demanded, slamming the door as Joseph cranked up the handle at the front and the engine jumped to life. He took the handle out and climbed in beside her, closing his own door more gently. The car moved away, and she changed gear with practiced ease.

"We're going home to see what Appleton knows about where the car went," Joseph replied.

"Father wouldn't have told him." She steered with panache around the corner and into the main road from Cherry Hinton back toward St. Giles.

"Doesn't Appleton still clean the car?" he asked.

She glanced at him sideways and increased speed.

He put out a hand to steady himself.

"Of course he does," she answered. "You think he'd have noticed something? Such as what?"

"We'll ask him. And from what Mrs. Channery said, Mother was there an hour and a half, so he can only have gone a certain distance. We ought to be able to narrow it down. If we ask, someone will have seen him. The Lanchester was rather noticeable."

"Yes!" she said exuberantly, pressing her foot down harder on the accelerator and sending the car forward at nearly fifty miles an hour.

Asking Appleton turned out to be a delicate matter. They found him in the garden staking up the last of the delphiniums, which were beginning to sag under their own weight.

"Alfred," Joseph began, "when my father returned from taking Mother to visit Mrs. Channery at Cherry Hinton, did you clean the car afterward?"

Appleton straightened up, his face dark. "O' course Oi cleaned the car, Mr. Joseph! An' checked the brakes an' the fuel an' the tires! If you think Oi din't—"

"I want to work out where he went!" Joseph said quickly, realizing what accusation Appleton had assumed. "I thought you might be able to help me, from anything you observed."

"Went?" Appleton was confused. "He took Mrs. Reavley to Cherry Hinton."

"Yes, I know. But he left her there and went somewhere else, then came back for her."

Appleton tied up the last sky-blue delphiniums absentmindedly and stepped out of the flower bed onto the path. "You think summin' happened to the car?"

"No, I think perhaps he saw someone, and I need to know who it was." He did not intend to tell Appleton more than that. "It's about three and a half miles from here to Cherry Hinton. Is there any way you can tell how much farther he went?"

"Course Oi can. Just got to look at the milometer. That'll tell you pretty exact. Course it won't say where to, only how far."

Joseph felt the silence settle into the hot garden with its motionless flowers, gaudy splashes of color, butterflies pinned like precarious ornaments onto the lilies.

"Did you see anything at all that would help us to know where they went?"

Appleton screwed up his face.

"Dust?" Joseph suggested. "Gravel? Mud? Clay? Peat, maybe? Or manure? Tar?"

"Loime," Appleton said slowly. "There was loime under the wheel arches. Et to wash it off."

"Lime kilns!" Joseph exclaimed. "He was gone an hour and a half altogether. How fast does the Lanchester go? Forty . . . fifty-five?"

"Mr. Reavley was a very good driver," Appleton said pointedly, looking at the path where Judith was coming toward them. "More loike thirty-five."

"I see."

Judith reached them and looked inquiringly from Joseph to Appleton and back again.

"Appleton found lime on the car," Joseph said to her. "Where are the nearest lime kilns, close enough to the road that the lime itself would be tracked across, so someone would pick it up?"

"There are lime kilns on the roads south and west out of Cherry Hinton itself," she answered. "Not east back to St. Giles or Cambridge, or north toward Teversham or Fen Ditton."

"So what lies south or west?" he said urgently.

"Over the Gog Magog hills? Stapleford, Great Shelford," she said thoughtfully, as if picturing the map in her mind. "To the west there's Fulbourn, or Great and Little Wilbraham. Where shall we start?"

"Shelford's only a couple of miles from here," he replied. "We could start there and work our way north and west. Thank you, Appleton."

"Yes, sir. Will there be anything else?" Appleton looked puzzled and faintly unhappy.

"No, thank you. Unless there's anything he might have said about where he went?"

"No, sir, not that Oi can think. Will you be taking the car out again, Miss Judith? Or shall Oi put it away?"

"We'll be going straight out, thank you," she replied firmly, turning back toward the house without waiting for Joseph.

"What shall we say to the people if we find out where he got the document?" she asked when they were on their way out of St. Giles again on the road southward, climbing almost immediately up into the shallow hills. She kept her eyes on the road ahead. "They'll know who we are, and they have to realize why we've come." It was a question, but there was no hesitation in her voice, and her hands were strong and comfortable on the wheel. If there was tension in her, she masked it completely.

He had not thought of that in detail; all that weighed on his mind was the compulsion to know the truth and silence the doubts.

"I don't know," he answered her. "Mrs. Channery was easy enough; it seemed like following Mother's footsteps. I suppose we could say he left something behind?"

"Like what?" she said with faint derision. "An umbrella? In the hottest, driest summer we've had in years! A coat? Gloves?"

"A picture," he answered, the solution coming to him the instant before he spoke. "He had a picture he was going to sell. Are they the people he was going to show it to?"

"That sounds reasonable. Yes . . . good." Unconsciously she increased the speed, and the car surged forward, all but clipping the edge of the grass on the side of the road.

"Judith!" he cried out involuntarily.

"Don't be stuffy!" she retorted, but she did slow down. She had been almost out of control, and she knew it even better than he did. What it took him longer to realize, and he did it with surprise, was that it was exuberance that drove her, the feeling that at last she was able to do something, however slight the chances of success. It was not fear, either of the process or of the discovery of facts she might find painful.

He was looking at the profile of her face, seeing the woman in her and beginning to understand how far behind the child had become, when she turned and shot him a glance and then a quick smile.

He drew breath to tell her to concentrate on the road, then knew it would be wrong. He smiled back and saw her shoulders relax.

They stopped in Shelford and asked, but no one had seen John Reavley on the Saturday before his death, and the yellow Lanchester was a car they would have remembered.

They had sandwiches and a glass of cider on the village green outside the pub at Stapleford.

He was not quite sure what to say, afraid in case his voice unintentionally carried disappointment. While he was still considering, she began the conversation, talking about various things, interesting but inconsequential. He felt himself gradually enjoying it, his mind following hers as she spoke of Russian theater, then Chinese pottery. She was full of opinions. He did not appreciate how hasty they were until it dawned on him that she was speaking to reassure him, to lend him the strength of normality and of not being the leader for a little while. It amazed him and embarrassed him a little, and yet there was a warmth to it that for an instant brought a sharp prickle to his eyes, and he was obliged to turn away.

If she noticed it, she affected not to.

Afterward they drove north again. They turned right on the Works Causeway, past the gravel pits and the clunch pit—named for the peculiar sticky local clay—and drove into the village of Fulbourn. It was nearly three o'clock, a bright afternoon with the heat shimmering up from the road. Even the cows in the fields sought the shade, and the dogs lying on the grass under the trees and hedges were panting contentedly.

They swung into the main village street and drew to a stop. It was almost deserted. Two boys of about seven or eight stared at them curiously. One of them had a ball clutched in a grubby hand, and he smiled, showing a gap where his front tooth was still growing in. He was obviously more interested in the car than in either of its occupants.

"Ever seen a yellow car?" Joseph asked him casually.

The boy stared at him.

"Do you want to look inside?" Judith offered.

The other boy backed away, but the gap-toothed one was braver or more curious. He nodded.

"Come on, then," she encouraged.

Step by step he came toward the car and then finally was persuaded to peer inside the open door while she explained to him what everything was and what it did. Finally she asked again if he had seen a yellow car.

He nodded slowly. "Yes, miss. Bigger'n this, but Oi never seed inside it."

"When was that?"

"Donno," he answered, still wide-eyed. "Way back."

And no matter how she tried, that was all he knew. She thanked him and reluctantly he allowed her to close the door. He gave her a beaming smile, then turned and ran away and disappeared into a crack between two cottages, closely followed by his companion.

"Hopeful," Judith said with more courage than belief. "We'll ask again."

They found an elderly couple out walking, and a man with a dog, strolling in a side lane, thoughtfully sucking at his pipe. None of them remembered a yellow car. Neither did anyone else in Fulbourn.

"We'll have to try Great and Little Wilbraham," Joseph said flatly. "Not very far." He glanced at her and saw the anxiety in her eyes. "Are you all right?"

"Of course!" she answered, staring back at him levelly. "Are you?"

He smiled at her, nodding, then started up the car again and climbed in. They headed back into Fulbourn and from there north across the railway line east to Great Wilbraham. The streets were quiet, towering trees motionless except for the topmost leaves flickering gently in the breeze. A flock of starlings swirled up in the sky. A tabby cat blinked sleepily on top of a flat gatepost. The peal of church bells sounded clear and mellow in the warm air, familiar, gentle as the smell of hay or the sunlight on the cobbles.

"Evensong," Joseph observed. "We'll have to wait. Would you like something to eat?"

"It's early for dinner," she answered.

"Tea?" he suggested. "Scones, raspberry jam, and clotted cream?"

They found a tea shop willing to serve them at this hour. Afterward they went back into the street and walked up toward the church just as the congregation was leaving.

It was not easy to approach someone gracefully, and Joseph was awaiting an opportunity when the vicar saw him and walked over, smiling at Judith and then speaking to Joseph.

"Good evening, sir. Another beautiful day. Sorry you're just too late for the service, but if I can be of any help?"

"Thank you." Joseph looked around with genuine appreciation at the ancient building, the worn gravestones leaning a little crookedly in the earth. The grass between was neatly mowed, here and there fresh flowers laid in love. "You have a beautiful church."

"We have," the vicar agreed happily. He looked to be in his forties, a round-faced man with a soft voice. "Lovely village. Would you care to look around?" His glance included Judith.

"Actually, I think my late father may have come here a little while ago," Joseph replied. "His car was rather distinctive, a yellow Lanchester."

"Oh, yes!" the vicar said with obvious pleasure. "Delightful gentleman." Then his face clouded. "Did you say 'late'? I'm so sorry. Please accept my sympathies. Such a nice man. Looking for a friend of his, a German gentleman. I directed him to Frog End, where he had just rented the house." He shook his head, biting his lip a little. "Really very sad. Takes a lot of faith sometimes, it really does. Poor gentleman was killed in an accident just after that himself."

Joseph was stunned. He was aware of Judith beside him drawing in her breath in a gasp. Her fingers dug into his arm. He tried to keep himself steady.

"Out walking about in the evening and must have slipped and fallen into Candle Ditch," the vicar went on sorrowfully. "Up where it meets the river near Fulbourn Fen." He shook his head a little. "He wouldn't know the area, of course. I suppose he hit his head on a stone or something. And you say your poor father died recently as well. I'm so sorry."

"Yes." Joseph found it difficult to gather his feelings in the face of this sudden very real compassion. Indifference woke anger, or a sense of isolation, and that was in some ways easier. "Did you know this German gentleman?"

An elderly couple passed; the vicar smiled at them but turned back to Joseph and Judith to indicate he was engaged, and the couple moved on.

"I did not know him closely, I regret to say," the vicar shook his head. They were still standing out on the road in the sun. "But it was actually I who rented him the house, on behalf of the owner, you know. An elderly lady who lives abroad now. Herr Reisenburg was a very clever gentleman, so I'm told, a philosopher of some sort—kept largely to himself. Melancholy sort of person." Grief filled his mild face. "Not that he wasn't very pleasant, but I sensed a certain trouble within him. At least that's what I thought. My wife tells me I imagine too much."

"I think perhaps you were correct, and it was sensitivity rather than imagination," Joseph said gently. "Did you say his name was Reisenburg?"

The vicar nodded. "Yes, that's right, Reisenburg. Very distinguished-looking gentleman he was, tall and a little stooping, and soft-spoken. Excellent English. He said he liked it here. . . ." He stopped with a sigh. "Oh, dear. So much pain sometimes. I gathered from the gentleman in the yellow car that they were friends. Corresponded with each other for years, he said. He thanked me and drove toward Frog End. That was all I saw of him." He looked a little shyly at Judith. "I'm so sorry."

"Thank you." Joseph swallowed, the tightness almost choking his throat. "My father was killed in a car accident the next day . . . and my mother along with him."

"How very terrible," the vicar said in little more than a whisper. "If you would like to be alone in the church for a while, I can see that no one disturbs you." His invitation included both of them, but it was Joseph he reached out to touch, placing his hand on Joseph's arm. "Trust in God, my dear friend. He knows our path and has walked every step before us."

Joseph hesitated. "Did Herr Reisenburg have any other friends that you are aware of? Someone I might speak to?"

The man's face crumpled in regret. "None that I saw. As I said, he kept very much to himself. One gentleman asked for him, apart from your father, at least so I am told, but that's all."

"Who was that?" Judith asked quickly.

"I'm afraid I don't know," the vicar replied. "It was the same day as your father, and frankly I rather think it was just someone else he must have spoken to. I'm sorry."

Joseph found himself too filled with grief to answer. But he also believed that in Herr Reisenburg he had found the source of the document, and that he too had paid for it with his life. There was now no possibility whatever that John Reavley was mistaken as to its importance. But where was it now, and who was behind it?

"Don't you have any idea what that document was?" Judith asked when they were in the car again and turning toward home. "You must have thought about it."

"Yes, of course I have, and I don't know," he replied. "I can't remember Father ever mentioning Reisenburg."

"Neither can I," she agreed. "But obviously they know each other, and it was really important, or he wouldn't have gone looking for him while Mother was with Maude Channery. Why do you think Reisenburg had the document?" She negotiated a long curve in the road with considerable skill, but Joseph found himself gripping his seat. "Do you suppose he stole it from someone?"

"It looks like it," he replied.

She gave a shudder. "And they murdered him for it, only he'd already given it to Father—so they murdered Father. What do you suppose they're going to do with it? If they got it back then, it's four weeks ago now, so why hasn't anything happened?" Her voice dropped. "Or has it, and we just don't know?"

He wanted to be able to answer her, but he had no idea what the truth would be.

She was waiting; he knew it by the turn of her head, the concentration in her face.

"Matthew thinks there may have been two copies," he said quietly. "It isn't that they need one so much as they can't let the other one be roaming around, in case it falls into the wrong hands. That's why they're still looking." Fear for her seized him with an almost physical pain. "For God's sake, Judith, be careful! If anyone—"

"I won't!" she cut across him. "Don't fuss, Joseph. I'm perfectly all right, and I'll stay all right. It isn't in the house, and they know that! For heaven's sake, they've looked thoroughly enough. Are you staying tonight?

And I'm not asking because I'm afraid—I'd just like to talk to you, that's all." She gave a gentle, almost patient little smile and avoided looking at him. "You're not much like Father most of the time, but now and then you are."

"Thank you," he said as unemotionally as he could, but he found he could not add anything. His throat was tight, and he needed to look away from her at the long slope of the fields and compose himself.

CHAPTER

THIRTEEN

Joseph waited up alone for Matthew to return from seeing Shanley Corcoran. It was almost midnight.

"Nothing," Matthew replied to the unspoken question. He looked tired, his fair hair blown by the wind, but under the brief flush of travel he was pale. "He can't help." He sat down in the chair opposite Joseph.

"Want anything to drink?" Joseph asked. Then, without waiting for an answer, he told Matthew what he and Judith had discovered about Reisenburg.

Matthew seized on it. "That must be it!" he said, enthusiasm lifting his voice. He sat forward eagerly, his eyes bright, attention suddenly focused again. "Poor devil! It looks as if they killed him for it as well. No proof, of course." He rubbed his hand over his face, pushing his hair back. "It looks as if it must be as dangerous as Father said. I wonder how Reisenburg got it, and where from!"

Joseph had been thinking about that all evening. "He might have been the courier for it," he said dubiously. "But I think it's far more likely he stole it, don't you?"

"But where was he taking it when they caught up with him?" Matthew inquired. "Not to Father, surely? Why? If he'd been in any sort of intelligence service, I'd know!" He made it a statement, but Joseph could see in his eyes that it was a question. The yellow lamplight cast shadows on his face, emphasizing the uncertainty in him.

Joseph crushed his own doubts with an effort of will. "I think he just knew Father," he replied. "The people he stole it from knew he had it and were after him. He passed it to the only honorable person he could. Father was here. There was no time to get to London, or to whoever he meant to deliver it."

"No more than chance?" Matthew said with a twist of his lips. The irony of it hurt.

"Perhaps he came this way because this was where Father lived," Joseph suggested. "It seems he knew Cambridgeshire—he took the house here."

"Whom was he intending to give it to?" Matthew stared ahead of him into the distance. "If only we could find that out!"

"I don't know how," Joseph replied. "Reisenburg is dead, and the house is let out to someone else. We drove past."

"At least we know where Father got it." Matthew sat back, relaxing his body at last. "That's a lot. For the first time there's a glimmer of sense!"

They stayed up another half hour, arguing more possibilities along with the chances of finding out more about Reisenburg, and then the family went to bed, as Matthew had to get up at six and drive early to London. Joseph was to go back to Cambridge at a much more agreeable hour.

Almost as soon as he entered the gate Joseph ran into Inspector Perth, looking pale, hunch-shouldered, and jumpy.

"Don't ask me!" he said before Joseph had even spoken. "Oi don't know who killed Mr. Allard, but so help me God, Oi mean to find out, if Oi have to take this place apart man by man!" And without waiting for a reply he strode off, leaving Joseph openmouthed.

He had left St. Giles before breakfast, and now he was hungry. He walked across the quad in the sun, and under the arch to the dining hall. The mood was sombre. No one was in the mood for talking. There were murmurs about Irish rebels in the streets of Dublin, and the possibility of sending in British troops to disarm them, perhaps even as soon as today.

Joseph was busy catching up on essay papers all morning, and when he had time for his own thoughts at all, it was for Reisenburg, lying in a Cambridgeshire grave, unknown to whoever loved or cared for him, murdered for a piece of paper. Could the document possibly be to do with some as yet unimagined horror in Ireland that would stain England's honor even more deeply than its dealings with that unhappy country had done already? The more he thought of it, the less likely it seemed. It must be something in Europe, surely. Sarajevo? Or something else? A socialist revolution? A giant upheaval of values such as the revolutions that had swept the continent in 1848?

He did not wish to go to the hall for luncheon, and bought himself a sandwich instead. Early in the afternoon he was crossing the quad back to his rooms when he saw Connie Thyer coming from the shadow of the arch. She looked harassed and a little flushed.

"Dr. Reavley! How nice to see you. Did you have a pleasant weekend?"

He smiled. "In many ways, yes, thank you." He was about to ask her if she had also, and stopped himself just in time. With Mary Allard still her guest, still waiting for justice and vengeance, how could she? "How are you?" he asked instead.

She closed her eyes for a moment, as if exhaustion had overtaken her. She opened them and smiled. "It gets worse," she said wearily. "Of course this wretched policeman has to ask everyone questions: who liked Sebastian and who didn't, and why." Her face suddenly pinched with unhappiness, and her eyes clouded. "But what he is finding is so ugly."

He waited. It seemed like minutes because he dreaded what she was going to say; he was prolonging the moment of ignorance, and yet he was pretending. He did know.

She sighed. "Of course he doesn't say what he's found, but one can't help knowing, because people talk. The young men feel so guilty. No one wants to speak ill of the dead, especially when his family is so close by. And then they are angry because they are placed in a situation where they can't do anything else."

He offered her his arm, and they walked very slowly, as if intending to go somewhere.

"And because they have been cornered into doing something they are ashamed of," she went on, "poor Eardslie is furious with himself, and

Morel is furious with Foubister, who must have said something dreadful, because he is so ashamed he won't look anyone in the face, especially Mary Allard." She glanced at him, and away again. "And I think Foubister is afraid Morel had something to do with it, or at the very least may be suspected. Rattray is just as afraid, but I think for himself, and Perth won't leave him alone. The poor boy looks wilder every day. Even I am beginning to think he must know something, but whether it is something that matters or not, I have no idea."

They moved from the temporary shade of the archway out into the next quad.

"What about Elwyn?" he asked. He was concerned for them all, but Elwyn particularly. He was a young man with far too much weight to bear.

"Oh, dear," she said softly, but her voice was full of emotion. "That is the one thing for which I really dislike Mary. I never had children of my own."

Was it pain in her voice, masked over the years, or simply a mild regret? He did not turn to look at her—that would be unpardonably intrusive—but he thought of her love affair with Beecher with a new clarity. Perhaps there was more to understand than he had imagined.

"I cannot know what her loss is," she went on, looking at the sunlight on the grass ahead of her, and the castellated roof against the blue of the sky. "But Elwyn is her son also, and she is indulging her own grief without any thought for him. Gerald is useless! He mopes around, most of the time saying nothing beyond agreeing with her. And I'm afraid he is helping himself to rather too much of Aidan's port! He is glassy-eyed more often than not, and it is not simply out of grief or exhaustion. Although Mary would be enough to exhaust anyone!"

Joseph kept step with her.

"Poor Elwyn is left to try to comfort his mother," she said, shaking her head. "He's attempting to shield her from the less pleasant truths that are emerging about Sebastian, who has reached the proportions of a saint in her mind. Anyone would think he had been martyred for a great cause rather than killed by some desperate person, in all likelihood goaded beyond endurance." She stopped, turning to face Joseph, her eyes wretched. "It isn't going to last. It can't!"

He was startled.

"She's going to find out one day, she has to!" she said so softly he had to lean toward her to catch the words. Her voice was tight with fear. "And then what can we do for her?" Her eyes searched his. "For any of them? She's built her whole world around Sebastian, and it's not real!" Then she sounded surprised at herself. "Sometimes I feel desperately sorry for him. How could anyone live up to what she believed of him? Do you suppose the pressure of it, his own knowledge of what he was really like, drove him to some of the ugly things he seems to have done? Is that possible?"

"I don't know," he said honestly. They were walking very slowly. "Perhaps. He was remarkably gifted, but he had flaws like any of us. Maybe they now look the greater because we hadn't known they were there."

"Was that our fault?" she asked earnestly. "I thought he was . . . golden. That he was superbly clever, and that his character was as beautiful as his face."

"And his dreams," he added. His own voice was hoarse for a second as grief overcame him for the loss not only of Sebastian, but for a kind of innocence in himself, for the lost comfort it carried with it. "And yes, it was my fault, certainly," he added. "I saw him as I wanted him to be, and I loved him for that. If I were less selfish, I would have loved him for what he was." He avoided meeting her eyes. "Perhaps you can destroy people by refusing to see their reality, offering love only on your own terms, which is that they be what you need them to be—for yourself, not for them." It was true, gouging out the last pretence inside him, leaving him raw.

She smiled very slightly, and her voice was very gentle. "You didn't do quite that, Joseph. You were his teacher, and you saw and encouraged the best in him. But you are an idealist. I daresay none of us are as fine as you think."

Again her love for Beecher rushed into his mind, and the hard, abrasive thought that Sebastian had known of it and used it to manipulate Beecher into things painfully against his nature.

"No," he agreed quietly. They had reached the shade of the next archway and he was glad of it. "I think I have learned that. I wish I could help you with Mary Allard, but I'm afraid she is too fragile to accept the truth without it breaking her. She is a hard, brittle woman who has built a shell around herself, and reality won't intrude easily. But I'll be here. And if that is any help at all, please turn to me whenever you wish."

"Thank you, I fear I will," she replied. "I can't see the end of this, and I admit it frightens me. I look at Elwyn and I wonder how long he can go on. She doesn't seem even to be aware of his presence, let alone do anything to comfort him! I admit, sometimes I am so angry I could slap her." She colored faintly; it made her face vivid and uniquely lovely. He was aware of her perfume, which was something delicate and flowery, and of the depth of color in her hair. "I'm sorry," she said under her breath. "It's very un-Christian of me, but I can't help it."

He smiled in spite of himself. "Sometimes I think we imagine Christ to be a lot less human than He was," he replied with conviction. "I'm sure He must feel like slapping us on occasion—when we bring our grief not only upon ourselves, but upon everyone around us as well."

She thanked him again with a sudden smile, then turned to walk away back into the sun toward the master's lodgings.

Joseph sensed the tension mounting all afternoon. He saw Rattray carrying a pile of books. He walked quickly and carelessly, tripping on an uneven paving stone at the north side of the quad and dropping everything onto the ground. He swore with white-lipped fury, and instead of helping him, another student sniggered with amusement, and a third told him off for it sarcastically.

It was left to Joseph to bend down and help.

He met a junior lecturer and encountered several sarcastic remarks to which he replied calmly, and in his annoyance unintentionally snubbed Gorley-Brown.

The ill feeling finally erupted at about four o'clock, and unfortunately it was in a corridor just outside one of the lecture halls. It began with

Foubister and Morel. Foubister had stopped to speak to Joseph about a recent translation he was unhappy with.

"I think it could have been better," he complained.

"The metaphor was a little forced," Joseph agreed.

"Sebastian said he thought it referred to a river, not the sea," Foubister suggested.

Morel came by and had gone only a few steps beyond when he realized what he had overheard. He stopped and turned, as if waiting to see what Joseph would say.

"Do you want something?" Foubister asked abruptly.

Morel smiled, but it was more a baring of the teeth. "Sounds as if you didn't hear Sebastian's translation of that," he replied. "That's the trouble when you only get bits! It doesn't fit together!"

Foubister went white. "Obviously you got it all!" he retaliated.

Now it was Morel's turn to change color, only it was the opposite way, blood rushing to his cheeks. "I admired his work! I never pretended otherwise!" His voice was rising. "I still knew he was a manipulative swine when he wanted to be, and I'm not going to be hypocrite enough to go around saying he was a saint now that he's dead. For God's sake, somebody murdered him!"

There was a roll of thunder overhead and a sudden, wild drumbeat of rain. No one had heard footsteps approach, and they were all jolted into embarrassment when they saw Elwyn only a couple of yards away. He looked bowed with exhaustion, and there were dark smudges under his eyes, as if he were bruised inside.

"Are you saying that means he must have deserved it, Morel?" he asked, his voice tight in his throat and rasping with the effort of controlling it.

Foubister stared at Morel curiously.

Joseph started to speak, then realized that his intervention would only make it worse. Morel would have to answer for himself, if he could make his voice heard above the drumming of the rain on the windows and the gush of water leaping from the guttering.

Morel took a deep breath. "No, of course I'm not!" he shouted above the roar. "But whoever did it must have believed they had a reason. It would be much more comfortable to think it was a lunatic from outside who broke in, but we know it wasn't. It was one of us—someone who knew him for at least a year. Face it! Somebody hated him enough to take a gun and shoot him."

"Jealousy," Elwyn said hoarsely.

Beecher emerged from the doorway of the lecture room, his face white. "For God's sake, be quiet!" he shouted. "You've all said more than enough!" He did not appear to see Joseph. "Go on back to your work! Get out!"

"Rubbish!" Morel exploded, ignoring Beecher completely. "That's absolute bloody rubbish! He was a charming, brilliant, conspiring, arrogant sod who enjoyed his power over people, and for once he went too far." He swung his arm wide, almost hitting Foubister. "He made you run errands like a boot boy. He took Rattray's girlfriend, just to show everyone that he could." He glanced at Beecher and away again. "He got away with all kinds of things nobody else did!" His voice was almost a scream above the rain.

"Shut up, Morel, you're drunk!" Beecher shouted at him. "Go and put your head under the cold tap before you make even more of a fool of yourself. Or go and stand in the rain!" He jerked his hand toward the streaming window.

"I'm not drunk!" Morel said bitterly. "The rest of you are! You don't have any idea what's going on!" He jabbed his finger viciously in no particular direction. "Perth does! That miserable little bastard can see through us all. It'll give him a kick to arrest one of us. Can't you see it in his face—the glee? He's positively smacking his lips."

"Then at least it'll be over!" Foubister yelled it as if it was an accusation.

"No, it won't, you fool!" Morel shouted back at him. "It won't ever be over! Do you think we can just go back to the way we were? You're an idiot!"

Foubister launched himself at Morel, but Beecher had seen it coming and caught him in full flight, staggering backward to pitch up hard against the wall, Foubister in his arms.

Outside the rain was still roaring and hissing over the rooftops and bouncing back off the ground.

Beecher straightened up and pushed Foubister away. Foubister swung around to face Morel, Joseph, and Elwyn. "Of course we won't be the same!" he choked, his voice a sob. "For a start, one of us will be hanged!"

Elwyn looked dazed, as if someone had hit him also.

Morel was white to the lips. "Better than going to war, which is where the rest of us will end up," he lashed back. "He was always afraid of that, wasn't he—our great Sebastian! He—"

Elwyn lurched forward and hit Morel as hard as he could, sending him staggering backward to strike his head and shoulders on the wall and slither to a heap on the floor.

"He wasn't a coward!" Elwyn gasped out the words, tears streaming down his face. "If you say that again, I'll kill you!" And he aimed another punch, but Morel saw it coming and stumbled out of the way.

Beecher was staring at Elwyn in disbelief.

Elwyn jerked forward again, and Joseph grasped his arms, exerting all his strength to hold him, surprised to find it sufficient. "That was stupid," he said coldly. "I think you had better go and sober up, too. If we don't see you again until tomorrow, that will be more than soon enough." Elwyn went slack, and Joseph let him go.

Beecher helped Morel to his feet.

Elwyn glared sullenly at Joseph, then turned and walked away.

Morel shook himself and winced, then mumbled something, touching his jaw tentatively and smearing blood across his mouth.

"Maybe that will teach you to keep a wiser tongue in your head," Joseph said unsympathetically.

Morel said nothing, but limped away.

"Coward . . . ?" Beecher turned the word over as if he had discovered a new and profound meaning in it.

"Everybody's afraid," Joseph responded, "except those who are too arrogant to realize the danger. It's an easy word to fling around, and it's guaranteed to hurt pretty well anyone."

"Yes . . . yes, it is," Beecher agreed. "And I don't know what the hell we're going to do about it. Isn't there anything worth salvaging out of this? God knows what!" He pushed his hair off his forehead, gave Joseph a sudden, bright, gentle smile, and went back the way he had come.

The rain had stopped as suddenly as it had started. The wet stones of the quad steamed, and everything smelled sharp and clean.

Joseph continued on to his rooms. But he knew that he needed to face the fact that he was afraid Sebastian might have been morally blackmailing Beecher. He had either to prove it to be true, and perhaps destroy one of the best friends he had ever had, or else to prove it untrue—or at least that he was innocent of Sebastian's death—and release them both from the fear that now invaded everything. He must not avoid it any longer.

He walked across the quad and into the shade of his own stairway. The conclusion that Beecher and Connie Thyer were in love had become inescapable, but without any proof, how could Sebastian have blackmailed Beecher? Was that a delusion, one of the many born of fear? Now was the time to find out.

He turned and walked very slowly back out again and across to the stair up to Sebastian's rooms. The door was locked, but he found the bedder, who let him in.

"You sure, Dr. Reavley?" she said unhappily, her face screwed up in anxiety. "I'n't nothin' in there as worth seein' now."

"Please open it, Mrs. Nunn," he repeated. "It'll be all right. There's something I need to find—if it's there."

She obeyed, still pursing her lips with doubt.

He went in slowly and closed the door behind him. It was silent. He drew in a deep breath. It smelled stale. The windows had been closed for over three weeks, and the heat had built up, motionless, suffocating. Yet he could not smell blood, and he expected to.

His eyes were drawn to the wall. He had to look because he could think of nothing else until he did. It was in his mind's eye whichever way he faced, even if his eyes were closed.

It was there, paler than he had remembered, brown rather than red. It looked old, like something that happened years ago. The chair was empty, the books still piled on the table and stacked on the shelves.

Of course Perth would have been through them, and everything else, the papers, the notes, even his clothes. He would have to, searching for anything that would point to who had killed him. Obviously he had found nothing.

Still his own hands turned automatically through the pages of the notes, held up each book and ruffled it to find anything loose, anything hidden. What was he expecting? A letter? Tickets to something, or somewhere?

When he found the photograph he barely looked at it. The only reason it caught his attention at all was because it was Connie Thyer and Beecher standing together, smiling at the camera. There were trees close to them, massive, smooth-trunked, autumnal. Beyond them there was a path winding away toward a drop to the river, and up again at the far side. It could be anywhere. A couple of miles away there was a place not unlike it.

He put it down and moved on. There were other photographs: Connie and her husband, even one of Connie and Joseph himself, and several of students and various young women. He thought one was Abigail, standing beside Rattray and laughing.

He went back to the picture of Connie and Beecher. Something about it was familiar. But he was sure he had never seen it before. It must be the place. If it was somewhere near here, then he would know it, even though it was not the same place as the other pictures.

He held it in his hand, staring at it, trying to recall the scenery around it, the bank of the river beyond the camera's eye. It went upward steeply. He could remember walking it—with Beecher. They had been eating apples and laughing about something, some long, rambling joke. It had been a bright day, the sun hot on their backs, the stream rattling loudly below them. Little stones loosened and fell into the pool, splashing. The shadows were cool under the trees. There had been wild garlic. They were heading uphill, toward the open moorland, with huge, wind-raked skies—Northumberland!

What had Connie been doing in Northumberland with Beecher? Almost before he had finished asking, the answer was whole in his mind. He remembered her taking a holiday late the previous summer, just after he had come to Cambridge. She had gone north to visit a relative, an aunt or something. And Beecher had gone walking alone; Joseph had been mourning Eleanor and refused even to think of such a thing. He needed to be busy, his mind occupied until exhaustion took over. The thought of so much wild, solitary beauty was too powerful to bear.

But where had Sebastian found the photograph? A dozen answers were possible: found during a visit to Beecher's rooms, slipped out of the pocket of a jacket left over a chair, or even from the contents of Connie's handbag when it tipped over.

Was that what had unnerved Beecher to the point he had so openly criticized Sebastian, and at the same time allowed him to get away with such slipshod, challenging behavior? He was afraid. This was proof.

He put it into his pocket and turned to leave. The room was stifling now, the air heavy, choking in the throat. He fancied he could smell the dried blood on the wall and in the cracks of the floorboards. Did one ever really get such things out?

It was time to face Beecher. He went out and closed the door behind him. He felt stiff and weary, dreading what was to come.

It was windless and hot in the late slanting sunlight as he crossed the quad and went in through the door on the far side and up the stairs to Beecher's rooms. He dreaded having to be so blunt about what was a private subject, but nothing was truly private anymore.

He reached the landing and was surprised to see Beecher's door slightly ajar. It was unusual because it was an invitation to anyone to interrupt whatever he was doing, and that was completely out of character.

"Beecher?" he called, pushing it a few inches wider. "Beecher?"

There was no answer. Could he have slipped out to see someone, intending to be back in a moment or two, and simply left the door ajar?

He did not like to go in uninvited. He was going to intrude painfully enough when it was inevitable. He called out again, and there was still no answer. He stood, expecting to hear Beecher's familiar step any minute, but there was no sound except the call of voices in the distance.

Then at last there were footsteps, light and quick. Joseph spun around. But it was Rattray coming down from the floor above.

"Have you seen Dr. Beecher?" Joseph asked.

"No, sir. I thought he was in his rooms. Are you sure he isn't?"

"Beecher!" Joseph called again, this time raising his voice considerably.

Still there was silence. But it would be most unlike Beecher to have gone out and left his door open. He pushed it wider and went inside. There was no one in the study, but the bedroom door beyond was also ajar. Joseph walked over and knocked on it. It swung open. Then he saw Beecher. He was leaning back in the bedroom chair, his head lolled against the wall behind him. He looked exactly as Sebastian had: the small hole in his right temple, the gaping wound on the other side, the blood drenching the wall. Only this time the revolver was on the floor where it had fallen from the dead hand.

For a moment Joseph could not move for horror. It lurched up inside him, and he had the thought that he was going to be sick. The room wavered, and there was a roar in his ears.

He breathed in deeply and tasted bile in his throat. Gradually he backed out of the door and through the outer room to find Rattray still waiting on the landing. Rattray saw his face and the words were hoarse on his lips. "What is it?"

"Dr. Beecher is dead." Joseph's voice sounded strangled, as if his lungs were paralyzed. "Go and get Perth . . . or . . . someone."

"Yes, sir." But for several seconds Rattray was unable to move.

Joseph closed the door to Beecher's rooms and stood for a moment gasping for air. Then his legs buckled and he collapsed onto the floor, leaning his back against the door lintel. His whole body was shuddering uncontrollably, and the tears ran down his face. It was too much; he could not bear it.

At last Rattray went, stumbling down the first two or three steps, and Joseph heard his feet all the way down, then a terrible silence.

It seemed an eternity of confusion, horror and soul-bruising misery until Perth arrived with Mitchell and, a couple of paces behind him, Aidan Thyer. They went in past Joseph, and a few moments later Thyer came out, gray-faced.

"I'm sorry, Reavley," he said gently. "This must be rotten for you. Did you guess?"

"What?" Joseph looked up at him slowly, dreading what he was going to say. His mind was whirling; thoughts slipped out of his grasp, no coherence to them, but he knew they were black with tragedy.

Thyer held out his hand. "Come on. You need a stiff shot of brandy. Come back to the house and I'll get . . ."

Oh, God! Joseph was appalled as one thought emerged from the rest: Connie! She would have to be told that Beecher was dead! Who should tell her? It was going to be unbearable for her, whoever it was, but what would be least terrible? Her husband . . . alone? Could she mask her own feelings for Beecher? Was it even conceivable that Thyer knew?

Had Beecher taken his own life, knowing that the truth would come out and that he'd be blamed for Sebastian's murder? Joseph refused even to think that he might actually have done it—but the possibility hung on the dark edges of his mind. Or was it Aidan Thyer who had made it look like suicide, standing there in front of him, with his grave face and pale hair, his hand outstretched to help Joseph to his feet?

The answer was something he could not evade. Yes, he should go to the house, whether it was he or Thyer who told Connie. She would need help. If he did not go and there was a further tragedy, he would be to blame.

He grasped Thyer's hand and allowed himself to be pulled to his feet, accepting Thyer's arm to steady himself until he found his balance.

"Thank you," he said huskily. "Yes, I think a stiff brandy would be very good."

Thyer nodded and led the way down the stairs, across the quad and through the archway toward the master's lodgings. Joseph's mind raced as he walked beside him a little dizzily, every step drawing him closer to the moment that would end Connie's happiness. Would she believe Beecher had killed Sebastian? Had she even known of the blackmail? Had Beecher told her, or had he borne it alone? Or had the photograph been his?

And might she think it was Aidan Thyer? If she did, then she might be terrified of him herself. But Joseph could not stay there forever to protect her. What could he say or do so that she would be safe after he left? It was his responsibility, because he was the only one who knew.

Nothing. There was nothing anyone could do to save her from ultimately having to face the husband she had betrayed, at heart if not more.

They were at the door. Thyer opened it and held it for Joseph, watching him with care in case he staggered and tripped. Did he really look so dreadful? He must. He certainly felt it. He was moving in a nightmare, as if his body did not belong to him.

It seemed interminable moments before Connie appeared. For seconds she did not realize there was anything wrong, and she said something pleasant about having tea. Then slowly the look on Thyer's face registered with her, and she looked at Joseph.

Thyer was about to speak. Joseph must act now. He stepped forward a couple of paces.

"Connie, I'm afraid something very dreadful has happened. I think you had better sit down . . . please . . ."

She hesitated a moment.

"Please," he urged.

Slowly she obeyed. "What is it?"

"Harry Beecher has killed himself," he said quietly. There was no way to make it any better or gentler. All he could do now was try to save her from a self-betraying reaction.

There was an instant's terrible silence, then the blood drained from her face. She stared at him.

He stepped between her and her husband, taking her hands in his as if he could hold her together, in some physical fashion bridging the gulf of aloneness. What he really wanted was to shield her from Thyer's sight.

"I'm so sorry," he went on. "I know you were as fond of him as I was, and it is the most awful shock, on top of everything else that has happened. It was very quick, a single shot. But no one yet knows why. I'm afraid there is bound to be speculation. We must prepare ourselves."

She drew in her breath in a stifled little cry, her eyes wide and empty. Did she understand that he knew about them, that he was saying all this to give her whatever protection there was?

Thyer was at his elbow with two glasses of brandy. Joseph straightened up to allow him to give one to Connie. Had he any idea? Looking at his white face and pinched mouth told him nothing. It might as easily have been only the horror of yet another tragedy in his college.

Joseph took the brandy offered to him and drank it, choking on the unaccustomed fire of it in his throat. Then he felt it blossom inside him with artificial warmth, and it did help. It steadied him, gave him a little strength, even though he knew it was only temporary, and changed nothing.

Thyer took over. "We don't know what happened yet," he was telling Connie. "The gun was there on the floor beside him. It looks as if it is maybe the end of all this."

She stared at him and started to say something, but the words died in her throat. She shook her head, whimpering in pain she would always have to conceal. No one would understand; no one would offer her sympathies or make allowances for her grief. She would have to bear it alone, even pretend it did not exist.

That was something Joseph could do for her; he could share his own loss of a friend, recall all the good things about him and let her borrow his grief. Without the embarrassment of saying so, or requiring any confession or acknowledgment from her, he could let her know that he understood.

He stayed a little longer. They made meaningless remarks. Thyer offered them each another brandy, and this time he had one himself as well. After about half an hour, Joseph left and walked in a daze of grief back to his own rooms for one of the worst nights he would ever endure. He sank into sleep at last a little before one, and was engulfed in nightmare. He slipped in and out of it until five, then woke with a tight, pounding headache. He got up, made himself a cup of tea and took two aspirins. He sat in the armchair and read from Dante's *Inferno*. The passage through hell was vaguely comforting; perhaps it was the power of Dante's vision, the music of the words, and the knowledge that even in the worst pain of the heart he was not alone.

Finally at eight o'clock he went outside. The weather was exactly as it had been nearly all summer—calm and still, with a slight heat haze on the town—but inside St. John's suddenly the pressure seemed to have lifted.

Joseph met Perth, who was setting out across the quad.

"Ah! Morning, Dr. Reavley," Perth said cheerfully. He still looked tired, shadows around his eyes, but his shoulders were squared and his step was lighter. "Shame about Dr. Beecher. Oi know he were a friend o' yours, but mebbe it's the best way. Clean end. No trial. Best for poor Mr. Allard's family, too. Now the public don't need to have all the details."

The words, with Perth's unquestioning assurance, crystallized the anger inside Joseph. All Perth knew was that Beecher was dead and the gun was found next to him, yet he was happy, almost gleeful, to take it for granted that he had killed Sebastian and then himself. Arguments boiled up in Joseph's mind, along with fury at Perth's willingness to believe without looking any further. What about the others? They had known Beecher for years. Was all that carried away as if by a single flash flood? He wanted to shout at Perth to stop, to think, to weigh and measure. It was nothing like the man Joseph had known! How dare Perth, or anyone, be so certain?

But then Joseph himself had not seen the affair with Connie Thyer, right under his nose! Or that Sebastian had seen it and was using it in subtle blackmail. How well did he know anyone?

And it was all hideously reasonable. The words died on his lips. He was really only angry because Perth was relieved. Everyone would be. The suspicion had stopped. They would be able to start rebuilding all the old friendships that had been the fabric of their lives.

"Are you so very sure?" he said thickly, his voice strained.

Perth shook his head. "Makes sense, Reverend. About the only answer what does—when you think on it."

Joseph said nothing. The courtyard seemed to waver around him, like a picture blurred by rain.

"Looks like the same gun," Perth went on. "When we test it, Oi reckon we'll find as it is. Was a Webley that killed Mr. Allard. Did Oi ever tell you that."

Joseph stared into space, trying not to visualize it. Whatever had happened to Beecher, the scholarly, dry-humored man he had known, the good friend, that he would have killed Sebastian to protect his own reputation? Or was it Connie's? Thyer could have overlooked it if no one knew. Such things happened often enough. But to have made it public would be different. No man could ignore that. Beecher would have lost his position, but he could have found another, even if not in such a prestigious university as Cambridge, if not even in England! Surely better anything rather than murder?

Or was it to protect Connie? Perhaps she would have been divorced by Thyer. But even that was something they could have lived with.

And would Sebastian really have sunk so low as to tell people? It would have ruined Connie and Beecher, and made Thyer the butt of pity. But it would have broken forever Sebastian's own image as a golden youth. Surely he would not have done that simply to exercise power?

"I'm sorry, Reverend," Perth said again. "Very sad thing, an' hard to believe it o' friends. That's the trouble with a calling like yours. Always reckoning the best o' folk. Comes a shock when you see the other side. Now for me, Oi'm afraid it's no shock at all." He sniffed. "Still a shame, though."

"Yes . . ." Joseph pulled his thoughts together. "Yes, of course it is. Good day, Inspector." Without waiting for a reply he walked away toward the dining hall. He did not want to eat, and he certainly did not want company, but it was like getting into cold water—better done quickly.

In the hall there was the same slightly hysterical air of relief. People launched into conversation, then stopped suddenly and burst into high-pitched, self-conscious laughter. They were not sure whether it was decent to show their happiness that the weight of suspicion was gone, but they dared to look at each other, because words were no longer guarded against hidden meaning. They spoke of the future; they even told jokes.

Joseph found it intolerable. After a couple of slices of toast and a single cup of tea, he excused himself and left. They were behaving as if Beecher had not been one of them, as if they had not lost a friend in the most hideous way imaginable. The moment real friendship was put to the test they cut and ran.

That judgment was unfair, but it would not leave his mind, for all the sensible reasoning he used. The hurt was too great.

He was not certain whether to go back to the master's lodgings or not. He did not want to intrude on Connie in what must be a time she would bear only because there was no possible alternative. One could not die purely from misery. He had discovered that after Eleanor's death.

But even if he did not go specifically to see Connie, he should speak to Mary now that Beecher's death was generally accepted as the close of the case. They would be leaving to go home, and if he waited, it might be too late; it would seem as if he were indifferent.

He was shown into the sitting room by the parlor maid, and a few moments later Connie appeared. She might have doubted within herself whether she should wear black or not, but even if she had considered that it might be too revealing of her emotions, she had cast aside such caution. She wore a fashionable silk dress with a deep sash and pleated tunic, black from neck to hem, and black shoes. Her face was as white as chalk.

"Good morning, Joseph," she said quietly. "I imagine you have come to see Mrs. Allard. She has her vengeance now, and she can leave." Her eyes expressed the fury and the pain she dared not speak aloud. She dropped her voice to a whisper. "Thank you for coming yesterday evening. I . . . I . . ."

"You don't need to thank me," he interrupted. "I liked him very much. He was my best friend, right from the beginning." He saw her eyes fill with tears, and it was almost impossible to continue, his own throat was so tight. He could scarcely breathe from the weight constricting his chest.

At that moment Mary Allard came in through the door.

"Oh, good morning, Dr. Reavley." She still looked proud and angry, and she was dressed in unrelieved black. It flattered her olive complexion but not her gaunt body. "It is good of you to come to wish us goodbye." There was a faint softening in her voice.

He could not think what to say to her. Nothing in her yielded or offered warmth.

"I hope the resolution of the matter will give you some measure of peace," he said, and an instant later wished he had not. In saying that, he had wished Beecher's death to give her peace, and he felt like a betrayer.

"Hardly," she snapped. "And I would not have expected you, of all people, to suggest it!"

Connie drew in her breath. She stared back at Joseph defensively. Her voice shook when she spoke. "You have been willing to allow it said that my son blackmailed this wretched man over some sin or other, God knows what—no one will tell me—and that he murdered Sebastian to keep him quiet." She was trembling with bewilderment and unanswered pain. "The suggestion is monstrous! Whatever he had done, or Sebastian knew about, Sebastian would never have put pressure upon him, except to persuade him to act honorably." She gave a little gulp. "Obviously that failed, and the miserable man murdered Sebastian in order to protect himself. Now not only has this damnable place taken my son's life, but you would like to take from him as well the very memory of who and what he was. You are beneath contempt! If I do not meet you again, Dr. Reavley, I shall be much better suited."

Her words were both arbitrary and unjust. He was angry enough to retaliate, but the words did not come easily.

"People will say what they wish to say, Mrs. Allard," he said stiffly, his mouth dry. "Or what they believe to be true. I cannot stop them, nor would I, any more than I can stop you saying whatever you wish to about Dr. Beecher, who was also my friend."

"Then you are unfortunate in your choice of friends, Dr. Reavley," she snapped. "You are naive, and think too well of many people, but not well enough of others. I think you would be better served by some long and deep contemplation of your own powers of judgment." She lifted her chin a trifle higher. "It was civil of you to come to wish us goodbye. No doubt you considered it your duty. Please accept that it is done, and feel no need to call upon us further. Good day."

"Thank you," Joseph said with unaccustomed sarcasm. "That puts my mind greatly at ease."

She swung round and glared at him.

"I beg your pardon?"

"I shall feel free not to call upon you again," he answered. "I am obliged to you."

She opened her mouth to make some reply, and to her fury the tears flooded her eyes. She swung around and marched out, black silk skirts crackling, shoulders stiff.

Joseph felt guilty, and angry, and thoroughly miserable.

"Don't," Connie whispered. "She deserved that. She has been behaving for three weeks as if she were the only person in the world who has ever been bereaved. My heart aches for her, but I can't like her!" She took in a long, deep breath and let it out in a sob. "Even less now."

He looked at her. "Nor I," he said gently, and they both stood there, smiling and blinking, trying not to weep.

* * *

Joseph spent the rest of the day in a haze of misery. At night he slept poorly and rose late, grief washing back over him like a returning tide. He missed breakfast altogether, and forced himself to go back to the dining hall for luncheon. He had expected the conversation still to be about Beecher's death. He was startled to find instead that it was about yesterday's newspaper headlines, added to by this morning's. Somehow he had not taken any notice until now.

"Troops?" he said, turning from one colleague to another. "Where?"

"Russia," Moulton replied to his left. "Over a million men. The czar mobilized them yesterday."

"For the love of heaven, why?" Joseph was stunned. A million men! It was shattering and absurd.

Moulton stared at him dourly. "Because two days ago Austria-Hungary declared war on Serbia," he replied. "And yesterday they bombed Belgrade."

"Bombed . . . !" The coldness went through Joseph as if someone had opened a door onto a freezing night. "Bombed Belgrade?"

Moulton's face was tight. "I'm afraid so. I suppose with poor Beecher's death no one mentioned it. Ridiculous, I know, but the death of someone we know seems worse than dozens or even hundreds of deaths of people we don't—poor devils. God only knows what'll happen next. It seems we can't stop it now."

"I'm afraid it looks as if war in Europe is inevitable," Gorley-Smith said from the other side, his long face very grave, the light shining on his bald head. "Can't say whether it'll drag us in or not. Don't see why it should."

Joseph was thinking of a million Russian soldiers and the czar's promise to support Serbia against Austria-Hungary.

"Makes our troops in the streets of Dublin look like a very small affair, doesn't it?" Moulton said wryly.

"What!" Joseph exclaimed.

"On Monday," Moulton told him, raising his wispy eyebrows. "We sent the troops in to disarm the rebels." He frowned. "You'll have to pull yourself together, Reavley. It seems Allard was a bit of a wrong 'un after all. And poor old Beecher lost his head completely. Woman's reputation, I suppose, or something of the sort."

"Of the sort," Addison said sourly from the other side of the table. "Never saw him with a woman, did you?"

Joseph jerked up and glared at him. "Well, if it were something worth blackmailing him about, you wouldn't, would you!" he snapped.

Gorley-Smith raised his glass. "Gentlemen, we have far larger and graver issues to concern ourselves with than one man's tragedy and a young man who, it appears, was not as good as we wished to believe. It seems that Europe is on the brink of war. A new darkness threatens us, unlike anything we have seen before. Perhaps in a few weeks young men all over the land will be facing a far different future."

"It won't touch England!" Addison said with contempt. "It'll be Austria-Hungary and east, or north if you count Russia."

"Since they've just mobilized over a million men, we can hardly discount them!" Gorley-Smith retorted.

"Still a long way from Dover," Moulton said with assurance, "let alone London. It won't happen. For one thing, think of the cost of it! The sheer destruction! The bankers will never let it come to that."

Addison leaned back, holding his wineglass in his hand, the light shining through the pale German white wine in it. "You're quite right. Of course they won't. Anyone who knows anything about international finance must realize that. They'll go to the brink, then reach some agreement. It's all just posturing. We're past that stage of development now. For God's sake, Europe is the highest civilization the world has ever seen. It's all saber rattling, nothing more."

The conversation swirled on around Joseph, but he barely listened. In his mind he saw not the oak-beamed dining hall, the windows with their centuries of stained-glass coats of arms, but instead the evening sun shining long and golden across the river. He saw Sebastian staring at the beauty of Cambridge—the architecture as well as the glories of the mind and the heart treasured down the centuries—and dreading the barbarity of war and all it would break in the spirit of mankind.

Joseph still found it impossible to believe that Sebastian had really been a grubby blackmailer. And Harry Beecher. How could he have killed Sebastian?

And was any of it tied to the murders of John and Alys Reavley? Had

Sebastian witnessed their deaths and known who was responsible? Or was that only a hideous coincidence? How could it have anything to do with Reisenburg and whoever had killed him?

Or the worst thought of all: Was Sebastian blackmailing Beecher not over Connie but over the Reavleys' deaths?

Or was there someone else who had taken advantage of Beecher's love affair to hide the fact that it was he whom Sebastian was blackmailing? Someone Sebastian had seen lay that string of caltrops across the road?

Or was Joseph simply trying, yet again, to avoid a truth he found too painful to believe? For all his proclaimed love of reason, the faith in God he professed aloud, was he a moral coward, without the courage to test the truth, or the real belief in anything but the facts he could see? Did he trust God at all? Was it a relationship of spirit to spirit? Or just an idea that lasted only until he tried to make it carry the weight of pain or despair?

He laid down his napkin and rose to his feet. "Excuse me. I have duties I must attend to. I'll see you at dinner." He did not wait for their startled response, but walked quickly across the floor and out of the door into the sun.

It was time he looked at Sebastian's murder without any evasion or protection for his own feelings. He must have at least that much honesty. Perhaps he had not really accepted it until now. His emotions were still trying to absorb the death of his parents.

He was walking aimlessly, but swiftly enough to distract anyone from speaking to him.

Sebastian had been shot early in the morning, before most people were up. According to Perth, it had been with a Webley revolver, probably like the one that had killed Beecher. No one had admitted ever seeing such a gun in college. So where had it come from? Whose was it?

Surely the fact of having such a thing indicated intent to kill. Where did one buy or steal a gun? It was certain beyond any reasonable doubt that the same gun had been used both times, so where had it been that the police had not found it?

He walked over the Bridge of Sighs and out into the sun again. He knew St. John's better than the police possibly could. Surely if he applied his mind to the problem, he could deduce where the gun had been.

He passed a couple of students strolling, deep in conversation. A man and a young woman in a punt drifted lazily along the river. Three young men sat on the grass, absorbed in conversation. Another sat alone, lost in a book. Peace soaked into the bones like the heat of the sun. If they had read the same news as Moulton and Gorley-Smith, they did not believe it.

Where could one hide a gun that it would be retrievable, and in a condition in which it could be used again? Not the river. And not where anyone else would find it, either casually or because they were looking for it.

He stopped on the path and stood facing the college. As always, its beauty filled him with pleasure. From the Bridge of Sighs the fine brick was met by white stone sheer down into the water. Further on there was a short stretch of grass sloping to the river. The walls were smooth except for the windows, all the way up to the crenellated edge of the roof with its dormers and high chimneys.

But Perth's men had been up there.

All except the master's lodgings. In deference to the Allards, they had merely looked at it from the next roof over, from where they could see everything. The drainpipes down were wide at the neck, to catch the runoff from the roof behind. An idea stabbed his mind. Was it possible? It was the one place, so far as he knew, where no one had looked.

Could Beecher have put it there after killing Sebastian? And could he have retrieved it again in time to take his own life with it? But even if Joseph was right, there would be no way to prove it now.

Perhaps he could deduce it if he tried. Where should he begin? With everyone's movements after the discovery of Sebastian's body. Anyone climbing on the roof of the master's lodgings would have risked being noticed, even at half past five in the morning. At this time of the year it was broad daylight.

He started to walk slowly.

Was it possible they had kept it somehow concealed temporarily and then put it in a safe place later? Had it been in the top of the downpipe, it would have taken only a few moments to place it: a quick visit to one of the attic rooms with a dormer window, open it wide, lean far out and drop the gun, perhaps wrapped in something. Even a scarf or a couple of handkerchiefs would disguise the outline, then a few leaves.

If that were the answer, then it could only have been done from the master's lodgings. He could not imagine it was one of the servants. That reduced it to Aidan and Connie Thyer, Beecher if he had seen Connie there, and whoever else might have visited.

Whoever it was had to have concealed the gun very soon after Sebastian's murder was committed, because the police had started the search within an hour of their arrival.

What would he have done were he in that situation? Hidden it in the undergrowth in the Fellows' Garden until he was free to go back and get into the master's lodgings unobserved.

And to retrieve it again? Perhaps much the same.

It came back to Connie and Aidan Thyer—and perhaps Beecher. He could not believe it was Connie, but the more he thought of it, the more likely did it become that it was Thyer. Perhaps it was he whom Sebastian had seen on the Hauxton Road. Perhaps it was even he who was behind the plot itself. He was a brilliant man with a position of far more power than most people realized. As master of a college in Cambridge, he had influence over many of the young men who would, in a generation's time, be the leaders of the nation. He was sowing seeds the world would reap.

Now that the thought was in Joseph's mind, he had to test it until it was proved one way or the other. And there was only one place to begin. He would hate doing it, but he could think of no alternative.

He walked slowly back to the Bridge of Sighs and into St. John's, then across the inner quad to the master's lodgings. Thyer himself would be in the library at this time in the early afternoon. He hoped Connie would be at home.

The parlor maid let him in, and he found Connie standing at the window staring out at the bright flowers in the Fellows' Garden. She made an effort to smile at him. "Thank you for coming yesterday," she said a little huskily. "It was kind of you." She did not explain what she meant, and turned away again almost immediately. "I'm relieved the Allards have gone home and Elwyn has moved back to his own rooms. But the house is unnaturally quiet now. It seems like silence rather than peace. Is that absurd?"

"No," he answered. He hated what he was about to do, the more so because if it proved anything at all, it might be something she would infinitely prefer not to know. "I need to ask you one or two questions. . . ." He hesitated, not sure how to address her. Her Christian name was too familiar; using it would be taking something of a liberty. And yet to address her as Mrs. Thyer was both cold and bitterly ironic.

She was only mildly curious. "About what?"

He must do it. He could feel his body stiff and he was standing awkwardly. "I found a photograph in Sebastian's rooms." He hated this. He saw her stiffen, and he knew instantly that she was aware of it and that it meant all that he had supposed. "You met Harry in Northumberland. I know the place it was taken. He and I walked there."

The tears filled her eyes. "He told me," she whispered, her voice choked. "I didn't go there to meet him. It was almost by accident." She gave an awkward, lopsided little shrug. "I should have stopped myself. I knew it was wrong, and I knew what it would lead to—but I wanted it so much! Just once to have . . ." She looked away from him. It was a moment before she was able to compose herself. "Some passer-by took the photograph. Harry kept it. It must have fallen out of his pocket when his coat was over the arm of the chair. He was frantic when he discovered it was gone. I didn't know Sebastian had it." Her face was touched with a rare, terrible anger. It frightened him.

"Connie . . ."

The expression vanished again, drowned in misery.

He had to go on; there were other things that he had to know. There was no more time to spend in patience. "About the morning Sebastian was murdered, and the day leading up to the time Harry died."

"I don't know anything useful." Her voice was flat again, emotion buried far below in a sea of pain too deep to dare touch.

"And about Sunday, the day the archduke and duchess were shot in Sarajevo," he went on.

She swung around. "Oh, God! You can't think Harry had anything to do with that! That's idiotic!"

"Of course I don't!" He denied it vehemently, but his mind went to the yellow Lanchester mangled and broken, and his parents' bodies covered with blood. Until the moment of saying it, the thought had not entered his mind that Beecher could be guilty of that, but now it was there, a tiny shard, like a dagger.

She was staring at him incredulously.

"No!" he said again, forcing a smile, this time in the face of the absurdity of Beecher being responsible for the assassination in Sarajevo. "I simply used that event to bring the day to your mind. If you remember, it was also the day my parents were killed."

"Oh!" She was stunned and utterly contrite, her face crumpled in pity. "Joseph, I'm so sorry. I had completely forgotten! With—" She took a deep breath and held it a moment. "With murder"—she forced herself to use the word—"here in college, an accidental death, even two, seems so much . . . cleaner. What is it you need to know? If I can tell you, of course I will."

Now was the moment to say what he had to. "I think someone may have seen what happened. Do you know where Harry was about noon that day?"

The color swept up her face. She must have felt its heat, because her eyes betrayed her as well. "Yes. It couldn't have been he," she said.

He could not let it go quite so delicately. "Are you certain, as a fact, not a belief?"

"Absolutely." She looked down, away from him.

"And the morning Sebastian was killed?" He chose the slightly softer word, blunting it where he could.

She turned a little to look out of the window again. "I got up early and walked along the Backs. I was with Harry. I can't prove it because we kept to the trees. We didn't want to be seen, and there are quite often other people around, mostly students, even at five or six."

"Then it is not possible that Harry could have killed Sebastian," he said, watching for the slightest shadow in her eyes or alteration in the rigidity of her body that would betray that she was lying to protect him, even now that he was dead.

She turned to face him, her eyes wide, brilliant. "How can you be sure?" she said, not daring yet to grasp the hope. "We didn't meet until nearly six. Sebastian could have been killed before that, couldn't he?" She was pale now, perhaps wondering if Beecher had come to her straight from having murdered the one man who threatened them both.

"Where did you meet?" he asked.

She was confused. "Where? I went over the Bridge of Sighs, because it's enclosed and no one would have seen me, then walked to the beginning of the trees. He was there."

"He didn't come to the lodgings?"

Her dark eyes widened. "Good heavens, of course not! We're not completely mad!"

"When was the next time he was there?"

"I don't know. Why? About two days, I think. I had the Allards by then, and everything was a nightmare."

A warmth began to ease inside him. Beecher had definitely not killed Sebastian, because he had had no time to hide the gun! Not if it had been on the master's roof—and the more he thought of it, the more certain he became that that was where it had been. "And before he shot himself?" he asked.

She stiffened again, her face white. "I saw him in the Fellows' Garden the evening before, just for a little while, almost fifteen minutes. Aidan was due home."

"Did he go inside?"

"No. Why?"

Should he tell her? Caution said not . . . but she had loved Beecher, and the thought that he had committed murder and then suicide was a bleeding wound inside her.

Yet if he explained, then she would work out for herself the only terrible alternative: that it was someone who had access to the roof of her house, her husband. She would be a danger to him then, and would he kill her, too?

Would she work it out, even if he did not tell her? No. It all depended upon the gun having been hidden on the roof. He dared not let her deduce it.

"I'm not sure," he lied. "When I'm certain, I'll tell you."

"Did Harry kill Sebastian?" Her voice was trembling, her face ashen.

Would she guess anyway? "No, he couldn't have," he answered. "But say nothing to anyone!" He made the warning sharp, a message of danger. "If he didn't, Connie, then someone else did! Someone who may kill you. Please, say nothing at all, to absolutely anyone . . . including the master! I may be wrong."

That, too, was a lie; Joseph had no doubt he was right. Aidan Thyer might kill, but he was certain in his heart that Harry Beecher had not. And if Connie had been out on the Backs early in the morning, then Aidan Thyer could have been anywhere; certainly he could have been in Sebastian's rooms. And Thyer could have killed Sebastian for the same reason—because he was blackmailing any or all of them over exposing Connie's affair.

Or it could have been Thyer Sebastian had seen on the Hauxton Road.

"Say nothing," he repeated even more urgently, touching her arm. Her wrist was slender under his fingers. His mouth was dry, his hands sweating. "Please—remember it is murder we are dealing with."

"Two murders?" she whispered.

"Perhaps," he replied. He did not say it could be four—or, if Reisenburg had been murdered also, then five.

She nodded.

He stayed only to give her a few words of assurance, then walked slowly back in the bright sun, cold in his flesh and his bones.

CHAPTER

FOURTEEN

Joseph walked slowly across the quad. The sun was hot in the early afternoon, but it felt airless. His clothes stuck to his skin. There were no clouds that he could see in the blue distance bounded by the crenellated tops of the walls, but it felt like thunder to come. The electricity of it was already inside him, an excitement and a fear that he was on the brink of the truth.

Where had Aidan Thyer been on the afternoon of Sunday, June 28? Whom could he ask that Thyer would not hear about it? Connie had been in the garden with Beecher. If Thyer had been on the Hauxton Road, where would he have told people he was? And who would remember now, over five weeks later?

He could not ask Connie; she would know why he was asking, and then no matter how hard she tried, it would surely be beyond her to conceal that knowledge from Thyer himself.

He was walking more and more slowly as he tried to make up his mind. Thyer had come late to the cricket match. Would Rattray, who had captained the St. John's side, know where he had been before that? It was worth asking him. He turned and went rapidly back in through the door at the farther side and up to Rattray's rooms. He was not there.

Ten minutes later Joseph found him in a corner of the library between the stacks, scanning the bottom shelf.

"Dr. Reavley! Are you looking for me, sir?" he asked, closing his place in the book in his hands.

"Yes, actually I was." Joseph bent to the floor, looking along the row curiously. They were on warfare and European history. He regarded Rattray's thin, anxious face.

Rattray bit his lip. "It looks pretty bad, sir," he said quietly. "The kaiser warned the czar yesterday that if Russia didn't stop within twenty-four hours, Germany would mobilize, too. Professor Moulton reckons they'll probably close the world stock exchanges pretty soon. Maybe even by Monday."

"It's a bank holiday," Joseph replied. "They'll have all weekend to think about it."

Rattray sat back on the floor, legs out in front of him. "Do you think so?" He rubbed the heel of his hand along his jaw. "God, it would be awful, wouldn't it? Who could imagine five weeks ago that some lunatic in a town in Serbia, of all places, taking a potshot at an archduke—and Austria's got loads of them—could blow up into this? Just a short time, barely more than a month, and the whole world's changed."

"Six weeks ago, nearly." Joseph found the thought strange, too. Then his parents had been alive. Six weeks ago tomorrow would be the Saturday John Reavley had driven the yellow Lanchester to Little Wilbraham and talked to Reisenburg—and found the document. That night he had telephoned Matthew in London. The next day he had been killed.

"We played cricket at Fenner's Field," he said aloud. "You captained the side. I remember being there, and Beecher, and the Master."

Rattray nodded.

"Sebastian wasn't," Joseph continued. "He was late coming back home. I expect the master wasn't pleased. He was one of our best bats."

"Rotten bowler, though." Rattray smiled. He looked close to tears, his voice a little thick. "No, the master was pretty cross when he did come, actually. Sort of caught him by surprise that Sebastian wasn't playing."

Joseph felt cold. "When he did come?"

"He was late, too!" Rattray pulled a slight face. "Don't know where he'd been, but he arrived in a hell of a temper. He said he'd been stuck on the side of Jesus Lane with a puncture, but I know he wasn't, because Dr. Beecher came that way and he'd have seen him." He sighed and looked away, blinking hard. "Unless, of course, you can't believe Dr. Beecher anymore. I just can't—I can't understand that!" He chewed painfully on his lower lip to stop it trembling. "Everything's sort of . . . slipping apart, isn't it? You know, I used to think Sebastian was pretty decent." He looked at Joseph. "He had some odd ideas—used to waffle on about peace, and that war was a sin against mankind, and that there wasn't anything in the world worth fighting for if it meant killing whole nations and filling the earth with hate."

He rubbed his jaw again, leaving a smudge of dust on it. "A bit too much, but still sane, still all right! I never thought he would do something really squalid, like blackmail. That's filthy! Beecher might have been doing something out of line, but he was a decent chap—I'd have staked anything you like on that." He pushed his hair back off his forehead in a gesture of infinite weariness. "I'm beginning to wonder if I really know very much at all."

Joseph understood his confusion profoundly. He was fighting his own way through the same desperation, trying to make sense of it and regain his own balance. But there was no time for the long, gentle conversations of comfort now. "Where do you think the master was?" he asked.

Rattray shrugged. "I've no idea. Or why he should say something that wasn't true."

"But he was in his car?" Joseph persisted.

"Yes, I saw him drive up in it. I was waiting for him."

"Thank you."

Rattray looked curious. "Why? What does it matter now? It's over. We were all wrong—you and me, everyone. Beecher's dead, and our quarrels don't amount to much if there's going to be war and we're all drawn into the biggest conflict in Europe. Do you suppose they'll ask for volunteers, sir?"

"I can't see that we'll be involved," Joseph replied. "It will be Austria, Russia, and perhaps Germany. It's still possible they're all just threatening, seeing who'll be the first to back down."

"Maybe," Rattray said without conviction.

Joseph thanked him again and went out of the library and back to the first quad to see Gorley-Smith. There was a vital question to ask now, and he dreaded the answer. He was surprised how deeply it cut into his emotions to believe that Aidan Thyer was guilty of killing John and Alys Reavley. And for what? That was something he still did not know.

He knocked on Gorley-Smith's door and stood impatiently until it was opened. Gorley-Smith looked tired and irritable. His hair was untidy, he had his jacket off, and his shirt was sticking to his body. It very obviously cost him some effort to be civil.

"If you came to apologize for dinner, it really doesn't matter," he said abruptly, and started to push the door shut again.

"I didn't," Joseph answered him. It was clear that there was going to be no opportunity for subtlety. "Beecher doesn't seem to have left any note, or wishes of any kind. . . ."

Gorley-Smith suppressed his momentary annoyance. "No, I don't suppose he did. Look, Reavley, I know he was a friend of yours, but he was obviously driven beyond his sanity by whatever it was that young Allard was pressuring him over, and I'd really rather not know the details. I don't think we should speculate." His face was filled with distaste and with the anxious desire to avoid embarrassment.

Joseph knew what was on his mind. "I was going to ask you," he said coldly, "if Beecher had any opportunity to speak to the master around about that time. He might have some ideas what we should do. As far as I know, Beecher had no close family, but there must be someone who ought to be informed as discreetly as possible, in the circumstances."

"Oh." Gorley-Smith was taken aback. "Actually, I don't think so. Whatever sent him over the edge must have been rather sudden, and as it so happens, I know the master was in a meeting for at least two hours before we heard about it, because I was there myself. I'm sorry, Reavley, but you'll have to look elsewhere."

"You're quite sure?" Joseph pressed. He wanted it to be true, and yet it made nonsense of the only answer he could think of.

"Yes, of course I'm sure," Gorley-Smith replied wearily. "Basildon went on interminably about some damned building fund, and I thought we were going to be there all day. It was mostly the master he was arguing with."

"I see." Joseph nodded. "Thank you."

Gorley-Smith shook his head in incomprehension and closed the door.

Once again Joseph made his way over the bridge to the Backs. The air was cooling at last, and the light shone through the flowers in rich colors like stained glass. The trees across the grass barely shimmered in the faint sunset wind, and there was no sound but the call of birds.

If Aidan Thyer had not killed Beecher, and Beecher had not killed Sebastian, then what was the answer?

He walked slowly, his feet silent on the dry grass. He passed into the shade of the trees. Here it smelled cooler, as if the greenness itself had a fragrance.

Who else could have put the gun on the roof of the master's lodgings? Or was he wrong about that after all? He went back to the beginning of all that he knew for certain. Elwyn had come to his rooms, almost hysterical with shock and grief, because he had gone to fetch Sebastian for an early morning walk by the river and found him shot to death. There was no gun there. Anyway, no one had ever suggested Sebastian had any reason on earth to take his own life. No one who knew him had ever imagined such a thing.

The police had been called and had searched everywhere for the gun, but had not found it. Everywhere except the funnel openings to the drainpipes on the master's roof.

Of course, it was always possible there was another answer he simply had not thought of. Maybe someone had quite casually walked out with the gun and put it in another college—or had given it to somebody else.

Except that unknown person had retrieved it with no difficulty in order to shoot Beecher.

Joseph concentrated on who could have shot Beecher and who might have wanted to. Everyone seemed to assume after Beecher's death that he had killed Sebastian. But had anyone assumed it before?

Mary Allard? She would have had the fury and the bitterness to kill.

But how would she have known where the gun was, or got herself to the roof for it?

Gerald Allard? No, he had not the passion, and he also would not have known where it was.

Joseph was opposite Trinity now. The wind was rising a little, whispering in the leaves above him, and here in their shade the light was fading rapidly.

Elwyn? He could not have killed Sebastian. He was accounted for in his own room at the time. Besides, he and Sebastian had been close, even for brothers, and so unalike as to have been rivals in very little. They admired each other's skills without especially wanting to possess them.

Nor could Elwyn have had anything to do with crashing the Lanchester. He had been in Cambridge all day.

But he had been in and out of the master's lodgings seeing his mother, trying to comfort her and offer her the support his father seemed incapable of giving. He could have retrieved the gun if he had known it was there.

But how could he have known? Had he seen it somewhere? Could Beecher have hidden it there? For whom? Connie? The thought was ugly, and the pain of it sat so tight in his chest he could hardly breathe. Had Beecher been protecting her?

And had Elwyn assumed it was Beecher who had shot Sebastian? That would have been motive enough to have killed him and deliberately left the gun there to make it seem like suicide, an admission of guilt.

Except that he was wrong.

In the shadows Joseph could hardly see the path at his feet, although there were echoes of light across the sky. He walked onto the grass again. Outside the avenue of trees there was still that tender, airy dusk that seems neither silver nor gray. He looked at the horizon to the east, where the depth of the coming night was a veil of indigo.

In the morning he would have to face Connie again and put it to the final test.

He slept badly and woke with a nagging headache. He had a hot cup of tea and two aspirins, and then as soon as he knew Aidan Thyer would have begun his college duties, he went across to the master's lodgings.

Connie was surprised to see him, but there was no shadow in her eyes. If anything, she seemed pleased.

"How are you, Joseph? You look tired. Have you had any breakfast? I'm sure Cook could make you something if you wish." They were in the sitting room with the light slanting in through the French windows.

His stomach was knotted far too tightly to eat, and the aspirins had not yet had much effect. "I have been thinking a great deal about what must have happened, and I've asked a few questions."

She looked puzzled, but there was neither hope nor fear in her face.

"The police never found the gun after Sebastian was killed," he said. "Although they believed they searched everywhere."

"They did," she confirmed. "Why do you say *believed*? Do you know of somewhere they didn't look? They were here. They searched the entire house."

"When?"

She thought for a moment. "I . . . I think we were about the last. I suppose they came here only as a matter of form. And at first Elwyn was here, because he was desperately shocked and grieved, and then of course his parents."

"Did they search the roof?"

Would she lie to protect herself, even if it was only to leave the matter closed? Was it she who had originally started the subtle suggestion that the love affair over which Beecher was blackmailed was not with her but with Sebastian himself? That was a repulsive thought. He pushed it away.

"They were up on the next roof," she replied thoughtfully, remembering it as she spoke. "They can see all of this one from there. It's not so big. Anyway, I really don't think anybody could have been up there. We would have heard. How can you hide a gun on a rooftop? It would be obvious."

"Not if it were poked barrel first into one of the funnels at the top of a downpipe," he said.

Her eyes widened. "You could reach those from the dormer windows. It could be anyone who was in this house!"

"Yes," he agreed.

"Aidan? Harry?"

"No." He shook his head. "Neither of them had the opportunity. Harry could not have killed Sebastian—you told me that yourself. Weren't you telling the truth?"

"Yes! Yes, I was!" she assured him. "You don't think Aidan? But why? Not over . . ." Again the blood flushed up her cheeks. "He doesn't know," she said huskily.

"What about Elwyn?" he asked her. "Could he have found the gun there and taken it to kill Beecher, believing Beecher had killed Sebastian?"

She stared at him, misery and grief swimming in her eyes.

"Could he?" he repeated.

"Yes." She nodded. "But how would he know it was there? Who killed Sebastian? I can't believe Aidan would have, and I know I didn't. And it wasn't Harry, so who was it?"

"I don't know," he admitted. "I'm right back to the beginning with that. Who else could have put the gun up there? He would have to have come through the house."

"No one," she said after a moment. "It must have been somewhere else. Unless . . ." She blinked several times. "Unless Aidan was hiding it for someone. Do you think he would have done that, and Elwyn knew?"

"Perhaps, but why?" And the moment the words were spoken he knew the answer. It was back to the document again, but he dared not tell her that. "Of course, it depends upon other things," he added.

She opened her mouth to ask, then changed her mind. "The police, the whole college, think that Harry killed Sebastian," she said instead. "And that when he thought they were about to arrest him, he killed himself." Her voice was shaking. "I wish I could prove that wasn't true. I loved him very much, but even if I hadn't, I don't think I could allow anyone to be blamed for something terrible if I could prove they were innocent."

"Then I think we had better go and tell Inspector Perth. I imagine we can find him at the police station in the town."

She hesitated only a moment. She might never have to do anything that would cost her more than this. Once the words were said, she could not ever return to this privacy, this safety of unknowing. Then she took a step forward, and he followed her out of the room and to the front door.

They walked to the police station. It was less than a mile, and at this hour in the morning it was still cool and fresh. The streets were busy with tradesmen, early deliveries, shoppers seeking a bargain. The footpath was bustling with people and the roadway loud with hooves of horses pulling wagons and drays, delivery carts, and a doctor's gig. There were several cars and a motor van with advertisements printed on the side, and, as always, dozens of bicycles. Only if one listened carefully did one hear a different tone in the voices or realize that conversations were not about the weather and there was no gossip. It was all news, carefully disguised anxiety, forced jokes.

Perth was busy upstairs, and they were obliged to wait over a quarter of an hour in tense, unhappy impatience. When he finally arrived, he was less than enthusiastic to see them, and only when Joseph insisted did he take them to a small, cluttered office where they could speak without being overheard.

"Oi don't know what you want, Reverend," Perth said with barely veiled impatience. He looked tired and anxious. "Oi can't help you. Oi'm very sorry about Mr. Beecher, but there's an end to it. Oi don't know if you've seen the papers this mornin', but the king o' the Belgians has gone against his own government and mobilized all his armies. There's a whole lot more at stake than any one man's reputation, sir, an' that's something we can't tossle about no more."

"Truth is always worth arguing about, Inspector Perth," Connie said gravely. "That's why we fight wars: to keep the right to rule ourselves and make our own laws, to be who we want to be and answer to no one but God. Dr. Beecher did not kill himself, and we believe we can prove it."

"Mrs. Thyer—" Perth began with exaggerated patience.

"You never found the gun, did you!" Joseph exclaimed. "Until it was by Dr. Beecher's body."

"No, we didn't," Perth admitted reluctantly, anger sharpening his voice. It was a failure he did not like having pointed out to him. "But he must have known where it was, because he got it back again!"

"Did you search his rooms?"

"O' course we did! We searched the whole college! You know that, sir. You saw us."

"There must be somewhere you missed," Joseph said reasonably. "The gun did not dematerialize and then reappear."

"Are you bein' sarcastic, sir?" Perth's eyes hardened.

"I am stating the obvious. It was somewhere that you did not look. I have spent some time considering where that could be. You looked on the roof, didn't you? I can remember seeing your men up there."

"Yes, we did, sir. Very thorough, we were. Not that there's a lot o' places on a roof as you could hide a gun. Quite a big thing, a revolver, an' not the same shape as anything else. Not to mention that metal shines in the sun."

"What about the bucket at the top of a drain pipe?" Joseph asked. "With the barrel pointing down and the top covered with, for example, an old handkerchief, suitably dusty, and a few leaves?"

"Very good, sir," Perth conceded. "That could be. Except we looked."

"How about the downpipes on the master's lodgings?" Joseph asked. "Did you look there, too?"

Perth stood absolutely still, his face frozen.

Joseph waited, aware of Connie holding her breath beside him.

"No," Perth said at last. "We reckoned . . . nobody'd be able to hoide anything there unless they went through the master's lodgings to do it. Are you saying as they did?" The last was addressed to Connie.

"Elwyn Allard was in and out of the house a great deal while his mother and father stayed with us," she replied, her voice very nearly steady. "He was there within an hour of Dr. Beecher being shot."

Perth stared at her. "If you're saying that he shot his brother, Mrs. Thyer, you got it wrong. We thought o' that. Lots of families don't get on all that well." He shook his head dismally. "Brother killing brother is as old as the Bible, if you'll excuse me saying so. But we know where he was, an' he couldn't've. You'd not understand the medical evidence, mebbe, but you'll have to trust us in that."

"And Dr. Beecher didn't do it, either," she said, her voice tight as if her throat would barely open. "He was with me." She ignored Perth's expression of incredulity. "I am perfectly aware of what time it was, and of the impropriety of it. I would not admit to it lightly, and I can barely imagine what my husband will feel if it has to be public—or what he will do. But I will not allow Dr. Beecher, or anyone else, to be branded for a crime they did not commit."

"Where were you . . . and Dr. Beecher, madam?" Perth asked, his face sour with disbelief, and perhaps disapproval.

Connie blushed, understanding his contempt. "On the Backs along the river, Inspector Perth. At this time of the year, as you say, the daylight hours are long, and it is a pleasant place if you wish to talk unobserved."

His expression was unreadable. "Very interesting, Oi'm sure. Why didn't you mention this before? Or has Dr. Beecher's reputation suddenly got so much more important to you?"

Her face tightened. She was white about the lips. Joseph could see how intensely she would like to have lashed back at Perth and withered him, but she had already given away her weapons. "Like others, I'm afraid I thought Sebastian Allard had been blackmailing him over his regard for me and the indiscretion of it for both of us," she replied. "I thought he had killed himself rather than have it exposed, which he believed was going to happen because of the investigation into Sebastian's murder."

"Then who did kill Sebastian, Mrs. Thyer?" Perth asked, leaning forward a little across the desk. "An' who put the gun down the drainpipe on your roof? You? If you'll excuse me saying so, we only got your word that Dr. Beecher was with you. Same as we only got his word that you was with him . . . an' he ain't here to back you up."

She understood perfectly, but her eyes did not waver from his. "I am aware of that, Inspector. I do not know who killed Sebastian, but it was not Dr. Beecher, and it was not I. But I believe that if you investigate a little further, you will find that Elwyn Allard shot Dr. Beecher, and you cannot find it difficult to understand why, since you yourself assumed that Dr. Beecher was guilty of killing Sebastian."

"Oi'm not sure as how Oi do believe it." Perth bit his lip. "But Oi suppose Oi'd better go back to St. John's an' ask around a bit more, leastways find out if anyone saw Elwyn near Dr. Beecher's rooms just before he were shot. But Oi still don't see how he could have known where the gun were if it were in the pipe from the roof of the master's lodgings!"

"The gun was on the floor, by Dr. Beecher's hand," Joseph said suddenly. "Did you do any tests to see if that was where and how it would fall if dropped from a man's hand after he was shot?"

"An' how would we do that, sir?" Perth asked dourly. "We can't hardly ask somebody to shoot theirselves to show us!"

"Haven't you ever seen suicides before?" Joseph was thinking rapidly. How on earth could he prove the truth he was more and more certain of with every moment? "Where do guns fall after the shock of death? A gun is heavy. If you shoot yourself in the head"—he carried on regardless of Connie's gasp—"you fall sideways. Does your arm go down as his was, and the gun slither out of your fingers? For that matter, were there any fingerprints on it?"

"Oi dunno, sir," Perth said sharply. "It was plain it was suicide to me, seeing as you yourself showed us that Sebastian Allard had been blackmailing him into doing all kinds o' favors for him, things as he wouldn't do o' hisself, an' ruining his name as a professor."

"Yes, I know that," Joseph said impatiently. "But I'm talking about proof. Think back on it now, with other possibilities in mind! Was that how a gun would fall?"

"Oi dunno, sir." Perth looked troubled. "Oi suppose it were a bit . . . awkward. But that ain't proof of anything. We dunno how he sat, nor what way he moved when he were shot. Begging your pardon, ma'am. Oi'd like to spare your feelings, but you ain't making it possible."

"I know that, Inspector," she said quietly, but her face was ashen.

Joseph's mind was racing urgently. "Surely, Inspector, if we could prove that the gun was in the bucket at the top of the drainpipe on the master's roof, that would also prove that Dr. Beecher could not have got it to shoot himself?"

"Yes, sir, it would. But how are we going to prove that? Guns don't leave nothin' behind, an' if it were there, likely it were wrapped in a cloth or something, to keep it from being seen, or getting wet."

Wet. The idea was like a lightning flare. "We had rain the day Beecher was killed!" Joseph almost shouted the words. "If there was a cloth around the gun, then the whole thing would have blocked the drain! There are barrels at the bottom of the drainpipes in the Fellows' Garden! If one of them is dry, that's your proof! And he would choose that side, because the other overlooks the quad, where it was far more exposed."

Perth stared at him. "Yes, sir, if it's clear now, Oi'd take that as proof." He started toward the door, barely waiting for them to follow. "We'd best go an' look now, before it rains again an' we've lost it all."

It was a short walk back to St. John's, and they did not speak as they dodged between pedestrians on the narrow footpaths. It was already getting warmer as the sun beat down on the stone.

They went in through the front gate past Mitchell, who looked startled and unhappy to see Perth again, then across the first quad, through the archway, and across the second. Then, since the gate was locked, as usual, they hurried through the master's lodgings into the Fellows' Garden.

Joseph felt his pulse quicken as they passed between the flowers, the perfume of them heavy in the stillness, and stopped in front of the first water barrel.

He glanced at Connie, and she back at him. His mouth was dry.

Perth looked into the barrel. "About a quarter full," he announced. "Near as Oi can tell."

Connie reached out and took Joseph's hand, gripping him hard.

Perth moved to the middle barrel and looked in. He stood still, a little bent.

Connie's fingers tightened.

Joseph felt his heart pounding.

"It's dry," Perth said huskily. He turned to look at Joseph, then Connie. "Better check the last one," he said softly. "Oi think you're right, Reverend. In fact, seems like for certain you are."

"If it's dry," Joseph pointed out, "then there was something wrapped around the gun. It might still be there, especially if there's still no water at all."

Perth stared at him, then very slowly he turned away and bent to peer up the drainpipe. "Reckon as there is an' all," he said, pursing his lips. "Come most o' the way down. Oi'll have to see if Oi can get it the rest."

"Can I help?" Joseph offered.

"No, thank you, sir. Oi'll do it myself," Perth insisted. He took his jacket off, reluctantly handing it to Joseph, then rolled up his shirtsleeve and poked his arm up the drainpipe.

There were several moments of frustrated silence while he wriggled without effort.

Connie walked over to the delphiniums and plucked out one of the canes that held them up. She returned with it and offered it to Perth.

"Thank you, madam," he said, tight-lipped, and extended a dirty hand to take it from her. Three minutes later he retrieved a piece of canvas awning like that used on the punts at night. It was almost a foot square, and there were smudges of oil near the middle. Perth held it to his nose and sniffed.

"Gun oil?" Joseph asked huskily.

"Yes, sir, I reckon so. Suppose Oi'd better go an' have a few words with Mr. Elwyn Allard."

"I'll come with you," Joseph said without hesitation. He turned to Connie. "I think you'd better stay here."

She did not argue. She let Joseph and Perth out of the side gate into the quad, then went back into the house.

Joseph followed Perth across toward Elwyn's rooms. He knew it would be desperately painful, the more so because he could understand the passion of hatred, the compulsion that had drawn Elwyn to defend his mother from grief. And perhaps also the hunger within him to do something sufficiently powerful to make her grateful to him, even if she did not know why. Then she might emerge from her obsession with Sebastian long enough to acknowledge that she still had one live son who was equally worthy of her love.

They found Elwyn in Morel's rooms. They were studying together, discussing alternative translations of a political speech. It was Morel who answered the door, startled to see Perth again.

"Sorry to disturb you, sir," Perth said grimly. "Oi understand Mr. Allard is here."

Morel turned just as Elwyn came up behind him.

"What is it?" Elwyn asked, glancing from Perth to Joseph and back again. If he was afraid, there was no sign of it in his face.

Joseph spoke before Perth could answer. "I think it would be a good idea if you were to come to the police station in town, Elwyn. There are a few questions you may be able to answer, and it would be better there."

Perth glanced at him, a flicker of annoyance across his face, but he conceded.

"If you want," Elwyn agreed, the tension greater in him now, too.

Morel looked at him, then at Joseph. Finally he turned to Elwyn. "Do you want me to come?"

"No, thank you, sir," Perth cut him off. "This is a family matter." He stepped back to block the stairway door. "This way, sir," he directed Elwyn.

"What is it?" Elwyn asked halfway down the steps.

Perth did not answer until they had reached the bottom and were outside in the quad.

"Oi'm taking you in for questioning, sir, regardin' the death o' Dr. Beecher. Oi thought it easier for you if Mr. Morel didn't have to know that at this point. If you give me your word to come without making a fuss, there'll be no need for 'andcuffs or anything like that."

Elwyn went white. "H-Handcuffs!" he stammered. He turned to Joseph.

"If you wish me to come with you, then of course I will," Joseph offered. "Or if you prefer me to contact your parents, or a lawyer, then I'll do that first."

"I . . ." Elwyn looked lost, stunned, as if he had never considered the possibility of this happening. He shook his head, bewildered.

"Mr. Allard's an adult, Reverend," Perth said coldly. "If he wants a lawyer, then o' course he can have one, but he don't need his parents, nor you. An' strictly speaking, sir, this in't your concern. We're grateful for your help an' all you've done, but Mr. Allard ain't going to give no trouble, so you could stay here at St. John's. Mebbe you'd be more use if you told the master what's happened, an' sent for Mr. an' Mrs. Allard."

"Mrs. Thyer will already have done that," Joseph pointed out, and saw the flash of annoyance on Perth's face as he realized. "I'll come with Elwyn, unless he would rather I didn't."

Elwyn hesitated, and it was that instant of indecision which made Joseph certain that he was guilty. He was frightened and confused, but he was not outraged.

Perth gave in, and they walked together into the shadow of the front gate, and out into the street on the far side.

At the police station it was a formal matter of charging Elwyn with the murder of Harry Beecher, to which he pleaded not guilty. On Joseph's advice, he refused to say anything further until he had a lawyer with him.

Gerald and Mary Allard arrived at St. John's an hour after Joseph returned. Mary was beside herself, her face contorted with fury. The moment Joseph walked into the sitting room at the master's lodgings, she swung around from Aidan Thyer, to whom she had been speaking, and glared at Joseph. Her thin body looked positively gaunt in its tight black silk, like a winter crow.

"This is monstrous!" she said, her voice strident. "Elwyn couldn't possibly have killed that wretched man! For heaven's sake, Beecher murdered Sebastian! When he knew you were closing in on him, he took his own life. Everybody knows that. Let Elwyn go immediately—with an apology for this idiotic mistake. Now!"

Joseph stood still. What could he tell her? One of her sons was dead and the other guilty of murder, even if he had done it in mistaken revenge.

"I'm sorry," he said to her—and he meant it profoundly, with a pain that throbbed inside him. "But they have proof."

"Nonsense!" she spat. "It is totally absurd. Gerald!"

Gerald came to stand almost level with her. He looked wretched; his skin was pale and blotchy and his eyes blurred. "Really, for God's sake, what is going on?" he demanded. "Beecher killed my son and now you have arrested my other son when quite obviously Beecher took his own life." He put out a hand tentatively as if to touch Mary, but she pulled away from him.

"No," Joseph said as gently as he could. He could not like Gerald, but he was fiercely sorry for him. "Beecher did not kill Sebastian. He was seen elsewhere at the time."

"You are lying!" Mary accused him furiously. Her face was ashen, with scarlet splashes on her cheeks. "Beecher was your friend, and you are lying to protect him. Who on earth would see Beecher anywhere at five o'clock in the morning? Unless he was in bed with somebody? And if he was, then she is a whore, and her word is worth nothing!"

"Mary . . . ," Gerald began, then faltered under her withering glance.

"He was out walking," Joseph replied. "And the gun that killed Sebastian was hidden where only a limited number of people could have placed it or retrieved it."

"Beecher!" Mary said with scalding triumph. "Naturally! It is the only answer that makes sense."

"No," Joseph told her. "He might have been able to hide it there, but he could not have retrieved it. Elwyn could have."

"It's still ridiculous," she asserted, her whole body so tense she was shuddering. "If he had known where it was, he would have told the police! It might have led to the arrest of whoever killed Sebastian. Or are you insane enough to believe he did that, too?"

"No. I know he didn't. I don't know who did," he admitted. "And I believe that Elwyn sincerely thought it was Beecher and that the law could not touch him."

"Then he was justified!" she said savagely. "He killed a murderer!"

"He killed someone he thought was a murderer," Joseph corrected. "And he was mistaken."

"You're wrong," she insisted, but she turned away from him. Her voice rose, shrill with desperation, as if the world no longer made sense. "Beecher must have done it! Elwyn is morally innocent of any crime, and I shall see to it that he doesn't suffer."

Joseph looked past her at Aidan Thyer, and again the darkness filled his mind that it could have been he who was behind the document, and perhaps Sebastian's death. He looked pale and tired today, the lines in his face deeper.

Did he know about Connie and Beecher? Had he always known? Joseph stared at him, searching, but there was nothing in Thyer's eyes to betray him.

"Dr. Reavley?" Gerald said tentatively. "Would you . . . would you do what you can for Elwyn? I mean, I wish he would . . . you are a person of standing here . . . the police will . . ." He floundered helplessly.

"Yes, of course I will," Joseph agreed. "Do you have legal representation in Cambridge?"

"Oh, yes . . . I meant as a . . . I don't know . . . as a friend . . ."

"Yes. If you wish, I'll go right away."

"Yes . . . please do. I'll stay here with my wife."

"I'm going to Elwyn!" Mary shouted at him.

"No, you are not," Gerald answered, unusually firmly for him. "You are staying here."

"I . . ." she began.

"You are staying here," he repeated, catching hold of her arm as she lunged forward, and bringing her to a stop. "You have done enough harm already."

She swiveled around and gaped at him in stupefaction, fury and pain struggling in her face. But she did not argue.

Joseph bade goodbye to them and went out again.

Perth placed no barrier to Joseph seeing Elwyn alone in the police cell. It was late afternoon, and the shadows were lengthening. The room smelled stale, of old fears and miseries.

Elwyn sat on one of the two wooden chairs and Joseph on the other, a bare, scarred table between them.

"Is Mother all right?" Elwyn asked as soon as the door was closed and they were alone. He was very pale, and the shadows around his eyes looked like bruises.

"She is very angry," Joseph replied truthfully. "She found it hard to accept that you could be guilty of Beecher's death, but when she could no longer avoid it, she believed that you had just cause and were morally innocent."

The rigidity eased out of Elwyn's shoulders. His skin looked oddly dead, as if it would be cold to touch.

"Your father will engage a lawyer for you," Joseph went on. "But is there anything I can do, as a friend?"

Elwyn looked down at his hands on the table. "Look after Mother as much as you can," he answered. "She cares so much. You wouldn't understand if you hadn't seen Aunt Aline. She is Mother's older sister. She always does everything right, and first. And she boasts about it all the time. Her sons win everything, and she makes us feel as if we'll never be as clever or as important. I think she's always been like that. She made it . . ." He stopped suddenly, realizing it was all pointless now. He drew in his breath. And went on more quietly. "You cared about Sebastian; you saw the best in him. Go on caring, and don't let them say he was a coward." He looked up quickly, searching Joseph's face.

"I've never heard anyone say he was a coward," Joseph replied. "No one has even suggested it. He was arrogant and at times manipulative. He enjoyed the power his charm gave him. But I think, in time, even that will be forgotten, and people will choose to remember only what was good."

Elwyn nodded briefly and brushed his hand across his face. He looked desperately weary.

Joseph ached with pity for him. Too much had been asked of him, far too much. His brother had been idolized, and Mary, in her grief, had expected Elwyn to ignore his own pain and carry hers for her, defend her from the truth and bear the weight of her emotions. And as far as Joseph knew, she had given him nothing back, not even her gratitude or her approval. Only now, when it was far too late, did she consider him and prepare to defend him. In a way it was her passion that had driven Elwyn to seek such a terrible revenge—as it turned out, a mistaken one.

The truth was still to be found. Someone else had put the gun in the drainpipe after killing Sebastian, someone with access to the master's lodgings. Connie, in order to protect her reputation and thus all her marriage gave her? Or Aidan Thyer, because it was he whom Sebastian had seen on the Hauxton Road when the Lanchester crashed? Perhaps this was the last chance for Joseph to ask, and the moment when Elwyn had nothing left to lose and would tell him if he knew.

"Elwyn . . . ?"

Elwyn moved slightly in acknowledgment, but he did not look up.

"Elwyn, how did you find the gun?"

"What? Oh . . . I saw it."

"Out of the upstairs window?"

"Yes. Why? What does it matter now?"

"It matters to me. Dr. Beecher didn't put it there, did he? Was it Mr. Thyer—or Mrs. Thyer? Did you see?"

Joseph waited. It seemed almost a battle of wills.

"Yes, I did," Elwyn said at last. "It *was* Dr. Beecher."

"Then he did it for someone else," Joseph told him, knowing the blow he was dealing him, but it was a truth he could not hide forever. "Dr. Beecher did not kill Sebastian. He couldn't have. He was somewhere else, and he has a witness to prove it."

Elwyn's body was rigid, his eyes hollow, almost black in the fading light of the room. "Somewhere else?" he whispered in horror—but it was not disbelief. Joseph saw it in him the moment before he tried to mask it, and for an instant they saw in each other that terrible understanding that can never be taken back.

Then Joseph looked away, the knowledge burned into him. Elwyn had known Beecher had not killed Sebastian! Then why had he shot Beecher? To protect whom? Not Connie. Aidan Thyer? Had Sebastian seen Thyer on the Hauxton Road and told Elwyn before he was killed? Was that why Elwyn would not speak, even now? Was it even conceivable that he had killed Beecher on Thyer's orders, rather than be killed himself? The thoughts whirled in Joseph's mind like leaves in a storm—chaotic, battering. Was this all part of the plot John Reavley had discovered in Reisenburg's document? And was it going to cost Elwyn Allard his life as well?

He closed his eyes. "I'll help you if I can, Elwyn," he said softly. "But so help me God, I don't know how!"

"You can't," Elwyn whispered, covering his face with his hands. "It's too late."

CHAPTER

FIFTEEN

Joseph woke up late on Sunday morning, his mind still consumed with Elwyn's last words to him and with the picture of the young man's utter despair. And yet Elwyn was determined to hide some secret of Sebastian's death, even at this cost. Joseph had turned it over and over in his wakeful hours, grasping and losing, finding nothing that made sense.

It was the second of August, and he still did not know who had killed his parents, what the document was, or what had happened to it. He had tried, and every answer had evaporated the moment he framed it. But John and Alys Reavley were dead, and so were Sebastian Allard, the German Reisenburg, and now Harry Beecher. And poor Elwyn might well be, when the fullness of the law had run its course. Joseph knew of no way to help any of it.

Tomorrow was a bank holiday; he should go back to St. Giles and spend it with Judith. He had been too overwhelmed in the last few days even to write to her, or to Hannah.

He got up slowly, shaved, and dressed, but he did not go down to the dining hall for breakfast. He was not hungry, and certainly he did not want to face Moulton or any other of his colleagues. He was not going to explain about Elwyn or discuss the matter. It was a consuming tragedy, but it was a private one. The Allards had more than enough to bear without the added scourge of other people's speculation.

He spent the morning tidying up various books and papers, then writing a long letter to Hannah, which he knew said little of any meaning—it was simply a way of keeping in touch. He went to the eleven o'clock service in the chapel, and found it washed over him without giving him any of the deep comfort he needed. But he had not honestly expected that it would. Perhaps he knew the words so well that he no longer heard them. Even the perfection of the music seemed irrelevant to the world of everyday life, the disillusion and all the loss he knew of around him.

He saw Connie Thyer briefly in the afternoon, but she had only a few minutes to talk. Again she was overtaken by the growing hysteria of Mary Allard and the futility of attempting to help, and yet she was obliged by circumstances and her own sense of pity to try.

Joseph walked out of the front gate and ambled aimlessly along the nearly deserted streets of the town. All the shops were closed in Sabbath decency. The few people he saw were soberly dressed and merely nodded to him respectfully as they passed.

Without intending to, he found himself on Jesus Lane, and instinctively turned right down Emmanuel Road. He strolled past Christ's Pieces and eventually across St. Andrews Street, along to Downing Street toward Corpus Christi and the river again.

He was not really thinking so much as letting things run through his mind. It was still teeming with questions, and he had no idea where to find a thread to begin untangling even one answer. Perhaps it began with who had killed Sebastian, and why.

The longest day of summer was well past, and by half past six he was tired and thirsty, and the sun was lowering in the west. Maybe he had come to the pub near the millpond intentionally, even if it had not been consciously in his mind. He would be able to sit down here and have supper and a long, cool drink. In time he could make the opportunity to talk with Flora Whickham again. If Sebastian had known anything about the crash of the Lanchester, then she would be the one person he might have told, other than Elwyn, and there was no chance that Joseph could draw it out of him. He was locked inside his own misery and grief, and perhaps fear as well. If he held that lethal knowledge, it could be the catalyst for his own death if he spoke it aloud to anyone. And why should he trust Joseph? So far he had succeeded in nothing except proving that Beecher did not kill Sebastian or take his own life.

The pub was quiet—a few older men sitting over pints of ale, faces grim, voices subdued. The landlord moved among them quietly, filling tankards, wiping tables. Even for Flora there were no jokes.

Joseph had cold game pie with fresh tomatoes, pickles, and vegetables, then raspberries and clotted cream. The other tables were empty and the air was already hazed with gold when at last he was able to gain Flora's attention undivided. It was deserted now, and the landlord granted her an early evening.

She seemed quite willing to walk along the Backs under the trees in the fading light. There was no one on the river, at least on this stretch, and the leaves flickered in the barest breeze. One minute they were green and shadowed, the next opaque gold. There was little sound but a whispering of the wind, no voices, no laughter.

"Is it true that Sebastian's brother killed Dr. Beecher?" Flora asked him.

"Yes, I'm afraid it is."

"In revenge over Sebastian?"

"No. Dr. Beecher didn't kill Sebastian, and Elwyn knew that."

She frowned, the golden light making her hair a halo around her troubled face. "Then why?" she asked. "He loved Sebastian, you know." She shook her head a little. "He din't hero-worship him; he knew his faults, even though he didn't understand him much. They was a lot different." She stared ahead of her at the light across the smooth sweep of the grass, the tiny motes of dust swirling in the air, the sun gilding the flat surface of the water. "If there's going to be a war, an' it seems loike from what people say that there is, then Elwyn would have gone to fight. He would have thought it was his duty an' honor. But Sebastian would have done anything on earth to prevent it."

"Did Elwyn know that?"

"Oi think so." She waited a moment or two before she continued. "He din't understand how much Sebastian cared, though. No one else did."

"Not even Miss Coopersmith?" he asked gently. He did not know if

Flora knew of her, but even if she had not, she surely never hoped for more from Sebastian than friendship, at the very most. The least would have been something grubbier and far less worthy.

"Oi think she knew something," she said, looking away from him. "But it made her feel bad. She come to me after his death. She wanted me to say nothing, to save his good name, an' Oi suppose his family from bein' hurt." Her mouth pulled a little at the corners, her face soft with pity. "He din't love her, an' she knew it. She thought he moight come to in time. Oi can't think how awful that must be. But she still wanted to protect him."

Joseph tried to imagine the same scene, the proud, almost plain Regina in her elegant mourning black, facing the barmaid with the oval face and the shining, almost pre-Raphaelite hair and asking her to keep silent over her friendship with Sebastian, to save his reputation. And perhaps something to salvage a little of her public pride, if not privately, to know he had preferred Flora as a confidante.

"Did he care about it so much?" he asked aloud, remembering his own conversation with Sebastian, only a few yards from here. It had been intense, there would be no question of that, but was it fears and dreams or a will to do anything? Flora had spoken of doing. "Was it really more than words?"

She stared at the grass in the fading light, and her voice was very low. "It were a passion in him," she said. "In the end it were the most important thing in his loife . . . keep the peace, look after all this beauty what's come to us from the past. He was terrified o' war—not just the foighting an' bombing." She lifted her head a little and gazed across the shining river at the towers of the intricate, immeasurably lovely buildings and the limpid sky beyond. "The power to break an' smash an' burn, but the killing o' the spirit most o' all. When we've broke civilization, what have we got left inside us? The strength an' the dreams to start over again? No, we haven't. In smashing up all we got left o' what's wise, an' lovely, an' speaks to what's holy inside us, we break ourselves, too. We get to be savages, but without the excuses that savages have for it."

He heard Sebastian's words echoed in hers, exactly as if it had been he again, walking silent-footed in this exquisite evening.

She turned to face him. "Do you understand?" she said urgently. It seemed to matter to her that he did.

For that reason he needed to answer her honestly. "That depends upon what you are prepared to do to avoid war."

"Does it?" she demanded. "Ain't it worth anything at all?"

"Did Sebastian think so?"

"Yes! Oi . . ." She seemed troubled, looking away from him. "What d'you mean, it depends? What could be worse'n that? He told me about some of the things in the Boer War." She shuddered almost convulsively, hugging her arms around herself. "The concentration camps, what happened to some o' the women an' children," she said in a whisper. "If you do that to people, what is there left for you when you come home, even if you won?"

"I don't know," he confessed, finding himself cold as well. "But I've come to the point where I can't believe that appeasement is the answer. Few sane people want to fight, but perhaps we have to."

"Oi think mebbe that was what scared him." She stood still on the grass. They were opposite Trinity; St. John's was dark against the sunset, and there was only a tiny sliver of light on the water under the bridge. "He was terrible upset over something the last few days. He couldn't sleep; Oi think he was afraid to. It was as if he had a pain inside him that were so deep he weren't never free of it. After that shooting in Serbia 'e were so close to despair that Oi was scared for him . . . Oi mean real scared! It was as if for 'im there were nothing out there but darkness. Oi tried to comfort him, but Oi din't manage." She looked back at Joseph, her eyes full of grief. "Is it a wicked thing to say . . . sometimes Oi'm almost glad he din't live to see this . . . 'cos we're going to war, aren't we? All of us."

"I think so," he said quietly. It seemed a ridiculous conversation with the tremendous sunset dying on the horizon, the evening air full of the perfume of grass, no sound but the murmur of leaves and a whirl of starlings thrown up against the translucent blue of the sky. Surely this was the very soul of peace, generations mounting to this pinnacle of civilization. How could it ever be broken?

"He tried so hard!" There were tears of anger and pity in her voice.

"He belonged to a very big sort o' club fighting for peace, all over the world. An' he would have done anything for 'em."

Something tugged at his mind. "Oh? Who were they?"

She shook her head quickly. "Oi dunno. He wouldn't tell me. But they had big ideas he was terribly excited about, that would stop the war that's coming now." She knotted her hands together, her head bowed. "Oi'm glad he din't have to see this! His dreams was so big, an' so good, he couldn't bear seeing 'em come to nothing. He went almost mad just thinking o' it, before they killed him. Oi've thought sometimes if that was why they did it." She looked up and searched Joseph's face. "Do you think there's anyone so wicked they'd want war enough to kill him in case he stopped it?"

He did not answer. His voice was trapped inside him, his chest so tight it filled him with pain. Was that the plot his father had stumbled on? Had Sebastian known about it all the time? What price was it they were prepared to pay for a peace that John Reavley had believed would ruin England's honor?

Flora was walking again, down over the slope of the grass toward the river, perhaps because the light was fading so rapidly she needed to be away from the trees to see where she was going. She belonged in the landscape, her blemishless skin like gold in the last echoes of the light, her hair an aureole around her head.

He caught up with her. "I'll walk back with you," he offered.

She smiled and shook her head. "It ain't late. If Oi can't go through the college, Oi'll walk along the street. But thank you."

He did not argue. He must see Elwyn. He was the only one who could answer the questions that burned in his mind, and there was no time to wait. The darkness was not only in the sky and the air, but in the heart as well.

He did not go back to St. John's but cut across the nearest bridge back through Trinity to the street again, and walked as fast as he could toward the police station. His mind was still whirling, his thoughts chaotic, the same questions beating insistently, demanding answers.

He had to see Elwyn, whomever he had to waken, whatever reason or excuse he had to give.

The streets were deserted, the lamps like uncertain moons shedding a yellow glare on the paving stones. His footsteps sounded hollow, rapid, slipping a little now and then.

He reached the police station and saw the lights were on. Good. There were people, perhaps still working. The doors were unlocked, and he went straight in. There was a man at the desk, but Joseph ignored him, hearing the voice calling after him as he strode into the room beyond, where Perth was remonstrating with Gerald and Mary Allard and a man in a dark suit who was presumably their solicitor.

They turned as Joseph came in. Perth looked harassed and so tired that his eyes were red-rimmed. "Reverend—" he started.

"I need to speak to Elwyn," Joseph said, hearing a thread of desperation in his voice. If the solicitor got to him first, then he might never hear the truth.

"You can't!" Mary refused savagely. "I forbid it. You have brought nothing but ill to my family, and—"

Joseph turned to Perth. "I think he may know something about Sebastian's death. Please! It matters very much!"

They stared at him. There was no yielding in Mary's face, and the solicitor moved half a step closer to her, as if in support. Gerald remained motionless.

"I think Sebastian knew about the death of my parents!" Joseph said, panic coursing through him, threatening to slip out of control. "Please!"

Perth made a decision. "You stay here!" he ordered the Allards and the solicitor. "You come wi' me," he said to Joseph. "If he wants to see you, then you can." And without waiting for possible argument, he went out of the room with Joseph on his heels.

It was only a short distance to the cells where Elwyn was being held, and in a few minutes they were at the door. The key was on a hook outside. Perth took it off and inserted it into the lock and turned it. He pushed it open and stopped, frozen.

Joseph was a step behind him, and taller. He saw Elwyn over Perth's shoulder. He was hanging from the bars of the high window, the noose around his neck made from the strips of his shirt plaited together, strong enough to hold his weight and strangle the air from his lungs.

Perth lunged forward, crying out, although barely a sound escaped his lips.

Joseph thought he was going to be sick. Emotion—pity and relief—overwhelmed him with a crushing force. He barely felt the tears running down his face.

Perth was scrambling to untie Elwyn, fingers clumsy, tearing at the knots, breaking his nails, his breath rasping in his throat.

Joseph saw the letter on the cot and went to it. There was nothing he or anyone could do for Elwyn. The envelope was addressed to him. He opened it, before Perth or anyone else should tell him he couldn't.

He read it:

Dear Dr. Reavley,

Sebastian was dead when I got to his room that morning; the gun was on the floor. I knew he had killed himself, but I thought it was because he was afraid of going to war. He always believed we would. It looks now as if he was right. But I didn't read his letter until afterward, when it was too late. All I could think of was hiding his suicide. Mother could not have lived with the knowledge that he was a coward. You know that, because you know her.

I took the gun and hid it in the bucket at the top of the drainpipe in the master's house. I never meant anyone to be blamed, but it all got away from me.

Dr. Beecher must have realized. You heard what he said on the landing, about Sebastian and courage. By then I'd read his letter, but it was too late. I'm so sorry, so terribly sorry. There is nothing left now. At least this is the truth,

Elwyn Allard

Wrapped inside it was another letter, on different paper, and in Sebastian's hand:

Dear Dr. Reavley,

I thought I knew the answer. Peace—peace at any price. War in Europe could slaughter millions; what is one life or two to save so many? I believed that, and I would have given my own life gladly. I wanted to keep all the beauty. Perhaps it isn't possible, and we'll have to fight after all.

I was in London when I heard the document had been stolen. I came back to Cambridge that night. They gave me a gun, but I made the caltrops myself, out of fence wire. Then it would look like an accident. Much better. It wasn't difficult, just tedious.

I went out on a bicycle the next day, left it in a field. It was all very simple—and more terrible than anything I could have imagined. You think of millions and the mind is devastated. You see two who lie broken, the spirit gone, and it tears the soul apart. The reality of blood and pain is so very different from the idea. I can't live with who I am now.

I wish it hadn't been your parents, Joseph. I'm so sorry, sorrier than anything will heal.

Sebastian

Joseph stared at the paper. It explained everything. In their own way Sebastian and Elwyn were so alike: blind, heroic, self-destructive, and in the end futile. The war would happen anyway.

Perth laid Elwyn on the floor, gently, a blanket under his head, as if it mattered. He was staring up at Joseph, his face gray.

"It's not your fault," Joseph said. "At least this way there doesn't have to be a trial."

Perth gasped. He tried to say something, but it ended in a sob.

Joseph put Elwyn's letter back on the cot and kept Sebastian's.

"I'll go and tell them." He found his mouth dry. What words could he possibly find? He walked out and back the short distance. Perth could send for somebody to help him.

As soon as he was in the room Mary stepped forward and drew in her breath to demand an explanation. Then she saw his face and realized with terror that there was something more hideously wrong.

Gerald moved behind her and put his hands on her shoulders.

"I'm sorry," Joseph said quietly. "Elwyn has admitted to killing Dr. Beecher, because Beecher realized the truth of Sebastian's death."

"No!" Mary said stridently, trying to raise her arms and snatch herself away from Gerald's grip.

Joseph stood still. There was no way to avoid it. He felt as if he were pronouncing a sentence of death upon her. "Sebastian took his own life. No one murdered him. Elwyn did not want you to know that, so he took the gun and made it look like murder—to protect you. I'm sorry."

She stood paralyzed. "No," she said quite quietly. "That isn't true. It's a conspiracy!"

Gerald's face puckered slowly as understanding broke something inside him. He let go of Mary and staggered backward to collapse onto one of the wooden chairs.

The solicitor looked totally helpless.

"No!" Mary repeated. "No!" Her voice rose. *"No!"*

Perth appeared in the doorway. "I've sent for a doctor. . . ."

Mary swung round. "He's alive! I knew it!"

"No," he said huskily. "For you. I'm sorry."

She stood swaying.

Joseph reached to help her, and she lashed out at him as her legs buckled. She caught his face, but it was only a glancing blow.

"You'd better go, sir," Perth said quietly. There was no anger in his face, only pity and an immense weariness.

Joseph understood and walked out into the cool, shrouding darkness and the protection of the night. He needed solitude.

The next day, August 3, Mitchell brought him the newspaper early.

"There's going to be war, sir," he said somberly. "No way we can help it now. Russia invaded Germany yesterday, and the Germans have gone into France, Luxembourg, and Switzerland. Navy's mobilized, and troops are guarding the rail lines and ammunition supplies and so on. Reckon it's come, Dr. Reavley. God help us."

"Yes, Mitchell, I suppose it has," Joseph answered. The reality of it choked like an absence of air, heavy and tight in his lungs.

"You'll be going home, sir?" It was a statement.

"Yes, Mitchell. There really isn't anything to do here for the moment. I should be with my sister."

"Yes, sir."

Before leaving he called briefly on Connie. There was very little to say. He could not tell her about Sebastian, and anyway, when he looked at her, he thought of Beecher. He knew what it was like to lose the only person you could imagine loving, and exactly how it felt to face the endless stretch ahead. All he could do was smile at her and say something about the war.

"I suppose many of them will enlist as officers," she said quietly, her eyes misted over, staring at the sunlight on the walls of the garden.

"Probably," he agreed. "The best—if it comes to that."

She turned to look at him. "Do you think there's any hope it won't?"

"I don't know," he admitted.

He stayed only a moment longer, wanting to say something about Beecher, but she understood it all. She had known him perhaps even better than he had, and would miss him even more. In the end he simply said goodbye and went to find the master to say goodbye to him for the time being.

Afterward he had barely reached the center of the outer quad when he met Matthew coming in through the main gate. He looked pale and tired, as if he had been up most of the night. His fair hair was a little sun-bleached across the front, and he was wearing uniform.

"Do you want a lift home?" he asked.

"Yes . . . please." Joseph hesitated only a moment, wondering if Matthew wanted a cup of tea or anything else before he went on the last few miles. But the answer was in his face.

Ten minutes later they were on the road again. It hardly seemed different from any summer weekend. The lanes were thick with leaf, the harvest fields ripe, here and there stippled with the burning scarlet of poppies. The swallows were gathering.

With a heavy heart Joseph told Matthew what had happened the previous night. He could remember Elwyn's letter, and he still had Sebastian's. He read it as they drove. It needed no explanation, no added comments. When he had finished he folded it and put it back in his pocket. He looked at Matthew. His brother's face was heavy with pain, and anger for the sorrow and the futility of it. He glanced sideways at Joseph for a moment. It was a look of compassion, wordless and deep.

"You're right," Matthew agreed quietly, swinging round the curve of the road into St. Giles and seeing the street ahead of them deserted. "There's nothing either of us can do now. Poor devils. All so bloody pointless. I suppose you've still got no idea what happened to the document?"

"No," Joseph said bleakly. "I'd have told you."

"Yes, of course. And I still don't know who's behind it . . . unless it is Aidan Thyer, as you suggest. Damn! I liked him."

"So did I. I'm beginning to realize how little that means," Joseph said ruefully.

Matthew shot him a glance as he turned right off the main street toward the house. "What are you going to do now? Archie'll stay at sea as usual. He won't have a choice. And I'll keep on with the SIS, naturally. But what about you?" His brow was furrowed slightly, concern in his eyes.

"I don't know," Joseph admitted.

Matthew pulled the car up in front of the house, its tires crunching on the gravel. A moment later Judith opened the front door, relief flooding her face. She took the steps in two strides and hugged Joseph and then Matthew before turning to go back inside.

Walking out over the soft grass in the garden under the apple trees, they told her about Elwyn and Sebastian. She was stunned; rage, pity, confusion washed over her like storm waves, leaving her dizzy.

It was a late and somber lunch, eaten in an agreed silence, each willing to be alone with his or her thoughts. It was one of those strange, interminable occasions when time stands still. The sound of cutlery on the china of a plate was deafening.

Today, tomorrow, one day soon, Joseph would have to make his decision. He was thirty-five. He did not have to fight. He could claim all kinds of exemptions and no one would object. Life had to continue at home: there were sermons to be preached, people to be christened or married or buried, the sick and the troubled to be visited.

There were raspberries for dessert. He ate his slowly, savoring the sweetness of them, as if he would not have them again. He felt as if Matthew and Judith expected him to say something, but he had no idea what, and he was saved by Matthew interrupting his indecision.

"I've been thinking," he said slowly. "I don't know what armaments we have, not in detail. I do know it's not enough. We may be asked to give up anything we have that works. I don't know if anyone will want them, but they might."

"It's not going to be that bad! Is it?" Judith looked very pale, her eyes frightened. "I mean . . ."

"No, of course it isn't!" Joseph rushed in. He glared warningly at Matthew.

"They may ask us for guns," Matthew said stiffly. "I shan't be home, and I don't know whether you will or not." He looked at Joseph, pushing his chair back as he spoke, and standing up. "There are at least two shotguns, one new one and an old one that may not be up to much. And there's the punt gun."

"You could stop an elephant with that!" Judith said wryly. "But only if it was coming at you across the fens and you just happened to be out punting at the time."

Matthew pushed the chair back in at the table. "I'll get it out anyway. It'll probably be of use to someone."

Joseph went with him, not out of any interest in guns—he loathed them—but for something to do. "You don't need to frighten her like that!" he criticized. "For God's sake, use some sense!"

"She's better off knowing," was all Matthew replied.

The guns were kept in a locked cupboard in the study. Matthew took the key from his ring and opened it. Inside were the three guns he had mentioned, and a very old target pistol. He looked at them one by one, breaking the shotguns and examining them.

"Have you decided yet what you're going to do?" he asked, squinting down one of the barrels.

Joseph did not answer. The thoughts in his head had been forming into immovable shapes for far longer than he had realized. They had already cut off every line of retreat from the inevitable. Now he was forced to acknowledge it.

Matthew looked down the other barrel, then straightened the gun again. He picked up the second gun and broke it. "You haven't much time, Joe," he said gently. "It won't be more than another day or two."

Joseph hoped he might be guessing. It was a last grasp at innocence, and it failed. He understood Sebastian's fear. Perhaps that was what he had seen in him that had found the deepest echo within himself, the helpless pity for suffering he could not reach, even to ease. It overwhelmed him. The anger of war horrified him, the ability to hate, to make one's life's aim the death of another . . . for any cause at all. If he became part of it, it would drown him.

Matthew picked up the big punt gun. It was an awkward thing, long-barreled and muzzle-loaded. It did not break in the middle like a shotgun, but it was lethal over the short distances at which it could be aimed and used.

"Damn!" he said irritably, peering up the barrel. "I can't see a thing! Whoever designed these bloody guns should be made to look after them. I don't know whether it's working or not. Do you remember the last time anybody used it?"

Joseph was not listening. His mind was back in the hospital where he had started his medical training—the injuries, the pain, the deaths he could not prevent.

"Joe!" Matthew said savagely. "Damn it! Pay attention! Pass that rod and let me see if this is clean or not!"

Joseph passed over the rod obediently, and Matthew rammed it up the barrel of the punt gun.

"There's something up here," he said impatiently. "It's . . ." Very slowly he lowered his hands, still holding the gun. "It's paper," he said huskily. "It's a roll of paper."

Joseph felt the sweat break out on his skin and go cold. "Hold the gun!" he ordered him, taking the rod from Matthew and beginning to tease very gently. He found his hands were shaking, as was the barrel of the punt gun in Matthew's grip.

It took him nearly ten minutes to prise the paper out without tearing it, and then unroll it and hold it open. It was in German. They read it together.

It was an agreement between the kaiser and King George V, the terms of which were shatteringly simple. Britain would stand aside and allow Germany to invade and conquer Belgium, France, and of course Luxembourg, saving the hundreds of thousands of lives that would be lost in trying to defend them.

In return, a new Anglo-German empire would be formed with unassailable power on land and sea. The riches of the world would be divided between them: Africa, India, the Far East, and best of all, America.

The surgery of war would be swift and almost painless, the reward beyond measure. The document was signed by the kaiser, and obviously had been on its way to the king for countersignature.

"God almighty!" Matthew said hoarsely. "It's . . . it's monstrous! It's . . ."

"It's what Father died to prevent," Joseph said, tears choking his voice. It was the one thing he had believed that had stood fast and whole through all the loss. His father had been right. Nothing had misled or deceived him; he had been right. It spread a peace through Joseph, a kind of certainty at the core. "And perhaps he succeeded," he went on aloud. "There will be war. God knows how many will die, but England gave her word to Belgium, and she will not betray it. That would be worse than death."

Matthew rubbed his hands over his face. "Who's behind it?" He was weary, but in him, too, there was something stronger within, a doubt, a vulnerability gone.

"I don't know," Joseph said. "Someone in Germany close to the kaiser, very clever, with a great deal of vision and power. And more importantly to us, someone here in England, too, who was going to get it to the king—and damn nearly did."

"I know." Matthew shook his head. "It could be anyone. Chetwin . . . Shearing himself, I suppose. Even Sandwell! I don't know, either."

"Or anyone else we haven't even thought of," Joseph added.

Matthew stared at him. "But whoever it is, he's brilliant and ruthless, and he's still out there."

"But he's failed. . . ."

"He won't accept failure." Matthew bit his lip, his voice tight, his face almost bloodless. "A man who could dream up this won't stop here. He'll have contingency plans, other ideas. And he's far from alone. He has allies, other naive dreamers, wounded idealists, the disaffected, the ambitious. We never know who they are until it's too late. But by God, I'll put every spare minute I've got into hunting him down. I'll follow every trail, wherever it goes, whoever it touches, until I've got him. If we don't, he'll destory everything we care about."

Something in the words crystalized the knowledge in Joseph's mind, and it became undeniable, sealed forever. Whatever he felt, regardless of mind or heart, horror or his own weakness to achieve anything of use, he must join the war. If honor, faith, any values, human or divine, were to be kept, then there was no escape. He would do everything he could. He would learn to preserve his emotions apart, not to feel the rage or the pity; then he could survive.

"I'll join the army," he said aloud. "As a chaplain." It was an absolute statement, no question, no alteration possible. "I won't fight, but I'll be there. I'll help."

Matthew smiled, his face softening to an extraordinary gentleness. In his eyes was something that Joseph recognized with amazement as pride.

"Thought you would," Matthew said quietly.

Somewhere far away in the house the telephone rang.

The light outside was softening, turning hazy.

"What are we going to do with this?" Matthew asked, looking at the document.

"Put it back in the gun," Joseph answered without hesitation. "We may want it one day. No one would believe its existence without seeing it. They didn't find it here before, and they looked. That's as safe as anywhere. Disable the gun where they'll see it, and then no one will think to use it."

Matthew regarded the old gun ruefully. "I hate to do that," he said, but even as he spoke, he removed the firing pin.

Joseph rolled up the document again and pushed it down the barrel, using the rod to jam it in as far as possible.

They had just finished when Judith came to the door, her face pale.

"Who was it?" Joseph asked.

"It was for Matthew," she said a little jerkily. "It was Mr. Shearing. Sir

Edward Grey said in Parliament that if Germany invades Belgium, then Great Britain will honor the treaty to safeguard Belgian neutrality and we will be at war. He wants you back as soon as we know." She took a deep, shuddering breath. "It will happen, won't it?"

"Yes," Joseph answered. "It will." He glanced at Matthew.

Matthew nodded.

"We found the document Father died for," he said to Judith. "You'd better come to the sitting room and we'll tell you about it."

She stood motionless. "What is it?" she demanded. "Where was it? Why didn't we find it before?"

"In the punt gun," Joseph told her. "It was every bit as terrible as he said . . . more."

"I want to see it!" she said without moving.

Matthew drew in his breath.

"I want to!" she repeated.

It was Joseph who went to the gun and very carefully started to lever the paper out again. Matthew held the gun to help him. Finally he had it. He unrolled it and opened it for Judith.

She took it in her hands and read it slowly.

Instead of fear in her face there was a kind of fierce, hurting pride. The tears stood out in her eyes, and she ignored them as they slid down her cheeks. She looked up at them. "So he was right!"

"Oh, yes!" Joseph found his own voice choked. "Typical of Father—he understated it. It would have changed the whole world and made England the most dishonorable nation in the annals of history. It might have saved lives, or not—but only in the short term. In the end the cost would be beyond counting or measuring. There are things we have to fight for. . . ."

She nodded and turned away, walking back to the sitting room. The sun was sinking already, casting long shadows.

Joseph and Matthew carefully replaced the treaty yet again, then went after her.

They sat quietly together, remembering, while the light lasted, all the moments they had shared, past laughter, the happier times woven into the fabric of memory to shine in the darkness ahead.

Later Shearing telephoned again. Matthew answered it and listened.

"Yes," he said at length. "Yes, sir. Of course. I'll be there first thing in the morning." He hung up and turned to Joseph and Judith. "Germany has declared war on France—and is massed to invade Belgium. When it happens, we will send Germany an ultimatum, which, of course, they will refuse. By midnight tomorrow we shall be at war. Grey said, 'The lamps are going out all over Europe. We shall not see them lit again in our lifetime.' "

"Perhaps not." Joseph took a deep breath. "We shall have to carry our own light . . . the best we can."

Judith buried her head in his shoulder, and Matthew reached out around her to take Joseph's hand and grip it.